AGENT OF ROME

THE

FAR SHORE

AGENT OF ROME

THE FAR SHORE

NICK BROWN

HODDER &
STOUGHTON

First published in Great Britain in 2013 by Hodder & Stoughton
An Hachette UK company

1

Copyright © Nick Brown 2013

Map © Rosie Collins 2013

A CIP catalogue record for this title is available from the British Library.

Hardback ISBN 978 1 444 71491 3

Typeset in Plantin Light by Palimpsest Book Production Limited,
Falkirk, Stirlingshire

Printed and bound by CPI Group (UK) Ltd, Croydon, CR0 4YY

Hodder & Stoughton policy is to use papers that are natural, renewable
and recyclable products and made from wood grown in sustainable forests.
The logging and manufacturing processes are expected to conform to
the environmental regulations of the country of origin.

Hodder & Stoughton Ltd
338 Euston Road
London NW1 3BH

www.hodder.co.uk

For David Grossman
Without whom . . .

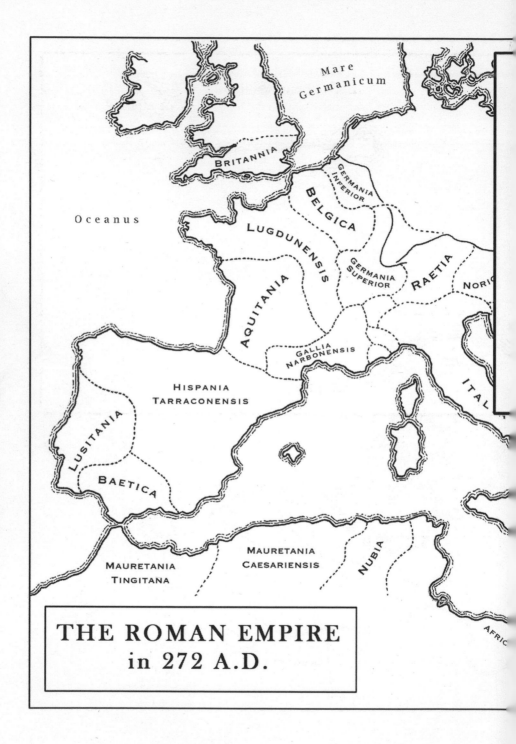

Mare
Germanicum

BRITANNIA

GERMANIA
INFERIOR

Oceanus

BELGICA

LUGDUNENSIS

GERMANIA
SUPERIOR

RAETIA

NORIC

AQUITANIA

GALLIA
NARBONENSIS

ITAL

HISPANIA
TARRACONENSIS

LUSITANIA

BAETICA

MAURETANIA
TINGITANA

MAURETANIA
CAESARIENSIS

NUBIA

AFRIC

THE ROMAN EMPIRE
in 272 A.D.

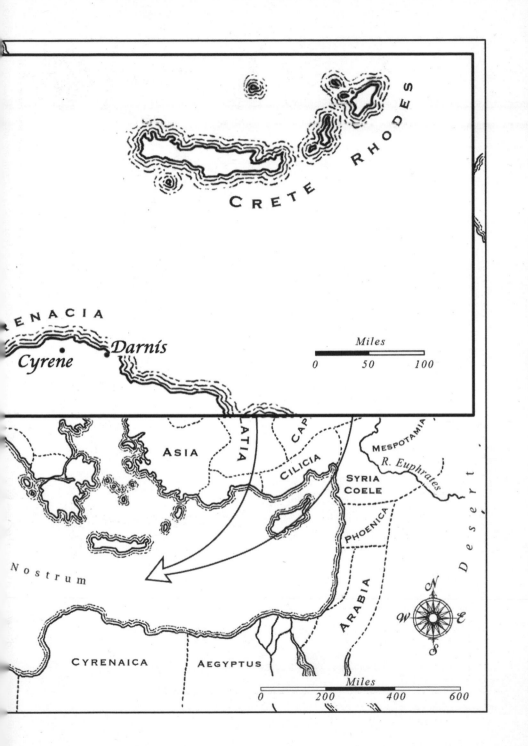

CRETE

RHODES

RENACIA

Cyrene Darnis

Miles

0   50   100

ASIA

ATIA

CAP

CILICIA

MESPOTAMIA

R. Euphrates

SYRIA
COELE

PHOENICA

Nostrum

ARABIA

Desert

N

W   E

S

CYRENAICA   AEGYPTUS

Miles

0   200   400   600

TIMES OF THE DAY

The Romans divided day and night into twelve hours each, so the length of an hour varied according to the time of year.

On Rhodes, in early winter, the first hour of the day would have begun at approximately 06.45.

The seventh hour of the day always began at midday.

The first hour of night would have begun at approximately 17.00.

MONEY

Four sesterces (a coin made of brass) were worth one denarius.

Twenty-five denarii (a coin made partially of silver) were worth one aureus (partially gold).

Cilicia, October AD 272

The noise reached its peak as the procession passed under the arched gate, then settled into a tumult of clapping, cheering and crying. Soldiers in gleaming bronze helmets and armour lined the road, holding back the crowd. Children clung to their parents' legs and looked up; the lucky few able to reach a roof or high window looked down. Leading the way were four mounted soldiers carrying spears trailing red and yellow streamers. Behind them came a plump, long-haired herald, bellowing an insistent refrain: 'People of Karanda, welcome our returning leader! Hail Prince Orycus! Hail the Prince!'

Orycus and his horse were covered in flowers thrown by the crowd. Clad in a pristine white tunic and cape, he sat high in his saddle, gracing his people with restrained smiles and nods. Close by were two attendants with heavily laden horses and two aged priests in long, flowing robes that hung close to the ground. Then came six armoured cavalrymen bearing circular shields and lances.

Bringing up the rear were three individuals who seemed entirely out of place with the rest of the procession. In the middle was Cassius Quintius Corbulo: a tall, lean, fair-skinned man who didn't look anything like old enough for the scarlet cloak and crested helmet of an officer of the Roman Army. To Cassius's left was his servant Simo: an older fellow of similar height but considerably more width, wearing a pale woollen tunic and a well-travelled pair of sandals. He had a kind, friendly face and looked as if he could barely resist the temptation to wave to the

3

onlookers. Cassius's bodyguard Indavara seemed to be the least comfortable in the saddle. He was the shortest of the three but altogether more muscular and his sleeveless tunic showed off a pair of remarkably solid arms laced with scars. His thick black hair didn't quite cover his left ear, the top half of which was missing. He caught Cassius's eye and nodded forward at the prince with a sneer.

'Looks quite the part now, doesn't he?'

Cassius shrugged as Indavara continued:

'Lucky they didn't see him hiding behind trees every time we met someone on the road, or starting at every sound.'

'We all have our roles to play,' replied Cassius, almost having to shout to make himself heard. 'You too. Watch these windows for archers.'

'Their man said there'd be no danger once we were inside the walls.'

'I know numbers aren't your strong point, but how many people do you think are here?'

'I don't know,' said Indavara. 'Thousands.'

'Exactly. And it only takes one. We've got Orycus this far. We don't want to lose him now.'

The ensuing half-hour was tense and chaotic, and Cassius let out a long sigh of relief when the procession finally reached the palace. The building barely deserved the name but then Karanda didn't seem like much of a city and – as Indavara had pointed out – Orycus certainly didn't seem like much of a prince. The palace was a three-storey structure built of timber and reminded Cassius of a large, not particularly luxurious inn. Roughly made standards hung from poles over the main entrance, where a number of well-dressed dignitaries had gathered. More soldiers were stationed along the path from the entrance to the front of the courtyard, where the prince had just dismounted. With a final wave to the crowd, Orycus strode towards the palace. He was met by a hulking, white-bearded man who gripped the hand offered to him, then escorted the prince inside. There was a groan from the watching horde, which was soon being dispersed by the soldiers.

'Break it up there! Off you go!'

'Back to your homes! Back to work!'

Cassius slid wearily to the ground, then unbuckled his chinstrap and removed his helmet. 'Thank the gods that's over with. He's someone else's problem now. A good night's rest, then we can be on our way.'

Indavara dropped down next to him and stretched out his arms. Simo dismounted and immediately set about removing saddlebags.

Tutting at the commoners bustling past, Cassius glanced up at the darkening sky and the foreboding mountains beyond the city walls. Strands of grey cloud drifted past the high, jagged crags and a light drizzle began to fall.

'Sir? Sir?' said a voice in Greek.

Cassius saw a small man pushing his way through the crowd. 'Officer Corbulo?'

'Yes.'

The man straightened his tunic and the thick silver chain around his neck. 'I am Speaker Malacus Argunt of the grand council. Karanda welcomes the envoy of Rome.'

Cassius rather liked the sound of that. He gripped forearms with Argunt, who, like most provincials, was too delicate and too quick with the gesture.

'Thank you, Speaker Argunt.'

Cassius always made a point of repeating back the names of anyone he met who occupied a position of authority. It created a good impression and invariably ensured he would remember the name.

Argunt waved a pair of servants forward. 'We shall stable your horses at once. I've arranged a room for you in the palace.' He cast a vaguely distasteful look at Indavara. 'Three wasn't it?'

'Three, yes.'

'If you come with me, sir. First Minister Vyedra would like to see you now.'

'Of course.'

Cassius turned to Indavara, who was already removing his weapons from his saddle. 'Help Simo with the gear, would you?'

Indavara nodded.

Cassius followed Argunt back through the crowd.

First Minister Vyedra turned out to be the white-bearded man who had greeted the prince. Speaker Argunt completed the introductions then left the large reception room, which was on the second floor of the palace, overlooking the courtyard. As a servant took Cassius's cloak and helmet, Vyedra gestured to two couches by a broad window.

'Thank you. A moment,' said Cassius. He took off the leather satchel he carried over his left shoulder and put it down on the floor, then removed the diagonal sword belt from his right shoulder. 'Don't think I need this.'

The servant added the heavy sword to his load and hurried away into an anteroom. Cassius waited for Vyedra to lower his substantial frame on to one of the couches, then picked up the satchel and sat opposite him. Another servant – a middle-aged woman – appeared and placed a wooden tray on the table between the couches. She took from it a plate of cakes, a jug and two fine glasses. Her hand was shaking as she poured wine into each glass, then handed them to the men.

Cassius looked down at the street beyond the courtyard, where scores of the city folk were still gathered. 'They seem reluctant to leave.'

'All of Karanda rejoices,' replied Vyedra. 'We owe you a great debt. With the prince returned to us, the House of Tarebe will live on.'

'All of Karanda?' queried Cassius, resting the glass on his knee. 'I was told the people of this enclave – Solba – oppose his family's rule. Isn't that why we had to escort him home in secret?'

'The threat from Solba has been somewhat overstated in certain quarters. But it is better to be safe than sorry, is it not?'

'Indeed. I did try to explain that to the prince, but he took a rather dim view of my methods.'

'Staying in out-of-the-way inns with beds crawling with mites?'

'Those sound like his words.'

'And having him dress as your clerk until you were close to the city?'

'Rather inventive that, I thought.'

Vyedra made a valiant attempt not to smile.

The servant offered each man the plate of cakes but both refused. She replaced the plate on the table and left.

'So, regarding the new arrangement with the governor in Tarsus,' continued Cassius. 'Tragic that the king wasn't able to sign it before his death, but now that the prince has been safely returned, it is essential that the agreement be ratified.'

Cassius unbuckled the satchel. 'I have it here. I require your signature and – once he is king – Orycus's too. I shall then have it sent back to the governor, for immediate implementation.'

Cassius took a sheet of paper from a thin leather folder and handed it over. Vyedra held it up to the light as he read. Cassius sipped on his wine (not watered enough considering the early hour) and glanced at the badly stuffed stag's head mounted on the wall behind the minister. Though cross-eyed, it seemed to be staring right at him.

Vyedra read aloud: 'We are to send a monthly report on the activities of the bandits to the north of our territory; hand over any prisoners captured for interrogation; and take action if their activities present a serious threat to communications or trade.'

'Rome faces many threats from without its borders. We simply haven't the resources to address all the problems within.'

Vyedra showed no sign that he had heard Cassius. His breathing – already laboured – became even louder. 'Our annual tribute is also to be increased? And our commitment of men?'

The first minister lowered the sheet and glared at his guest. Strictly speaking it was none of Cassius's concern; he was simply the messenger, but he knew that if the agreement wasn't signed, his commander – Aulus Celatus Abascantius of the Imperial Security Service – would be less than impressed.

'With the greatest respect, First Minister, I shall remind you that if it hadn't been for the intervention of the Roman Army, your royal family would be without an heir.'

'And I shall remind you, Officer Corbulo, that it was the failure of that same army to provide an escort for the royal party – through an area known for brigandage – that resulted in the death of the prince's father and brother. If the king hadn't been *summoned* to Tarsus by the governor, this whole disaster could have been avoided!'

Vyedra's cheeks were turning red.

Cassius had strict orders not to reveal that four-fifths of the province's forces were tied up in a crucial campaign against the Goths, nor that Imperial Security had organised Orycus's return because there were no legionaries available to do it.

'Will you sign the agreement, First Minister? And advise Orycus to do the same?'

Vyedra shook his head. 'His Majesty King Adricus would never have accepted these conditions.'

Cassius took a last sip of wine, then replaced the glass on the table. He'd overheard an interesting conversation in Tarsus when they'd taken charge of the prince. He hadn't intended on making use of the information unless the first minister proved recalcitrant, but it seemed that moment had arrived. He hunched forward and spoke quietly so that the servants wouldn't hear him.

'I'm told that the prince was found hiding in a latrine – unarmed and shivering in his nightshirt. He admitted to the tribune who found him that he'd fled as soon as the raiders struck.' Cassius turned towards the window. 'I'm sure you agree it would be most unfortunate if such a tale were to reach the people.'

Vyedra pursed his lips. Beads of sweat had formed on his brow. After a moment, he glanced down at the agreement and sighed.

Cassius smiled. 'Is there a pen around here anywhere?'

The coronation took place that afternoon, in what was known locally as the Great Square. Cassius slept through the whole thing, only to be woken by an impressive cheer when the deed was done. Half an hour later, a scowling First Minister Vyedra returned the agreement, now complete with Orycus's signature.

Cassius was glad there had been no invitation to the coronation, but later a messenger arrived with a note from Speaker Argunt, requesting that he join the celebratory banquet in the palace's Great Hall.

'Great? It's not even that big,' observed Indavara as they joined the end of the queue.

'Everything's relative, isn't it?' replied Cassius, yawning. 'It's probably the biggest chamber in the city, so to these people it's the Great Hall. Or – to take another example – I don't feel especially proud of knowing my times tables up to fifty, whereas you'd be happy if you could manage four times three.'

After a considerable pause, Indavara said, 'Twelve.'

'Very good. Simo's getting somewhere with you after all.'

Ahead of them were guests in bright tunics and thick furs; many of the women had elaborate floral arrangements woven into their hair. Silent attendants waited outside as their masters and mistresses filed through the door.

'Anyway,' added Cassius, 'you should count yourself fortunate to be here at all. I was offered only two seats. Lucky for you Simo's busy mending my saddle.'

'Should be a good feed at least.'

Cassius noted how grimy Indavara's tunic was. 'Don't you have anything cleaner?'

'Hardly a mark on it.'

Cassius couldn't wear his helmet in most of the low-roofed chambers and corridors of the palace, so he'd left it in his room. Assuming the hall would be hot, he'd left his cloak there too, and wore only his best long-sleeved scarlet tunic. Simo had also given his boots a good shine and fished out one of his favourite belt buckles – a circular silver plate with an image of the goddess Tyche, a memento from Antioch.

By the time they reached the door, Cassius realised all the men were removing their weapons. Two soldiers were taking the sword belts and knives and hanging them on wall-mounted pegs. Speaker Argunt was overseeing operations and coaxing the last of the guests inside.

'A tradition, you understand,' he explained as Cassius and Indavara handed over their daggers. 'The Great Hall is where views are exchanged, not blows. Only the monarch may bring his blade into the room.'

Just as they were about to enter, a youth trotted up to Speaker Argunt. He bowed his head, then offered a rolled-up sheet of paper wrapped in cloth. 'Just arrived by army dispatch, sir. For the officer.'

Argunt slid the letter out of the cloth. It was tied with twine and the wax seal remained intact. He read the single line of writing on the outside. 'So it is.'

Cassius took the letter and examined the wax seal. It carried the emblem of the Governor of Syria – almost certainly from Abascantius.

'I trust that the rider and his mount will be accommodated?' he said.

'Of course,' replied Argunt.

'Good. I have some post requiring delivery to the capital. He'll need to leave first thing.'

'As you wish,' said Argunt, gesturing towards the doorway.

They were the last guests to enter. The hall was lit by a multitude of glowing braziers mounted on three-legged stands. In the middle of the chamber was an impressive wooden throne facing a long row of tables that extended around on both sides to form a U. The guests – perhaps fifty in all – were standing behind their chairs, speaking excitedly. A dozen soldiers had been stationed around the hall. They were wearing tunics striped with red and yellow and, without any weapons to wield, held their arms stiffly by their sides. A serving girl directed Cassius and Indavara to their seats – the last two on the right side of the U. Feeling the eyes of the local elite upon him, Cassius clasped his hands behind his back and moved at a stately pace.

'Stay behind me, oaf,' he whispered as Indavara sped up, keen to investigate the tables of food that lined the walls. When they reached their seats, Cassius made sure he got the chair one in from the end.

'I shall take this,' he told Indavara, 'in fear of the prospect of having you as my only source of conversation for the next few hours.'

Indavara shrugged and stood behind his own chair.

Speaker Argunt entered the hall and went to speak to First Minister Vyedra.

Cassius turned to face the man to his right. He was old, crook-backed and bald, hanging on to the chair and staring vacantly at the empty throne.

'What happens now?' Cassius asked him.

No reaction. Cassius bent closer to his ear. 'What happens now?'

Again, nothing.

Cassius sighed and glanced at Indavara. 'You've nothing to say either, I suppose?'

The bodyguard ignored him too.

'By Jupiter,' said Cassius. 'I thought you might gradually begin to pick up the concept of polite conversation, but I see all my efforts of the last few weeks have been in vain.'

Indavara frowned.

'Look at Simo,' Cassius continued. 'He's only a slave but he and I can talk about all manner of things for hours: art, politics, religion. And think about where we are – a mountain kingdom most people will never have the chance to see. And what we're doing – playing a part in important affairs of state. Have you no observations, no thoughts to share?'

Indavara considered this for a moment before replying. 'Dinner smells good.'

'By the gods.'

Cassius looked down at the letter in his hand and decided he couldn't wait any longer. Sweat prickled the skin above his mouth as he scratched away the wax with his fingernails. He felt certain it contained details of his next assignment – what awful mission had Abascantius found for him now? Keeping his hands behind the chair, he unrolled the page and started reading.

Indavara turned round and inspected the food. There were platters of steaming roasted meat with the fat still sizzling, big wheels of cheese, bowls full of dried fruits and nuts, and silver trays piled high with cakes.

Argunt, Vyedra and several other grandly-dressed men lined up beside the throne. The room quietened.

'What does it say?' whispered Indavara, brushing his hair from his face as he looked down at the letter.

Cassius was smiling. 'It's from Master Abascantius. We have been tasked with a simple errand. We're to journey to the island of Rhodes, pick up some important papers, then return to Antioch.'

'An island?' said Indavara. 'Oh no. That means going on a ship.'

'Nothing gets past you, does it?'

'And picking up papers? Sounds even more boring than this job.'

'Nothing wrong with "boring",' replied Cassius, rolling up the letter and tucking it behind his belt. 'Highly underrated.'

First Minister Vyedra waited until there was absolute silence before he spoke. 'Assembled guests, esteemed members of the grand council, priests of the High Temple; we gather here in the Great Hall this night to honour our new king.'

Vyedra paused, and Argunt initiated a long round of applause.

'Blessed are the gods,' the first minister continued when quiet returned. 'Blessed are the gods that have delivered his excellency from the jaws of death. Blessed are the gods that smile upon Karanda.'

At this, two priests opposite the throne (whom Cassius now realised were the pair who'd earlier joined the procession) began an incantation in the local language. When they finished, the assembled city folk answered with a brief affirmation.

'This will take probably go on for hours,' Cassius whispered, 'and not even a mouthful of wine yet.'

Vyedra, Argunt and the others went to stand in front of the table opposite the priests, then turned round.

'Now we welcome him,' stated Vyedra in the same portentous tone he had adopted throughout. The nobles dropped down on one knee, closely followed by everyone else except the two priests.

Cassius did so too, prompting Indavara to reluctantly comply.

Vyedra spoke again: 'Keeper of the Winter Crown, Guardian of the High Temple, I present to you, his people, King Orycus the Fifth.'

Cassius and Indavara looked over the edge of the table as Orycus entered. The two guards flanking him took up positions on either side of the door. The king was wearing a long, purple cloak with a gem-studded silver crown nestling in his curly hair. Strutting slowly, he rounded the throne and stood in front of it.

'Hail, King Orycus!' roared Vyedra.

'Hail, King Orycus!' came the reply.

The new monarch took a step backwards and sat down.

Cassius noticed a servant close to the priests moving around. One of the holy men glared at him.

'We bow to you, our king,' announced Vyedra.

Indavara nudged Cassius. 'Not me.'

All the locals bowed their heads, including the priests this time.

Cassius was still watching the servant. The man bowed briefly, then turned and picked up something from one of the food tables. Cassius looked over his shoulder. On every plate with a joint of meat was a long, sharp carving knife.

He pointed across the hall. 'Indavara, there!'

'Quiet,' said someone to their right.

The servant leapt between the two priests and on to the table. The orange light of the braziers sparked off the blade in his hand.

Indavara was already on his feet and running.

Cassius stood up as the assassin leapt again, this time over the kneeling dignitaries.

Indavara pounded across the flagstones towards the throne.

Some of the guards were moving but none stood a chance of getting there in time.

Neither will Indavara.

Cassius picked up a large, empty wooden jug and threw it at the assassin. The jug bounced once, then skittered into the man's ankle. He stumbled and fell to one knee, skidding on the smooth stone floor. As he struggled back up again, he shouted: 'For Solba!'

King Orycus shrank back into the throne.

The quicker guards were still yards away.

The assassin raised the blade high and jabbed it down at the king's neck.

His arm froze in mid-air.

Eyes wide, the assassin looked down at the big, scarred hand gripping his wrist. He couldn't see the second hand but he could feel the fingers digging into his neck.

Indavara held him there as the guards closed in around them. Before he could do anything more, the assassin cried out. Indavara watched as blood seeped from the corner of the man's mouth. He looked down and saw the king's red-streaked blade slide out of the assailant's gut.

The man shuddered then suddenly went limp. Indavara let go and the guards took hold of him. The face of the would-be assassin was impossibly young, his cheeks marked with the spots of a teenager. Indavara backed away from the throne, leaving the king standing there alone, holding the bloodied sword in his hand.

'All praise the king!' came a shout from somewhere.

'All praise the king!'

Suddenly everyone was shouting.

Cassius hurried over to Indavara, who shook his head when their eyes met.

'That was too close.'

'Could have been the shortest reign in history,' replied Cassius. 'Good work.'

'Good work by whoever threw that jug. Slowed him down just enough.'

'It was me. I threw it.'

'You?'

The soldiers half dragged, half carried the assassin out of the hall, leaving a trail of blood on the flagstones.

Speaker Argunt came over and gripped their arms in turn. It took him a while to get out any words. 'All of Karanda thanks you both. What speed of thought and action.'

Cassius turned to Indavara, who gave a rare nod of approval.

Vyedra came past and grabbed one of the older soldiers.

'Four men to stand by the king. I want every one of these servants replaced. And take anything that looks like a weapon outside. The meat can be cut in the kitchens.'

Speaker Argunt then tried to address the crowd but with his diminutive height, few people could see him, let alone hear him. One of the soldiers had taken the blade from the king, who had sat down and now looked rather dazed, his crown in his lap. After a few moments, he put it back on, stood up and raised his hand. Even the servants being herded out of the room and the soldiers herding them stood still and silent. Orycus beckoned Argunt forward, then whispered in his ear. The older man spoke:

'Clear a space at the table there! The king will eat with our Roman friends.'

The crowd answered with a roar.

It was in fact more than an hour before Cassius and Indavara actually got to eat something. They were seated on either side of the king, who apologised for his conduct during the journey, raised a brief but heartfelt toast to them, then left. The mood in the hall became considerably more rowdy and people began to queue up to thank Cassius and Indavara personally. Some of the ladies present also offered enthusiastic kisses.

Only when this duty was complete were they free to fill their plates. Cassius found he had rather lost his appetite after all the excitement. He managed a bit of cheese and a few little cakes, then settled for supping his wine. The local concoction was unusual – sweet and fortified with spices – but he swiftly acquired a taste for it. Indavara used the wine only to slosh down his food; he was already on to his second plateful.

Speaker Argunt sidled up and knelt by Cassius's chair. 'Word is spreading across the city. The people will bring gifts and flowers for you in the morning.'

'That's very kind.'

Argunt leaned in closer. 'You not only saved the king, but also made him appear a hero.'

'The gods have smiled upon us this night.'

'Indeed. Though not on First Minister Vyedra, I fear. The king has had him arrested and appointed me in his stead.'

'Really? Why?'

'He was in charge of security.'

With a wink, Argunt stood up and walked away. Before Cassius could take another sip of wine, a rather voluptuous woman of about forty hurried over. She was wearing a fox fur around her neck and sweating profusely.

'Centurion, I am the Countess Sifke. May I too offer my profound thanks for your heroic actions.'

Cassius's actual title was 'officer' but he often chose not to correct the error.

'Thank you, Countess.'

She looked past Cassius at Indavara, who was stripping a greasy chicken leg with his teeth.

'You too, of course, young man.'

Indavara answered with a grunt.

'What a throw, sir,' the countess continued. 'Worthy of an Olympiad.'

'You should see me with a javelin, madam.'

Indavara grunted a different kind of grunt.

'I wonder, sir,' said the countess, 'would you like to come and join my party? I'm here with my four daughters. They would be enchanted to meet you.'

Cassius glanced over at the girls: three black heads of hair and one red, and fair faces too, watching coyly from a corner.

'Likewise, I'm sure. We will be over presently.'

The countess smiled and wobbled her way back to her table.

Indavara put down the chicken leg and stood up to inspect the rest of the food.

Cassius gave him a napkin. 'Clean yourself up.'

'Why?' asked Indavara, wiping his chin.

Cassius aimed a thumb towards the corner.

The bodyguard grinned when he saw the girls.

'Come,' said Cassius, grabbing his wine as he stood. 'Time to enjoy the warm embrace of a grateful nation.'

I

Rhodes, November AD 272

Even as the ship finally slid alongside the quay, as the yelling sailors tied off the mooring ropes and fixed the gangplank, the dozen passengers remained by the side-rail. They stood in a line, gazing across the harbour, though the object of their fascination had been visible for hours, soon after the island's high mountains materialised out of the morning mist.

'Half the bronze in the world, they say.'

'Two hundred feet high it was.'

'I heard three hundred.'

'You could get a thousand men inside it.'

'Probably more.'

'And to think it's just lain there like that for five hundred years.'

'Five hundred and fifty, actually,' said Cassius.

It was a remarkable sight, but he was struggling not to be slightly underwhelmed. Hadn't someone told him the statue once stood astride the port; that high-masted ships sailed between the sun-god Helios's legs? Looking back at the narrow breakwaters that enclosed the harbour, he now saw how ridiculous this notion was.

The statue was in fact about a mile back from the water, built upon an enormous stone platform. The god appeared to have been cut off at the knees. The body had fallen to the left and now lay face down on the ground. The right arm – originally held up, supposedly shielding the god's eyes from the sun – now seemed to cover the face, as if protecting it from further assault. In the centuries since an earthquake had toppled the statue, numerous buildings had sprung up around it.

'Men *made* that?' Indavara enquired, his hands resting on the side-rail.

'No,' said one of the other passengers, a fat-necked merchant in a garish green tunic. 'The locals try to claim credit for it, but it was the gods. And it was them that brought it down too.'

Cassius glanced at Indavara and shook his head.

'How? How could men *make* that?' asked the bodyguard.

'I don't know the specifics,' Cassius replied. 'I'm no engineer. But it was a man named Chares who designed the whole thing. I think he was a sculptor.'

'Must have had big hands,' scoffed the merchant. Several of the others laughed.

Cassius turned to him. 'Tell me this then: why would the gods create such a statue of just *one* of them?'

'Perhaps it was Helios himself – to remind the people of his power.'

'Then why create it only to bring it down fifty years later?'

'Perhaps that was the work of another god. A jealous god.'

Cassius gave an ironic smile, then nodded at the sparkling white columns of the ancient citadel on the hill above the city. 'So who built that?'

The merchant shrugged.

Cassius gestured at an equally impressive temple lower down the slopes. 'And that?'

'Men. But those are just buildings. Look at it!'

The merchant pointed at the statue – the vast expanse of gleaming bronze that shone out among the pale buildings. '*That* is the work of a higher power! How could a man – or even hundreds of men – create such a thing?'

'I don't know *how*, but they did it. Mainly because they wanted to outdo the Athenians, as I recall. Haven't you read Pliny?'

The merchant said nothing.

'You must have visited Rome at least – seen the Colosseum? Why it's ten times the size!'

'Ah yes, of course. Rome, Rome, Rome. You must always have the biggest and best of everything.' The merchant pointed at the

20

statue again and smiled smugly. 'But there's nothing like *that* in Rome, is there?'

The conversation had been in Greek. As the merchant walked away across the deck, Cassius switched to Latin:

'Bloody provincials.' He turned to the others. 'Come, you two.'

Simo already had a saddlebag over each shoulder and now picked up several empty water skins.

Indavara was still at the side-rail, staring at the statue. 'How? How could they *build* it?'

'By Jupiter. Listen, what about the arena you fought in? Who built that?'

Indavara looked down at the water, and the clumps of weed and driftwood that littered the harbour. 'I never really thought about it.'

'I daresay. Come on.'

Cassius and Indavara picked up the remainder of their gear. The three of them had to wait for a gap in the stream of porters and sailors lugging bales of wool and heavy clay pots. Cassius was first on to the gangplank.

'I think that temple halfway up the hill is for Asclepius,' he told Simo over his shoulder. 'I shall have to take a look at that too.'

'You do seem excited to be here, sir.'

'Well why not, Simo?' replied Cassius, stepping on to the quay. 'This city is a seat of fine culture, philosophy and art in particular. There are some wonderful—'

He stood still, waiting for the strange feeling in his legs and the dizziness to subside. It had taken them seven long days to reach Rhodes from the Cilician port of Anemurium. Considering the season, the weather had been kind but – as ever – Cassius was glad to be back on dry land. He moved away from the sailors and sat down on a barrel on the far side of the quay.

'Are you all right, sir?' asked Simo.

'Better than Indavara, by the looks of it.'

The bodyguard dropped his bags next to Simo. He staggered, put his hands out to steady himself and took some deep breaths.

It had been his longest trip on a ship. He didn't suffer from the seasickness that usually afflicted Cassius but had made little progress in overcoming his fear of large expanses of water.

Simo, meanwhile, remained utterly unaffected. He had eaten and slept well and maintained his usual healthy glow. Though he'd little experience of sailing, he put his affinity for the sea down to his Gaulish forefathers; they'd been fishermen.

Cassius took a drink from his canteen and surveyed their bags.

'Look at all this. I doubt we'll get it all on three horses.'

It was a recurring problem. Simo kept his personal belongings to an absolute minimum, but Cassius needed quite a variety of clothing and there were other items – his bathing oils, pillows and collection of belt buckles for example – that he simply couldn't do without. Other objects that took up a lot of space included his helmet and mail shirt, not to mention footwear ranging from felt slippers to hobnailed marching boots.

In addition, Simo always insisted on making sure they had plenty of spare cloths, blankets and towels. He had, however, judged to perfection the amount they would consume during the trip and there was nothing left but half a skin of wine.

Indavara would have been considered an exceptionally light traveller were it not for his collection of weapons and equipment. Having received a silver ingot upon the successful completion of their first assignment, he'd already spent more than a quarter of his newly acquired wealth. Only his battered wooden fighting stave remained from their last outing in Syria. He'd spent two days scouring the markets of Antioch and was now equipped with a new bow, sword and mail shirt. All three items had been purchased from suppliers used by the Roman Army.

The composite bow was five feet long, made of wood, hide and sinew. Indavara also had a quiver with sixteen arrows and numerous tools for maintenance. He kept the whole lot in a long leather bag.

The sword was standard military issue but of a rather old-fashioned design, and he'd had to look hard for one as short and light as he wanted. It reminded him of the first weapon he'd fought with in the arena. He could still move easily when wearing it and the blade was perfect for close-quarter work. He'd opted for a piece with a ridged bone handle and a solid wooden pommel – always useful for a non-lethal blow to the head. He had yet to draw the sword in anger.

The mail shirt wasn't quite up to the standard of Cassius's (copper alloy was incredibly expensive), but the bronze rings provided solid protection and felt relatively comfortable when worn over the accompanying padded undershirt.

Cassius took his sword belt from Simo and slipped it over his right shoulder so that the sword hung over his left hip. His weapon was also new: a long, broad blade with a brass eagle's head on the hilt and elaborate swirls embossed on the scabbard. He winced as the strap tugged at his neck.

Indavara shook his head. 'Have you even tried wielding that? You'd probably need to train for a month just to hold it up.'

'I think we've been through this, bodyguard.'

'Just saying, that's all. If there's some spare time, we shall see what you can do with it.'

'At the earliest opportunity.'

Cassius had so far resisted Indavara's attempts at instruction but there was no denying it made sense. In truth, he would just as soon have carried the lightest blade possible, but most officers now seemed to favour these ostentatious weapons.

'Helmet, sir?' asked Simo.

'I suppose I must. Always helps get things done quicker, doesn't it?'

Cassius took the hated helmet from Simo and pulled it on, glad that it was at least more sufferable in the cooler months of the year. Simo reached up and straightened the red horsehair bristles on the transverse crest. Leaving the chinstrap untied, Cassius checked the clasp on his cloak, an item of clothing he wasn't wearing solely for effect; there was a brisk breeze running into the harbour.

'Grab a porter, Simo. I can't be seen carrying things in the city.'

As the Gaul hurried away, Cassius looked over at Indavara, now again weighed down with his bags.

'Perhaps you could have spent some of that silver on a third tunic.'

'Why do I need more than two?'

'I shall not waste my breath on a reply to that.'

Simo returned with a young lad, who instantly set about grabbing saddlebags.

'Know where the nearest army way station is?' Cassius asked him.

'No, sir.'

'Wonderful. Well, shouldn't be far away.'

Cassius set off down the side of the crowded quay. It was difficult to maintain one's dignity on such occasions and he forced himself to move slowly, though anyone who saw him coming took care to stay out of his way. Not for the first time, he was reminded of the parallels between life as an army officer and his youthful forays into acting, not to mention his two years studying to be an orator. So much of professional life was an act. One donned the clothes, then played the part.

Once off the quay, they came to the low sea wall that ran round the harbour. The rest of the waterfront was relatively quiet; though a hundred or more had gathered to meet the freighter, there was little sailing done at this time of year. The only other cluster of people in view were at a ramshackle market squeezed between the sea wall and the road.

'Good afternoon. Can I help you?'

Cassius turned to see a man of about forty with wavy, greying hair and a practised smile. He was wearing a heavy cloak over an immaculate toga. Behind him were three male attendants.

'Gaius Vilsonius,' stated the man. 'I'm a member of the city assembly, amongst other things.'

They gripped forearms.

'Officer Cassius Quintius Corbulo.'

Cassius only mentioned Imperial Security to civilians if he thought it to his advantage, which was rarely the case.

'First time on Rhodes?'

'It is.'

Vilsonius pointed at the statue. 'What do you think of our big bronze friend?'

He spoke in perfect, accentless Latin; almost certainly raised in Rome.

'Most impressive,' replied Cassius.

'Take a closer look if you have a moment. Much quieter now the tourist season's past. There are usually a few artists over there – they'll do a good likeness of you with the statue in the background. Rather talented some of them. What brings you here so late in the year?'

As Vilsonius and Cassius spoke, the six others with them stood in silence.

'Just army business. Supply issues – all rather boring I'm afraid. But I hope to have a good look around the island.'

'Oh you must, you must.'

'I wonder if you can help me. I'm looking for the nearest way station.'

'You've not far to go.' Vilsonius pointed west along the road. 'Just down there. For some reason they insisted on putting it close to the fish market. Luckily there's a bit of wind today.'

'Indeed. Good day, sir.'

'Good day to you.'

The fish market was a hundred yards down the road. There was barely enough room to get a cart between the stalls and the row of two-storey villas opposite the sea wall. The dwellings were sturdily built of some local stone: uniformly white, with rust-coloured roofs. Their proximity to the elements clearly took its toll; there was a lot of peeling paint and missing tiles.

'Get your sea perch!' yelled one of the market vendors. 'Get your perch here. Last ten – got to get rid of them.'

It was early afternoon, so most of the fish had gone but, as they walked by, the trio examined what was left.

'What's that?' exclaimed Indavara as he passed the last stall.

25

Lying on a stone slab was a broad, grey fish about five feet long. The last foot was its blade-like snout.

'At a guess, I'd say a swordfish,' replied Cassius.

'Quite right, sir,' said Simo. 'Very tasty with some lemon and a few herbs.'

'Perhaps we can get some for dinner,' said Cassius, heading across the road to the way station with something of a spring in his step. Cilicia had been difficult and tiring, the sea crossing equally arduous, and he was glad both were behind him. He'd always hoped to visit Rhodes at some point in his life and it felt good to be in a new city, hopefully with a little time to explore.

The way station was marked by a solid bronze plaque engraved with the legend 'SPQR'. Without being told, Simo retrieved Cassius's ceremonial spearhead from a saddlebag and handed it to him.

'Wait here a moment,' he told the others as he hurried inside. Ahead of him was a long corridor. Immediately to the right was a shadowy room where a young clerk sat slumped at an empty desk. He had clearly been dozing but stood up with creditable speed as Cassius strode in.

'Officer Corbulo.'

'Yes, sir. Good afternoon, sir.'

The clerk – who was no more than sixteen – looked at the three-foot spearhead, which identified Cassius as a member of a governor's staff. The fact that the title engraved on the badge was that of the Governor of Syria was irrelevant; any man in possession of a spearhead was considered to be of a rank equivalent to a centurion.

Cassius heard someone marching down the corridor towards them.

'I require lodgings for three,' he told the clerk, removing his helmet. 'Tonight and possibly longer. Is there space here?'

'Er, yes, sir. Yes, that should be fine.'

'Afternoon, sir.'

Cassius turned to find a broad, middle-aged soldier behind him.

'Optio Clemens, sir. The lad will go and get the maid to prepare those rooms for you.'

The clerk warily rounded them and jogged along the corridor. Clemens glanced at the spearhead. 'Might I ask why you're here, sir?'

'I'm with Imperial Security,' Cassius replied, smoothing down his hair. 'Here to see Master Augustus Marius Memor. Can you direct me to his villa?'

Not many people would have noticed the subtle change in Clemens's expression once he heard the young officer before him was a 'grain man'. Legionaries generally maintained a dim view of the Service, believing it to be a corrupt organisation full of liars and thieves not courageous or honourable enough for real soldiering. Cassius did notice.

'I can,' Clemens answered evenly. 'He likes to keep himself to himself as a rule – for obvious reasons. We get plenty of post for him.'

'Nothing for me, by the way?'

'No, sir.'

Apart from accommodating and assisting army officers, the key function of a way station was to facilitate the delivery of the imperial post.

'Here, sir, I can show you the way?'

Clemens reached under the desk and pulled out a roll of thick paper. 'You came in on that freighter, I presume?'

'Indeed.'

Clemens gestured towards the grilled window. 'This is known as the Great Harbour. The one to the north is the Little Harbour, though they're actually about the same size now.'

Clemens pointed at the map. 'The road out front runs all the way along the sea wall. Follow it to the east. Then, when you reach the edge of the harbour here, turn south – inland along the Via Alexandria. You'll eventually reach the village of Amyndios about here. Memor's place is a hundred yards short of the square. There's no plaque on the gate but it's the biggest villa there and has an orchard of peach trees.'

'How far?'

'Four miles or so.'

'How many hours of light left?'

Clemens hurried to the doorway and looked out. 'Perhaps three.'

The optio glanced at the others and the pile of bags.

'We'll need some horses,' said Cassius, now behind him in the corridor.

'Let's get your men and your gear inside, sir, then I'll take you through to the stables.'

———◄8►———

Leaving Simo to settle in, Cassius and Indavara were soon heading back past the fish market, this time on horseback. Clemens only had one legionary with him at the way station but they'd swiftly saddled up the mounts and the optio assured Cassius that their rooms would be ready within the hour.

Cassius always tried to be as reasonable as possible with common soldiers – especially when he was dependent on their cooperation – but it was usually an uphill battle. Their suspicion of the Service was deeply ingrained – with some justification he knew – but it pained him to be repeatedly judged so harshly by men he'd just met. All things considered, Clemens had been exceptionally polite and helpful. Cassius wondered what he and the legionary would be saying now.

'So who's this man we're going to see?' Indavara asked as they passed a little fishing boat coming in alongside the quay.

Cassius shook his head. 'Do you remember anything I've taught you? Straighten your back and ease your grip on the reins. You'll pull the poor thing's teeth out if you're not careful.'

Indavara rolled his eyes.

'Open your fingers – you're not holding a sword.'

Cassius waited for him to comply before answering the question. 'We are going to visit Augustus Marius Memor – the Service's second in command beneath Chief Pulcher. As I understand it,

28

he's in charge of affairs in Africa and the East. We're to take some documents to Abascantius back in Antioch. I imagine he's keen to get them before winter sets in.'

'Africa is close to here?'

'South – a few hundred miles. In fact I believe the god Helios was Egyptian.'

'Why do so many wild animals come from Africa?'

Cassius sighed. He often felt like a teacher when talking to Indavara. 'I've no idea. Fewer people perhaps. More space and food for them.'

'I'd like to see a lion,' said Indavara.

'You never had to fight one?' Cassius asked.

'No.'

'I saw one once, but it was in a menagerie. Mangy old thing.'

'I'd like to see a crocodile too,' Indavara continued. 'And a rhinoceros. I once heard of a fight between a rhinoceros and three bulls. They chained them together.'

'People do love to see animals tear bits out of each other.'

Cassius pointed towards a patch of beach where twenty or so men stood in a circle, watching a pair of fighting cocks. Outside the circle were other birds in cages. Feathers shed by the anxious creatures covered the sand.

'Not only animals,' Indavara said as they came to the end of the sea wall.

'Here's the turn.'

Cassius led the way as they rounded a corner and headed up a slight incline along the Via Alexandria. This was an area of warehouses and boatyards and fishermen's huts. A pair of old women sat on a bench, stitching a thick net as they watched the riders pass.

'What was it like? The arena?' Cassius asked. 'You never really talk about it.'

Indavara cast a weary sideways glance at him but eventually relented. 'Quick. It was always over so quick. For months you'd just wait and train. Then suddenly you were told you were fighting – in a few days, or even the next day. You had to be ready. And not just your body.' Indavara tapped his head. 'I saw men shout

29

at themselves for hours before a contest, even bang their skulls against the wall until the blood ran. Others would just sit and cry. By the time they had to actually fight, they had nothing left in them. I remember one man killed himself just before he was to go up. Shoved a latrine sponge down his throat.'

'By the gods. And you – how did you prepare?'

'Did as little as I could. The night before there was always a big meal – drink too if you wanted it. I never even went. Once the day came, I'd try and sleep, do a few exercises just before I was taken up.'

'Sleep? How could you sleep?'

'As long as I'm not on a boat I can always sleep.'

'But thinking about it, what you faced . . .'

Indavara shrugged. 'It was coming – whatever I thought. Nothing I could do except try to get through it. One old boy, he said to me: "They're the cats. We're the mice. They'll play with us, then leave us in pieces, bleeding on the ground."'

Cassius eased his horse closer to Indavara's. It was rare for the bodyguard to string more than a few sentences together, especially about himself.

'Must have been terrible.'

'You'll never know.'

'I'm not a complete innocent. I have been in combat. I told you about the fort.'

'Not the same.'

'I saw a lot of death. And I thought I was going to die.'

'Not the same.'

'Neither is it entirely different.'

Indavara shifted in his saddle so he could better face Cassius. 'Why were you there?'

'We were defending the province against rebels. I told you before.'

'So there was a reason. A reason to fight.'

Cassius conceded with a tilt of his head. 'Point taken.'

It was a while before he spoke again. 'Have you ever thought about joining the army?'

30

'Trying to get rid of me already?' replied Indavara.

'I mean in the future. I'm sure they'd be glad to have someone with your abilities. Money's pretty good, and there's no shortage of enemies to fight. Good way to stay sharp.'

'I'm a freedman now. Isn't a soldier just another type of slave?'

Cassius wasn't about to argue with that. One of the few benefits of life in the Service was that he enjoyed far more personal freedom even than a senior field officer with the legions.

'Another good point, Indavara. We'll make an orator of you yet.'

The Via Alexandria took them through rows of closely packed town houses and past several pretty sanctuaries. They saw the Temple of Dionysus too, and a hundred followers gathered in the courtyard, reciting chants led by a quartet of priests.

The houses began to thin out as they continued along the wide, paved road and into the countryside. The wind increased and the high poplars that lined the road began to rustle and sway. Cassius shivered and pulled his cloak tighter around him. Indavara, who owned a cloak but never seemed to wear it, was still in his sleeveless tunic.

'You *have* to be cold.'

Indavara shook his head.

'Showing off your muscles more important, eh?'

'That's good coming from a man with *that* sword.'

Cassius reckoned Optio Clemens had got his distances correct. He could see the village square up ahead as they came to a big property on the left. The plot must have taken up a square mile and was separated from the road by a three-foot stone wall. The villa reminded Cassius of his family home: a sprawling structure made up of different blocks, all with dazzling white walls and immaculate tiled roofs. In the middle of the central section facing the road was a grand doorway flanked by columns. A meandering path led from the door

31

through the peach trees Clemens had mentioned and down to a gate. The trees were bare, but still identifiable by their dark, spindly limbs. The gate was narrow and set under a high arch built into the wall. Further down the road was a second gate, broad enough for carts and leading to a wide track that ran round to the rear of the villa.

As they dismounted beside the arch, a young servant opened the gate. 'Sir, are you from the magistrate's office?'

'No,' Cassius replied, putting on his helmet. 'My name's Corbulo. I'm here to see Master Memor. Is he at home?'

The servant chewed his lip and examined both Cassius and Indavara before glancing back at the villa. 'Would you wait here a moment, sir?'

'If I must.'

The servant hurried back through the gate, securing the latch before running up the path through the orchard. He suddenly stopped and shouted back at Cassius. 'Sir, sorry, what was the name again?'

'Corbulo!'

Cassius looked over at Indavara and shrugged as he retrieved the spearhead from the single saddlebag Simo had attached. Indavara took the horses over to a patch of lush grass to graze.

The lad soon returned in the wake of a much older man wearing a pale blue tunic. As he came closer, Cassius saw that he was at least fifty: short, dark-skinned, with as much white in his beard as black.

'Officer, please,' said the man, opening the gate wide. As Cassius came forward, he bowed. 'My name is Trogus, I am steward of this household.'

'Corbulo, Imperial Security. Is Master Memor here? Will he see me?'

'That . . . will not be possible, sir.'

'Might I ask why?'

Trogus looked up. His eyes were swollen and red. 'Master Memor was found dead this morning, sir.'

Cassius took a breath. 'Great gods. What happened?'

'They – they got inside the villa.' Trogus's eyelids flickered as he spoke. 'Last night.'

'They? What do you mean "they"?'

'Whoever they were. They – they – cut off his head. They cut off his head and they took it.' Trogus's voice dropped to a shaky whisper. 'Why would they take his head?'

II

It took a while for the steward to regain control of himself, during which time the young servant began to weep.

'You'd better come inside, sir,' Trogus said eventually. 'We shall put your mounts in the stable.'

Without being told, the lad trotted over to Indavara and took the reins, then led the horses up the road towards the other gate.

'What's going on?' Indavara asked as they followed Trogus through the orchard.

'Memor's dead,' Cassius replied, rubbing a knuckle against his brow. 'Murdered.'

'What? Why?'

'How in Hades would I know?'

Cassius stared up at the grey sky. How long had he been on the island? Two hours at the most. And already the prospect of a pleasant, uneventful stay had gone up in flames.

But his mind was already working, and there was in fact one unavoidable answer to Indavara's question. As second in command of the Imperial Security Service, Memor's list of enemies would be long and varied.

Cassius took off his helmet and cradled it under his left arm, the spearhead still in his right hand. As they approached the open door, he noticed the veins of gold leaf running down the marble columns. Whatever problems Augustus Marius Memor had faced, financial trouble didn't seem to be one of them.

Trogus stood aside and gestured for Cassius and Indavara to enter, but then came a noise that froze the men where they stood: a terrible, high-pitched wail. For a moment, nothing was said; Cassius was stunned by the desperation and pain he'd heard.

'Mistress Marta,' Trogus explained. 'The surgeon is with her but he's been unable to calm her down.'

'Your master's wife?' asked Cassius as they stepped inside.

'No, sir. His youngest daughter.'

The big reception room was well lit by a square glass skylight. Subtle frescoes adorned two of the walls – one an exotic garden, the other the Seven Hills of Rome. There were also half a dozen mounted white busts. Cassius recognised four faces immediately: Caesar, Hadrian, Trajan and Domitian – founder of the Service. Excluding the entrance, doorways led off from the room in three directions. Several servants, male and female, were standing to the right, inspecting the new arrivals.

'Are there other men in the family?' Cassius asked Trogus.

'Unfortunately not, sir. And Mistress Leonita – my master's wife – is in ill health and confined to her bed. The surgeon has seen her too. I believe she's sleeping now.'

Indavara caught Cassius's eye and nodded down at the rug on which they were standing. Close to the doorway was a dark stain.

'He was killed here?' Cassius asked.

'No, sir. The doorman – Ligur.' Trogus lowered his voice. 'His throat was cut.'

'Where's the body?' Cassius asked, matching the steward's hushed tones.

'I had it taken to an outhouse this morning, sir. Master Memor too.'

'And what—'

'You! Who are you?'

The servants parted and a young woman appeared, striding towards Cassius. She was tall and long-limbed, her statuesque frame at odds with the delicate features of her face. Her skin was pale, similar in colour to her modest tunic and long, flowing stola. Her glossy brown hair had been hastily piled up on her head with several vicious-looking pins.

Marching along behind her were two big men, labourers by the looks of them.

'Mistress Annia,' Trogus said quietly. 'My master's eldest daughter.'

She stopped two yards from Cassius and fixed the steward with an imperious stare. 'Why have you let these men into the house without consulting me?'

'My apologies, Mistress,' said Trogus with a bow. 'This is Master Corbulo. He's with the Service. He was coming to fetch some documents.'

Cassius held up the spearhead, turning it so that the young lady could see the badge.

She glanced at it, then at him. Unlike Trogus and many of the servants, there was no sign she had been crying. She looked past Cassius at Indavara, who was still standing in the doorway. 'And him?'

'My bodyguard,' replied Cassius. 'May I offer my condolences. This is—'

Annia wasn't listening; she too had noted the bloodstained rug. Cassius was astonished by what happened next. She grabbed Trogus by the collar with one hand and pointed down at the rug with the other.

'Look at that!' she shrieked. 'Look at it, you old fool. Do you intend to just leave that there for my sister to see every time she walks past? Take it away! Take it away and burn it.'

'At once, Mistress.'

Annia let go of the steward. Before he could move away, she reached out and flattened the ruffled front of his tunic. Then she just stood there, shoulders hunched, head bowed.

Trogus waved the servants forward to help him with the rug. 'Young lady, if I may.'

Annia shut her eyes for a moment, then turned to Cassius. 'Yes?' she said softly.

'I would be very surprised indeed if the local magistrate wouldn't be interested in seeing that.' He pointed at the rug. 'And anything else pertaining to what occurred here.'

'Well we don't know what the magistrate wants because he isn't here, is he? Why don't you make yourself useful and go and fetch him?'

Cassius bit his tongue and reminded himself that the girl had just lost her father. He took a breath before answering. 'Where is he?'

'We don't know,' Annia said bitterly.

'I sent a messenger to the city this morning, sir,' added Trogus. 'Apparently he was in Lindos overnight. His office said he would come as soon as possible.'

Annia cast a despairing look out of the door. 'The sun will be down soon. Will you help?'

'I will do what I can, of course,' Cassius replied. 'Clearly we don't have much time left today, but if Trogus here can tell me exactly what happened, I can perhaps consult with the magistrate in the morning. We might at least get the investigation moving.'

One of the female servants anxiously approached Annia.

'What is it?' she snapped.

'Your mother, Mistress. She's awake. She's calling for you.'

Annia squeezed her eyes shut again, then looked up at Cassius.

'What do you do with the Service?'

'Generally whatever is required of me. I work for Aulus Celatus Abascantius. I am assigned to the office of the Governor—'

'Of Syria. I know. I *can* read. I know that name – Abascantius. My father mentioned him.'

Annia came closer. 'I want to know who did this. I want to know who did this and why and I want them found and I want them killed.'

Cassius held up his hands. 'As I said, miss, I will do what I can.'

Annia examined Cassius's face once more, then addressed Trogus.

'Give him whatever he needs.'

As she left, Cassius put his helmet and the spearhead down on a nearby table.

'Get rid of these people,' he told Trogus.

With a couple of gestures, the steward cleared the room.

'It is not sensible to have a woman in charge of a household at a time like this,' Cassius told him. 'They are not by nature

37

suited to such demands. Are there no relatives or friends who can take over here?'

'There is a cousin of Mistress Leonita but he lives in Ixia at the other end of the island. I've despatched a message but it will take him at least two days to get here. I'm afraid Mistress Annia has always been rather wilful, sir.'

'Evidently.'

'Without a male heir and with his wife so ill, Master Memor has treated her more like a son in some ways. He had so much work to occupy him and was often away. In practice Mistress Annia has run the household for several years.'

'I see. How old is she?'

'Nineteen.'

Cassius was surprised. She was old to still be living at home; had Memor married her off at a good young age there might at least have been a man around to help the family.

'Well, she needs to calm herself down. Now, tell me what happened, Trogus.'

'Yes, sir. Perhaps we should start in the study. That's where . . . where Master Memor was killed.'

'Very well.'

Trogus led them across the reception room and out through a portico with rooms to the left and a courtyard to the right. Several servants were gathered on the other side of the courtyard, outside what looked like the kitchen. A few barked orders from Trogus scattered them.

He stopped at the third room along. Unlike the other two, it was fitted with a wooden door and a lock. The steward pushed the door open and hesitantly entered, Cassius and Indavara behind him. In the middle of the little room was a hardwood desk facing a couch to the right. Next to the desk was a chair, the seat of which was dark with blood, as was the tasselled rug beneath. The desk had been cleared and cleaned. A stack of paper sheets and waxed tablets had been moved to the couch.

'He was found here,' said Trogus. 'By one of the serving girls

– just after dawn. Those screams. I thought the world was about to end.'

'He was killed sitting down?' Cassius asked.

'Yes. The . . . the body was still . . . upright. But . . . without the head. Please excuse—'

The steward rushed past them and out into the courtyard, sucking in air.

Cassius kept his gaze on the corridor. 'He – or they – must have been damned quiet and damned quick to get inside and kill him in his chair. A professional. The taking of the head suggests another party required proof the job had been done.'

'Strange that he came in through the front door,' said Indavara.

'Stranger still that the doorman seems to have let him in.'

'Might have been known to him. Might have been known to Memor.'

'Indeed.'

Trogus returned to the room. 'My apologies.'

'Was the door shut?' asked Cassius.

'I believe it was slightly ajar. The girl knocked, then opened it when there was no answer.'

'So had he woken early?'

'No. He was still wearing his tunic. He had stayed up. Nothing unusual. Often he would only sleep for a couple of hours at night then take his rest in the afternoon. As usual he insisted I turn in before him.'

'And this doorman? I'm assuming he was reliable?'

'Ligur had been with us for many years.'

'There's a viewing hatch in the front door isn't there?'

'Yes.'

'And didn't I see a lantern? You keep it alight all night?'

'We do. It was up to Ligur to keep it burning.'

'So he would have known who he was letting in?'

'I suppose he must have, yes. Which is odd, because my master didn't take kindly to unannounced visitations, certainly not at night. He insisted that people always made an appointment in advance. No such arrangement was made.'

'There's a knocker on the door too, isn't there? How loud is it?'
Trogus looked confused.

'My point is,' Cassius continued, 'would anyone else have heard it other than Ligur?'

'No, sir. No one else even knew there'd been a visitor. The sleeping quarters are towards the rear of the house. There is also a bell but that wasn't rung. Ligur had a chair next to the door. He would have heard any approach.'

'The main gate doesn't have a lock. Presumably you don't bother because the walls are so low?'

'That's right, sir. And the rear of the property backs on to open fields. Only the horse yard is fenced.'

'But the rest of the house?'

'Always secured at night, sir. Seven separate locked doors, including the front. I checked every one myself before retiring.'

'When would that have been?'

'The second hour of night.'

Cassius glanced at the bloodstained chair. 'And the maid found him at dawn. So it could have happened at any time in between. Had Memor been involved in any disputes with people on the island? Do you know of anyone with reason to harm him?'

'No. My master had an excellent reputation here. His work kept him very busy but he contributed funds to the village council, the assemblies in Rhodes and Lindos, and to more temples than I can recall.'

'And what of his work?'

'Master Memor generally kept that side of his affairs between himself and his colleagues within the Service, sir.'

'He hadn't spoken of any specific or current threats to him?'

'No, sir.'

'And his recent behaviour?'

'He had been worried about his wife's condition but I can think of nothing else.'

Cassius took a long breath. 'All right, I think we should see the bodies now. But first you must get together as many of the male staff as you can, then send them out on to the streets of the village. They needn't mention the murder but they must ask anyone they come across about any sightings of strangers over the last few days – people behaving suspiciously, especially close to the villa or the grounds. They must speak to anyone and everyone: children, slaves, whoever. Tell them to get back here within the hour.'

'At once, sir.'

Trogus hurried away towards the reception room and was soon shouting orders.

Two serving girls walked across the courtyard, arms over each other's shoulders, sobbing into handkerchiefs.

'You'd think it was one of their own family had been killed,' muttered Indavara.

'Don't assume their tears are for their master,' said Cassius. 'Who knows what the future holds for a houschold with only a girl left to run things?'

He looked at the pile of papers on the couch. 'I wonder if the documents for Abascantius are in there. I shall have to write to him and Chief Pulcher. I hope the weather holds; they must be informed.'

'Might they know something about what happened here?'

'Perhaps. But we wouldn't receive a reply for at least two weeks, probably a lot longer.' Cassius shook his head. 'No, yet again the gods have conspired to ensure I am the one left in the shit.'

Indavara wandered off to the left side of the room, moving slowly, eyes trained on the ground.

'Yes, I suppose we should have a look round,' said Cassius, walking over to the couch to examine the papers. There were a lot of letters, some of them clearly encoded. If there was time, he would have to go through it all. Perhaps the whole lot could just be sent to Chief Pulcher. How many issues had Memor been dealing with? Scores by the looks of it. Was one in particular connected to his death?

Cassius found nothing of interest on the bare tiled floor between the couch and the shelves that lined the right-hand wall. On the shelves themselves there were more objects than books – mainly

41

candles, ornaments and religious icons. The few tomes were standard reference works – mainly geographical and political.

'Nothing over here,' said Indavara.

'Here neither.'

'What's that?'

Indavara pointed at the wall opposite the door, and the only fresco in the room. It looked rather old and had been composed in dark oils. Only when he moved closer did Cassius realise that it depicted a black sky, a huge wave and a ruined strip of coast.

'Ah. I suspect that's a representation of a disaster that struck the island about a century ago. An earthquake caused a giant wave that wiped out much of the city.' Cassius turned to Indavara. 'A single, sudden event that left utter devastation in its wake. Seems rather apt.'

———8———

Most of the space in the outhouse was taken up by firewood and sacks of animal feed, but beyond the largest pile of timber was a big table. Poking out from beneath a blanket were the feet of the two dead men. Ligur, the doorman – by the far the bigger of the two – still had his sandals on. Only one of Memor's slippers remained.

Trogus stopped just inside the doorway and didn't seem keen to venture any further. Cassius and Indavara walked past him. There was no smell yet, only the musty odour of the wood. Indavara took hold of the blanket, waited for a nod from Cassius, then pulled it away.

They barely noticed the larger of the two corpses. Their eyes were drawn instantly to the headless body of Augustus Marius Memor. Dark blood and tissues of yellow and pink had congealed around the uneven cut that had severed his neck two inches above his collarbone. Thick maroon streaks lined the throat and chest, colouring most of the white tunic. His arms hung straight by his sides but the fingers were clawed and contorted – his last moments of resistance frozen for ever.

42

Memor had been slim, with pale skin and thick black hair upon his arms and legs.

Indavara walked round the table and looked down at the neck.

'Not many cuts. Done quickly but done well. Probably slit the throat then worked back from there. Short, strong blade. Wide dagger perhaps.' He glanced at the sheathed weapon on Cassius's belt. 'Like yours.'

Cassius had taken a moment to compose himself. He walked the other way round the table, past Ligur's head, and looked down at Memor. He was glad he hadn't known him; he tried to put aside the fact that the butchered form before him had once been a man. He let his eyes run over the body, looking for anything else they might use.

Indavara had already moved on.

'Ah,' he said. 'Look here.'

Cassius turned and looked down at the doorman. Despite the blood, two separate rents in his throat could clearly be seen. Stuck to the wounds were a few fibres from the rug.

'Ligur was found on his front, Trogus?'

'Yes,' replied the steward, still keeping his distance.

'So he probably turned his back on the assassin. He *must* have known him, must have felt safe. Same blade?'

'Think so,' said Indavara.

Cassius squeezed past him and squatted beside the table, inspecting the wounds from the side. 'See the angle of the cuts?'

Indavara knelt down. 'I see it. The killer had to reach up to slice his neck. He might have been shorter.'

'Quite a lot shorter.'

'Left-handed too.'

'How can you tell?'

'The cuts are thicker to the right, where the blade first punctured the skin.'

'So they are. You're rather good at this. I suppose you've seen more weapons and wounds than most.'

Indavara shrugged.

'See anything else?' Cassius said. 'On either of them?'

43

Indavara checked both men's hands. Cassius went to look at their feet. Other than the fact that Ligur's were dirty and Memor's were spotless there was nothing of note.

'No scratches on their fingers or broken nails,' observed Indavara. 'Neither of them had a chance to put up a fight.'

Cassius pointed down at the blanket. 'Put that back, would you?'

He found Trogus pacing around outside. Opposite the outhouse were the stables. Cassius' and Indavara's mounts had been tied to a rail and were slurping water from a trough. The horses in the stalls behind them watched the new arrivals and sniffed the air.

'What now, sir?' asked Trogus.

'Before the men come back I would like to see Mistress Annia.'

'I shall pass on your request at once, sir.'

'Also, those papers in the study. Presumably Memor had a lot of other documentation?'

'Yes. I believe most of it is in wooden boxes up in his bedroom.'

'I see.'

Just as Trogus was about to head back into the villa, Cassius held up a hand. 'One more thing. I need you to compile a list of men on the island known either to Ligur or Memor, or to both of them. I am especially interested in short, left-handed individuals.'

III

Having sent Indavara to look over the rest of the property, Cassius waited for Annia on a chilly stone bench in one corner of the courtyard. The sun was hovering over the roof opposite him and the shadows were long; they would have to head back to the city soon.

She came out through the kitchen door and hurried over to him. Cassius again noticed how well she carried herself, how purposefully she moved. That high chin and haughty manner were rather off-putting but there was no denying the pleasing proportions of her body, nor the sculptured lines of her face. He stood and waited for her to sit at the other end of the bench before retaking his seat, adjusting his cloak to ensure it wasn't touching the ground.

Annia was now wearing a black woollen cape, which she pulled tight over her chest. 'I asked the surgeon to go out and help the servants. The villagers might take more notice of him.'

'A good idea, miss. How are your sister and mother faring?'

Annia looked down at the ground. 'My mother is weak in body, my sister in mind. I've long learnt to expect little help from them.'

Cassius was surprised by the cold detachment in her voice; surely this was just the trials of the day talking.

'This is a terrible time for you all,' he said. 'May I formally offer my condolences.'

'Thank you.'

'I'm afraid I have some questions about your father.'

'Ask. Ask whatever you have to.'

'Trogus seems to know little of his work. Did he have a clerk

45

or an assistant of any kind, someone who might be able to tell me more?'

'My father almost always worked alone. Occasionally Trogus or I would take some dictation for him, but he said that the affairs of state were not matters to be shared. When he wasn't travelling he spent hours writing reports for Rome or dealing with his post. Sometimes we wouldn't see him between dawn and dusk.'

'Do you know of any recent issues, any mention of a possible threat?'

'No. But if he had thought he was in danger, I'm sure he would have told Trogus. Ligur too; he wasn't just a doorman, he would often travel with my father as his bodyguard. He was a legionary – he served with my father many years ago.'

'I see. And what of Master Memor's behaviour – anything out of the ordinary, anything to suggest he was in fear for his life? Think carefully.'

Annia took a moment, then shook her head. 'Not at all. In fact he seemed unusually relaxed. Last week he asked Marta and me to sing for him. And yesterday he took his long walk.'

'*Long* walk?'

'Yes, he went every morning. Usually a shorter route, sometimes a longer one around the lake.'

'Away from the property?'

'Yes, it's about five miles.'

'And he would walk every morning?'

'Without fail.'

'Alone?'

'Always – he said the day went a little easier if he'd time to prepare for it.'

Cassius looked away.

'What is it?' Annia asked.

'It seems to me that time was of the essence for the assassin. Had he watched the house for only a day he would have discovered a perfect opportunity to kill your father with minimal risk. And if he arrived very recently, I'll be surprised if he wouldn't want to leave with similar haste. It's late in the year; I can't believe he'd risk trapping himself on the island for the winter months. We shall focus our efforts on the port tomorrow. There can't be that many ships sailing in early November.'

'I shall come down myself at dawn.'

Cassius decided to snuff out this idea immediately; the last thing he needed was a woman – this one in particular – getting in the way.

'That won't be necessary.'

'Necessary? How well do you know this island, Master . . .'

'Corbulo.'

'Yes. Well?'

'I've been here only a day, miss, but it is my duty to investigate this matter for the Service. Please, leave it in my hands. I promise to keep you informed.'

'What if you catch the assassin? What will you do with him?'

Her replies were so quick, so pointed. Cassius was unused to speaking to a woman who refused to give up the initiative in a conversation.

'Miss, you must accept the possibility that we may not be able to find him.'

'But if you do?'

'I shall consult my superiors.'

'No.'

Cassius's patience was rapidly wearing thin.

'There will be no waiting around for weeks on end,' Annia continued, her eyes now bright and wet with tears. 'If you find him I want to see him. And then I want him killed. And I want to be there when it's done. Is that understood?'

'With the greatest of respect, Miss Annia, I do not answer to you.'

'What rank do you hold in the Service?'

Cassius couldn't believe what he was hearing. The extremes of female behaviour were nothing new to him – he had three older sisters after all – but even taking into account the horrors of the day, this girl's presumptuousness and arrogance were exceptional indeed.

'Nominally that of centurion,' he replied. 'Not that it should be of concern to you.'

'My father was deputy commander of the Service for almost a decade. He was dining with prefects and senators and protecting the Empire when you were nothing but a boy.'

Cassius took a calming breath, then stood. 'Your men will be coming back soon. I shall see if there's any more to be learnt here, then return to the city. You and your family have my deepest sympathies, but if you address me like that again, I shall leave the investigation to the local magistrate and depart for Antioch at once.'

'You wouldn't dare. Your superiors—'

'My superiors are a long, long way away. I am prepared to do all I can to help you, but I do not see why I should be subjected to such impertinence. Good day to you, *miss*.'

Annia didn't reply. As he reached the portico, Cassius heard her strike the bench.

———8———

Half an hour later, he stood with Indavara and Trogus by the front door as the men filed through the gate and up to the villa. The sun was setting now, deep orange colouring the towers and roofs of the high citadel to the north.

Indavara had just returned from checking the rest of the villa. He'd established that there were indeed numerous ways to approach the building from the rear, but with all the doors locked it would have been extremely difficult to get inside.

As the men came to a halt, the surgeon – a balding, well-attired fellow – hurried forward. 'I'm afraid I didn't turn up anything useful myself, but I believe some of the men have information to report. I must see how Mistress Leonita is.'

'Thank you, sir,' said Trogus.

As the surgeon went inside, Cassius turned to the men. 'Now, if you think you've heard something of interest, raise your hand. Do not worry about whether a matter seems trivial. I shall decide what is important or relevant.'

Of the eleven male staff, five raised their hands.

Cassius started with the man furthest to the left, an aged individual with striking white hair. 'You first.'

'Sir, a lady in one of the villas opposite said she'd seen two strangers loitering by the gate three days ago – they were there for more than an hour.'

'Did you get a description?' asked Cassius.

'She only saw them from—'

Trogus interrupted. 'They were tradesmen with an appointment to see me. We had guests so I had to keep them waiting. Men of good repute.'

The old servant bowed. 'My apologies, Steward.'

'Not necessary,' said Cassius. 'That's exactly the type of thing I want to hear about. Next.'

A younger man wearing a leather apron over his tunic spoke up.

'Esdras the shepherd saw a group of men out by the lake last week. Said they looked like thieves.'

Another of the men interjected: 'Sir, Esdras thinks everyone looks like thieves.'

Cassius considered what Annia had told him about her father's daily walks. 'You're quite right to mention it, but given the circumstances of the murder, it's probably not relevant.'

He pointed at the third man. 'You.'

'Sir, it's something I saw myself.'

'Go on.'

'I took a cart into town yesterday to buy some tiles. Coming round a bend about a half-mile out of the village I nearly ran over this man on foot. He was almost in the middle of the road. I gave him a right mouthful but he didn't say a word – just kept walking. Had this big sack over his shoulder.'

'What did you see of him?' asked Cassius.

'Not a lot, sir. He was wearing a hooded cloak. There was quite a wind blowing.'

Trogus came close to Cassius and whispered to him: 'I don't mean to make up your mind for you, sir, but Cimber there rather likes the sound of his own voice – I knew he would come out with something. The Via Alexandria is the main road to the south of the island, including Lindos. Travellers from the port come through Amyndios almost every day.'

'One other thing, sir,' volunteered Cimber, raising a hand. 'He had on a nice pair of leather boots.'

'So?' said Cassius.

'I noticed because they didn't seem to go with his cloak – tatty thing. And that old sack too. Nice pair of boots they were. Shiny and new.'

'All right – who's next?'

The fourth member of the staff to speak was a lad of about fourteen. 'Sir, some of the women down at the tannery were talking about a girl who was in the village this week. She came past several times and seemed very interested in the villa. Apparently she was asking about Master Memor – whether he was currently in residence or not.'

'Description?' asked Cassius.

'She was about twenty, sir. Long, curly hair. Very pretty they said.'

'They didn't recognise her?'

'No, sir.'

'Officer Corbulo,' said Trogus, 'could I speak to you for a moment?'

Cassius followed the steward, who didn't stop until he'd reached the edge of the orchard, well away from both the men and the villa.

'What is it?'

The steward scratched at his beard with his fingernails. 'Sir, I must ask that this matter remain between us.'

'Of course. Hurry up, man.'

'About three years ago, Master Memor had a brief affair with one of the serving girls: Aelia was her name. Long, curly hair. Very, very pretty. She began to believe the relationship was more than it was. She became rather unstable – threatened to tell Mistress Leonita of my master's indiscretions. Of course we had to let her go but she didn't take it well. Eventually Ligur and I had to pack up her things and escort her off the property. We pretended she'd been caught stealing. I gave her some money to disappear. Luckily the ladies of the house knew nothing of the truth.'

'And what?' demanded Cassius. 'You're not seriously suggesting that this girl returned three years later to wreak her revenge; visited the villa in the depths of the night, slashed the throat of an ex-legionary twice her size, then beheaded Master Memor.'

'I know it sounds ridiculous, sir, but that's not all. She left Rhodes shortly after she left here, but I heard a while ago that she'd returned to the island. She could be rather wild – always falling out with the other girls. Terrible temper.'

'Trogus, it's simply not possible.'

'Please, sir, I've not finished. I just remembered – how she stuck out when the girls were sat in a row weaving. She was left-handed.'

Cassius, who had bowed his head while listening to Trogus, straightened up and beckoned to Indavara. As he jogged towards them, Trogus continued:

'Sir, if this matter were to come out—'

'Yes, yes. I know.'

'What is it?' asked Indavara.

'Could a woman have carried out the killings?'

The bodyguard's disbelieving grin faded quickly when he saw Cassius was serious. 'It's possible, I suppose. The way it was done needed more skill than strength. Would explain the height difference.'

Cassius turned to Trogus. 'Do you know where she might be?'

'Her family were from Birrenia – a village about ten miles away.'

The steward scratched at his beard again and stared out at the road. 'By Jupiter, can it really be?'

'We don't know anything for certain yet,' warned Cassius.

'Shall I have your horses fetched, sir?' asked Trogus.

'Do so.'

The steward hurried back to the men and sent off two of the stable lads. The others were left standing in a line, whispering to one another.

'A woman? Really?' said Indavara quietly as he and Cassius returned to the front door.

'I know, but what else do we have to go on?'

Cassius addressed the men again: 'There was one more hand up. Who's yet to speak?'

One of the big labourers who'd appeared earlier with Annia stepped forward. 'Me, sir. It's not about a stranger or anything, I just thought it was odd.'

'Speak.'

'I saw old Astrah just now, a priest from the Temple of Dionysus. I said nothing of the murder but he asked if all was well at the house. He saw Master Memor last night and said he hadn't seemed quite himself.'

'I know Astrah,' added Trogus. 'Friendly old boy. Master Memor knew him too.'

'What did he mean "not himself"?' Cassius asked the labourer.

'Astrah was on his way home from closing up the temple – about the third hour of night. He saw Master Memor in the garden. He hailed him but Master Memor just raised a hand and continued up to the house.'

Frowning, Cassius turned to Trogus. 'You said he often worked through the night, but why would he be outside? Might he have been preoccupied or concerned about something?'

'It's possible, sir. He did sometimes take a glass of wine and a walk in the orchard, but never at night. He had the courtyard next to his study if he wanted some air.'

'A meeting perhaps? This girl even.'

Trogus shrugged.

The labourer came closer. 'Sir, Astrah mentioned something even stranger. He said Master Memor was in full uniform – helmet, crest, everything.'

'What?' said Trogus.

'That's impossible,' said another of the servants. 'Master's metal is all with me. I cleaned and oiled it yesterday. It's still in my cupboard.'

'By the gods, it was *him*,' said Cassius. 'The old priest thought it was Memor but it was *him*.' He pointed at Cimber, the man who'd spoken earlier. 'The hooded stranger *he* saw yesterday. That's what he was carrying in the sack; that's why he had those boots on; and that's why Ligur let him in. The bastard was dressed as a centurion.'

——■8■——

Two hours after sunset, they arrived back at the way station. Following the sea wall across the harbour, they heard the songs and laughter of merry sailors. The choppy water bumped the vessels tied to the quay and the wind rattled rigging and rope. Unfortunately, the onshore breeze wasn't quite strong enough to do away with the odour of rotting fish.

Cassius and Indavara led the horses along a narrow alley and into the small courtyard between the way station and the stables. A bleary-eyed Optio Clemens appeared from the rear door, holding a lantern. Cassius told him he needed to speak with him at once. While the optio summoned the legionary to deal with the horses, Cassius and Indavara went in to the little parlour.

Simo had a pan of warm wine ready. He greeted the returning pair and poured each of them a generous measure.

'Nice stuff, this, sir. A local concoction – I believe there's myrrh in it.'

Cassius took a long sip.

Simo examined his face. 'Are you all right, sir?'

'No, Simo, I'm not. I trust my bed's ready?'

'Of course, sir.'

'Prepare my writing materials. Best ink and paper.'

'Yes, sir.'

Simo hurried away.

'Need me?' asked Indavara.

'No, go ahead.'

53

The bodyguard took his wine with him.

'Well, sir?' asked Clemens as he returned to the parlour.

Cassius gestured to the bench in front of the hearth. They sat down and he described what had occurred in Amyndios. Clemens looked aghast when he heard the grisly details and seemed stunned that such a thing could occur on the island.

Cassius instructed him to send a message to the magistrate, enquiring about what action he had taken so far and suggesting that he prevent any seagoing ships from leaving the port. Clemens was also to gather every available soldier and bring them to the way station. As was his right, Cassius intended to requisition the troops for as long as he needed them. All this was to be carried out within the first hour of the day.

'How many legionaries will you be able to get?' Cassius asked.

'Only my century – the Fifth – is permanently stationed in the city, sir. The barracks are close to the citadel but most of them are away rebuilding a bridge down in Camiros. Perhaps a dozen or so.'

'And the magistrate? How many sergeants does he have?'

'Quite a few, but I wouldn't rely on too much cooperation from that quarter.'

'Why not?'

'The magistrate is elected by the people; a sop to the Rhodian Assembly. His name is Nariad. Well connected but rather ineffectual, and he's not known for considering demands from the army a priority.'

'We're talking about the murder of the Service's second in command. He is bound by imperial law to assist me.'

'Fair enough, sir. It's just that the locals think a little differently here. They're very fond of reminding us that Rhodes was a naval power before we knew one end of a ship from the other. I've had half a dozen different postings in my time and, believe me, it's not your typical province.'

'Well, as long as I can depend on you and your men. I shall give detailed instructions in the morning.'

'Sir.' Clemens laid his hands across his ample gut and stared into the burning coals of the fire. 'Beheaded. By Mars.'

'You've not heard of any disputes involving Memor?'

'Not one. As I said, we hardly ever saw him unless he was leaving or returning. He used to send one of his men to collect the post. He always seemed a decent enough sort to me.'

'Even for a "grain man"?'

Clemens glanced anxiously at his superior.

Cassius continued: 'How were relations between Memor and the other officers here?'

'I don't know if Master Memor ever even visited the barracks. He certainly didn't advertise his presence. I think he said to me once that's why he liked it here – he was left alone to get on with his job.'

'Yes. I think he'd come to feel very safe here. Too safe, in fact.'

Cassius stood up, took a last swig of wine and left the mug on the table. 'Get some sleep, Clemens. I want you up before the sun.'

He walked out of the parlour and turned left. There were four small bedrooms in the way station. Indavara was sleeping in the one closest to the parlour, Cassius and Simo in the second. There was only one bed, so – not for the first time – Simo would have to make do with a pile of blankets on the floor.

The Gaul was sitting on the bed with a wooden writing board on his lap, mixing some ink. Beside him were two sheets of paper and Cassius's best silver pen – a gift from his father for his sixteenth birthday. Cassius undid the clasp that held his cloak together, took it off and threw it on to a chair – the only other piece of furniture in the room. To this he added his sword belt, then his main belt.

He slumped down next to Simo. Stretching out his legs he tried to lie back on the bed but it was too narrow to get comfortable. Simo placed a pillow under his master's head.

'Indavara told me what happened, sir. That poor family. It's beyond belief.'

'Quite horrible. But applying a little cold logic to the situation, the event itself is actually not that incredible. Can you imagine the number of people someone in Memor's position might have accused, imprisoned, exiled or had killed over the years?'

The Gaul looked shocked.

'Come on, Simo. I think you've heard enough from me to know that the Service rarely attracts the most wholesome of characters. No, what's beyond belief is that I should arrive here on Rhodes the day after the murder is committed, thereby ensuring I have to deal with the whole ghastly mess.'

Cassius blew out his cheeks and stared at the ceiling.

'Perhaps this letter can wait until morning, sir.'

'*Letters*, actually. No. I shall be busy enough tomorrow. In any case, they're both finished.' Cassius tapped his head. 'I did them on the way back. Only about two hundred words each. We shall be done in an hour.'

'I take it you'd like me to write, then, sir.'

'Your handwriting's better than mine anyway. Ready?'

Simo tested the nib on the writing block. A spot of ink came out. He placed the first of the sheets on the block and raised the pen.

'Ready, sir.'

IV

Less than an hour after dawn, the Great Harbour was alive with activity. Fishing boats cast off from the quay, stores opened their doors and the locals converged on another freighter that had arrived late the previous evening. Several hours of rain during the night had left puddles on the streets and a clammy cold in the air.

Cassius jumped up on to the sea wall. He looked to the north, towards the Little Harbour, and saw the masts of at least twenty seagoing vessels. Simo was over there somewhere, trying to find ships heading in the right direction. It was unlikely the letters to Abascantius and Chief Pulcher would follow a direct route but – for a fee – a willing captain would deliver them to an army way station and the imperial post would do the rest. Simo had already tried the Great Harbour but of the dozen ships there, eight were now ensconced for the winter, two were undergoing repairs and two were heading in the wrong direction.

Cassius glanced up at the tightly packed buildings on the terraced hillside below the citadel. Clemens was up there somewhere, fetching men from the barracks, and Cassius was impatiently awaiting his return. The optio had sent the message to the magistrate's office but there was still no reply.

Dropping to the ground, Cassius picked his way through a group of women cleaning up the remnants of yesterday's market – mostly stinking fish remains and clumps of straw. He found Indavara in the way-station parlour, tearing a corner off a loaf. The still unseen maid had left out some breakfast on the table.

'Morning,' said the bodyguard.

'Unlikely to be a good one, I'm afraid.'

'We're off round the ships, then?'

'Indeed.' Cassius half filled a mug with wine then topped it up with water.

'You said there won't be many on the move this time of year,' added Indavara. 'Shouldn't be that hard.'

'Yes, but it's not just the big ships. There are these coasters that make runs to the nearby islands or the mainland – it's only fifty miles or so to Lycia or Asia Minor. Then there are the other ports on the island – Lindos, for example.'

'Ah.'

'But there should be a harbour master around who can help us find out which ships have left and which are about to leave. Hopefully, Simo's already tracked him down.'

Cassius took a dried fig from a plate.

'Sir!'

He looked along the corridor to see Clemens waving at him from the road. Behind him were some legionaries.

'Bring them round to the courtyard!'

'Yes, sir.'

Cassius ate the fig and washed it down with wine. 'Bring those, would you?'

Indavara picked up a pile of small squares of paper from the table. Cassius pulled on his helmet, then checked his belt and straightened his cloak. He motioned for Indavara to go outside first, then stationed himself on the parlour doorstep while the legionaries filed into the courtyard. With a few swift orders, Clemens got the men into line.

Cassius stood with his feet well apart, hands on his belt, his chin high; the stance he always used when addressing troops. He counted eleven of them. There was no need for helmets or armour but their other equipment seemed in good repair; always an encouraging sign. There was no long hair, no bushy beards, and no evidence of drunkenness.

'Good morning, men. I am Officer Cassius Quintius Corbulo, Imperial Security.'

To their credit, not one of the legionaries' faces betrayed

what Cassius imagined would be a colourful array of mental retorts.

'You know now of the death of Master Augustus Marius Memor. This murder was carried out the night before last, and I believe the assassin left – or will be intending to leave – Rhodes as soon as possible. We must find out whatever we can about this man. We have at least established the following: he is probably left-handed, probably short, and he was seen wearing a hooded cloak and good-quality boots. He was also carrying a sack, and inside was what he used to disguise himself and carry out the killing – a centurion's outfit. It's likely he is a stranger here and that he arrived recently. You men know the city – you must scour the harbour, the inns, the taverns, the stores. Talk to captains, sailors, innkeepers – anyone and everyone. The main details of his appearance are written here, so there's no excuse for forgetting them.'

While Indavara handed out the scraps of paper, some of the less subtle legionaries inspected his disfigured ear.

'Remember,' said Cassius. 'Short, left-handed, hooded cloak, fine leather boots, carrying a sack. Can everyone read?'

'Not me, sir,' volunteered one of the men. 'But I can remember it well enough,' he added, before repeating the description verbatim.

'Excellent.'

Though cooperative, the men didn't seem particularly enamoured with their task, not that soldiers ever did, unless women, drink or treasure were involved.

'An additional incentive for you,' Cassius announced, 'courtesy of Imperial Security. Ten denarii to any man who gives me information I can use. And tell the people on the streets they'll get half as much for the same. If this man's still here I want him found, and I want him found today. Clemens will divide you up and tell you which areas you are to cover. We shall reconvene later. Any questions? No? On your way then.'

The legionaries followed Clemens out of the courtyard, rather too slowly for Cassius's liking. He clapped his hands together. 'Let's get to it then! A little more urgency, gentlemen!'

Clemens led the way with a trot, which the soldiers reluctantly matched.

'We should be off too,' Cassius told Indavara as they hurried back to their rooms. 'See how Simo's getting on.'

While Indavara went to fetch his weapons, Cassius grabbed the leather satchel Abascantius had given him in Syria. It was very well made (deer-hide according to Simo) and ideal for carrying papers and other essentials. Cassius insisted that Simo always kept a few key items inside: some paper and charcoal for making notes, a small fire-starting kit, a couple of candles and a miniature sundial. He'd also had the Gaul stitch in a secret pocket that contained five gold aurei, commenting, 'You never know when you might need a good bribe.' The satchel was also just about big enough to accommodate the spearhead, though the tip stuck out of one end. Cassius placed it inside and slung the satchel over his shoulder.

He sighed. One of the worst things about army life was constantly being weighed down with equipment, as if the helmet and sword belt weren't uncomfortable enough. Riding helped ease the load but was impractical for the day ahead. Cassius sighed again. Thoughts of temples and libraries and works of art were but a distant memory now.

———◆8◆———

They met Simo a hundred yards up the road. Despite the stiff breeze, the Gaul was sweating, carrying his cloak in one hand as he hurried along the sea wall.

'Well?' asked Cassius, handing over the satchel.

'Apologies, sir, I was unable to find a suitable ship there either. Most of them are staying in port too.'

'Wonderful. What about the harbour master?'

'I did find his office, sir, but there was only a clerk there. Apparently, because things are very quiet at this time of year, the harbour master takes every fourth day off. This is one of them. I found him at a tavern called The Anchor, but he refused to speak to me. Sir, I am sorry.'

'He'll be the sorry one. Take me to this tavern at once.'

The trio walked on along the wall and it soon became obvious that the names of the harbours were even more misleading than they first appeared. The Little Harbour was indeed about the same size as the Great Harbour – and also enclosed by long breakwaters running out to the west and north – but it was far busier and more developed. Almost every space on the high concrete wharves was occupied by large vessels of a hundred feet or more. Squeezed in between them were smaller skiffs and tenders, often tied up two or three abreast.

They left the road and cut across one of the wharves, between a stack of barrels and a massive wooden wheel. Next to it were a pile of long timbers, coiled lengths of thick rope and four huge pulleys.

'What's that thing?' asked Indavara.

'A crane,' said Cassius. 'The wheel is mounted on a stand and connected to a rope that runs up an arm and down to the load. Slaves stand inside the wheel and walk; the wheel turns and the crane lifts the load. Quite ingenious.'

'Just like mice in a cage,' said Indavara, more to Simo than to Cassius.

'I can think of worse jobs,' said Cassius. 'On days like this I'd be quite happy to do nothing but walk.'

Indavara snorted. 'Oh yes, it's so easy – the life of a slave.'

'I don't say it's easy, but in some ways it's *easier*. Less responsibility, for one.'

Indavara shook his head. 'What do you reckon, Simo?'

Simo glanced warily at Cassius, who shrugged.

'Answer if you wish.'

'Whatever one's station in life, one will have problems, I suppose,' Simo said eventually. 'The Lord Jesus taught us that we should think first of others, those in suffering, the poor—'

'Well done, Indavara,' said Cassius, 'you've got him started now.'

The bodyguard moved closer to Simo. 'You Christians believe that everyone is equal, yes?'

'We believe God values us all equally, and that we will all face the final judgement if we wish to reach the kingdom.'

Indavara jabbed a finger at Cassius. 'But how can you be equal if you belong to *him*?'

'One's station in life is not as important as how one conducts oneself,' Simo explained.

'What?'

Cassius held up a hand. 'Indavara, not now. We have enough to occupy us today. Leave the religion and philosophy for another occasion – you'll give yourself a headache.'

—8—

They passed several moored ships – including a flat-hulled dredging barge – and reached the far side of the Little Harbour. Most of the buildings were high, red-brick warehouses, but clustered around a crossroads were some low structures more like the houses that faced the Great Harbour. The road that ran along the north side of the port continued into the heart of the city, then up, zigzagging across the terraced slopes before reaching the citadel.

'That's the harbour master's office, sir,' said Simo, pointing to what looked like a storefront. 'Two doors down is the tavern.'

They negotiated a long queue outside a money changer's, waited for a well-laden cart to rumble past, then crossed the road to the tavern. Were it not for the people outside, Cassius would have assumed The Anchor was closed. Several of the windows were boarded up and the roof had a quarter of its tiles missing. A painted sign had been stripped of all colour by the elements, though there was a rusty iron anchor by the door. Of the two tables outside, one was in fact a converted half of a rowing boat. Sitting inside were three lads throwing pebbles at a gull. The other table was occupied by four men playing some kind of board game. They were a rough-looking bunch: bearded, grizzled and tanned.

'Which one's the harbour master?' Cassius asked Simo.

62

'The older man, sir. Wearing the felt cap.'

'Hang back to start with,' Cassius told Indavara. 'If he doesn't cooperate, make your presence known. But let's avoid any unpleasantness if possible.'

The harbour master threw three dice and moved his glass counter. He and the other players were still discussing the move when the trio approached the table. The harbour master glanced up at Simo and rolled his eyes. 'You again.'

'And me, this time,' said Cassius. 'I'm sure Simo told you who his master was. Are you in the habit of ignoring requests from officers of the Roman Army?'

Before the harbour master could answer, another man spoke up. 'On his day off, he's in the habit of ignoring everything except the next game of Twelve Lines or the next cup of Lindos's best.'

Two of the others found this hilarious.

The harbour master turned to Cassius. 'What's the problem?'

Cassius was already annoyed; the man hadn't addressed him as 'sir'.

'I'll tell you that when you've stood up and accompanied me back to your office. A most important matter. I haven't time to waste.'

'My clerk will tell you all you need to know.'

'Not good enough.'

The harbour master sipped his wine and gave a resigned shake of his head. The man who'd made the quip pointed at Cassius's helmet.

'I can see you're Roman, but we ain't.' He pointed in turn at his friends, starting with the harbour master: 'Rhodian, Egyptian, Spanish, and I'm Carthaginian.'

'Forget it, Korinth,' said the harbour master, collecting up his pile of coins. 'We can play later.'

Korinth, whose muscled bulk strained against his undersized tunic, had strange dark tattoos circling his neck and wrists. His right cheek had been disfigured by a burn – a curiously angular slab of smooth, orange skin. He put a hand on the harbour master's shoulder.

'Stay where you are. It's your day off.'

'I don't care if it's Saturnalia,' said Cassius. 'A man has been killed. A very important man.'

'This man,' replied Korinth. 'Roman, I take it?'

'If you were born free in the Empire, so are you. As are we all.'

Korinth and the others laughed at this. The harbour master restricted himself to a grin. Cassius felt his face reddening.

'He'll come when he's finished his game,' said Korinth, running a hand through his wild tangle of hair.

Cassius turned slightly to his right.

Indavara got the message. He stepped forward and kicked the table, knocking drinks, coins and the board flying.

'Looks like the game's over,' he said.

One of the men looked down at his wine-soaked tunic. 'You son of a bitch.'

Korinth jumped up and made a grab for Indavara. Unfortunately for him, his legs were between the bench and table, so when Indavara swiped his hand away then pushed him in the chest, he went flying backwards, hitting the ground hard.

'Uff!'

The other three scrambled free of the table.

'All right that's enough!' yelled Cassius as he and Simo got out of the way. The harbour master put his hands up. The man with the wet tunic helped Korinth to his feet and the pair advanced side by side, eyeing Indavara. The bodyguard was armed with both dagger and sword but he reached over his shoulder and pulled the stave from his back.

'I suggest you two calm down and walk away,' advised Cassius.

By now the young lads and several passers-by had gathered to watch the impending fight. Cassius looked around but couldn't see any of the soldiers nearby.

Korinth didn't have a dagger on his belt, but hanging from his neck on a length of twine was a five-inch rope-spike. These were usually used for untying knots, but as he pulled it off over his head it was evident to all that he had a different application

64

in mind. His friend drew his dagger – a narrow but sharp blade – and spat at Indavara's feet.

Shouts from the other side of the road. Four young men wielding wooden clubs were sprinting towards the tavern. Behind them was an older man. He was unarmed, holding only the bulky chain around his neck.

Indavara spun round and saw the four men bearing down on him. He glanced at Cassius, who was backing away, still trying to work out what was going on. Apparently facing threats from both sides, Indavara decided to take matters into his own hands.

He turned back to the sailors, adjusted his grip on the stave and shoved it straight into the gut of the man with the dagger. The man's mouth formed a wide O as he dropped on to his backside. Holding the rope-spike out in front of him, Korinth sprang forward.

His progress was instantly halted as the stave struck him on the chest with a hollow crack. Arms flailing, he flew back into the table. The impact snapped a plank and sent a jug of wine flying into the wall of the tavern. It exploded spectacularly.

'Stop!' shouted Cassius.

Indavara – who had already spun back round towards the road again – nodded at the advancing men. 'Why don't you tell them!'

The men showed no sign of stopping, and Indavara had no intention of letting them get in the first blow. He came out to meet the lead man and swung two-handed at his shoulder. The clubbing blow knocked his foe clean off his feet and into one of the others, who was sent sprawling to the ground. The other two skidded to a halt.

'I said stop!'

Cassius ran over and got between them and Indavara. 'All of you, stop!'

'What's going on here?' asked the older fellow, bustling his way between the others, two more men coming up behind him. Cassius now noticed the object attached to his neck chain – a silver rendering of a familiar design of club.

'You the magistrate?' Cassius asked.

'Of course. I am Gratus Nariad: Chief Inspector of Markets, Chief Inspector of Harbours and Chief Inspector of the Municipality. Who in the name of the gods are you?'

'Corbulo, Imperial Security,' Cassius replied, gesturing up at his helmet. 'Didn't you receive a message from Optio Clemens?'

'No.'

'Aaagh! Shit!' cried the guard Indavara had struck. 'I think he broke my arm.'

The other man sat next to him, staring down at the cuts and scrapes on his hands.

Korinth had recovered himself for a second time. He rubbed his chest, then picked up his rope-spike and staggered towards Indavara. 'You little bastard.'

'Indavara, over here,' instructed Cassius.

Indavara didn't move an inch.

'Magistrate,' said Cassius, 'I want that man arrested. Now.'

'What?'

'He attacked my bodyguard. Tell your sergeants to arrest him.'

'You one-eared whoreson,' growled Korinth, bringing the spike up level with his face. 'I'll take off the other one too, make you look nice and even.'

'Don't mention his ear,' Cassius warned.

The magistrate was staring at the combatants, frozen by indecision. Cassius yelled at him: 'By the authority of the Imperial Roman Army, I order you to arrest that man at once!'

At last, the magistrate acted.

'All right. Do it,' he said, pushing his sergeants forward.

Cassius took hold of Indavara by the shoulders. The bodyguard shook him off but got out of the sergeants' way.

'Don't make this worse than it already is, man,' the magistrate told the enraged sailor.

The harbour master spoke up too: 'He's right, Korinth. Put it down. There's no real harm done yet.'

Korinth was breathing hard, teeth set in a snarl, but after a few moments he lowered the spike.

One of the sergeants came forward. 'Hand it over.'

Korinth gave the young sergeant the weapon but he was still glaring at Indavara. 'You better hope we don't meet again.'

Indavara gave a crooked smile as he lowered the stave, then slung it over his back. 'I thought sailors were supposed to be tough. Stick to tying ropes, friend.'

Korinth made another lunge for him but by this time he was surrounded by the sergeants. After a brief struggle, they locked his arms by his side.

'You have a cell?' asked Cassius.

'Yes.'

The magistrate pointed at Korinth. 'Take him back to headquarters.'

'Him too,' said Cassius pointing at the second sailor, who was hunched over, retching.

'Why?'

'He pulled a knife on us.'

'Very well. Men – him too.'

The other sailor straightened up and came forward voluntarily. 'All right. I'm coming.' He shook his head. 'Drinking in the morning. Why do I do it?'

The four uninjured sergeants escorted Korinth and his friend away through the small crowd that had gathered. The magistrate instructed the other two to get up, then puffed out his chest. 'You people move along. I am Chief Inspector of the Municipality and I command it. Move along there! Move along!'

The crowd reluctantly broke up, all except the boys, who were still staring at Indavara. Cassius strode over to the harbour master and poked him in the arm. 'Get back to your office. I want to see all your documentation regarding arrivals and departures for the last week. Understood?'

'It's all right,' added the magistrate. 'You can do as the officer says.'

'Yes, sirs,' said the harbour master before trotting away.

'Might I have a word?' said Cassius.

The magistrate followed him into the narrow alley between the tavern and the house next door.

'What was the name again?'

'Nariad. And yours?'

'Corbulo.'

Nariad was a slender man with a long, curved nose and a thick head of oiled black hair. His cloak was lined with silver braid and he had rings on most of his fingers.

Cassius took the spearhead out of his satchel and held it so that the point was only a couple of inches from Nariad's chin. 'Know what this is?'

The magistrate's eyes almost crossed as he looked down. 'Of course,' he gulped.

'Then you'll know that it obliges any official or soldier I encounter to lend me assistance: immediate and unquestioning assistance – not that I would even need to be involved if you'd done your job in the first place. Tell me why you aren't in Amyndios right now, investigating the death of Augustus Marius Memor.'

'I was planning to ride over later this morning. A tragedy. A great loss.'

Nariad failed to imbue his words with even a vestige of genuine concern.

'Not a tragedy,' said Cassius. 'A killing. The murder of the second in command of the Imperial Security Service.'

Nariad seemed to regain a little nerve. He reached for the small silver club on the chain round his neck and held it up. 'I wonder, young man, do you know what *this* is? You seem to imagine I have nothing else to concern me.'

'This investigation *must* take precedence. You say you didn't receive the message sent by Optio Clemens on my behalf?'

'I was out of the city most of yesterday and last night. As well as the assembly meeting tomorrow, I have an outbreak of pestilence on the east of the island to deal with. I cannot be everywhere at once! In fact, it's lucky for you that my men and I happened to be passing.'

Cassius almost laughed. 'By the great gods. How much did you pay for your position? It clearly wasn't attained through merit.'

Nariad looked genuinely shocked. 'You can't talk to me like that! I shall go straight to the governor.'

Cassius was in no mood for compromise; he knew he held the upper hand. 'Were this a bigger, more important city, in a bigger, more important province, that might concern me. But if I inform Chief Pulcher that you not only failed to take charge of this investigation with appropriate haste, but also obstructed my efforts, it will take more than the help of some second-rate governor to save you. I don't even know the man's name. But I see you know Pulcher's.'

The colour had drained from Nariad's face. It wasn't the first time Cassius had invoked his ultimate superior, and the response was invariably the same. Abascantius had assured him that the chief was a noble man and a true patriot, but Pulcher's reputation was that of a ruthless spymaster, a man who would do anything he considered necessary to safeguard the interests of the Empire. He had served four emperors and brought down generals, governors and senators in his time.

'I have a signed letter of authorisation from him,' Cassius continued. 'Would you like to see it?'

He did have such a letter, though it was actually back at the way station.

'No, no,' replied Nariad. 'That won't be necessary. After a moment's reflection I see that you're right, Officer. I have been lax.'

Cassius marched out of the alley. He was too angry to draw any satisfaction from the exchange; the whole incident had wasted more valuable time.

'Tell me, Officer,' said Nariad, hurrying after him. 'How *is* the investigation progressing? What exactly can I do to help?'

V

'I apologise, sir,' said the harbour master, removing his cap and turning it in his hands as Cassius, Indavara and Simo walked into his office. 'I should have come when you asked me to. Now Korinth and Magga are in trouble on my account.'

'Indeed they are,' Cassius replied. 'And you're damned lucky not to be joining them. You do however have an immediate chance to redeem yourself. What's your name?'

'Akritos.'

The harbour master was standing behind a rickety desk stained with oil and wax. Also present was his young clerk, who was by a shelf stacked with boxes of documentation. Mounted on the wall were several bronze plaques with statements in Greek reinforcing the authority of the harbour master under local and imperial law.

'First, tell me this,' said Cassius. 'Have any ships left this morning?'

Akritos turned to the clerk, who shook his head.

'Lucky,' said Cassius. 'Especially for Nariad.'

The magistrate had left, now promising to devote all available resources to the investigation.

'Anything *scheduled* to leave today?' asked Cassius.

The clerk stepped forward. 'An Egyptian freighter was supposed to be leaving first thing, sir. Captain hasn't been in yet though.'

'So they're still here?'

'Yes, sir.'

'We keep a good lookout,' added Akritos, pointing to a ladder at the rear of the room running up to a hatch. 'Plus they have

70

to come and pay their wharf dues and organise a tow-out if they need one.'

Cassius glanced down at the open leather-bound book on the desk. 'Is that what I asked for?'

'It is.'

'You keep a record of *every* departure or arrival?'

'Only for ships – which are vessels with a hold wider than eight yards.'

'Show me the departures from yesterday,' Cassius instructed.

Akritos struggled to find the right page amongst the loose sheets yet to be tied into the book. The clerk swiftly took over and located it.

'Here, sir,' said the young man. 'Six vessels in all.'

'Really?' queried Cassius. 'At this time of year?'

'That's because of Phalalis,' replied the harbour master, 'the old boy the captains go to for their weather. He said there'd be pretty clear skies for three days so a few of them made a run for it yesterday. Might not get another chance this season.'

Cassius grabbed the page. The clerk had made notes for each of the six vessels, with details of the captain's name; time and date of arrival and departure; origin and destination; type and amount of cargo; and wharf dues paid.

'Nothing on passengers,' he said to himself. Typically, those seeking transportation aboard ship simply asked around and made arrangements with cooperative captains; Cassius had done precisely that when organising their journey from Cilicia.

He sat down on the chair Simo had brought over for him. 'Come round here, you two.'

Cassius placed his finger next to the first of the six entries. 'The *Chios*, captained by one Placcus Onginus. Arrived from Miletus at the ninth hour on the second, left at the first hour on the fifth – yesterday – bound for Seleucia. Cargo unloaded: dried fish, dried fruit and iron implements. Cargo loaded: wine and figs. You don't take notes on taxes paid?'

Before they could answer there was a knock on the office door. Akritos waved the clerk over to deal with the man standing there.

'Not our job, sir,' he told Cassius. 'That's down to the revenue people.'

'Nariad's office.'

'Correct.'

'So they actually go on board?'

'Yes, sir.'

'Then they might know which ships had passengers?'

'They might, sir. They usually only check the cargo though.'

Cassius looked back at the page and examined the rest of the entries. 'Why is there a space between the first four ships and the last two?'

'Last two are what a sailing man would call coasters, sir, but with big holds, so we have to take their details.'

'This second coaster. It arrived three days ago and unloaded four dozen barrels of oil but didn't take anything on board.' Cassius checked the other entries. 'All the other vessels took on considerable loads.'

'Of course,' said Akritos, 'you're throwing money away with an empty hold.'

'So it's unusual?'

'Very.'

Cassius looked back at the page. 'And why is there no listing for the time of departure?'

The clerk had by now dealt with the visitor so returned to the desk.

'Ah yes, sorry, sir, that's the *Scyros* – they had a problem with their rudder. They were supposed to go yesterday but—'

'You mean it's still here?'

'Yes, sir,' replied the clerk. 'I believe they're bound for Macedonia.'

Akritos grunted.

'What?' asked Cassius.

'Long way home – in a ship that small at this time of year.'

'You think it's a lie?'

'Either that or they're braver men than me.'

'Maybe they don't have any choice.'

Cassius stood up and handed the page to Simo. 'You're going to show me this ship,' he told the clerk. 'Akritos, I want you to spread the word. No seagoing vessel is to leave without my express permission. Understood?'

Akritos put his cap back on. 'Sir, you'll need Magistrate Nariad's authorisation for that.'

'Consider it given.'

— 8 —

A light rain began to fall as they strode along the coast road, now accompanied by a pair of legionaries Cassius had collared. The *Scyros* was moored some distance away, beyond the last of the warehouses, close to where the wharf became the northern breakwater.

'Looks like this weather forecaster was wrong,' Cassius said to the clerk.

'Yes, sir. Just a cloudburst I think, though. The sailors really do listen to him. He makes more money than the augurs.'

'Officer! Officer Corbulo!'

Cassius turned to see a covered carriage approaching at speed. Next to the driver was the diminutive figure of Trogus, waving frantically. Cassius and the others moved off the road as the driver brought the horses to a stop.

'Wonderful,' muttered Cassius when he saw that sitting under the carriage's fabric roof were young Mistress Annia and someone he presumed to be her maid – a sweet-looking girl of about the same age. The driver got down and steadied the horses.

'Morning, sir.'

'Trogus.'

Annia had a little more colour about her than the previous day but was wrapped up in the same black cape. 'Good day, Officer Corbulo.'

'Good day, miss.'

'How are things proceeding?'

'Well at least they *are* proceeding now. I had a frank exchange

73

of views with Magistrate Nariad and he is cooperating fully. His sergeants are assisting the legionaries to see if anyone recalls anything about the assassin. I am trying to establish the man's movements.'

'And?'

'Nothing yet. But the day is young.'

Annia looked past him at the others. 'Where are you going now?'

'Just making enquiries.'

'Are you concerned with one ship in particular? You know my father had a lot of dealings in Africa, you might look for ships from there.'

'Miss, I really must get on. Perhaps if you return to the villa – I shall ensure you're kept abreast of any developments.'

'No, no. I can't wait around there all day.'

'Perhaps a visit to the governor then, to make sure he also understands the gravity of the situation?'

Cassius noticed Trogus wince but as long as the girl was out of his way, he didn't care.

'Perhaps,' replied Annia. 'Shall we arrange a meeting for later?'

'I really don't know where I'll be. But don't worry, I promise to keep you apprised.'

Annia leant over the side of the carriage and ushered Cassius closer. 'If you need money, please just ask,' she said quietly. 'Whatever is required.'

In truth, this was one area where her help might prove useful. Cassius had only his own money with him, and there were no senior army administrators in the city from whom he could secure funds.

'I shall, miss. Thank you.'

'Please do your best for us.'

Though the distinctly unladylike attitude remained, Cassius was relieved to note the improvement in her manner.

'Of course.'

———8———

74

The *Scyros* was a broad, high-sided vessel about seventy feet long. The yard had been raised and the brown mainsail hung beneath it, bunched up like a huge curtain. Close to the stern were four crewmen working on the ship's tiller, talking in a language Cassius didn't recognise. Aside from the fact that they were all dark-skinned, black-haired and wearing long, beltless tunics, Cassius could deduce little from the sailors' appearance. Noticing the visitors, they looked up at the wharf.

'We are coming aboard,' he announced in Greek.

The men said nothing but watched in mild surprise as Cassius ordered the soldiers on first. Between the ship and the wharf were large fenders made from sacks filled with dried bark. The soldiers negotiated these then dropped on to the deck. As Cassius and the others followed, one of the sailors spoke.

'Gaulish?' suggested the clerk.

'No,' said Simo.

'Who's in charge here?' asked Cassius.

The crewmen stared at him blankly.

'Where – is – your – captain?' Cassius asked, changing to Latin.

He could make nothing out of the garbled reply.

'I think he said he's not here,' suggested the clerk.

'How can they sail to Rhodes and not speak a word of Greek or Latin? It's damned odd.'

One of the legionaries had wandered away to inspect the rest of the ship. 'Sir, I think I heard something below.'

Dragging his eyes from the shadowy main hatch, Cassius turned to the talkative sailor. 'Is – someone – down – there?'

The sailor shrugged, then gestured towards the hatch. The other three glanced anxiously at one another.

'Draw swords, you two,' Cassius told the legionaries. 'If there's someone below I want them brought up. Swiftly now.'

'Yes, sir.' The older of the two led the way down the steps, blade angled downwards.

Cassius waved Indavara forward to keep watch on the sailors, then walked over to the hatch as the legionaries reached the bottom.

'Bloody dark down here, sir.'

'You see anything?'

'Not much, just— Hey!'

'What is it?'

Cassius's only answer was the sound of a struggle. He was halfway down the steps when the legionaries reappeared out of the gloom. They each had a hand on a short individual attired like the other sailors.

'Got another one, sir.'

'You speak Greek?' demanded Cassius. 'Latin?'

The man's response was to try to wrench his arms free, but he soon desisted when the older legionary waved his sword in his face. 'Want some of that, short-arse?'

'You keep looking,' Cassius told the younger legionary.

'Yes, sir.'

'Bring him.'

Cassius retreated up the steps. As soon as the fifth sailor cleared the hatch, he started babbling at his compatriots.

'Quiet!' Cassius shouted.

The older legionary held the man by the collar and kept his sword close to his neck.

'Centurion! Sir!'

The ten men on the deck of the *Scyros* looked up at the wharf. Standing there with a coil of rope over his shoulder was a man of about forty. He looked rather shocked.

'Might I ask what's going on here? I am Nepius Ahala, master of this vessel.'

'Just making enquiries,' Cassius said calmly, keen to avoid letting another tense situation spiral out of control. 'Come down here, would you?'

Leaving the rope on the wharf, Ahala nimbly negotiated the fenders and strode over to Cassius. He was a striking man: broad-shouldered and handsome, with a light beard and thick, greying hair.

'Surely there's no need for blades here, sir,' he said, continuing in Latin.

'I'll be the judge of that,' replied Cassius. 'Is there anyone else on board?'

Ahala exchanged a few words with his men in the mysterious language. 'No. I have six more crew but they're fetching water.'

'Why do none of them speak Latin or Greek?'

'Why would they? I recruit them from my home town, not far from Barcino.'

'Ah,' said Cassius. 'Spanish.'

'Aquitanian, we call it.'

'You were supposed to leave yesterday, correct?'

'That's right. Bit of rudder trouble. What's all this about anyway?'

'Where are you headed?'

Though Cassius kept the questions coming, Ahala showed no sign of unease.

'To Demetrias in Macedonia. Quite a long trip.'

'And dangerous at this time of year.'

Ahala shrugged. 'I've done it before. Basically a matter of hopping from one island to the other, then along the coast in stages.'

'Why is your hold empty?'

'We're bound to meet some bad weather somewhere, so we're better off without a big load.'

'That's horseshit, sir,' interjected the older legionary. 'These captains squeeze in everything they can to make a profit.'

'Experienced seaman, are you, soldier?' asked Ahala.

'Watch your mouth,' retorted the legionary.

'I've already made my money on this trip,' explained the captain. 'Which won't count for a lot if we're sunk on the way home.'

'Sir, I've got something!' cried the other legionary, still down below. He stomped up the steps holding a heavy-looking sack tied at the top with twine. 'Didn't you say something about a sack, sir? Found this near where we found the man.'

Cassius and the others all stared at the captain. He suddenly laughed.

'Something amusing?' Cassius asked.

Ahala put a hand on the curved dagger at his belt. 'May I?'

'Sir,' warned the older legionary.

Cassius examined the captain's face and made a swift decision. 'Go ahead.'

'You'll find a hundred and forty-nine more of these if you keep looking.'

Ahala jabbed the dagger into the sack, then pulled it out. Sand spilled from the hole on to the deck. The captain sheathed his dagger. 'Ballast.'

Cassius looked at the crew. 'Where were your men on the night before last?'

'Here. Sleeping.'

'You're sure of that?'

'Absolutely. I bed down near the hatch so none of them can sneak into town for a drink.'

'All right. One last thing. Line your men up.'

As Ahala gave the orders, Cassius waved the legionaries up to the wharf. 'Go. We're done here.'

The soldier who'd argued with Ahala shook his head. 'You're just going to leave it at that, sir?'

'You don't get paid enough to make decisions, legionary. Off the ship.'

'Should I translate?' asked Ahala, now standing with his men.

'Yes,' Cassius replied, pulling a coin from the money bag attached to his belt. 'Tell them to catch this with one hand.'

'As you wish,' replied the bemused captain.

Cassius went along the line. Four of the men caught the coin cleanly and the last one dropped it but they all had one thing in common.

'Right-handed,' said Indavara. 'But what about the other sailors who aren't here?'

Cassius shook his head. 'We're wasting our time. My fault for jumping to flawed conclusions. Why would the killer masquerade as part of a crew? He wouldn't even be able to decide when to make his escape. No, we're looking for a man on his own. Come on.'

'Apologies for the intrusion,' he said as they passed Ahala. He wouldn't normally have bothered, but the captain had been exceptionally good-natured about the whole thing.

'No harm done, Officer,' said Ahala with a smile. 'Always happy to assist imperial officials.'

'I'm sure.'

Cassius was last off the ship. As they marched back towards the town, the covered carriage reappeared on the road, overtaking a slow-moving wagon and speeding past the warehouses towards them.

'Gods,' said Cassius. 'What is it now?'

The two legionaries laughed when the carriage came to a stop – squeezed in between the two young ladies was the portly Optio Clemens.

Annia waved at Cassius. 'Officer, this man was looking for you so I thought we'd help out.'

'Very thoughtful, miss,' said the red-faced optio.

'Ha ha! Lady Clemens out for a ride!' cried the younger legionary. The older man was already guffawing.

Cassius shoved the loudmouth in the shoulder, swiftly bringing him to his senses. 'Shut your mouth, idiot,' he snapped, before turning to Clemens. 'What is it?'

'One of the men has got a sighting from the day before yesterday. Sounds right. Short man, with the hood and the sack.'

'Where?'

'Coming out of a shipping agent's office.'

'Who saw him?'

'Cobbler with a store opposite.' Clemens grinned. 'He noticed the boots.'

VI

A quarter of an hour later, a quite sizeable group of people were gathered outside the shipping agent's office: Clemens and four legionaries, three city sergeants, the harbour master's clerk, Mistress Annia and her entourage, and half a dozen curious passers-by.

Cassius – waiting impatiently as the agent examined an array of waxed tablets – looked out through the doorway at Annia. Alone in the carriage, she stared out at the sea, seemingly unconcerned by the harsh wind lashing her face, or the errant strands of hair whipping about her neck.

The agent was named Sudrenus; a wealthy-looking Greek who didn't seem accustomed to clerical work. His two employees were both ill with some coughing sickness, so he was having to man the office himself. His family owned and managed a fleet of mid-size freighters that ran routes all across the eastern Mediterranean.

He glanced at the street. 'Must they all stand around like that? It's not good for business.'

'The quicker you are, the quicker they'll be gone,' said Cassius. 'The witness did seem sure he saw the man leaving here two days ago.'

'Yes, yes. I just have to find the right tablet.'

Though it had cost him fifteen denarii (ten for the legionary, five for the cobbler), Cassius was fairly certain the sighting was genuine. The man had described a brand new pair of the hobnailed, front-laced boots worn by legionaries and officers across the Empire. 'Just like yours, sir, only newer,' he'd said. Such boots were expensive, and would indeed have looked out of place with the rest of the assassin's garb. Unfortunately, the cobbler had been so entranced by the suspect's footwear he couldn't recall much else, though confirmed he was on the short side.

'Here it is,' said Sudrenus, tapping a tablet, 'just the *Lebadea* in on that day. Arrived from Paphos in the morning and left bound for Halicarnassus in the afternoon.'

'Go on.'

Cassius was sitting on the other side of Sudrenus's high, marble desk, at right angles to the door, with Simo and Indavara standing behind him. The only thing the well-appointed office had in common with the harbour master's was the bronze plaques on the wall. The tiled floor was covered with thick, oriental rugs and there were two little statues – one of Zeus, one of Poseidon – mounted on miniature columns at the back of the room.

'Er . . . the cargo was a load of red clay and . . . what's that? Ah yes, grain. That cretin Herma – I can hardly read his writing.'

'The load isn't important,' Cassius replied sharply. 'Passengers.'

'Yes. Three men gave payment.' The Greek looked up. 'I insist a record is kept, so that none of the captains take backhanders.'

'And?'

'First, one Carius Asina. Wife and family included. Paid and signed.'

'You know the name?' asked Cassius.

'Can't say I do.'

Without turning round, Cassius pointed at the door. 'Simo, go and repeat the name Carius Asina to that lot outside. Somebody might know it. Next, Sudrenus?'

'No name. Just one initial – D. No signature.'

Cassius leant forward over the desk and looked at the D.

'That could be our man. Who did you say was manning the office that day?'

'Herma.'

'Where does he live?'

'No idea.'

81

'What? One of your employees?'

Sudrenus shrugged. 'What do I care where he lives?'

'Excuse me, sir,' said Simo from the door. Knowing the Gaul wouldn't disturb him without good reason, Cassius got up and walked over. All eyes were on him as Optio Clemens came forward.

'Sir, Carius Asina is a member of the Rhodes Assembly. From one of the old families. Has a lot of land around Hippoteia.'

'Where's that? Close?'

'No, sir. Middle of the island.'

Cassius heard a curse from inside the office.

Sudrenus slapped the tablet. 'Bloody Herma! Useless little worm!'

'What's the problem?' asked Cassius, returning inside.

'The third passenger was Drusus Viator. I expressly told my staff not to allow that man to set foot on one of our vessels.'

'Why?'

'He was charged with theft and tax evasion by the municipal court earlier in the year.'

Cassius was smiling as he hurried back to the door and waved the city sergeants forward. 'Anyone know a man by the name of Drusus Viator? A thief, apparently.'

Two of the men shook their heads. The third man spoke: 'I was with the arrest party. We had to chase him halfway across the Great Harbour.'

Annia had climbed down from the carriage and was now listening intently to the conversation. 'This man,' she said. 'It was *him*?'

'I don't think so,' replied Cassius. 'But another man on the ship didn't leave a name, and this Viator might have seen him. If he was on the ship with him all the way from Paphos he may even have spoken to him.'

He turned to the sergeant. 'Do you know where Viator lives?'

'I do, sir. Little townhouse not far from Helios.'

'Where's that?'

'He means the *statue* of Helios,' said Annia impatiently.

Cassius resisted the urge to order her back into the carriage.

'Right,' he told the sergeant. 'You shall take us there at once. Clemens, I need you to find out what you can about this Asina fellow – he may not have returned home immediately. If he or any of his family are still around we need to speak to them at once. Tell the rest of your men to keep looking. Just because we have a lead here doesn't mean there aren't others. And we now know something else – our man might have gone by a name beginning with D. Also, I need two of your men.'

'Sir.'

Clemens took the other two legionaries with him and marched away along the street. Cassius led the other two into the office.

Sudrenus looked up.

'These men are going to find your slave,' Cassius said. 'Give them all the help you can – I need to see him at once.'

'Very well,' the Greek replied wearily.

'You get hold of him, you bring him to me,' Cassius told the legionaries. 'I don't care if you have to drag him out of bed.'

Once back outside, he found Annia questioning the sergeant about Drusus Viator. Cassius held up his hand before the sergeant could answer. 'That's really none of your concern, miss. I did ask you to leave this matter in my hands.'

Annia gestured to the carriage. 'Please, Officer. We can get you to the Helios in no time.'

Cassius looked around. As well as Simo, Indavara and the three sergeants, Trogus, the driver and Annia's maid were also standing there, listening in.

'Give us a moment,' Cassius said irritably. As the others moved away, Annia stared back at him, arms folded across her chest. Cassius could quite happily have slapped her, but settled for leaning in close and addressing her in an urgent whisper.

'Miss, I do not intend to try and apprehend a known criminal by arriving at his house in a carriage with two *women* in tow. It is time for you to remember your place and stay out of my way.'

Annia matched his whisper but replaced urgency with defiance.

'You, sir, are not in a position to tell me what my place is. The only man capable of doing that is dead.'

Cassius straightened up and took a breath. The girl really was quite infuriating.

'I ask you again, miss, will you just allow me to do my job?'

Annia took a long time to reply. 'Very well.'

She aimed a finger at Trogus. He, the driver and the maid climbed back on to the carriage.

'But I want to know something,' Annia added. 'It's possible the assassin has already left the island, yes?'

'Several vessels departed yesterday. We must establish whether he was on one of them.'

'And if he was? Will you charter a vessel and follow that ship?'

'That is one possibility, yes. We might also look to the navy for assistance.'

'I see. I apologise for getting in your way, Officer. Knowing my place has never been a great strength of mine.'

This first flash of humility came as a surprise to Cassius. He followed Annia the few steps to the carriage, then offered her his hand as she climbed up.

The driver waited for a rider coming up from the harbour to pass, then turned into the road and followed him. As the carriage trundled away, Cassius glanced at Indavara and rolled his eyes.

'Women, eh, sir?' said one of the young sergeants. Cassius knew he should admonish him for his cheek but he couldn't resist the reply.

'Ladies are worse.'

——8——

Crouching behind a cart loaded with bundles of dried reeds, Cassius, Indavara, Simo and the three sergeants looked across the street at Drusus Viator's villa. It was situated in a mainly residential area on the slopes above the Little Harbour; the third of three identical properties squeezed in between a bakery to the left and a tree-lined sanctuary to the right. The columns on either side of the front door seemed rather grandiose for a one-storey building with probably only three or four rooms.

'Sure it's that one?' asked Cassius.

'Definitely, sir,' replied Auspex, the sergeant who'd arrested Viator before. 'He went flying out the back when our men rang the front-door bell.'

'Indavara, remember the glass factory in Antioch?'

The bodyguard pointed to a little scar on his neck.

'Ah,' said Cassius.

'I'll take the back,' said Indavara, who always became more vocal and animated with the prospect of a bit of excitement.

'Don't go overboard – we just need to talk to this man. Auspex, you go with him. Be careful not to show yourselves but be ready to act.'

'And you,' said Indavara as he and Auspex walked casually away along the pavement. When they were well away from the villa, they hurried across the street and disappeared around the far side of the sanctuary.

'Now listen,' Cassius told the other sergeants as he removed his sword belt. 'You two be ready as well, but stay well hidden.'

Cassius would have preferred to send the men in, but their surly demeanour, identically short haircuts and bulky physiques were an absolute giveaway; better not to alarm the man if he had a tendency to run. He handed one of the men his sword-belt.

'Simo, give him my helmet and the satchel too. You're coming with me.'

As Simo handed them over, Cassius eyed the Gaul's belt and tutted.

'How many times have I told you about carrying a dagger, yet still you defy me?'

'I simply haven't the need for a weapon, sir.'

'Lucky bloody you.'

Cassius turned to the sergeants for one last word. 'If it goes to shit, be quick.'

He pulled his cream-coloured cloak tight around his collar. His tunic could still be seen underneath but red wasn't exclusively the preserve of the army, so he hoped Viator would take it for no more than a bold statement of style.

'Come on, Simo.'

Cassius walked across the street and up on to the pavement, twitching as he felt sweat gathering under his armpits.

The villa's wooden door was fitted with an expensive iron lock. Next to it was a bell on a chain. Cassius rang it and the door opened surprisingly quickly. Standing there – holding a broom taller than him – was a lad of about ten.

'Viator residence?'

'Who's asking?'

The only thing that stopped Cassius cuffing the boy round the ear was the man who appeared behind him.

'Keep at your work.'

As the lad withdrew, the man pushed the door back towards Cassius so that it was only slightly ajar. He was about thirty, lean and wiry, with long, greasy hair tied into a tail. He took a quick look at Simo and a longer one at Cassius.

'You Drusus Viator?' Cassius asked with as friendly a smile as he could summon.

'I reckon you know that as you're standing at my door,' replied Viator with a scowl. 'More to the point, who are you?'

'My name is Cassius Corbulo. I'm working on behalf of—'

Viator took a brief look over Cassius's shoulder then slammed the door in his face.

Cassius spun round. One of the overzealous sergeants was by the side of the cart, clearly visible. He shrugged.

'Idiot!'

Viator shouted from inside: 'Where's the key?'

Cassius grabbed the latch and lifted it, then pressed himself against the door. It opened six inches.

'Get some weight on it, Simo.'

Overcoming his initial hesitation, the Gaul leant against the door. Cassius waved the sergeants forward.

Viator slammed back into the door and got the latch down.

'Balls!'

86

Cassius pressed his fingers under the latch and tried to force it upward again. 'Damn it, Simo, push harder!'

The sergeants arrived and swiftly took over, one knocking the latch up with his cudgel, the other bashing his shoulder into the door. As it momentarily swung open, he shoved his foot into the gap.

'Got it!'

Cassius retreated, suddenly feeling rather useless. There was no way to see inside the villa – both windows at the front were shuttered. Simo picked up Cassius's cloak, which had come off and fallen to the ground.

'I'll fetch the rest of your gear, sir,' said the Gaul, pointing across the street.

'Tell the others to come in the back, sir!' shouted one of the sergeants, his face tight with effort as he leant against the door.

Cassius ran past the half-dozen people who'd stopped to watch the struggle and along the side of the sanctuary. Though the wall surrounding it was only knee-height, planted just inside were tall, closely packed conifers. Cassius reached the corner and turned left. The sanctuary faced a square with a few market stalls and a fountain. He'd just passed the arched entrance when one of the sergeants shouted, 'We're in!'

Cassius stopped, unsure whether to go forward or back.

'Where is he?' came another shout.

'There – the window!'

Cassius pressed on to the far corner and looked along the road behind the villas; it was empty apart from a tethered mule at the rear of the bakery.

'Indavara?'

No response. Cassius shouted louder. Because of his damaged left ear, Indavara's hearing wasn't always the best. Still no response.

But then came the slap-slap-slap of sandal on stone. Cassius turned and saw Viator sprint out of the sanctuary and across the square.

'Out the side – of course,' he muttered. 'Shit.'

Tightening his belt two notches, he set off after him.

'Here!' he cried over his shoulder as he ran. 'He's here!'

Cassius still had his dagger on his belt and was relieved to see that the thief didn't seem to have a weapon. He also had the advantage of his strong, well-worn-in boots, and though Viator's loping stride suggested he wouldn't be easily caught, his sandals would slow him down.

Skirting the busy market stalls, Cassius passed the fountain just as Viator nipped into a narrow alley between two apartment blocks. Moments before he reached it, Cassius took a quick look back across the square. He glimpsed two figures coming out of the sanctuary, but couldn't tell who they were.

Shouts from the windows above echoed along the alley. Viator – arms and legs pumping – hadn't taken a single look back. Glad he'd checked his boots before they approached the villa, Cassius lengthened his stride.

Viator charged past a sleeping mongrel. The dog woke, scrambled to its feet, chased him for a few yards, then gave up. It was still barking when Cassius leapt over the top of it, catching it on the ear. His leading foot landed on wet ground beneath a gutter and he skidded to a stop, only just maintaining his balance. Fully expecting to feel canine teeth sink into his trailing leg, he was relieved to get under way again unscathed.

Across a perpendicular alley and between two more blocks. Someone somewhere was yelling curses in Greek. More obstacles: rotting firewood piled up to the right, then a line of rusting braziers, several of which lay across the alley. Concentrating on his footing as he jumped over the last one, Cassius then looked forward. Viator had reached the next street, and a large obstacle of his own.

Two gentlemen in litters were being carried from right to left up the slope. Viator turned sideways as he ran, aiming to go between them. The toga-clad man lying in the first litter cursed at the thief as he splashed through an unexpectedly deep puddle, then stumbled into the two strapping slaves at the rear. Despite the impact, they each kept one hand on the litter and their master off the ground.

Viator didn't fare so well. Bouncing off the bigger men, he pirouetted towards the slaves at the front of the second litter. One of them – a big African with arms wider than Viator's legs – decided on a pre-emptive strike. He shoved the thief in the shoulder, sending him careering into the alley opposite. Viator finally lost his balance and fell.

The occupants of the now stationary litters were not happy.

'Bloody disgrace!'

'Never a sergeant around when you need one!'

Cassius reached the end of the alley. The stern frown of the gentleman in the first litter suddenly became a smile.

'Oh. Good morning, Officer—'

'Corbulo. Good morning, Gaius Vilsonius,' said Cassius, recognising the helpful assemblyman they had met on their arrival at the Great Harbour.

Vilsonius's frown returned as Cassius dropped to the ground in front of him then crawled under the litter. As his hands slid on the wet, grimy flagstones, Cassius looked up to see Viator back on his feet and running again. Dragging himself clear of the litter, Cassius bolted after him.

'Hope you catch him!' cried Vilsonius.

The next alley was wider, and in the distance were the great bronze legs and fallen body of the Helios. Closer, a swathe of people were swarming past the end of the alley, also heading uphill.

'Look out!' cried another toga clad fellow as his retinue divided to let Cassius through.

'Sorry!'

Twenty yards ahead, Viator had reached the crowd. There were men, women and children – three or four hundred at least – all wearing blue capes over their clothing and all holding bottles or jars in two hands. Viator squeezed his way into the mass of bodies.

The worshippers were reciting a chant after every beat of a drum. 'All praise Poseidon, Mover of the Sea, God of the Deep.'

Cassius peered over their heads and caught a glimpse of Viator's long hair. 'Stop that man!'

There were a few curious looks but the worshippers were more interested in not spilling their libations. Cassius glanced to his left and saw that they were converging on the arched entrance of a high-walled temple.

'I said stop him! I am an—'

Cassius belatedly realised he was just a man in a red tunic, with no sword or helmet to mark him out as an army officer.

'All praise Poseidon, Mover of the Sea, God of the Deep.'

Though they spoke slowly and softly, the combined volume of the hundreds of voices was remarkably loud.

Mainly because of his height, Cassius was able to keep track of Viator, who was now about a third of the way through the crowd. A priest carrying a staff was glaring at the thief, but imploring the worshippers to continue their chant.

'All praise Poseidon, Mover of the Sea, God of the Deep.'

'Sorry,' said Cassius, as he cut in front of a young girl. He darted forward again but then found himself in the middle of a group of rough-looking youths. Without a word – and without spilling a drop of their libations – they communicated their displeasure by knocking him forward with their shoulders.

'I'm very sorry, but I must—'

An elbow in the ribs silenced him. He got his hands high and tried to wriggle free but was carried along by the human tide. A shove in his back spun him around and on towards the temple. It was a while before he could even turn long enough to catch sight of Viator.

The thief had somehow forced his way through; he was almost at the edge of the crowd.

—◼8◼▶—

Indavara stopped at the other end of the alley. With his rangy frame and brown hair, Cassius stood out amongst the locals, but he was soon lost from view as the worshippers pressed on up the hill.

The three sergeants arrived together.

'We can cut around,' said Auspex between breaths.

'You two go that way,' said Indavara pointing to the right, down the slope.

He and Auspex sprinted away to the left, nipping neatly past the two litters bearing Gaius Vilsonius and his friend.

'Too late as usual!'

Indavara accelerated to get ahead of a line of water carriers filing out of a doorway.

'Next right!' yelled Auspex.

Indavara rounded the corner and found himself on a narrow street that led down to another entrance at the side of the temple complex. Beyond an iron gate were the sparkling white columns and imposing walls of the building itself. The gate was open but standing either side of it were two priests – one young, one old – wearing long white robes.

'Coming through!' shouted Indavara. To his surprise, the priests moved together, blocking his path. He only just stopped in time and Auspex almost ran into him.

Indavara turned to the young sergeant. 'Tell them!'

'Er, in the name of the magistrate, you must allow us past, we are chasing a criminal.'

'Only the Purified can use this entrance,' said the older of the two priests.

'The what?' said Indavara.

'He means priests,' said Auspex. 'Perhaps we should find another way.'

'No chance.'

Indavara walked straight at the priests.

The younger of the two turned aside to let him through but the older man stood his ground and grabbed Indavara by the arm.

'You cannot enter by this gate.'

'I'm not going to do anything bad,' Indavara replied. 'I just want to pass through. Let go, you old fool!'

'This is outrageous.' The grey-bearded priest turned to the sergeant. 'Do something, you imbecile.'

Auspex shrugged.

'Let go of my arm or I'll kick you,' said Indavara.

'What?'

'You heard me.'

'How dare you threaten one of the Purified!'

Instead of letting go, the priest grabbed Indavara by both arms and shook him. 'You are not pure. You shall not pass!'

Indavara kicked him on the shin just below his right knee. Not hard. But hard enough.

With a high-pitched shriek, the old priest staggered backwards. The younger man went to his aid, while Auspex looked on, open-mouthed.

'Can't say I didn't warn you,' Indavara said as he ran through the gateway.

'The wrath of Poseidon upon you!' bellowed the priest. 'Poseidon! Poseidon!'

'Never heard of him,' Indavara muttered.

The crowd slowed as those at the front reached the main gate. Feeling rather battered and bruised, Cassius squeezed past a family and a group of old women and reached the comparative safety of a statueless plinth to the right of the gate. Pressing his back against the marble he slid sideways to his left until he was finally able to extricate himself from the mass of worshippers.

Assuming Viator was long gone, he took a moment to get his bearings and catch his breath. He then heard an extremely refined but extremely loud voice:

'That's him! That's the one. Almost knocked me over.'

Cassius looked up to see Viator struggling to get away from a red-faced young man who had hold of his arm.

'Keep him there, Gavros! I shall find a sergeant!' cried the old man standing close to the warring pair. He too was wearing a blue cape and holding a libation.

Cassius ran towards them.

Having sprinted along the side of the temple, Indavara halted by the steps that led up to the cavernous entrance. To his right – directly opposite the steps – was the main gate, where a dozen priests marshalled the faithful. On the other side of the temple were the gardens: a sprawling space decorated with vividly coloured bushes and luxuriant trees. Unnoticed by the busy priests, Indavara jogged past the temple looking for a way back on to the street. The gardens and the rest of the complex were enclosed by a twenty-foot red-brick wall. To the right, a dozen artisans – some on the ground, some up ladders – were at work, filling holes in the cement. He hurried over to a pair of them.

'Sure you should be in here, mate?' said one.

'How do I get to the other side of this wall?'

'You can't from here. There's only the main gate and the Priest Gate open today.'

The second man cast a suspicious glance at Indavara, especially the sword at his belt and the stave over his back. 'What are you doing in here?'

Indavara turned back towards the temple and saw four more priests coming down the steps.

'Er, I'm with the Magistrate's Office. Chief Inspector of . . . Ladders. I think I'll start here.'

By the time the suspicious labourer replied he was already on the third rung.

'What are you doing?'

'Just testing it. Hold it steady for me. Yes, good so far.'

Wincing at his own words, Indavara carried on climbing. All the other men had stopped working to watch him. He was halfway up the wall when he heard shouts to his right. The two priests from the side gate had appeared, the old man yelling at his colleagues exiting the temple. He stopped for a moment to rub his shin and noticed Indavara. Apparently forgetting his injury and showing impressive speed, he lifted his robes and ran, still shouting.

Indavara doubled his pace. A protruding nail end sliced his right thumb but he pressed on. Eight rungs to go. Trying to ignore the shouts from below, he looked up. Five rungs. Four.

93

A sudden, jarring impact; and the ladder slipped a yard down the wall. Indavara lost his footing but managed to hang on. Then the ladder lurched to the right, and only by wedging his boot against the wall did he stop it tipping over. Glancing downwards, he saw the aged priest was there, shaking the ladder for all he was worth.

'Old bastard!'

He looked up again. The top of the ladder was three feet from the top of the wall. He clambered up, set one boot on the penultimate rung, the other on the last rung, and threw himself upward. As his arms came down on the brick, a startled pigeon flew away in a flurry of feathers and shit, most of which landed on Indavara's hands. He levered himself up, got a knee over the edge, and hauled himself on to the top of the wall. He turned round just in time to watch the ladder crash to the ground, narrowly missing one of the labourers. Wiping his hands on his tunic, he waved at the priest.

The old man shook a fist at him.

———◆8◆———

Cassius was only feet away when the desperate Viator swung an elbow into his captor's face. The thief sprang away and the young man fell back, blood already streaming from his nose. As Cassius passed him, the old gentleman was already admonishing his attendant.

On they ran again; under a grand arch decorated with scenes of ancient battles and on to a wide gravelled path that ran down to the grassed area in front of the Helios. Lining the path were artists displaying their work on easels and a handful of middle-aged tourists milling around. There was also a party of well-dressed children sitting by the chain-link fence that surrounded the sun god, sketching the statue's feet.

As he came down the slope, Cassius looked beyond the Helios and cursed. At the end of the path, about a hundred yards away, was what looked like a cloth market. There were scores of people in amongst the densely packed stalls and hanging lengths of fabric. If Viator made it there, he'd never find him, especially as neither Indavara nor the useless city sergeants had been able to keep up.

Cassius accelerated.

—■8■—

For several moments, Indavara had done nothing but stare in amazement at the two sections of the gargantuan figure. The head of the Helios – which was about the size of a cart – was to his left, ears and tufts of hair ingeniously crafted from the bronze. The shoulder was only a little below the level of the wall, while the tops of the knees on the standing section were a good twenty feet higher. The vast, curved slabs of metal seemed darker up close, like a polished hardwood.

'Hey, what are you doing up there?' There were also labourers at work on the other side of the wall and the closest of them was halfway up a ladder to Indavara's left. There was another unoccupied ladder close by.

Shouts from below. He saw Viator scattering the tourists before disappearing behind the huge platform that supported the statue's legs. Indavara was impressed to see Cassius not that far behind.

'At least he can run.'

Looking along the path, Indavara saw the cloth market and reached the same conclusion as Cassius. He crawled along the wall to the ladder. Taking in a few angles and distances, he turned around and lowered himself on to it.

'Get off there!' shouted the labourer.

Doubt struck Indavara – the result of the soft life he was leading these days, he knew – but then he recalled an incident from their last outing in Antioch; a blind leap from twice this height.

He twisted his neck and glimpsed Viator, still sprinting hard.
Got to go now.

95

Gripping the sides of the ladder with both hands, he braced his right foot against the wall and pushed out.

———◆◦◆———

Cassius reckoned he was gaining.

Viator had just lost a sandal but the cloth market was close.

Cassius got ready for one last burst. He would go for his legs and bring him down.

———◆◦◆———

As air rushed past his ears, Indavara steeled himself for the impact. He expected to hit the statue's left shoulder, then slide down to the ground and run around the head.

But the ladder had picked up tremendous speed; as it struck the shoulder, he was propelled straight on to the Helios' back, landing with enough impetus to send him sliding across the slick metal. He only began to slow as he reached the right shoulder. Rolling over to try to stop himself, he then found himself careening down the statue's right arm on his backside.

———◆◦◆———

Cassius looked on in amazement as Indavara – apparently appearing from nowhere – landed on the ground just ahead of Viator. He dusted himself off, stepped neatly over the fence and stuck out a leg.

Stealing a glance back at Cassius, Viator didn't even see him. He fell face first on to the ground, mirroring the statue's pose. As he tried to scramble away, Indavara picked him up: one hand on his collar, one hand on his belt. He spun him round and shoved him back against the sun god's forearm, which reached higher than both their heads.

'Where in Hades did you come from?' asked Cassius.

Indavara shrugged, one hand still on Viator's collar. 'Short cut.'

As he momentarily turned away, the thief drew his fist back.

'Watch him!' cried Cassius.

Before the second word was out of his mouth, Indavara had shifted his hand to Viator's head and slapped it hard against the bronze.

'Ow!'

'Don't do that again.'

Indavara backed up and stood beside Cassius.

Still rubbing his head, Viator glared at them. 'Who are you two, anyway?'

'Make way! Make way!'

The tourists and schoolchildren parted and Auspex and the other sergeants jogged forward. Behind them were three angry-looking middle-aged priests and a tall, balding man in a purple-striped toga.

'This is Procurator Liburnias,' explained Auspex. 'He was attending the ceremony at the temple.'

Cassius gave a little bow and patted his hair down. 'Sir.'

'All right then, you two,' said the procurator sternly. 'Who kicked the priest?'

VII

The forum was full, not of local politicians but cleaners, readying the building for the assembly meeting the next morning. The women scrubbed floors, walls, columns and steps, while men kept them supplied with pails of steaming water. Cassius hurried along the portico, a neat and colourful garden to his left, a dozen of the women to his right. Eleven were on their knees, attending to already immaculate tiles. The twelfth was a sour-faced and voluble overseer. 'Not slow, not quick, an even pace; don't move on till you can see your face!'

Despite his foul mood, Cassius couldn't help smiling – he remembered his mother repeating the same chant to the maids at his home in Ravenna. Noticing how dirty his hands were, he stopped a water carrier and dipped them in his pail. Once the worst of the grime was gone, he hurried on towards the anteroom where Indavara and Auspex were keeping watch on Drusus Viator.

Cassius had just concluded a rather tense meeting with Procurator Liburnias. Though ostensibly in charge of financial affairs, Liburnias was the second most powerful man in the city after the governor, who – rather fortuitously – was busy elsewhere. Without the spearhead and his letters to reinforce his authority, Cassius been forced to rely on his diplomatic skills (plus the odd oratorical flourish) and he thought he'd done rather well.

Halfway through the meeting, a letter had arrived from the high priest of the temple of Poseidon, calling for court proceedings and a flogging for Indavara. Cassius had done his best to plead the bodyguard's case, quickly moving the conversation on to the brutal nature of Memor's murder, the suffering of his grief-stricken family and the crucial importance of apprehending

Viator. He had also dropped Chief Pulcher's name into the mix a couple of times for good measure. Even so, it was a good half an hour before he could extricate himself, promising the Service would make a sizeable contribution to the Temple of Poseidon. Liburnias had suggested that Indavara keep his head down. The word was already out about the one-eared thug who'd assaulted one of the Purified, and the procurator seemed sure that some of the younger, more headstrong followers would be out for blood.

Wondering where exactly Simo had got to, Cassius jogged to the end of the portico and turned right. The anteroom was empty apart from a row of upturned benches. Indavara and Auspex were standing over Drusus Viator, who was sitting against the wall below the only window. Cassius walked straight up to him.

'Tell me what I want to know and you'll be home in an hour. Or I can hand you over to Magistrate Nariad and suggest he take a very good look into your affairs.'

'He didn't find anything last time; he won't find anything now,' Viator said calmly, legs stretched out in front of him, one sandal by his side.

'Oh, he will,' replied Cassius. 'Even in the unlikely event that there's nothing *to* find. I'll make sure of it.'

Viator smirked, as if he'd heard such speeches a thousand times before.

Cassius took another step towards him. 'You returned to Rhodes from Paphos on the *Lebadea*, correct?'

'I might have.'

Cassius lashed a kick at him, the toe of his boot catching the thief on his ankle bone. Viator cried out and looked as shocked as Cassius felt.

He had no idea why he'd done it. Actually he knew exactly why – monumental levels of frustration and anger with recent events – but the kick had been instinctive and he hated to lose control of himself, especially in front of Indavara. Still, the man deserved it.

'Curses on you, Roman,' hissed the thief.

'Listen to me, you stupid piece of shit. I don't care about your pathetic little dealings. All I want to know is whether you spoke to someone aboard that ship. He was probably travelling alone. A small man, with a hooded cloak, wearing army boots and carrying a sack.'

Viator stared back at him. Cassius imagined he'd had plenty of worse kickings.

'What's it worth?'

Indavara came forward, the stave in his hand.

'It's worth not getting your head smashed in!' Cassius yelled. *'Did you see him?'*

Viator waved a hand. 'All right, Roman. You can call off your dog. I saw him. Don't remember any boots though.'

'Did you speak to him?'

'A bit. Just to make conversation. There was just me, him and some rich type with his wife and brats.'

'Did you get a name?'

'Dio.'

'What did he look like?'

'Normal.'

Cassius shook his head. 'Short?'

'Shortish.'

'Well built?'

'No. Slight.'

'Hair colour?'

'Normal. Dark.'

'Handsome? Ugly?'

Viator screwed up his face. 'How should I know?'

'Eyes?'

'Yes. Two.'

Cassius almost kicked him again. 'What colour, dolt?'

'I don't know!'

'Did he tell you anything else about himself?'

Viator seemed amused by the idea. 'No. Me neither.'

'So what did you talk about?'

Viator shrugged. 'The weather. He didn't say much.'

'Think,' Cassius insisted. 'What else?'

'Once he found out I was from Rhodes, he did ask about a few things.'

Cassius knelt down in front of the thief. 'Such as?'

'The ports, ships, different routes. I think he wanted to go to Crete.'

'Crete. You're sure?'

'He mentioned a few places, but yes, mainly Crete.'

'You recall nothing else?'

'No.'

Cassius stood up and turned to Auspex. 'Take him outside and let him go.'

'That's it, sir?'

'That's it. I appreciate your help.'

Auspex seemed unused to statements of gratitude. 'Thank you, sir.'

Indavara put the stave back over his shoulder and followed Cassius out of the anteroom. 'Crete's an island, right?'

'Yes,' replied Cassius as they passed under the portico and on to the path that led around the side of the forum. 'To the south-west. I'll have to see Simo and check the list, but if memory serves one of the ships that left yesterday was bound for there.'

'So we're going after him?'

'What choice do I have? Cassius said irritably, massaging his brow as they walked. 'By Jupiter, that fat bastard Abascantius – he has the power of a god when it comes to making my life difficult.'

'How far to Crete?'

'More than a hundred miles. Plus this Dio has a day's head start, and the weather's only going to get worse. But neither of those is likely to be our biggest problem.'

'What is?'

'Finding a captain willing to take us.'

——◆8◆——

'Asdribar. Maybe.'

'Who's he?' asked Cassius, wiping sweat away from above his mouth. It was over a mile from the forum to the Great Harbour; he and Indavara had marched through the city, stopping only twice to get directions. Cassius had been headed for the harbour master's office but they'd run into the young clerk and the three of them were now sheltering from the rain under a snack-stall awning.

'Carthaginian captain, sir,' replied the youth. 'He's got an old freighter: the *Fortuna Redux*. I can't see anyone else being too keen with the weather closing in, but from what I've heard he'll pretty much take anyone anywhere – for the right price.'

'There's Simo,' announced Indavara, looking out across the street. Before Cassius could tell him to, he ran out into the rain to fetch him.

'He's reliable, this Asdribar?'

The clerk grinned. 'I don't know if that's the first word that comes to mind, sir. He's had a few run-ins with the authorities. The last magistrate tried to get him into court half a dozen times but Asdribar always wriggled out of it. And I believe Nariad tried to have the *Fortuna* declared unseaworthy but Asdribar got the fishermen to blockade the harbour for a day, so that didn't work out either. His crew are an . . . interesting bunch, but I'm told there are none better when it comes to real sea sailing – the "out of sight" stuff as they call it.'

'As in out of the sight of land?'

'Yes, sir.'

Cassius felt a chill run down his spine, and he knew it wasn't just cooling sweat. The recent trip from Cilicia had been only his third sea voyage. The first two had taken him across the eastern Mediterranean to Syria, first from Ravenna, then from Cyzicus. Though there had been the odd short period when land wasn't visible, captains generally tried to keep as close to the coast as possible for ease of navigation. The thought of venturing south into the vast swathes of the Great Green Sea was nothing short of terrifying.

'Are all you all right, sir?' asked the clerk.

'Fine. Where would I find this character?'

'The *Fortuna* is moored out on the east side of the Great Harbour. Quite a walk, sir. But Asdribar's sailing master is an old chap . . . well I don't know his real name, but everyone calls him Squint. He can usually be found in The Sea Serpent. Just a stone's throw from the army way station. Can't miss it.'

The stallholder leant over his counter. 'You two going to buy anything?'

'I will,' said Indavara, ducking under the awning with Simo not far behind. As he went to inspect the cakes on display, Cassius glared at the big Gaul.

'Where in the name of the gods have you been?'

'My apologies, sir,' Simo replied breathily. 'Thank the Lord I found you.'

'Forget the Lord, Simo, you can thank Indavara – who just happened to spot you. Where did you disappear to?'

'I tried to keep pace, sir, but with all this—'

Simo was carrying his master's sword-belt, helmet, cloak and satchel, which still had the spearhead sticking out of it.

'And look at my gear,' Cassius said. 'Soaking wet!'

'I'm really very sorry, sir. The cloak should be fine. I treated it with oil just the other day. I'm sure—'

'I mean look at you, Simo.'

Thanks to a combination of sweat and rain, the Gaul's tunic was clinging to his rather large stomach.

'You're simply too fat. With the type of work we're involved in, it's just not good enough. I shall have to put you on some sort of training regime. We shall start at the earliest opportunity.'

'Where have I heard that before?' said Indavara, turning from the counter with a large raisin cake in his hand.

'Just give me that bloody page,' Cassius told the Gaul.

'Page, sir?'

'From the harbour master's logbook!'

'Might I be excused, sir?' asked the clerk as Simo rummaged in the satchel.

'No you may not. Invariably something violent happens when I go to inns looking for people, so you can introduce me to this sailor if he's there.'

'I only really know him to pass a good day, sir.'

'That's good enough.'

Cassius took the page from Simo and examined it. 'Here. The *Cartenna*. Arrived last week, left yesterday bound for Crete, third hour.' Cassius turned to the clerk. 'You know the ship?'

'I do, sir. Been in a few times. The captain came in and paid his wharf dues first thing and they set off not long after.'

'Do you know if Crete was his final destination?'

'I don't, sir.'

'Right, once you've taken me to this inn, go back to Akritos. Simo, you're to go with him. Pay him a denarius when you're done.'

'Yes, sir.'

'My sincere thanks, sir,' offered the clerk.

'I want to know everything there is to know about the *Cartenna*: routes they follow, shipping agents they work with, and – most importantly of all – who was on there. Go to Nariad's revenue people if you have to. There, a chance to redeem yourself, Simo.'

'Thank you, sir.'

'Now hand me that cloak.'

—8—

A quarter of an hour later, Cassius and Indavara were ensconced in a booth in one corner of The Sea Serpent. With its small, grilled windows and the overcast sky outside, the inn was shrouded in gloom. Even so, it was easy to see that every one of the two dozen patrons made his living on the water: weathered faces; sun-bleached hair; thick, marked, blistered fingers. A group in one corner were on to the third verse of some nautical song. From what Cassius could gather, the tune celebrated the end of the sailing season and expressed gratitude to the gods that the singers had survived it.

Even though it was barely midday, the man sitting opposite him was nursing a huge mug of wine. 'Squint' was well named;

104

Cassius could have picked him out even amongst his fellow seamen. His left eye was almost completely closed, his right bloodshot and yellowed. His thick beard – like his wispy hair – was the colour of fresh snow, apart from the strands dyed wine-red above his mouth. His arms lay on the table, encircling his mug. The wrinkled, leathery skin was reminiscent of old fruit and made it hard to read the words tattooed in green ink between his elbows and wrists. Cassius had decided it was probably a list of the ships he'd served on.

'You wanted to talk, Roman,' he croaked. 'Talk.'

'Tell me about the *Fortuna Redux*.'

'You've never heard of her, boy?'

'Should I have?' Cassius replied impatiently, moving his wet cloak to the side of the bench he was sharing with Indavara.

'The *Fortuna*'s the ship that did the Carthago Nova run in twelve days.'

'I'm sure that's very impressive, but what I really want to know is whether your vessel is available for hire.'

'Now?'

'Immediately. I need to get to Crete. Just three passengers but we must leave today.'

'That's up to the captain, boy.'

'Would you mind not calling me "boy". I'm an officer of the Roman Army, with a rank equivalent to centurion.'

Squint took a noisy slurp from his mug before answering. 'Well done, lad.'

Indavara chuckled.

'I need to see this captain of yours at once,' insisted Cassius. 'What's his name – Asdribar?'

'That's right.'

'Will you take me to him?'

Squint raised his mug. 'Soon as I've finished this.'

The innkeeper came to the table and gave Cassius and Indavara the glasses of hot wine they'd ordered.

'Drink up quickly,' Cassius told Indavara, as he undid the top of his money bag.

The inn door clattered open. A gust of wind blew in and a bottle smashed on the floor. Tutting, the innkeeper looked at the mess next to his bar.

The booth was the fourth of four situated to the right of the door, which Cassius and Indavara were facing away from. Cassius turned, leant round the side of the booth and watched five men walk in. The innkeeper pointed at the first of them: a squat, buck-toothed ruffian with two swords on his belt.

'Rassus, you're barred – remember!'

'I'm not here for drink. We're after this foreigner – he beat up an old priest at the temple of Poseidon. Sergeants aren't doing shit so we and the rest of the guild have decided to deal with him ourselves.'

Cassius turned back and looked at Indavara, who mouthed: 'Hardly touched him.'

'Big bastard apparently,' added Rassus, 'but he's easily recognised – only got one ear. Anyone seen him?'

Because of where he was sitting, Indavara's disfigured left ear was visible only to Squint and the innkeeper. Squint didn't appear to have noticed.

Cassius felt Indavara reaching for his sword. He put his hand on the bodyguard's wrist and glanced up at the innkeeper.

'Well?' said Rassus. 'No one seen nothing?'

The innkeeper looked at Indavara. He had noticed the ear. Turning his attention to Cassius, he widened his eyes speculatively.

Cassius reached into his money bag and placed three denarii on the corner of the table.

The innkeeper looked at the money, then back at the gang.

Cassius added three more denarii.

'No one's seen this cocksucker then?' demanded Rassus. 'He must have been round the port.'

The innkeeper looked back at Cassius and subtly held out four fingers.

Shaking his head, Cassius added four more coins.

At last, the innkeeper spoke up: 'That sounds like a no to me. Why don't you go and disturb someone else's customers?'

With a grunt, Rassus and his cronies left. As the door slammed shut, Indavara moved his hand away from his sword. Cassius leant back and sighed.

Squint finished off his wine and set down his mug. He then watched in amazement as the innkeeper slid the ten silver coins off the table into his hand and walked away, smirking.

The old sailor tapped his mug. '*This* was only a sesterce.'

Cassius shrugged. 'Inflation.'

Despite its supposedly legendary reputation, at first sight the *Fortuna Redux* didn't particularly impress. The ship was small for a freighter and the green paint of the hull had faded almost to grey. Under the bowsprit was a wooden rendering of Fortuna herself. The goddess had lost her nose and one breast and the only trace of colour left was the odd patch of yellow in her hair. In fact, she was really only identifiable by the outstretched hands cupping a stack of coins.

'Ninety-five-foot long, twenty-three wide,' stated Squint proudly as they walked along the narrow breakwater towards the vessel's stern. 'With a deep keel to keep her upright.'

'Always helps,' observed Cassius.

'She can carry a hundred tons fully laden and make seven knots with all her sails up and a fair wind.'

'Sure it's ready to leave today?' asked Cassius.

'Maybe – if the captain says yes and we can get the crew together. See the tall mast? We had it extended a few years back.'

'Doesn't that make the ship more unstable?'

'A bit, but worth it for the extra speed.'

Unlike the freighter they'd arrived on, the *Fortuna* also had a second, smaller mast, close to the bow. At about forty feet, it was half the size of the main mast and virtually identical in dimensions to the yard, which was currently lying on the deck.

Despite its condition, Cassius had to acknowledge there was a certain elegance to the ship's design, with its sleek lines and sharp, narrow bow. The hull also tapered slightly towards the stern but was made broader by the winglike housings for the steering rudders. Tied to the rear of the ship was a solidly built tender about fifteen feet long.

The sternpost was more conventional than the bow: a goose-head design with two blue dots for the eyes. Forward of this was the deckhouse, one of the largest Cassius had seen. It was six feet high and stretched across almost the entire width of the deck. There were small windows on either side and a door more befitting a villa than a ship.

'That's the captain's quarters,' said Squint as he led them across a slippery, squeaking gangplank. 'I'll see if I can rouse him.'

Ten feet forward of the deckhouse was the main hatch, currently protected from the rain by a tent-like cover. Voices drifted up from below.

The deckhouse door opened and lamp smoke swirled out into the damp air. Squint said a few words then moved aside. Standing in the doorway was a bald, strong-jawed, blue-eyed man with the type of face it was difficult not to look at. He smiled at Cassius.

'This must be my lucky day. Good afternoon, sir.'

'Good afternoon, Captain. Might I speak with you?'

'Of course,' replied Asdribar warmly. 'However – and you must forgive the pun – I'm afraid you've missed the boat if you wish to hire the *Fortuna*.'

'Oh.'

'Yes, I'm afraid I couldn't possibly refuse the terms offered, nor a lady in need of assistance.'

Asdribar stepped on to the deck.

Annia came to the door. Despite the vaguely apologetic smile, that fierce determination hadn't left her eyes.

Cassius ran a hand through his rain-soaked hair.

'Caesar's balls.'

VIII

The deckhouse of the *Fortuna Redux* was a miracle of compact design. Immediately to the right of the door was a sturdy hard-wood table and a stool fixed to the floor. Strewn around a big abacus in the middle of the table were dozens of paper sheets. Above was a rack stuffed with multicoloured flags. Running along the rear of the deckhouse were two narrow, high-sided beds. To the left was another table – this one accommodating jugs, bottles and a bowl of dried fruit. Above it was a cloth hammock slung between two hooks. Every other inch of space was occupied either by an exotic memento or a piece of nautical equipment, some more easily identifiable than others.

Asdribar had just sat down on the stool next to the door, Squint standing beside him. Annia and her maid were sitting on the first bed, Trogus and Indavara on the second, while Cassius and Simo leant against the other table. Cassius had to stretch his legs out to keep his head from touching the roof.

'So where are we going, Officer?' asked Annia, looking keenly up at him.

'I shall address the "we" part of that statement in a moment,' replied Cassius. 'But as far as the assassin goes, my best guess is that he departed yesterday aboard a ship named the *Cartenna*, bound for Crete.'

'Guess?' queried Annia.

'Perhaps you have another theory, miss?'

'Not at all. I would just like to know on what this guess is based.'

Cassius noted a slight grin from Asdribar. Despite the weather, the captain was dressed in only a thin, grey tunic. Though he must have been well over forty, his light beard was jet black, and his bronzed body that of an athlete half his age.

'Further enquiries are being made,' said Cassius, 'but I have questioned this Viator character. It seems the assassin goes by the name of Dio and was interested in travelling on to Crete. I cannot be certain, but it is an educated guess, at least.'

'I see,' said Annia.

Cassius addressed Asdribar. 'The *Cartenna* left yesterday morning. What chance do we have of catching her?'

The captain ran a contemplative finger down his jaw. 'We've a northerly coming in now, which isn't bad, but yesterday it was more to the east so they'll have had a nice run.'

'About a hundred and fifty miles – Crete?'

'More like two hundred to Cnossus, which is where most ships will put in.'

Cassius grimaced.

'That's good, isn't it?' suggested Annia. 'The further it is, the more chance we have of catching them on the open sea. Once the ship reaches land, this man might disappear.'

'I suppose that's true,' said Asdribar.

Cassius couldn't deny the logic but he was more concerned by the fact that Annia was still saying 'we'.

'Which route would you take?' she asked the captain. 'East or west?'

Asdribar turned to Squint, who was twisting the end of his beard with his fingers.

'If this cloud is setting in, west would be better,' said the old sailor. 'Keep us away from Krapathos.'

'What's at Krapathos?' asked Cassius.

'Nothing special,' replied Asdribar. 'But it's an island, with other smaller islands around it, and it's in our way if we go east around Rhodes. The problem at this time of year is not just the rain, it's the cloud and the mist – they make navigation very difficult. We have another big problem, actually, my—'

'Captain,' interrupted Annia. 'What's the earliest we could leave?'

Cassius was on the verge of sending the others outside and putting an immediate end to this charade.

'Well,' said Asdribar, 'we must clear the port in daylight. It'll be a struggle to get my crew together and some supplies on board, but I'll make it happen. When can you be ready, miss?'

'Two or three hours.'

'And you, sir?' asked the Carthaginian.

'Whenever,' Cassius replied curtly.

'Excellent,' said Asdribar. 'Might I suggest the tenth hour then? If you wish to be present for the ceremonials, come a little earlier.'

'Very good,' said Annia, getting up. 'Thank you, Captain.'

Cassius caught Asdribar's eye. 'Might I speak to the young lady alone for a moment?'

Asdribar turned to Annia, who nodded. 'Of course.'

Cassius directed Simo and Indavara outside and waited for the others to leave. Annia's maid, Clara, stayed sitting and stared down at her lap.

Walking over to Annia, Cassius had to bow his head, which made him feel rather foolish. 'Miss, these ridiculous notions must end here. You will not be accompanying us.'

'As Captain Asdribar's client, surely it is *I* who decides who shall accompany *me*.'

Cassius could see little sense in arguing with the girl; a debate could not be conducted in the absence of reason.

'Very well, then. I shall certainly not plead my case. I would much rather stay here on the island, wait for a little good weather, then take the next vessel heading east.'

He made for the door.

'Officer Corbulo, my apologies,' Annia said quickly. 'It is only your hard work and insight that have allowed any progress at all. Please – the investigation cannot continue without you.'

Cassius, who had no real intention of actually leaving, stopped and turned round.

'You have accomplished a great deal in only a few hours,' Annia continued. 'And I'm confident you can bring this affair to a conclusion.'

Cassius had never met anyone who didn't respond well to a bit of praise and he certainly didn't consider himself an exception. 'Young lady, I admire your determination to see your father's murderer caught, but there is no practical reason for you to come. Apart from anything else, your family need you here.'

'You will not change my mind, sir.'

Cassius wasn't sure if it was the stuffy, oily air of the deckhouse or the trials of the day, but the pain that had been seeping out from behind his eyes and across his head for the past hour had doubled in the last few moments. He clenched his right fist and smacked it into his left palm. 'By Jupiter, see sense, will you?'

Fear flashed into Annia's eyes and she took half a step backward.

'This is no place for a woman,' Cassius added. 'Who knows what we might face?'

Annia took a moment to compose herself before replying. 'You recall the island the captain spoke of – Krapathos? I sailed to it last summer with three friends. My father first took me out on the lake when I was little more than a baby. I have made passage to Alexandria and Athens and Ephesus. I have spent more than a hundred days at sea and—'

Cassius held up a hand. 'How much did you pay the captain?'

'We agreed to four aurei a day.'

'Thank you. I shall outbid you, and then there really is no need for you to be aboard.'

'I don't think you have the money, sir. You said earlier you might need something from me.'

Cassius couldn't fault the smart little bitch there – he had no chance of finding enough coin elsewhere at such short notice.

'Well, miss, as you clearly do not hold me in sufficient esteem to accept my counsel, I shall waste no more of my breath.'

'I do respect you, Officer Corbulo. And you can be assured that I will not interfere.'

Cassius almost laughed when he heard that.

'You will be here at the tenth hour?' Annia asked.

'I shall consider my position very, very carefully before arriving at a decision.'

'Please, sir. Your presence is essential. You have shown yourself to be most capable.'

Cassius was sick of the sound of her voice but he had one final thing to say. 'Forgive me, miss, but what if your father were here? What do you think *he* would advise?'

'That I am certain of. He would want me to follow that man to the very ends of the earth – until I'd seen him burnt to ash or put under the ground. And I will not rest until it's done.'

———8———

The flying boot smashed into the door, narrowly missing Simo, who had just returned to the way station. Cassius kicked off his other boot, then poured himself a mug of wine and slumped down on the bed.

'One day on land. One day! Now back on a bloody boat.'

As Simo retrieved the boot, Indavara wandered out of his room to see what was going on.

Cassius pointed at him. 'And as if that's not bad enough, this genius decides to attack a priest at the temple of Poseidon just before we're about to embark on an already dangerous sea journey!'

'I thought Neptune was god of the sea,' said Indavara.

'By the gods, listen to him.'

'They're really the same,' Simo explained quietly, putting the boots neatly together on the floor. 'Poseidon is the Greek version, Neptune the Roman.'

'Oh,' said Indavara, before returning to his room.

Cassius shut his eyes and rubbed his temples.

'One of your headaches, sir?' asked Simo.

'Of course.'

'Would you like to hear how I got on with the harbour master's clerk?'

Cassius drank and gestured for him to continue.

'There isn't much to report, I'm afraid.' Simo produced a sheet of paper. 'Though I did take some notes.'

'Hurry up, man.'

'The *Cartenna* is a private vessel, owned and captained by a Thracian named Aradates. He has worked with various shipping agents in Rhodes and elsewhere and has a good reputation. This opinion is supported by Magistrate Nariad's men, and we spoke to the inspector who went aboard the *Cartenna* when it arrived. He saw nothing suspicious but confirmed that the ship was definitely headed to Crete and he believed Aradates planned to winter there. No one knew anything about any passengers but Aradates is known to take them if adequately paid.'

'We might surmise, then, that if Dio was aboard, this Aradates has no idea he has helped an assassin make his escape.'

Cassius looked up at the roof and shivered.

'Are you cold, sir?'

'No. Just thinking about what Dio might have been carrying with him.'

Simo looked confused.

'Proof of his work,' Cassius explained.

The Gaul realised what he meant. 'Oh, Lord. It is the work of the beast Satan, sir.'

'Blame your mysterious evil-doer if you wish, Simo, but I'll wager this killer was hired by a flesh and blood man with good reason to want Memor dead.'

'Sir, I was also able to find a ship to take your correspondence – a coaster in the Little Harbour bound for Ephesus. The captain was away but one of the crew was certain they would leave when the weather next cleared. I don't think we'll do any better, sir. Optio Clemens can pass your letters on to the captain for us.'

'Yes, organise that.'

'Already done, sir.'

'Ah. At least I can rely on you, Simo.'

The big Gaul looked down at the pile of saddlebags and clothes on the floor. 'I suppose I should get us packed up, sir.'

Cassius sighed. 'Yes. I suppose you should.'

As Simo began folding blankets, Cassius refilled his mug from the jug he had taken from the parlour.

'Are you sure that's wise, sir, what with your head? And you know how your stomach can be onboard ship.'

'Don't even talk about it. I'm trying to enjoy my last few moments on dry land.'

Cassius walked out into the corridor. 'By the gods, Simo, that girl Annia. She is quite impossible. Just wouldn't listen to reason.'

'She does seem very forward, sir.'

'I'll say. Needs a firm hand, that one.'

'Pretty though,' said Indavara, as he gathered his bags by the door.

'Nothing special,' replied Cassius. 'And one soon forgets the fair face when she opens her mouth. My sisters are all girls with minds of their own – my mother made sure of that. But they know their place – my father made sure of *that*.'

'I think she's pretty.'

'Well there'll be plenty of time onboard the ship, Indavara. You should make an approach; charm her with your sophistication and wit like you did those girls in Karanda. I could use a good laugh.'

Indavara reddened as he attended to an errant bootlace. 'That wasn't my fault.'

'Well it wasn't me who told crude jokes and spilt wine all over them.'

'Roman!'

Cassius turned to see the diminutive, bow-legged figure of Squint shuffling down the corridor towards him.

'Why don't you just use "sir"? It's shorter and far more polite.'

'We have a problem,' said the old sailor, peering up at him.

Cassius leant back against the door frame and took another swig of wine. 'Surely it's not possible for this day to get any worse.'

'It's our deck-chief,' Squint explained. 'He was thrown in prison this morning.'

Cassius had neither the time nor the energy for a trip to the cells, where – according to Squint – Korinth was to be held until the next session of the municipal court. He therefore had to write a note to Magistrate Nariad explaining the situation, and was rather glad he wouldn't have to do so in person. It seemed almost laughable, having insisted the man be detained in the first place, but Squint was sure that Asdribar couldn't possibly leave port without his deck-chief. Watching from the way station entrance as the old sailor hurried away clutching the note, Cassius wondered how many more sly tricks the gods were planning to play on him before the day was out.

A waving hand appeared and he was relieved to see Clemens marching along the sea wall. As soon as the burly optio reached the way station, Cassius swiftly related the events of the last few hours.

As instructed, Clemens had been trying to locate Carius Asina. 'I eventually found an administrator at the forum who knows him well. Asina and his family left for their estate as soon as they returned. We can get a message to them but—'

'No, no, there's no time for that,' Cassius interjected. 'And probably no need. I doubt they could offer any more information about this Dio than Viator did. What about Sudrenus's slave?'

'He lives in a fishing village on the other side of the citadel – quite a way along the coast. I sent one of the men on horseback to question him but I doubt he'll be back before you leave.'

'Right. Anything else?'

'No. I went round most of the inns but nobody remembers him. By the way, is your bodyguard here?'

'Yes. Why?'

'This incident at the temple of Poseidon. Lot of talk about it. Some very angry people. It's probably just as well that you're leaving.'

Just then a young legionary shot out of an alley and ran over to them. Cassius didn't recognise him.

'Sir. Another sighting – a fisherman whose boat was moored up next to the *Cartenna*. There *was* a passenger. The crew had him sit on the wharf for an hour while they cleaned the decks. The fisherman noticed the sack *and* the boots.'

'He's sure?'

'Yes, sir.'

'Good work,' Cassius told the legionary. 'I'll make sure you get your due.'

'Thank you, sir.'

'I may as well round the men up then,' said Clemens. 'Get them back to barracks.'

Cassius nodded. 'Yes. You – and they – did well for me. It's appreciated.'

'You wouldn't believe me if I told you I was a keen supporter of the Service, sir, but no Roman deserves what happened to Memor. It's his poor wife and those girls I feel for. I hope you find the son of a bitch. Best of luck.'

Once he'd shaken forearms with Cassius, Clemens and the legionary set off back along the sea wall. Cassius returned to the way station. Simo had gone to buy provisions for the journey, leaving Indavara to pile the last of their gear in the little room by the door.

'Now listen,' Cassius told him. 'Assuming they let this Korinth character out, we're going to be stuck on a boat with him for the next few days. Can I rely on you to keep control of yourself?'

'Who started it?'

'All right, but evidently he's a pretty fiery fellow. Just stay out of his way.'

Finished with the bags, Indavara leant back against the wall by the window.

'You're becoming a bit of a liability, my man,' said Cassius.

'What do you mean?'

'You're causing me more problems than you solve.'

Indavara shook his head but said nothing.

'I mean kicking a priest,' Cassius continued. 'Whoever heard of such a thing?'

'We got Viator, didn't we?'

'I almost had him anyway.'

'And what would you have done if you'd caught him? Talk him into surrender?'

'Very funny.'

Indavara crossed the room, stepped over one of the saddlebags and stood close to Cassius. 'You know something, Corbulo?'

Cassius felt his throat dry. Indavara hardly ever addressed him by name.

'One day I might not be around when you need someone scared or beaten up, or you pick a fight with the wrong people. And then you really will have a problem, won't you?'

Indavara held Cassius's gaze a moment longer then walked past him and out on to the street.

IX

In the murky gloom of early evening, with a light rain still falling, the passengers and crew of the *Fortuna Redux* stood in a line behind the deckhouse, waiting for Asdribar to begin the leaving ceremony.

The start of the tenth hour had just passed but, to Cassius's surprise, the Carthaginian had managed to get the ship in some sort of order and assemble his crew. The full complement was twenty, but various individuals had already departed for different parts of the island so he was now down to twelve. Apart from Squint and Korinth, his other senior man was Opilio: a veteran of the Roman fleets about the same age as his captain. He seemed to be in charge of everything that went on below decks and had been supervising the loading of supplies. The other nine members of the crew were as rough and eclectic a bunch as Cassius had seen. He'd already heard conversations in four different languages, though it seemed Asdribar insisted on Greek for anything relating to the ship.

Cassius had hoped Annia might have a late change of heart, but she and Clara had already taken over the deckhouse by the time he, Indavara and Simo arrived. He'd briefly considered a last appeal to the girl but not only did he think it would fall on deaf ears, he simply hadn't the energy for it. The long, taxing day had sapped his strength and all he wanted to do was go below and get settled in. Unlike many freighters, the *Fortuna* had four small cabins close to the stern, one of which Asdribar had put aside for them. They were yet to see their quarters; their gear was still piled up next to the hatch.

The captain was standing behind the two altars situated

119

between the deckhouse and the stern. Both comprising cubes of stone mounted in wooden frames, one altar was inscribed with dedications in numerous languages while the other was stained pink with blood from sacrificed animals. Several cockerels had been brought aboard and one would be killed as a symbol of gratitude when they next reached port.

'We shall begin,' said the Carthaginian in Greek.

Cassius, Indavara and Simo stood to his right, with Annia and Clara (holding a parasol over her mistress) separating them from the crew. Asdribar had suggested to Cassius that they take a moment with Korinth and Indavara, but Cassius thought it best just to keep them apart, for the remainder of the day at least.

'First, to the God of the Deep, Great Poseidon.'

Cassius was relieved to see no reaction from the crew. Even if Poseidon had been offended, the other gods were undoubtedly smiling on Indavara if none of the sailors had heard what he'd done to that priest.

Squint came forward with a jug and placed it on the altar.

'This we give to you, Great Poseidon,' said Asdribar, 'so that we may in return see fair winds and calm seas.' He spoke quietly – his voice barely audible above the low hiss of the rain striking the water – but invested his words with a compelling gravitas. 'We humbly beg that you will be merciful, and see us safely on our way.'

He picked up the jug of wine, walked to the stern and poured it into the water. When he returned to the altar, Squint took the jug and handed the captain a little wooden bowl, which he placed on top of the inscribed stone.

'Now, to the goddess Fortuna, whose name this vessel carries, and to whom we offer our riches, so that the vagaries of luck may favour us. Come and give, so that you shall receive the best and avoid the worst.'

One by one, the crew came forward and dropped a coin into the bowl. Annia did the same, prompting Cassius to wonder where she was keeping the rest of her money – several large bags, surely. He, Simo and Indavara each added a sesterce to the bowl.

With Korinth holding a cloth cover over the altar, Squint poured thick, scented oil over the coins. He then lit a match from a lantern and set the oil alight. As it sizzled and spat, Asdribar dropped the coins into the water.

'Now I honour the gods of Carthage.'

The captain shut his eyes and spoke a few sentences in Punic.

Then came the turn of Opilio, who placed a small libation on the altar. 'To Jupiter, great god, all offerings and prayers. I beg for favour and deliverance.'

Asdribar glanced at another of the crew. 'And we acknowledge our friend Desenna. He worships the Hebrew god and will make his own prayers.'

Cassius was surprised to see the other crewmen turn to this man Desenna and nod respectfully. With the ceremony over, Asdribar suggested that Annia and Clara retire to the deckhouse while the crew made final preparations. The two young women picked their way past assorted ropes and sailbags, holding their stolas up above the wet deck. Korinth and another man looked on and shook their heads. Cassius watched Annia and Clara as they entered the deckhouse. He couldn't be entirely sure because of the rain, but the maid seemed to be crying.

'Ridiculous,' he whispered to himself. 'Utterly ridiculous.'

'Whose is this crap?' yelled Korinth, now standing by the hatch, staring down at the unstowed gear.

Cassius walked over to him. 'Ours.'

'Get it below.'

With a steely glance at Indavara, Korinth headed forward to join the men dragging the immense mainsail bag towards the mast.

'Best do as the man says,' Cassius told the others.

Even though he did his part, weighing himself down with saddlebags and a sack of food, it took return journeys from Simo and Indavara to get everything down the steps.

The upper hold of the ship was comparatively high; Cassius could almost stand up straight. Stacked up on the right side were hundreds of the twig bales he'd seen used for separating and protecting fragile cargo. To the left was a big pile of timber and a carpenter's table.

Opilio – who was apparently known as the hold-chief – came down the steps at speed. He was a squat, solidly built character clad in a grubby tunic. Not the most attractive of men, he was also the unfortunate owner of a flat nose, unruly teeth and thinning, straggly hair.

'This way, sir,' he said, picking up two skins of water and hurrying along the passageway behind the steps towards the stern. The three of them grabbed what they could and followed him. Directly ahead was what looked like the galley, with two cabins on each side of the passageway. Opilio stopped at the second room on the right. 'We had some salt pork hanging in here so you'll have to forgive the smell.'

The cabin was tiny; by Cassius's estimation about eight feet by seven. There was one bed, with a straw mattress no more than two inches thick. The head of the bed was against the far wall, under a porthole from which water was dripping.

Opilio put down the skins and squeezed past Cassius. 'I'll be in the galley if you need anything, sir.'

As he left, Cassius turned to Simo. 'At least there's one cheerful member of the crew.'

Opilio stuck his head back in the doorway. 'Only because I just heard what we're getting paid, sir. I'm usually a right miserable bastard.'

Korinth arrived outside with a woven basket of clothes in his hand. He dropped it in the room opposite, then strode back along the passageway.

Indavara picked up his bags. 'I'll find a space somewhere else. There's no room for all of us in here anyway.'

'As you wish,' replied Cassius.

'Did you have a falling-out, sir?' asked Simo when Indavara had gone.

'Of sorts. You know what he's like.'

'At least he's rather more sociable now, sir. You must remember how he was when we first met? It's only been a matter of months.'

Cassius went and stood by the porthole for a little fresh air as the Gaul brought in the last of the bags. 'It's just that he never seems to think. Just does the first thing that comes into his head.'

'Some might regard that as an admirable trait for a man in his profession, sir.'

'I suppose. What about his numbers and letters?'

'We've not had a lot of time, sir, but I'd say he's no worse or better than anyone else starting an education.'

'And he's still not spoken to you of his family, his past?'

'Not a word, sir. I have tried on occasion but he always changes the subject or goes quiet.'

'I must admit I'm curious,' replied Cassius. 'Think about it – all we know is that he was a gladiator in Pietas Julia, ended up travelling east, then fell into the employ of Abascantius. Try again, Simo.'

'I don't think I'll get anywhere, sir.'

'Well I certainly won't. Just try.'

A small group had gathered on the dock to see off the freighter, including half a dozen women, a couple of whom had children with them. They didn't look particularly happy that their menfolk were departing; neither did the sailors.

The start of the eleventh hour was well past, and though the rain had stopped, a blanket of low, grey cloud lay over Rhodes and the sea beyond. The wind had increased too, chopping the water into steep, angular waves.

The *Fortuna*'s deck was now clear, except for the mainsail and the yard, which would be raised once the ship was out of the harbour. Two towing tugs – twenty-foot dories each manned by eight strapping oarsmen – were sculling around in front of the ship. Akritos the harbour master was in one of them and had just overseen the tying of thick ropes to iron rings mounted on the freighter's bow.

Keen to escape the malodorous cabin, Cassius was standing

123

close to the mast on the shore side, his thickest woollen cloak over his shoulders. He could have blamed any number of things for the bitter churning in his stomach but suspected the prospect of a long, perilous sea journey was the main culprit.

Two hundred miles. *Two hundred*. In November. And ships were so slow, and so dependent on the elements. The only advantage was that when you slept – if you slept – you might awake to find another thirty or forty miles had been covered. Cassius just hoped the seasickness wouldn't be too bad. Later he would find his figurine of Neptune and offer a proper prayer of his own.

'Watch yourself there, sir.'

Cassius stood aside as one of the crew came past him and up to the side-rail. The sailor caught a rope thrown by Korinth, who was untying the lines holding the ship against the wharf. Squint, meanwhile, was now standing on a small platform between the deckhouse and the main hatch. He already had a hand on each of the tiller bars, which were connected by a complicated system of sockets and timbers to the two steering rudders on either side of the ship's stern. Asdribar was standing just ahead of the veteran, arms crossed. The harbour master waved to him.

'Ready at the stern?' the captain cried.

'Ready here!' answered one of the sailors.

'Ready at the bow?'

'Ready here!'

'Cast her off!'

Korinth and three of the crew pushed the ship away from the wharf, then jumped aboard.

Asdribar called out to Akritos: 'Heave on!'

'Heave on!'

Cassius ran a finger across his chin. The stubble on his face could stay now; it would keep his face warm and a ship was no place for a shave with an iron razor, even if carried out by Simo's steady hand. He watched as the towing lines pulled tight and the *Fortuna* began to move. Though dwarfed by the freighter, the dories were soon pulling her along at quite a clip towards the harbour entrance.

'Officer Corbulo.'

Cassius turned to see Annia beside him. She had her own thick cloak wrapped around her and had done something with her stola to keep the embroidered hem above the deck.

'Miss.'

Neither of them said anything else for a while. Then some of the sailors started throwing colourful insults at the oarsmen, who fired back equally imaginative retorts. It was rather awkward, standing there with the young lady as curses fouled the air.

'They have a competition in the summer,' Annia said eventually.

'Sorry?'

'The dories – they race across the harbour. People make bets.'

'Ah. How are your quarters, miss?'

'They'll do. It's good of the captain to give up his deckhouse for us.'

Cassius doubted there was much Asdribar wouldn't give up for a hundred denarii a day. Besides, the presence of the two young women was likely to be enough of a distraction for the crew. Better that they stay out of the way.

'Do you think we'll find this . . . Dio?'

She said the name with her eyes closed, as if she could barely stand to utter it.

'The soldiers found another witness who confirmed he was on the *Cartenna*. If we can catch up, or at least arrive not too long after in Cnossus, I believe there's a good chance, yes.'

'I suppose it might not end there. With him, I mean.'

'Possibly not.'

'It was an assassination. Someone hired him, paid him, that's why he—'

'Yes, miss. It may be complicated. And difficult.' Cassius turned to face her. 'It's not too late. One of those rowing boats can take you and your maid back. I can send you word as soon as I know more.'

Cassius half expected another fiery response, but Annia looked down at the deck and replied quietly, 'I will not sit and wait. It would drive me mad. I must know.'

Cassius could understand that at least.

'I believe the great gods are with us,' Annia added.

'I hope so, miss.'

He looked at her. The cold had drawn all the colour from her already pale face, whitening even her lips, but this allowed her emerald eyes to shine all the brighter. There was a certain beauty to her, he had to admit.

'Don't get cold on my account, miss.'

Annia gave an awkward little half-smile. She looked out past the breakwater, at the rocky coast of the island. 'This time two days ago he was alive.'

Cassius could think of no fitting maxim, no appropriate words of sympathy. Recalling the picture in Memor's study, he glanced back at the city and imagined that huge wave striking. He shivered.

Just then, the crew began to cheer and shout. They were all looking up at the three gulls that had just landed in the rigging.

'A good omen,' said Annia.

'Is it?' Cassius replied. 'There are so many – I lose track.'

'The great gods *are* with us. I feel it.' She turned away and walked back along the deck, passing Indavara as he came up through the hatch.

'Get settled in?'

With a barely perceptible nod, Indavara stopped beside him and looked morosely out at the dark blue sea.

'Sorry there wasn't room in the cabin,' Cassius said as the *Fortuna* neared the harbour entrance. 'You all right?' he added, keen to build bridges after Indavara's outburst at the way station.

'It really was stupid, what I did, wasn't it?'

'What do you mean?' asked Cassius.

'Kicking that priest. What if I have offended this god? He controls the sea and the wind. He could make a storm. He could sink the ship.'

'Calm yourself,' Cassius replied. 'You saw the ceremony. There's more gods watching over this ship than any I've been on and it's named after your Fortuna.'

Indavara was still gazing at the sea. 'I've heard there are creatures under the water bigger than any on land. Bigger than an elephant even.'

'Corbulo!'

Asdribar was gesturing to the left. All the crew had turned that way.

'Turn to port!' exclaimed the Carthaginian. 'Don't look at the wreck.'

This superstition Cassius had heard of; looking at a sunken ship was supposed to bring ill fortune. He had noted the weed-covered mast sticking out of the water just outside the harbour the previous day.

Korinth dropped the rope he was coiling and stalked towards them, scratching at his scarred face. 'Turn! Both of you! Or do you want to curse us all?'

'Which way's port again?' asked Indavara.

'Left,' said Cassius.

They turned away from the wreck. Slowly.

Korinth shot them a final glare, then returned to the stern.

Cassius and Indavara exchanged a smile.

'I really don't know why these sailors can't just use left and right,' said Cassius. 'Makes them feel special, I suppose.'

'What's right?'

'Starboard.'

'That's it.'

'By the way,' said Cassius, 'I've decided you're quite correct. It's ridiculous for me to depend on you all the time. I have a sword and I need to be able to use it properly. A ship is hardly an ideal training ground but perhaps we can at least go over a few basics. It's been a long time.'

'We can start tomorrow.'

As the towing dories passed through the harbour entrance and beyond the breakwaters, the sea became rougher. Akritos's cries were lost on the wind and trivial japes were long forgotten as the oarsmen dug deep with their oars to pull the freighter clear. The towing rope tightened and slackened as the three vessels were thrown around and Korinth came forward to monitor the iron rings now jolting in their mounts.

Only when they were a good fifty yards out did Akritos yell, 'Ready to cast off?', cupping his hands around his mouth to make himself heard.

'Ready!' answered Asdribar.

The men reversed their oars and propelled their boats back towards the freighter. Once they were close enough, the sailors untied the ropes and threw them back to the dories. Akritos directed the two boats upwind of the *Fortuna*, then had the men ship their oars, allowing them a welcome rest before heading back into the harbour. They still found enough breath to shout, and the wind carried their words to all on deck.

'May Poseidon smile!'

'Fair wind! Fair way!'

'Fortuna's best!'

Those of Asdribar's crew who weren't at work solemnly raised their hands to their fellow seamen.

'Raise the foresail!' ordered the captain.

Korinth and another man took hold of a thick rope and hauled the sail up hand over hand. It was tiny compared to the mainsail but all the pair's strength was required to get it to the top of the foremast.

'Bear away!' ordered Asdribar.

The freighter had been wallowing in the disturbed water beyond the harbour, but as the foresail filled, she began to pick up speed, bow aiming at the northern cape of Rhodes.

Cassius put a hand to his stomach. He was beginning to feel the first pangs of nausea.

'Grey,' observed Indavara. 'Grey everywhere.'

'Well you know why it's cloudy, of course.'

'The season?'

'No, no. Apparently someone' – he looked at Indavara – 'decided it would be a good idea to slide around on a statue of the sun god this afternoon. The god is offended, and hides his rays from us.'

Indavara's face froze.

'I'm joking,' Cassius said.

The bodyguard gulped and gazed up at the sky.

'Seriously,' Cassius added. 'I am joking.'

Simo came out of the hatch with a mug in each hand. He did extremely well to reach the mast having spilt only a little of the steaming wine.

'Thank you,' said Indavara.

'From Opilio,' said Simo. 'Not sure if it will be good or bad for your stomach, sir.'

'Might help me sleep at least.'

'The ship's name,' said Indavara after he'd taken his first sip. 'Fortuna I know. But *Fortuna Redux*. What does it mean?'

'Good luck that brings you home,' explained Simo.

Cassius raised his mug. 'Here's hoping, eh?'

X

Indavara lay in the darkness, head propped against one of his bags, watching the crewmen come up and down through the hatch. It was always hard to work out how much time had passed on a ship; might have been two hours since they left the harbour, might have been four.

And so much noise. The hull striking the waves. Flapping sails. Squeaking blocks. Groaning ropes and stays. It did seem a little quieter now though. From what he could gather, the mainsail was up, and he knew ships went better through the water once that was done.

Try as he might, Indavara couldn't stop thinking about the water. That lethal, formless void. Sometimes, when he found himself in the middle of an expanse of sea, he felt as if he might faint, and he wished some great hand would reach down from the clouds, pick him up and place him back on dry land. Night was even worse. Those scattered wave crests glittering in the moonlight. The sound of the water sliding by. Inescapable thoughts of what was around him, under him.

Indavara pulled the blanket up to his chin. He'd found a nice little space for himself next to the stack of twig bales. It would be noisy and busy by the hatch, but he preferred to be close to it in case anything happened. His bags were neatly arranged behind him and to his left, leaving just enough space for his blanket and hardly enough room to turn over. That was how he liked it; the bed in his cell under the arena at Pietas Julia had been narrow and he found he still barely moved during the night.

The last person he'd seen on the steps was Korinth. Like the others who'd come past, the sailor hadn't even noticed he was lying there. Indavara wasn't too worried about him. He'd handled him once, he could handle him again. Even so, he would sleep with his right hand resting on his dagger hilt – but then he usually did that anyway.

With all that had happened since they'd arrived on Rhodes, he was surprised to find it was the young lady Annia who kept forcing her way into his thoughts. That happened with women. You saw one, perhaps only for a few moments, and then you just kept thinking about her. Like Galla, that girl back in Antioch. He'd only seen her twice – and she took money so it was hard to know if she'd really liked him – but he thought about her a lot too.

But this Annia. She really was pretty. You could tell because she'd been through a terrible shock and she wasn't trying to look good, but she still did. She was probably almost as tall as him but he didn't mind that. She was so graceful, so feminine.

Indavara didn't think he could go and talk to her. That would be difficult. She had lost her father. He didn't know what to say to women at the best of times and this certainly wasn't that. Perhaps if they saw each other on deck *she* might talk to *him*.

He had managed a good wash before they left the way station and now reminded himself to keep putting on that scent Simo had given him. He'd hated the smell at first but now he quite liked it. Simo was always on at him about that sort of thing. Must get clean when you have the chance, must use soap, must wash your clothes.

But he was a good man, Simo, and a patient teacher. Indavara didn't understand why he himself could do some things without even thinking about it, yet found words and numbers so difficult. He had to do his sums hundreds of times just to remember them and even then it wasn't that satisfying. Not like writing. Writing was incredible. He could make his name look the same almost every time now. To think people wrote whole books!

Corbulo said he was planning to write several. Indavara was sure he could do it. He was annoying at times – most of the time actually – but he was clever. There was no doubt about that.

And he did seem to know a bit about women. He'd been a bastard that night in Karanda though, telling Indavara he had the manners of a – what was it? – Thracian muck-chucker; that he'd never get any girls if he couldn't learn how to behave. The woman had laughed along with him until Indavara had walked away.

That was when he hated Corbulo the most. When he made him feel a fool. Because it was as if he'd forgotten what Indavara had done for him – not once, but twice.

Saved him. Saved his life. Corbulo had done the same for him of course, that day at the river, but Indavara had thought a thing like that might bring two men together; make them friends. But it hardly ever felt like that. Perhaps when Corbulo had bought him the silver-plated figurine of the goddess Fortuna. Perhaps then. Indavara still had the gift, though he made a point of keeping it hidden when Corbulo was around. He preferred the old, small marble figurine he was holding in his hand.

His fingers had worn the stone smooth and he knew every edge, every contour. He imagined that the woman who'd thrown it to him at the end of his tenth fight had looked like Annia.

Indavara gripped the figurine tight and tried to focus on his prayer. Prayers weren't easy. He'd memorised a few bits he'd heard other people say but he couldn't ask Simo about it because he didn't want to seem stupid. He could at least usually find a way to say what he wanted to now.

'Fair Fortuna,' he whispered, 'Goddess Most High . . .'

———◆———

The galley of the *Fortuna Redux* was noisy, smelly and smoky. The noise was a combination of shouted conversation, rattling pots and pans, and a bubbling iron cauldron. The smell was an exotic mix of spices, barley and charcoal smoke. Cassius was surprised to see the cauldron was mounted on a metal grill in the middle of a hearth that wouldn't have looked out of place in a farmhouse. All around it were tiles covering the timber walls to reduce the risk of fire. Cut into the ceiling was a smoke hole that opened up behind the deckhouse.

'Check that barley!' Opilio yelled over his shoulder. He was standing over a wooden counter, chopping vegetables with a cleaver.

Desenna – the Jew – was kneeling by the hearth, rearranging the coals beneath the grill with a poker. 'Just checked it!'

'Check again.'

Shaking his head, Desenna stood up and dipped a long-handled spoon into the cauldron.

'They're missing the pail!' snapped Opilio. 'Wake up, Tarkel.'

The third member of the galley crew was a skinny lad of thirteen or fourteen. He was squatting by the counter, trying to catch the vegetable offcuts coming his way.

Simo, who was standing in front of a huge water barrel, suddenly noticed his master. 'Sorry, sir, won't be a moment.'

Opilio turned round. 'Ah, sir's getting impatient for his wine.'

Cassius stepped inside the doorway. 'Seems to help with my stomach.'

Opilio took a mug from Simo and went over to the hearth, then picked up a small pan of wine next to the cauldron. 'You'll be all right for the moment, sir. We've a calm sea. That's why we've got to cook up as much as we can now. The captain likes a proper hot meal.'

Being stuck in this tiny space, preparing food in bad weather, was about as appalling a job of work as Cassius could imagine.

Having filled the mug, Opilio handed it to him. 'I'll keep that pan warm for you, sir. In case you'd like a bit more later.'

'Much appreciated.'

Cassius and Simo left the galley. Even though the sea was indeed calm, it was generally necessary to keep a steadying hand on something solid. As they reached the cabin, the young maid Clara came down the steps, looking pale and anxious. Clutched over her impressive chest was a leather case. 'Master Corbulo, sir?'

'Yes? Ah – that will be those documents.'

Before Annia had returned to Amyndios to prepare for the journey, Cassius had asked her to collect the papers from her father's study.

The maid gave him the case.

'Clara, isn't it?' asked Cassius, smiling.

'Yes, sir.'

The ship suddenly pitched and she reached for the wall.

Cassius took hold of her arm and steadied her. 'Careful there. Your mistress is all right?'

Clara was trying hard not to look at him. 'Yes, sir.'

'Well,' Cassius said, 'a difficult time for her. You too, I expect.'

'Yes, sir.'

She pushed some strands of hair away from her face.

Despite his reservations, Cassius suddenly felt glad she was on the ship (purely from an aesthetic point of view). There was nothing worse than not having any women to look at – another occupational hazard of army life.

'Well. You'd best get back to her.'

One more 'Yes, sir' and off she went.

'Curvy little thing,' said Opilio as Clara's sandals disappeared up the steps.

Cassius turned round and saw that all three of the galley crew had gathered by the doorway.

'I like a woman with a bit of meat on her bones.'

Cassius found the comment rather distasteful but couldn't help laughing as Opilio gleefully rubbed his hands together then led the others back to work.

Noting the disapproval on Simo's face, Cassius entered the cabin and sat down on the bed. He didn't know a lot about Christian beliefs regarding sexual relations but – without ever saying a word – Simo had made it clear to him that base talk and casual assignations were not looked on favourably.

Cassius looked at the leather case in his hands. 'I expect all Memor's papers will go to Chief Pulcher eventually. We can at least see if there's anything useful here.'

He had to stretch his hand wide to hold the whole sheaf of

134

paper inside the case. He gave approximately a quarter to Simo and took a similar amount for himself.

'What exactly are we looking for, sir?'

'Names. Anyone involved in the cases and issues Memor was handling with a reason to want him dead. If something looks relevant, put it to one side.'

———8———

An hour later, Cassius had learnt more about the Imperial Security Service than he had from a dozen conversations with Abascantius. His commanding officer was, to all intents and purposes, a spy, with one eye on Rome's enemies and another on its ruling elite – the military in particular. That was how he did things, and that was what he thought was expected of him. But Cassius also knew that other agents were involved in field operations, intelligence work, tax collection, even running prisons. And some still fulfilled the traditional role of procuring and distributing supplies to the legions, though this was invariably a cover for other intrigues.

So Cassius had expected to find lots of orders. Orders *for* Memor, from Chief Pulcher in Rome; and orders *from* Memor to his numerous subordinates in Africa and the East.

There were such letters. And reports too, information received from those same subordinates: legion troop numbers, enemy fleet-size estimations, budget summaries, intelligence reports, even a few maps.

But most of the sheets – two-thirds by Cassius's reckoning – were letters from individuals *outside* the Service. Some were military personnel, some members of the governor's staff, others ordinary citizens, in provinces ranging from Mauretania to Arabia, Galatia to Egypt. And the majority of these letter-writers had one clear aim in mind: to get other people into trouble.

Many of the missives were so similar that Cassius began to skim-read, and variations of the same sentiment appeared again and again.

I feel this disgraceful conduct must be brought to your attention.
He has undermined our authority with the local populace.
He takes money from someone every hour of every day.
He is considered by his peers to be a liability.
My recommendation is that he be removed from his post.
This scandal could damage the reputation of the governor.
I can provide further evidence if necessary.
I am sure you will take appropriate action.

'There do seem to be a lot of complaints, sir,' observed Simo.

'I'll say. I've not seen this much tale-telling since I was at school. He seems to have ignored most of it.'

Memor had employed a simple procedure. He would write either 'No Action' or a brief note to himself at the bottom of each letter. On a number of occasions he had written an abbreviation that Cassius soon realised stood for 'Retain For Possible Later Use'.

He knew Abascantius employed a similar technique in Syria: accumulating potentially damaging information on as many people as he could, in case he needed leverage over them in the future.

'Well, we can probably discount anything where Memor took no action. And we can ignore anything very recent. The assassin and his employers would have needed some time to plan the killing.' Cassius glanced at the smaller pile of papers Simo had made. 'Anything interesting?'

'Several arrest orders, sir, from Chief Pulcher in Rome. And some copies of requests by Master Memor – asking for information about certain individuals.'

'I've much the same kind of thing. We shall start on the list of names tomorrow. In the event that we can't track this Dio, we'll at least have other avenues to follow.'

Cassius dropped his papers and the case on to Simo's blanket. As the Gaul set about tidying them up, he lay back against the wall and put his hands behind his head, interlocking his fingers.

'Clever – doing it now. The ports will close up for the winter.

Most of the roads are already mud, and soon there'll be snow and ice. By the gods, this might be part of an attack on the Service itself. What if Pulcher and the other senior officers have been targeted too?'

'Is that really possible, sir?'

'Consider history, Simo. How many emperors have been knocked off before their time? Don't recall many slipping merrily into retirement, do you? Perhaps someone somewhere decided the Service has held sway for too long. By Jupiter, for once I wish Abascantius were here. He'd know what to do.'

'Knowing what to do has never been a problem for you before, sir. I don't suppose it will be now.'

Cassius felt rather heartened by this comment, even if it was only from Simo. Generally compliant though he was, the Gaul never toadied. If he gave a compliment, he meant it.

'I remember the fort, sir,' Simo continued. 'Alauran.'

'I don't think either of us is ever likely to forget it.'

Simo put the papers down for a moment. 'That first day or two, sir. I kept thinking you would give up. Perhaps even run away. But you just kept going and going and going. Until it was over.'

Cassius could think of no reply to that.

'Why don't you wear your silver medal, sir? I could clean it up for you.'

Cassius felt his spirits drop instantly. 'Do you know how many times I actually used my blade in that fort, Simo?'

'No.'

'Once. Against a wounded man lying at my feet. And I couldn't even despatch *him*. I told you before. If it wasn't for the others – Strabo, Avso, Serenus, all of them – I would never have accepted that medal. It is theirs. Not mine.'

Cassius stood. 'I shall go and get a little air before bed. Put another blanket on for me.'

'Yes, sir.'

———✴———

The sky had cleared, leaving only thin banks of cloud far away to the east, and the half-moon cast a shimmering glow across the sea. The wind had lessened, but there was still enough to fill the sails, driving the *Fortuna Redux* along the western coast of Rhodes. The dark bulk of the island could be felt as much as seen. Almost directly opposite the ship was a group of lights.

'Where's that?' Cassius asked Asdribar, turning from the siderail. The captain was sitting on a chair that had somehow been attached to the deck just ahead of the steering position. Behind him stood Korinth, one hand on each tiller, eyes fixed on the bow.

'Camiros,' answered the Carthaginian without looking. He was slumped back in the chair, which came complete with several cushions. On the deck by his bare feet was a wooden plate with the remains of his dinner. 'I can hear your corner flapping, Nigrinus! Bring it in a bit.'

Cassius could just about see the crewman sitting to the left of the mast, hands gripping the foresail line.

'That'll do you!' the captain added when the flapping ceased.

Squint was also on deck, inspecting the mainsail. Cassius had been below when they'd raised the yard but looking at the sprawling rig now, it was hard to believe the reduced crew had accomplished it.

'Where might we be by morning?' Cassius asked.

Asdribar ran a hand across his brown dome of a head. 'I'll be happy if Rhodes is well behind us when the sun comes up.'

'Oh.'

'Big island,' Asdribar explained.

Apparently happy with the rig, Squint bade the others goodnight and disappeared down the steps.

'Will you be retiring soon, Captain?' asked Cassius.

'Not the first night. I always stay up the first night. Maybe the second, third and fourth too on this trip.'

'Why? Because it's so late in the season?'

'It's not late in the season, Officer. It's *after* the season. Long after. This is what old salts call the Dark Time – when a storm can come out of nowhere, knock your mast down and leave you drifting in fog for days on end. Weeks even.'

Cassius knew such talk wouldn't help him sleep but he couldn't curtail his curiosity. 'But you've been out in November before?'

'I have. Three times.'

'Only three? How long have you been sailing?'

'Not sure exactly. But I think Maximinus Thrax was emperor. How long's that?'

'About thirty-five years.'

'There you go then.'

'And how were the other trips?' Cassius asked, preferring not to dwell on the implications of what Asdribar had told him.

'Two of them were fine – well, eventually. We got home safe at least.'

'And the other?'

'Now that *was* a long time ago. I was a deckhand on the *Alka* – old grain ship out of Tingi. The army needed us to transport auxiliaries across the straits from Mauretania to Calpe. We started in clear skies, with barely enough to make two or three knots. A mile off the Spanish coast, a squall hit us. Whole sky turned black. Couldn't keep your eyes open for the rain. We couldn't get the yard down quick enough. The port arm snapped off and spliced us through the foredeck. The hold filled up like that.' Asdribar clicked his fingers. 'And the *Alka*, she went down quicker than an alley girl with the rent due. I found myself a cork float and jumped off the stern. Got picked up by a fishing boat two hours later. Back on dry land in three.'

'And the other men?'

'Eight of the crew made it too. One of them – nasty old Greek – he thought he'd try and take my float off me, but I put him off that idea pretty quick.'

'The auxiliaries?'

'Not one. Didn't have a chance weighed down with all their fighting gear. All went straight to the god of the deep. But I reckon he didn't want them because pretty soon they started popping up all over. Hundreds of them there was. Pop – one here. Pop – one there. One of them came up right next to me with his big old white face. Nearly went under myself when I saw that.'

Cassius took a long breath, and wished he hadn't started the conversation.

'But that was just the once,' Asdribar added. 'Like I said – the other two times were fine.'

Cassius headed for the hatch. 'Good night.'

'Night, Officer,' replied the captain. 'Sleep well.'

XI

The only spacious, private area on the *Fortuna Redux* was the main hold. With the hatch cover pulled to one side, it was well lit by the bright morning sunshine and once a few amphorae and barrels had been shifted, there was a square area about fifteen feet wide. Dawn had brought a few extra knots of wind but the sea remained calm and – apart from the occasional judder or pitch – it was relatively easy to stand.

Cassius glanced towards the stern to check there were no prying eyes behind the twig bales and timber. Thankfully, the seasickness still hadn't struck in earnest. Ascribing this to Opilio's hot wine, he'd already downed a big mugful with his breakfast. It was now the third hour, and he'd been pleased to discover that Rhodes was indeed now well behind them, with the *Fortuna* powering along at a good five knots.

Arriving in the hold, he'd found Indavara shooting arrows into a barrel lid. The bodyguard had been alternating hands and seemed to enjoy the challenge presented by the movements of the ship.

'Right,' he said, putting the bow down, 'let's have a look at this thing, then.'

Cassius handed over his sword belt. Indavara drew the blade and put the belt and scabbard on top of a barrel. Casting a disparaging look at the eagle head, he ran his eyes over the rest of the weapon. 'Not even runnelled.'

'What are runnels again?' Cassius enquired.

'Curved hollows along the flat. Lets air in when the blade slides into flesh. Makes it easier to pull it out.'

'Ah.'

For a brief moment, Cassius felt as if nausea might strike after all.

Indavara shook his head. 'Heavy as a trident. And just as unwieldy.'

He threw it to Cassius, who managed to grab the hilt.

Indavara looked at Cassius's forearms. 'I've seen teenage girls with bigger wrists than you.'

Cassius glared at him but the bodyguard persisted: 'Tell me they were like that when you finished your training.'

Cassius begrudgingly shook his head. He had lost a lot of bulk – muscle especially – in the last two years. Never a big eater, his only real form of exercise had been swimming.

'You need building up,' said Indavara. 'Start with the blade close to the deck, then raise it up until your arm's horizontal. Do twenty.'

'Very well.'

Cassius did as he was told. Upon reaching the twentieth swing, he winced, and instantly wished he hadn't.

'Too much for you, Officer?'

'Enjoying this, aren't you?'

Indavara shrugged. 'I always knew legionary training was piss-easy compared to what we fighters did, but it's still hard to believe *you* got through.'

'Oh I got through – don't worry about that. All sixty days.'

Cassius was suddenly assailed by one of his most shameful memories – crying into his pillow at the end of at least the first twenty of those days. He aimed the sword at Indavara. 'Don't get too full of yourself, bodyguard – you'd have been heading home on day three.'

'What happens on day three?'

'Half-mile swim.'

Cassius's triumphant grin didn't last long. The ship pitched suddenly and they both lurched towards the bow.

'Do you want to do this, or not?' asked Indavara when the vessel was steady again.

'Go ahead.'

'Now swing it side to side. Plant your feet. Don't twist your body.'

'I thought you were supposed to keep your feet moving.'

'We're strengthening your sword arm, not working on technique.'

When this exercise was done, Indavara ordered diagonal swings – left to right, then right to left.

'Here's what you must do,' he instructed when Cassius had finished. 'Fifty of all four variations – when you wake up, and before you go to bed.'

'Before bed? I'll be covered in sweat.'

'Not after a week or two.'

'Very well. Now, how about teaching me something useful? Some of your gladiator tricks.'

'Forget tricks. We can't do much on here anyway with the ship moving around. Do you have enough money for a new sword?'

'Not really.'

'If you sold that thing?'

'I'm not selling this! I spent half an afternoon haggling for it.'

Indavara shook his head despairingly. 'You said you'd been in a battle once – at this fort. How did you get on? Be honest.'

Cassius looked down at the deck. 'I couldn't think. I was so slow. My mind just . . . emptied.'

Indavara walked over to the row of barrels on the right side of the hold. 'We may as well sit down.'

'What? Why?'

'To talk.'

'You're supposed to be showing me how to fight.'

'Before that we must talk.'

With a sigh, Cassius picked up his sword belt and sheathed the blade. 'This is a first. *You* insisting that *I* talk.'

He sat down on a barrel next to Indavara. One of the crewmen passed by and looked down at them. Beyond him, the sky was a reassuring shade of blue.

'Did you do any hand to hand in training?' asked Indavara.

'A bit.'

'You wrestled when you were younger?'

'I gave it up as soon as I could.' Cassius made a face. 'All that oil and sweat. The only man I'm prepared to embrace is my father – and I don't particularly enjoy that.'

Indavara rolled his eyes. 'Hand to hand is difficult. And something tells me you won't be a natural. If you're caught without a weapon, always try and improvise. I never use my fists if I can avoid it.' He held out his fingers. 'Remember how precious these are. If you can't grip and hold you're in trouble. Boots are useful.' He tapped his boot on the deck. 'I nailed a bit of hardwood on to the front of these. Very nasty on the shin or knee.'

'Ingenious.'

'You should probably just concentrate on dagger and sword for now. But you'll have to start looking after them.'

'Simo *does* look after them. They're immaculate.'

'Simo doesn't look after them, he makes them look nice. Show me your dagger.'

Cassius drew it from the sheath on his belt. The standard-issue legionary's blade was ten inches long, three wide and topped by a triangular tip.

'They're almost like little swords, these army things,' said Indavara as he took it. 'Good weapon in the right hands.' He aimed the knife at Cassius's sword. 'More useful than that bloody thing.'

Indavara drew his own dagger, which was both shorter and narrower. He held each weapon by the handle, then dropped them blade first on to the deck. Indavara's stuck fast. Cassius's dagger bounced off and clattered to one side.

'Not sharp enough. I'll show you how to get it right.' He picked up the dagger and examined it. 'Hardly been touched.'

Cassius shrugged. 'I told you before – I don't like blades. I don't like holding them, using them. I don't even like wearing them.'

Indavara stood and turned to face him. 'So what? You'll just give up your life? If a man comes at you, you'll just let him gut you?'

'No, but—'

'There *has* to be a little fight in you. You clobbered that bastard Scaurus on the river that day.'

'That's true. I did hate that man.'

'Forget hate,' said Indavara. 'What about some thief that jumps out of the shadows? There won't be time to hate him – he'll already have stuck some cold metal into you. Did you ever cut anyone?'

'Once,' said Cassius. 'At the fort. A Palmyran.'

'I've seen men – not many, but a few – who would rather get cut themselves than do it to someone else. If you're like that, I won't be able to help you.'

'I'm not. Definitely not.'

'Just tell yourself: it's him or me. You value your life – you'll fight.'

'Him or me.'

Indavara nodded. 'Him or me.'

———8———

After an hour more of instruction, Cassius spent the rest of the morning working through Memor's documents with Simo. So by the time he finished his lunch, he was more than ready for some fresh air. Emerging from the hatch, he found everybody else on deck, the crew busy to a man, the other four passengers taking advantage of the continuing good weather. Though the sky was more grey than blue, there was hardly a trace of cloud. The wind was still from the west and strong enough to keep the *Fortuna* ploughing towards Crete.

Apart from Squint (steering), Asdribar (standing with Annia and Clara) and those manning the sails, the rest of the crew were sitting in a circle between the hatch and the mast. Under the supervision of Korinth and Opilio, the men were repairing a sail: cutting out damaged sections, then stitching replacements into the thick linen. Like the other sails, it had been dyed a watery blue.

Simo and Indavara were sitting against the side-rail on the

starboard side. Simo was reading from a little book. Cassius guessed it would be one of his precious religious tomes, and he made a mental note to tell him to be careful – there was no sense advertising his Christian beliefs to the superstitious, omen-obsessed sailors. Indavara was intently studying a piece of paper. He looked up and saw Cassius, then nudged Simo. Cassius held up a hand, indicating the Gaul should stay where he was.

Asdribar was leaning back against the port side-rail, arms crossed, a picture of relaxation. Annia and Clara were next to him, facing the sea.

'Afternoon,' said the captain as Cassius approached.

'Officer Corbulo,' said Annia. Clara gave a little bow. She was wearing a plain stola over her tunic. Her mistress's was a pretty yellow.

'Good afternoon to you.'

Cassius looked past them, at an island to the south.

'That's Krapathos,' Annia explained.

'Ah.'

'The young lady has sailed there herself,' added Asdribar.

'Yes, she told me,' replied Cassius. 'Rather impressive.'

'Very, I should say.'

'Captain!'

The cry came from the bow, where the lad Tarkel was pointing at something in the distance.

'Excuse me.'

Asdribar hurried away.

Annia looked at the sails. 'The gods have given us a fair wind.'

'Indeed,' replied Cassius, joining her at the side-rail. 'Let's hope it stays that way.'

As the women continued to gaze at the sea, Cassius gazed at them. Though they were both clad in several layers, the wind pressed the material against them, outlining their breasts and hips. Cassius considered himself an expert at ogling women without being noticed and he switched his gaze the moment Annia turned to him.

'You do seem very young for the Service, Officer Corbulo.'

'Swift promotion, I suppose,' Cassius replied. Which was true, in a way.

'A great honour, is it not? To dedicate your life to protecting the Empire and the Emperor.'

'It is, miss.'

'I know what some people think of the Service – some of the people in Rome, on Rhodes too. But I know the worth of the work. My father gave up a lot – time with us, his family. All for Rome.'

Smiling politely, Cassius thought about Memor's relationship with the maid. Evidently the man had been skilled at letting his family see only what he wanted them to. Cassius hoped they never found out about the affair (or *affairs* – there were probably more) but he feared it would be far harder to insulate Annia from the realities of her father's work. It seemed circumspect to prepare her for some unpleasant revelations.

'The Service's work is important, of course, but the results can often be very grave, for those found to be working at odds to the Emperor's interests.'

Annia surprised him with her answer. 'We reap what we sow, isn't that what they say?'

Cassius reckoned the expression might prove even more apt when applied to her father's fate.

Annia looked down at the dark blue water sliding by. 'I can think of nothing else. Nothing. Trogus stopped me going into the study – stopped me seeing my father. I hated him at the time, but now I'm glad he did it.'

Cassius recalled what he and Indavara had seen in the outhouse. 'Trogus was quite correct, miss.'

'Clara here tells me I should keep busy, but I can't clear my mind. She's tried needlework, games, poems, songs, books.'

Cassius looked past Annia at the maid, who cast a concerned glance at her mistress, then flicked her long, dark hair away from her neck.

'What do you read, miss?' Cassius asked. The more he spoke to Annia, the less annoying she seemed. He found he wanted to get to know her now.

'Some philosophy.'

'Really?'

Cassius tried very, very hard to keep any trace of sarcasm out of his voice but wasn't sure he had succeeded. He wondered if Annia had ever considered why there were no female philosophers, and that this fact might suggest she was overstretching herself.

'Really,' she replied sharply.

'As a native of Rhodes, it's to be expected, I suppose.'

'The island has been blessed with some imaginative thinkers.'

'Antonius of Rhodes, for example? An associate of Porphyry, isn't he?'

'He is,' said Annia. 'I once heard him speak.'

'I recall a friend going to hear Porphyry in Rome several years ago,' said Cassius. 'A follower of Plotinus, as I understand it.'

'So I believe.'

Cassius was somewhat taken aback. A young lady interested in philosophy! It wouldn't do to offend the girl, but he decided to assess the extent of her knowledge.

'Plotinus certainly examined some fascinating concepts. The idea of "the one", for example. An all-encompassing entity: not any one thing, yet the sum of all things. Interesting to compare it with standard Platonist thinking.'

Annia gave a little smile.

Cassius knew he had gone too far; he had embarrassed the poor girl.

'And?' she said.

'And?'

'How *would* you compare the two, Officer?'

'Er . . .'

Other than the fact that some of Plotinus's views were contrary to Plato's, Cassius knew only a few sketchy details. 'Well, this concept of "oneness" for example.'

'Yes?'

Clara was looking at him now too.

'Er . . . the relationship between "the one" and humanity.'

'Yes?'

How typical of her to press him. Cassius reached deep into the recesses of his memory and pulled out a few key phrases. He was far from sure, but he had to say something. 'Well, it's been a while, of course, but if memory serves, the argument centres on such fundamentals as the act of creation, the stages of perfection and the concepts of the demiurge and the dyad. Though that would be little more than a starting point for the discussion of course.'

Annia frowned. Cassius knew he'd made a fool of himself. Even if the girl had paid the slightest bit of attention to the speech she'd heard, she probably knew more than him.

'I can't remember much of the detail to be honest,' she said. 'It is all very confusing at times.'

'True, true,' Cassius replied, trying not to sigh with relief. 'Well, of course, oratory was my main area of study.'

'Ah,' said Annia. 'Now I *can* imagine you as an orator.'

'Really?'

'Oh certainly. You seem highly skilled in the art of saying a lot without answering the question.'

Clara's eyes grew wide and she looked away. Cassius was too surprised to even measure his own reaction and certainly not capable of an immediate reply.

'Just a jest, Officer,' Annia said with a placatory smile. 'Please don't take offence.'

'You are quick, miss,' Cassius said sourly. 'Very quick.'

'Please.' She placed a hand lightly on his arm. 'I apologise if I insulted you.'

Cassius's cheeks glowed. Looking down at those rather lovely green eyes, he felt himself relenting. But the rebuke still stung.

'How is it that you found yourself a soldier, sir?'

Cassius pulled his arm away.

'Officer!' Asdribar was on his way back from the bow.

'Perhaps you will tell me later,' said Annia.

'I think not,' Cassius shot back. 'It's a pity your maid couldn't find anything to distract you from your grief, miss, as you seem

149

to have concocted your own form of entertainment. I suggest that for both our benefits you stick to needlework from now on.'

Cassius turned away from her as Asdribar approached.

'Do you have any documentation with you?' asked the captain. 'An authorisation, that sort of thing?'

'Of course. Why?'

'There's a Roman warship ahead, coming up from the south. We first spotted her earlier this morning.'

'Right. And?'

'She's just altered course. To intercept us.'

'That shouldn't be a problem, should it?'

'Shouldn't be. No.'

Cassius found himself rather concerned by the doubt in the Carthaginian's voice. He was about to press him further when something heavy hit the deck. Looking over Asdribar's shoulder, he saw Indavara wiping water from his face and looking down at the sodden sheet in his hand. Korinth was standing over him, next to the bucket he'd just dropped by Indavara's feet.

'Oh. Sorry,' said the big sailor with a provocative grin.

Cassius half expected Indavara to fly at him but the bodyguard got up slowly, eyes fixed on the taller man.

Korinth scratched at the burnt section of his face, then waved him forward. 'Got no stave this time, have you? Unless you want to stick me with that blade, it'll have to be fists.'

'Calm yourself, lad!' yelled Squint. A couple of the other men bawled encouragement as Asdribar hurried over to intervene.

Indavara crossed his arms. 'I'm not going to break my fingers on your ugly snout.'

Korinth looked all set to go for him but by then Asdribar was between them.

'What did I tell you?' demanded the captain. 'Any more of that and your cut on this run drops from a sixth to a nothing. Got it?'

Korinth continued to glare at Indavara, who was wiping water off the sheet.

'Korinth!'

At last the sailor looked at his captain. Asdribar pointed towards the bow. With a final poisonous glare at Indavara, Korinth walked away.

———◆8◆———

The air of tension created by the incident was amplified by the approach of the warship. Not long after the vessel changed course, a sparkling light – apparently a sun-mirror – signalled a brief code that all the crewmen seemed to understand: 'Slow, and prepare for boarding.'

As the sailors furled the mainsail, Cassius joined the others on the starboard side to watch the warship approach.

'It's the *Armata*!' shouted young Tarkel as he coiled a line.

'Keep at your work,' ordered Squint, who was overseeing operations at the mast.

'What does it mean – *armata*?' asked Indavara.

'Armed,' said Cassius. 'As in ready for war.'

'Hopefully not with us,' Asdribar said ruefully as he passed by.

Cassius had been ruminating on what the harbour master's clerk had disclosed about the Carthaginian's reputation. He hurried after him.

'Captain?'

'Yes?'

'Should I be concerned? What would the navy want with the *Fortuna*?'

'Probably just a shakedown.'

'A what?'

'Officers looking to grab a few extras before heading home. Happens all the time.'

'Extras? Such as?'

'Whatever they can find. And taxes invented on the spot if they can't.'

'I presume there's nothing on board that shouldn't be?'

'That's what I'll be telling them.'

'Is it true?'

'That's what I'll be telling them.'

The blue eyes stared implacably back at Cassius, bright and clear in that bronzed face. Cassius decided it was probably best he didn't know.

'The authorisation,' Asdribar added. 'Might be wise to get it now.'

Cassius waved Simo over. 'Cloak, helmet and spearhead. My letters too. And be careful – I don't want them blowing over the side.'

As Simo made his way below, Tarkel scurried after him.

Korinth and a couple of the men lowered the foresail and the *Fortuna* drifted to a stop. Without any forward motion and the stabilising effect of full sails, the ship began to roll, an effect exacerbated by the yardarms projecting over each side.

Having taken some long, deep breaths, Cassius forced himself to focus on the warship. He had only ever seen such a vessel in dock, and never one this size. The sight of it reminded him of the first time he'd set eyes on a full legion camp in the field – that of the Fourth Legion stationed at Palmyra, Syria. Just like then, pride surged within him, and the warm glow of it seemed to burn the nausea away.

Cassius had been born just four years after the thousandth anniversary of the founding of Rome. At moments like this, and with a man like Aurelian now in command of the Empire, it was possible to forget the troubles in Gaul, the raiding Goths and rebels like Queen Zenobia. At moments like this, Cassius felt sure that what his father had told him all his life was true: Rome would endure another thousand years.

'And another thousand after that.'

'What?' said Indavara.

Cassius realised he had spoken aloud.

'Forget your giant creatures, Indavara,' he said, pointing at the warship. 'There's nothing in the sea mightier than that.'

As the *Armata* cut towards them, one big, oval eye stared out from above the metal ramming spike. There was no sense of grace or elegance about the warship's lines, just an angular, brutal efficiency. She seemed to lie low in the water, yet somehow glide across it. The hull was an ominous black, the deck the same bright red as the huge square standard hanging from the comparatively short mast. Sail power was strictly a secondary form of propulsion; for the watchers aboard the *Fortuna*, it was hard to concentrate on anything other than the scores of closely packed oars dipping in and out of the water with synchronised precision.

Cassius counted them. 'Twenty-two ranks of three. Must be a flagship. I wonder which fleet?'

'Alexandrian,' answered Tarkel as he knelt by the side-rail. In one hand was a sheet of paper held against a writing block, in the other a piece of charcoal. The lad gazed out at the *Armata* as he continued speaking. 'One hundred and fifty feet long, thirty wide. Full complement of crew: two hundred and five, including one hundred and thirty-two oarsmen and forty marines. Armed with ram, boarding bridge and grappling hooks, with capability for battle towers, ballistae and artillery. Normally escorts grain shipments. Wonder what she's doing out here.'

'Me too,' said Cassius quietly.

They could hear the ship now; the beating of the timing drums, the churning splashes of the oars. Gradually the beat slowed and the dip of the oars slowed with it until the warship eased to a stop about a hundred yards away.

Despite what Tarkel had said about the numbers aboard, Cassius could see little of the crew: not a trace of the oarsmen of course, and perhaps only a dozen men on deck, barely visible behind the high wooden barricades painted to resemble a line of shields. There was, however, activity at the rear: the ship's two tenders had been drawn up to the stern and men were climbing down rope ladders.

Cassius looked at Asdribar. The captain was standing close to Korinth, deep in discussion.

Annia came over to the side-rail. 'What could they want?'

Cassius studiously ignored her.

'Officer?'

'No idea.'

'I hope they won't keep us long,' Annia said. 'Perhaps they might even help us.'

Simo came up through the hatch with Cassius's gear. Cassius threw his cloak over his shoulders, then pulled on his helmet, tying the chinstrap tight. Leaving the spearhead with Simo for now, he took a little leather folder from him and tucked it carefully into his belt.

There were three letters inside. One was the authorisation issued several months earlier by Chief Pulcher, permitting him to join the governor's staff in Syria. The other two he had obtained before leaving Antioch for Cilicia. The first was from Abascantius, identifying Cassius as an officer of the Imperial Security Service and reminding the reader of the authority and privileges this afforded him. The second was from Prefect Oppius Julius Venator, commander of the Fourth Legion.

Venator had good cause to be glad that Cassius had brought the Persian banner affair to a successful conclusion and had readily acceded to his two requests: firstly that Cassius be officially assigned to the Fourth; secondly that the prefect write him a letter of recommendation. The former was largely a formality but the latter was – to Cassius – nothing short of invaluable.

It was a short note, just a few lines declaring that Venator knew Cassius to be a capable officer of good character and concluding with a request that the reader grant him favour and lend him assistance if required. The letter also happened to be the single most exciting piece of post Cassius had ever received; he had read it at least ten times before spending an indulgent night out to celebrate.

As well as being a prefect in charge of five and a half thousand men, Venator came from an extremely influential family thought to be the sixth or seventh richest in the Empire. He had uncles and brothers in the Senate and contacts in dozens of provinces. A written, formal association with such a man could secure influence, financial assistance and (most crucial of all) protection. Along with his mail shirt and the spearhead, the letter was one of Cassius's most prized possessions. His father had always told him a man is judged by four things: his words, his coins, his clothes and his letters.

As he watched the two tenders cast off from the *Armata*, Cassius hoped he wouldn't have to invoke either the letters or the spearhead. He'd never dealt with the navy before.

'What you sketching that bloody monstrosity for, boy?' asked Squint.

Tarkel ignored him.

'Let him draw,' said Opilio, who'd also come up on deck to see the warship.

When they were about fifty feet away, the tenders split up. The first continued slowly towards the starboard side of the *Fortuna*, while the other rounded the bow. The eight oarsmen in the first tender were sculling gently, just enough to keep the boat moving. In front of them were six marines clad in green tunics, wearing light leather armour with muscled chest plates. They also wore helmets, and three were armed with bows.

Apart from the oarsmen and marines, there was one other man in the tender. He had been sitting close to the bow but now stood up, one hand on the boat to steady himself. In the other hand was a short stick with a balled end, which Cassius knew to be the naval equivalent of a centurion's vine stick. He felt sure the officer must have noticed his crested helmet by now but there was no sign of acknowledgement. Cassius looked over his shoulder. The second tender was close to the port side.

'Listen carefully!' shouted the officer in Latin as Cassius turned back. 'Two men are to stand by at the stern to take our lines. The rest of you are to gather by the mast. Any man with a blade or other weapon must take it off and place it on the deck. Do so now!'

One of the older marines put his hand on his sword. The archers drew arrows and raised their bows.

Indavara turned to Cassius. 'Ready for war?'

XII

Once the two tenders had been secured, the marines hooked rope ladders over the stern and clambered up on to the *Fortuna*. Desenna and Korinth were the two sailors Asdribar had assigned to take the lines and as they withdrew to join the others, the Romans fanned out on either side of the deckhouse. Those without bows kept their hands by their sword hilts and stared hard at the group gathered by the mast. Unlike legionaries, the marines wore trousers under their tunics and long socks with their boots; instead of thick leather belts, their swords were slung from hardy lengths of cloth.

The officer was the last to appear. He was a small man, too small for his voluminous, richly coloured, dark blue cloak. The clasp on his left shoulder was in the shape of an oyster shell and had been polished to a high sheen. His greying hair had been recently combed and oiled, and resisted the wind well. Thumping the ball of the stick into his palm, he stopped by the pile of daggers next to the hatch and gestured for Cassius to come forward.

'What in the name of the great gods are you doing out here, young man?'

'Cassius Quintius Corbulo, sir. Long story, I'm afraid.'

The officer offered his hand and they shook forearms.

'Commander Sextus Viridius Ivmarus Litus, Imperial Vessel *Armata*, Imperial Fleet of Alexandria.'

'Might I ask why you hailed us, Commander?'

'You tell your tale first. I'm third in command of a flagship, which rates me well above any centurion.'

'I'm actually not a centurion, though my rank is equivalent. I'm with Imperial Security.'

Litus raised an eyebrow. 'This should be good. Speak.'

'I arrived on Rhodes two days ago. I was there to meet Augustus Marius Memor, a very senior officer within the Service. Upon visiting his home I discovered he had been murdered. I began an investigation at once and have good reason to believe that the assassin left yesterday aboard a vessel bound for Cnossus. This ship was hired and we set off after it.'

Litus looked past Cassius at the others. 'And the young lady?'

'Memor's daughter,' Cassius replied sheepishly. 'She insisted on coming.'

'My, my,' replied Litus, 'that is quite a tale.'

'As you can appreciate, sir, time is very much of the essence. I must ask – is there any possibility of assistance? Your vessel might be able to overhaul the ship we are pursuing.'

Litus gave the idea not a moment's consideration. 'Out of the question, I'm afraid. Apart from the dangers of the season – which mean my captain won't risk the *Armata* out here a day longer than necessary – we are in pursuit of our own prey. You are aware of the Emperor's campaign against Queen Zenobia of Palmyra?'

'Fully aware.'

'A certain faction of the local leadership in Egypt was rather favourable to her cause. They have been trying to stir up trouble for years and the Emperor has decided on decisive action. An arrest warrant was issued for their leader several days ago but the army failed to apprehend him. It is thought he made his escape by sea. We have been searching for his ship for the last three days.'

'I see.'

Litus took one neat little step to his right. 'Whoever is Asdribar – come here!'

As the Carthaginian strode forward, two of the marines came up close behind Litus.

'Departure papers,' instructed the Roman.

Asdribar reached inside the little bag on his belt and produced a small sheet, which he handed to Litus. The naval officer brushed dust off the paper, then read it.

'Seems to be in order,' he said, returning the sheet to Asdribar. 'I shall still have the ship searched. Must be thorough.' He turned to Cassius. 'I'm sure you understand.'

'Sir, I can vouch for this man and his crew. They couldn't possibly have been involved with this Egyptian – they were preparing to winter in Rhodes.'

'You can vouch for him, you say?'

Cassius glanced across at Asdribar, who was now looking rather uncomfortable.

'Yes,' Cassius said, barely convincing himself.

'Because one of my marines told me he recognises the name *Fortuna Redux*.' Litus tapped the balled stick against his thigh and fixed Asdribar with a provocative glare. 'Knows the captain's name. Knows what he is.'

'And what is that?' Asdribar asked defiantly.

Litus leant towards him. 'Address me without using "sir" again, and I'll have your *own* crew bind you with your *own* lines, then have you keelhauled under your *own* ship. Is that understood?'

Asdribar ground his teeth together before answering. 'Understood, sir.'

'Excellent.'

Litus ran a hand across the stiff strands of his hair. 'I could of course ask you about your cargo, ask you to declare any untaxed, undocumented goods, but in my experience such answers rarely elicit the truth, so these days I don't even bother. Let's see what we can find.'

Litus spun on his heels and addressed the marines. 'Four men to stay on deck. Four to the stern and work forwards; four to the bow and work back. Look everywhere. Go!'

The marines swiftly divided themselves, their boots thumping across the deck as they set about the search. With a smug grin for Asdribar, Litus adjusted his cloak and made for the mast.

Cassius blocked his path. 'Sir, is this really necessary?'

He thought Litus was about to shout at him, but the commander replied calmly.

'Absolutely. Despite our current involvement in this special

assignment, we of the Alexandrian mustn't neglect our funda-
mental duty: monitoring piracy and smuggling in these waters.
Millions are lost from the imperial coffers every year because of
ships like this' – Litus glanced back at Asdribar – 'and men like
him. That money must be recovered somehow.'

'Sir, I can't help feeling my superiors would be . . . disappointed
by your attitude. Master Memor was second in command of the
Service and we have a chance of catching his killer. We cannot
afford to lose even an hour. Perhaps if you were to look at my
letters. They are from Chief Pulcher in Rome, from Prefect
Venator of the Fourth—'

'These men have vouched for *you*, I presume.'

'Yes.'

Litus ran a hand across his hair once more. 'Keep your little
notes to yourself, Officer. Even assuming the men who wrote
them possess better judgement than you, they are *army* men. We
in the imperial fleet do things rather differently.'

He gestured for Cassius to move aside.

Cassius did so. 'You have made that very clear, Commander.'

While his marines continued their search, Litus walked over
to Annia, kissed her hand and offered his condolences. Annia
was polite at first, but as soon as Litus told her help from the
navy would not be forthcoming, she turned away from him and
refused to speak. Indavara and the sailors made no attempt to
hide their amusement.

'Strange girl,' muttered Litus as he wandered back towards
the stern.

One of the marines came up the steps. 'Sir, we've got a few
locked chests down here.'

'In here too,' added one of the men who'd been searching the
deckhouse.

Litus pointed at Asdribar, who had rejoined the sailors by the
mast.

'The marines want something opened – you open it.'

'The women are staying in the deckhouse,' said Cassius. 'Must
you rummage through their belongings too?'

Litus ignored him and kept his gaze on Asdribar. 'Hurry.'

Asdribar made his way across the deck past the Roman, who watched him all the way.

'He wants their undergarments!' cried a voice.

The crew bellowed with laughter. Clara put a hand to her mouth in shock. Annia smothered a smile.

Litus spun round, eyes blazing. 'Who said that? Who?'

He glanced at Cassius, who was fairly sure it had been Korinth. The deck-chief was standing with one hand on the mast, the other tucked into his belt.

'Who was it?' repeated Litus.

'No idea,' replied Cassius. 'Sorry.'

━━◼8▸━━

For the second time in two days, Cassius found himself waiting for a ship to be searched, though on this occasion an incriminating discovery would hinder the investigation rather than advance it. Quarter of an hour passed, and still the marines had found nothing. Annia walked to the bow and sat down with Clara, who brushed her mistress's hair while she stared out at the sea. This sight was quite enough to keep the crew occupied, not to mention the four marines still on deck. Litus tried hard not to look impatient, but began to glance anxiously at the *Armata* and pace round the hatch. The only person who seemed happy with the situation was young Tarkel. He knelt by the side-rail, charcoal in hand, happily drawing the warship.

One of the older marines came up through the hatch. 'I think we've got something, sir. Baldy kept staring at this stack of twig bales. Looks like a load stashed behind them.'

With a sly grin, Litus hurried down the steps.

Cassius wandered over to the hatch. The marines stationed by the deckhouse watched him but said nothing. Cassius glanced down into the shadowy interior. Litus was looking on as his men threw the twig bales aside and investigated what they'd found.

'Shit. They're empty,' said the older marine. 'Sorry, sir.'

160

'Show me that,' replied Litus. Ignoring Cassius, the commander came halfway up the steps and held a small vase up to the sunlight. He smiled. 'Ha! These are African red!'

'Sir?'

'Only the best clay money can buy, you peasant! See the insignia on the base? From Thuburbo Maius – the most prestigious centre of production. These will fetch twenty denarii a piece in Alexandria. Excellent. Quite excellent.'

'Can I go up on deck?' asked Asdribar.

'Of course, Captain,' replied Litus. 'I'm sure you need a little air. Oh – and thank you for your help.'

Asdribar came up the steps. Cassius tried to catch his eye but he walked back towards the crew, head down.

— ⊶8⊷ —

It didn't take long for the marines to load their booty. They loaded the clay vases into two barrels and lowered one into each of the tenders. In the meantime, Litus gave Asdribar permission to have the crew ready the ship.

With the first tender already heading back to the *Armata*, the commander then summoned Cassius and Asdribar to the stern. Only one marine from the other tender remained on board. He stood behind Litus as the Roman addressed the Carthaginian.

'Consider yourself lucky, most lucky, that I am in a generous mood. If this vessel weren't such a worthless piece of junk, I would take something else as a fine.'

Asdribar stared morosely at the deck.

'As it is,' Litus continued, 'confiscation of these undeclared goods will have to suffice.' He turned to Cassius. 'And so the fight against smuggling goes on.'

'And what a noble fight it is,' Cassius countered. 'I only hope this pointless delay doesn't prove crucial.'

Litus nodded down at the barrel below. 'Oh, far from pointless, Officer. Very far indeed.' He gathered his cloak about him. 'A small piece of advice, young man. If I were you, I would give

161

more careful consideration to my choice of travelling companions.'

With a helping hand from the marine, Litus negotiated the rope ladder and sat down in the bow of the tender. The marine unhooked the ladder and climbed nimbly down. Asdribar removed the line and threw it to him.

One of the oarsmen called out commands and the tender got under way. Grinning, Litus took one of the clay pots from the barrel and examined it. He waved to them. 'Farewell! Fair wind!'

Asdribar watched for a moment, then turned away. Cassius was astonished to see he was smiling.

───■8►───

Half an hour later, he found out why.

With the mainsail lowered and the foresail raised, the *Fortuna* was soon back up to speed. The *Armata* had departed as soon as the tenders returned and was now powering away to the east. The vessels were already more than a mile apart.

'Shall we, Captain?' asked Squint, when he was satisfied the yard and sails were set properly.

'Go ahead,' answered Asdribar, now back in his chair, examining the remarkably accurate sketch Tarkel had completed.

Squint and another sailor took two very long boathooks from a rack. Standing about six feet apart, they leant over the port side-rail and reached down. Korinth came over and stood between them.

'Don't you lose any,' Asdribar instructed.

'Got it?' Squint asked the other sailor.

'Got it.'

'Up we go.'

By now, Indavara, Simo, Annia and Clara had all come over to see what was going on. Korinth reached over the rail and took hold of something. The others dropped their boathooks and helped him. Moments later a dripping net was dragged over the side and lowered to the deck. Inside it were six small barrels and a few rocks.

'They look all right, Captain,' said Squint, breathing hard.

'Good. What about the others?'

Squint and the other man picked up their boathooks and crossed to the other side of the deck with Korinth.

Cassius was grinning. 'Crafty, Captain. Very crafty.'

Asdribar shrugged. 'An old trick. A couple of the marines were talking about checking the hull once they were done down below so I made sure they found the pots. What we in the trade call a "dummy discover". Luckily, that was enough for them.'

'Better to lose half your profits than all, I suppose.'

'Actually I doubt I've lost more than a few sesterces.'

'I don't follow, Captain,' said Annia.

'The vases are replicas, miss. Cheap Greek knock-offs. Packed on top of each other in those barrels like that, I doubt any of them will still be in one piece by the time they get back to Alexandria.'

Cassius smiled again as he thought of Litus's face when realisation dawned. 'What's in the barrels?'

'Rhodian cinnamon wine. Can't buy anything like it on Crete. I would have liked to have got forty barrels but there wasn't much time.'

'What's your profit on that?'

'Promise you won't tell anyone?'

'I promise.'

'Without export dues – and if we can find the right buyer in Cnossus – we'll double our money.'

'Nice,' said Cassius.

'When do you think we might be there?' Annia asked.

Asdribar squatted down and patted one of the barrels affectionately. 'If the wind stays as it is, perhaps this time tomorrow. In fact, in light of our continuing good luck with the weather and our recent narrow escape, I suggest we open one of these later. If the young lady will allow us to use the deckhouse for an hour or two, we can enjoy a post-dinner drink. Shall we say the second hour of night?'

XIII

The god's broad, muscled body was naked save for a loincloth. His long, flowing hair ran down over his shoulders to the star emblazoned on his chest. He stood with his trident thrust forward, proud and defiant.

The god fell backwards, and landed in beans and meat gravy.

'Balls. Sorry, Neptune.'

Cassius – who had accidentally knocked the little table as he sat down on the bed – righted the two-inch figurine and cleaned it off with his napkin. Also on the table was a plate complete with a small portion of every constituent of his dinner: barley broth, green beans, a chunk of pork, and some sweet berries. Cassius bowed his head and reminded himself to slow his speech; his mother always told him off for saying his prayers too quickly.

'This I give to you, Great Neptune, Lord of the Waves, God of the Deep. I thank you – and my stomach thanks you – for the favour you have shown us so far. In exchange for my offering, I ask for fair weather for the remainder of our journey. Thank you, Great Neptune, Lord of the Waves, God of the Deep.'

Simo – returning to the cabin with freshly washed plates – examined the hourglass. 'I believe that's the second hour, sir. Which buckle for your belt?'

'Oh you choose, Simo. It's hardly a dinner party.'

Cassius already had on his best scarlet tunic. He waited for Simo to select a buckle (a silver piece with a leaping fish) and attach it to a belt, then stood up. As Simo put the belt around his waist, Cassius noticed the Gaul had taken out one of his little books.

'Planning some reading?'

Simo buckled the belt. 'Yes, sir.'

'What's in there?'

'Teachings, sir. Lessons. I have committed almost half of it to memory.'

'Really? Very impressive.'

'When I have memorised the whole book I can advance to the next level, sir. I will be able to receive instruction directly.'

'I see. Simo, I meant to say – you should perhaps keep your beliefs to yourself while we're on board ship with this lot.'

'It might be that some of the men wish to hear of Christ's teachings, sir. They may wish to change the path of their lives, seek out the mysteries of the—'

Cassius held up a hand. 'Now, Simo, I've been over this with you before. I know you and your fellows think it's acceptable to tell others what they should believe, but I'm afraid most people don't see it like that. Keep it to yourself.'

There was a knock on the door and Opilio stuck his head in. 'Coming up for that drink then, sir?'

'It would appear so.'

'Enjoy yourself, Master Cassius,' said Simo.

'You sure you don't want to come along?'

'No. Thank you, sir.'

Cassius followed Opilio along the passageway.

'Not often we get a chance to sup with two young ladies in the captain's cabin,' said the hold-chief with a ribald grin. Cassius reckoned he was even uglier than Abascantius, which was quite a feat. It had often occurred to him that there were few worse fates than to be born utterly unattractive, and he'd even postulated that it might be better to be a handsome slave than an ugly freeman.

At the bottom of the steps they met Indavara, who was still moving some of the scattered twig bales away from his bed. Cassius noticed a pail of water there too.

'You coming along, Muscles?' asked Opilio.

'Yes.'

Indavara ran a hand through his hair, patting it down over his mutilated ear.

Cassius sniffed the air. 'Are you wearing scent?'

'What of it?'

'Nothing,' Cassius replied with a smile.

'I too am wearing a perfume,' Opilio announced. 'Essence of the kitchens. Very powerful.'

'Indeed it is,' replied Cassius.

'Come along then,' said the hold-chief, starting up the squeaking steps. 'I don't suppose you two have met Marcus Aurelius yet, have you?'

Cassius and Indavara exchanged bemused glances, then followed him.

The mystery of Marcus Aurelius was quickly solved.

'Ah yes,' said Asdribar when Opilio mentioned him, 'the oldest member of my crew.'

Cassius glanced at Squint when he heard this. The aged sailor was sitting to his right, next to Opilio, on one side of the table that had been moved into the middle of the deckhouse. Opposite the three men were Annia and Clara, each sitting on one of the beds. Annia's hair had been plaited and tied so as to resemble a little crown. Asdribar was at the end of the table, closest to the door. Cassius had made sure he avoided being next to Annia, leaving Indavara the seat at the other end. The bodyguard looked rather awkward, perched on a low stool, trying very hard not to gaze at the young lady to his left. Asdribar reached into a locker and pulled out a wooden box.

'I suppose I should have told you ladies – considering you've been sharing cabin space with him.'

As he put the box down on the table, Opilio and Clara moved their glasses out of the way. Everyone had already received a generous measure of the cinnamon wine. Asdribar looked around at his audience and took his time undoing the hook securing the little door on one side of the box.

'Move the light,' he told Squint, who pushed an oil lamp aside. 'He likes the dark, you see.'

Indavara and Clara hunched forward, fixated on the box. Annia – like Cassius – was trying to resist the Carthaginian's attempts at showmanship.

Asdribar opened the door. 'And here he is.'

'Here's what?' asked Indavara.

'We can't see anything,' said Annia.

Asdribar knocked the top of the box. Cassius found himself leaning across the table.

Suddenly, there was a loud crack from outside. All the non-sailors jumped and Cassius barely avoided spilling wine down his tunic.

'Just the yard shifting, sir!' came the shout from Korinth.

'I see it, I see it,' announced Clara.

A clawed, scaly leg appeared out of the shadows.

Opilio placed a handful of carrot tops on the table. 'I brought these for him.'

Indavara's jaw dropped as the little creature emerged from the box and took slow, tottering steps across the table. 'What *is* that?'

'Never seen one?' asked Cassius.

Indavara shook his head.

'It's a tortoise,' said Annia, as if it were impossible someone might not know such a thing.

'Remarkable animals,' Cassius observed. He remembered pestering his parents to buy him one as a boy, but they'd been unable to find any in Ravenna. 'They live to a good age, don't they?'

'Indeed they do, Officer,' replied Asdribar.

Cassius examined the enigmatic grins on the faces of the captain and his crewmen. 'What?'

'Guess how old he is,' said Opilio after a swig of wine.

'I'll give you a clue,' added Asdribar. 'He's older than Squint. Just.'

The old sailor took this in good humour, holding his glass up to the captain.

Cassius shrugged and decided to aim high. 'Sixty-five.'

Asdribar shook his head. 'Keep going.'

'Seventy,' said Annia.

'No.'

'Eighty,' offered Cassius.

'You've a way to go yet,' murmured Squint, rubbing his good eye with his fingers.

'One hundred!' yelled Clara, prompting laughter from Cassius and the sailors. Annia gave the maid a sharp look and pointed at her wine, indicating she'd already drunk enough.

'Marcus Aurelius,' Cassius said thoughtfully. 'He can't be.'

'He is,' said the captain. 'Named after the man made emperor in the year of his birth.'

'Which makes him one hundred and eleven.'

'Exactly right.'

Asdribar took the box off the table and sat down. Marcus Aurelius was now nibbling at the green fronds of the carrot tops.

'One hundred and eleven?' said Indavara. 'It's impossible.'

'It's not,' said Annia. 'One of the longest-lived creatures there are.'

'By Jupiter,' said Cassius, who'd been busy with a few calculations. 'There have been forty-four different emperors since then.'

'Yes, he's seen a lot of upheaval,' said Asdribar. 'Doesn't seem to bother him much though.' He turned to Clara. 'I tried to offer him a wage once but he wouldn't take a single coin.'

Clara giggled.

'How did you come by him?' Cassius asked.

'He came with the ship,' replied Asdribar. 'And he's been with us everywhere: up the great Egyptian river, through the gates of Byzantium, even out past the Pillars of Hercules.'

'You've seen the Great Ocean?' asked Cassius.

'Me and Squint both. What was it? Twelve, thirteen years ago now? Up to Portus Cale on the west coast of Spain.'

'What about Gaul and Britain?' Cassius asked.

'We didn't get that far.'

Squint cleared his throat and spoke up: 'A man sails too far past the Pillars, he sails beyond the reach of the gods, where worship and favour mean nothing. There is naught but the sea there; a huge, grey swell that rolls on for ever.'

Indavara took a long swig of wine.

'Still,' said Squint, with a little glance at Opilio. 'Can't really call yourself a sailor unless you've seen the Great Ocean with your own eyes.'

'The amount you go on about it, I feel like I've been there,' replied Opilio.

'Tell me,' said Cassius, leaning forward to address Asdribar. 'Commander Litus. Surely not all the navy men you come across are like that?'

'A shakedown,' replied Asdribar matter-of-factly. 'Just as I told you.'

'He was one of the worst,' added Opilio. 'Officers weren't that bad in my day.'

Squint made a noise that suggested he didn't agree.

'Exactly which part of the army are you from, Officer?' asked Asdribar. 'I'd not heard of this Imperial . . .'

'Security Service. As you know, Miss Annia's father was a very senior officer. The Service is – technically speaking – part of the army but in practice we often act independently. Basically we deal with specific threats to the Empire and the Emperor.'

Asdribar looked impressed. 'Interesting work?'

'Oh, certainly,' said Cassius. 'Eh, Indavara?'

Indavara looked mildly terrified at having to join the conversation.

'Yes,' he said. 'Interesting.'

'So Muscles here is your bodyguard?' asked Opilio.

'Indeed he is,' said Cassius, adjusting his tunic sleeve, which had somehow folded over on itself. 'And a damned good one at that.'

Indavara seemed rather embarrassed by the compliment but acknowledged it with a nod.

'I can believe it,' continued Opilio. 'Knocked our mouthy young deck-chief on his backside, so I hear.'

'That's water under the bridge now,' affirmed Asdribar.

'Quite right,' said Cassius. 'How many years were you with the navy, Opilio?'

'Twenty-two, would you believe?'

Annia spoke up: 'And you, Officer Corbulo, how long have you served?'

To Cassius, her implication seemed clear. Nonetheless, he did his best to answer politely.

'Nearly three years, miss. Why?'

'I just wondered.'

Cassius sipped his wine through pursed lips.

'One can experience a remarkable amount in three years,' he added. 'It has often occurred to me that, from within the walls of a home, a woman cannot possibly understand the travails of a man's life: the travel, the hardship, the burdens of duty.'

'I understood my father's travails,' Annia replied. 'He spoke to me of them often.'

The ensuing silence was broken by Asdribar.

'Twenty-two years,' he said, looking at Opilio. 'Why'd you leave again? Did someone actually *taste* your food?'

Squint chuckled.

'Ha ha,' said Opilio.

Asdribar stood up, slapped him on the shoulder, then began topping up the glasses.

'Take it slowly,' he told the passengers. 'Potent stuff if you're not used to it.'

When he got to Clara, Annia held up a hand. 'She's had enough.'

'Just a little, miss?' said Asdribar.

'A tiny bit, then. She's usually allowed nothing at all.'

Clara bowed to her mistress. Asdribar gave her more than a tiny bit.

Annia shuffled slightly to her right. She looked at Indavara for a moment, then spoke. 'I saw you with a page of writing earlier today. Are you studying something?'

Indavara looked about as fearful as Cassius had ever seen him but he eventually summoned a reply. 'Yes, miss. A few sums.'

'Ah, I see – and how are you getting on?'

'Look at Marcus go,' said Asdribar. The tortoise was now

munching his way through the carrot tops with some enthusiasm. 'At least *he* likes your food, Opilio.'

Squint then embarked on a long anecdote about a voyage where the ship's cook had poisoned most of the crew, and from there the three sailors took it in turns to try and impress young Clara with their nautical tales. Cassius joined in now and again but kept one ear on the other two. To his surprise, Indavara managed to keep the conversation going.

——■8■——

One hour and three large servings of Rhodian cinnamon wine later, Cassius was about ready to throw his glass at the wall. As if it wasn't enough that the infernal girl had twice mocked him that day, she was now making a fool of herself with Indavara. They hadn't stopped talking – mostly about reading and writing by the sounds of it – and Annia had made sure she didn't cast a single glance in Cassius's direction. It really was quite unseemly, a young lady from a family of standing like hers chattering away to a lowly bodyguard. She seemed to have forgotten herself entirely.

Cassius poured himself another drink. He spilt rather a lot of it on the floor but no one seemed to notice. The sailors were talking about gambling, chariot races in particular.

'What about gladiatorial contests?' he blurted out. 'Anybody ever bet on those?'

'Now and again,' replied Squint.

Cassius could feel Indavara's eyes on him but he said what he wanted to say anyway. 'My man here was a gladiator. Won twenty fights to gain his freedom.'

Even as the words left his mouth, Cassius knew he shouldn't have said them, but he had to do something to break Annia's apparent interest in Indavara. Surely even she would stop short of throwing herself at a man tarnished by the shame of slavery.

Indavara glared at him from beneath his dark fringe of hair.

'Is that true?' Annia asked him.

'Yes, miss.'

'How terrible.'

Cassius looked at her in disbelief, then wondered why he hadn't remembered that her behaviour seldom conformed to expectations.

'He doesn't really like to talk about it,' he said. 'Though I fancy you might get something out of him, miss.'

Cassius downed the rest of his wine.

'That might be enough of the Rhodian stuff for you tonight, Officer,' said Asdribar.

'Possibly, Captain. Possibly.'

When Cassius put his glass down on the table it sounded very loud. 'In fact, I think I shall retire.'

He stood up, then waited for the fog to recede from his eyes. 'That *is* strong stuff.'

He squeezed past Opilio and Squint and reached the door. 'Good night to you all. Clara, I must say – you really are rather pretty.'

The maid gave a shy smile, then looked at the floor.

'Marcus Aurelius, I must say – you really are not.'

While the sailors laughed, Cassius reached out and stroked the tortoise's shell. The round little head turned and looked back at him.

Opilio spoke up: 'He says neither will you be when you're a hundred and eleven.'

'True, true. Good night, Miss Annia, Indavara. I trust you will enjoy the rest of your evening.'

Asdribar stood up and opened the door for him. 'I shall accompany you to your cabin.'

'That's really not necessary.'

'Come, those steps are lethal.'

Once outside, the chilly wind did a little to clear Cassius's head. He took a long breath and looked around. Korinth was there, leaning languidly against the port side-rail watching Desenna, who was on the helm. The other men on deck were further forward and singing a melodic shanty in Greek

– something about distant ports and exotic treasures. Cassius looked up, and had to put his arms out to steady himself. At the top of the mast was the dim glow of a lantern. Above, the sky was clear. Cassius couldn't decide if the stars were blue or white.

'Beautiful night.'

'It is,' said Asdribar. 'Let's hope for a beautiful day tomorrow.'

He put a hand on Cassius's arm but Cassius shook it off.

'Honestly, Captain. I'm fine.'

'Very well, I shall just see you below then.'

Cassius stepped shakily over the tiller array and walked to the hatch, Asdribar close behind. As they made their way down the steps, Cassius kept a firm grip on the handrail.

'Was that really necessary?' asked the Carthaginian.

'What?' Cassius asked, though he knew.

'Bringing up the man's past like that. You mentioned the burdens of duty earlier. I doubt if my work – or yours – can ever constitute as great a burden as he carries. The shame aside, imagine what he must have endured as a gladiator.'

'I was simply informing her of the facts, Captain. If the young lady is happy to throw herself at a man such as him that's her choice.'

They arrived at the bottom of the steps.

'"A man such as him",' quoted Asdribar. 'Not an hour ago you were singing his praises. I gathered you were friends.'

'We are, of sorts. But he is a bodyguard. Mine. Not my equal.'

'I see.'

Cassius kept his hand on the rail.

Asdribar lowered his voice. 'Korinth was a slave, and I've known many other freedmen over the years. It weighs heavy on them.' Asdribar shook his head. 'He's told me some tales. I don't know that I would have survived it.'

Cassius considered this, though the wine made consideration something of a challenge. 'It's not that I'm without sympathy for what he must have been through. But he has never told Simo or me a single thing about his life before the arena, or even how he became a gladiator. Nothing. He might have been a thief, a murderer – anything.'

'Or he may simply have been a prisoner of war, or sold into it.'

'But we don't *know*,' Cassius insisted. 'It's hard to deal with such a man, call him a friend when – speaking truly – you know nothing of him.'

'Nothing? I thought you'd been together some while.'

'Only a few months actually, though a great deal has occurred in that time.'

'Many men don't speak of their past. What of his actions since you've known him? What do they tell you?'

Despite the drink, only a moment of thought took Cassius to his answer. 'He is a man of extraordinary bravery and skill. And on several occasions I have had more than good cause to be very grateful to him.'

'I shall say only this then, young sir. Given all that you've told me, I think you owe him an apology. Good night.'

Asdribar set off back up the steps.

Head buzzing, Cassius let out a long breath as he made for the cabin. Regrets were usually for the morning. Tonight they had come early.

XIV

Cassius missed the dolphins. While he lay in bed, battling a hangover and delaying the prospect of apologising to Indavara, three of the creatures appeared between the *Fortuna* and the Cretan shore. As Indavara joined Simo, Annia and Clara by the port side-rail, the crewmen – most of whom were still working on the damaged sail – stood up and performed a strange, formal bow towards the dolphins before sitting down again.

Asdribar got up out of his chair. 'May I, miss?' he asked, pointing at the deckhouse.

'Of course, Captain,' said Annia. She then turned to Indavara and Simo. 'Have you never seen them before?'

'No, miss,' replied Simo.

Indavara shook his head.

Asdribar returned holding a wicker box, which he put down on the deck out of the wind. Inside were dried flowers, some still with a little colour. 'We'll wait until they come close.'

'I've never heard of this custom,' said Annia.

'Essential for us sailors, miss.'

Asdribar put his elbows on the side-rail and watched as the dolphins sped towards the ship, fins cutting through the water. 'Messengers from the god of the deep. We give the flowers to show our thanks. Even when you're far, far out, when there's nothing but sea and not even a bird in the sky, they still come. He sends them to remind us we're not alone – to give us a little smile and cheer us up.'

'A smile?' said Indavara.

'It's true,' said Annia.

'Just watch them carefully, lad,' added Asdribar. 'You'll see it.'

The dolphins seemed to know they were being watched and came alongside the *Fortuna*, keeping pace for a while, then cutting away at an angle or speeding on to the bow.

'They're showing off!' cried Clara.

Asdribar gestured at the box. 'Miss, would you like to do the honours?'

'Of course,' Annia said. 'Thank you.'

'Clara?'

The maid eagerly knelt down by her mistress, who already had a handful of the flowers.

'Please don't take too much,' said the captain. 'That's got to last me until spring.'

As the flowers fluttered down on to the water, one of the dolphins came up a yard from the ship's hull. He turned over, showed the watchers his pale belly, then stuck his snub nose out of the water before disappearing into the depths again.

'He did smile, I saw it!' cried Indavara.

'What did I tell you?' said Asdribar.

The dolphins stayed until the third hour. Occasionally one of the four passengers would say something, but mostly they just watched them. Indavara began to think that perhaps sea voyages weren't so bad after all and, when he wasn't looking at the dolphins, he was glancing at Annia and wishing the journey would go on and on.

———◆8◆———

Five miles east of Cnossus, they spied a high-masted ship leaving the harbour. Cassius had just arrived on deck when Asdribar sent young Tarkel forward to the bow.

'Best eyes we have,' he explained.

The lad returned quickly. 'Heading west, Captain.'

'Sure of it?'

'Yes, sir.'

'Hope that's not the *Cartenna*,' said Cassius.

'Cnossus is a big port – bigger than Rhodes,' replied Asdribar.

'Transit station for a lot of grain and other crops. Probably just a freighter.'

'In November?'

'Weather's holding. Might be making a dash for Greece.'

'How long before we're in?'

'Hour or so. The gods have been kind. I've not often done that trip in under two days.'

Cassius looked at Crete. It was a huge island – more than a hundred and fifty miles long, almost forty across at its widest. Like Rhodes, it was dominated by a central ridge of mountains and the *Fortuna* was now opposite one of the highest peaks, a monstrous, dark crag Cassius estimated to be at least a mile high. Its lower slopes were bound by forest and mist; and some areas had been quarried, the earth stripped away to reveal angular sections of grey rock.

The island had been a Roman possession for more than three centuries, and though Cassius knew Asdribar was right about the volume of trade passing through Cnossus, Crete was generally considered to be a sleepy, peaceful corner of the Empire. Cassius looked along the coast, at a cove enclosed by high cliffs. The pale, striated faces of the cliffs were dotted with dozens of dark caverns. Cassius narrowed his eyes, and saw there were fires burning inside some of them. He imagined the man known as Dio standing there, Memor's head clutched in his hand, watching the ship approach.

Brushing aside such idle fantasy, Cassius considered the outcome of his morning's work. Despite the hangover, he had checked through more of Memor's documentation. The list of those with reason to want the man dead continued to grow, even though Cassius and Simo had examined only a fraction of his papers. Finding Dio therefore remained by far the best chance of making progress. Still gazing at the island, Cassius shook his head. If the assassin had gone to ground there, it might take weeks, even months, to find him.

'Captain, do you know what kind of army presence there is at Cnossus?'

'Not sure. I have seen legionaries around. And there's definitely a way station at the harbour.'

Cassius realised the time had come for him to speak to Indavara. The bodyguard was alone, sitting against the starboard side-rail, doing his sums on Asdribar's abacus. Annia and Clara were presumably in the deckhouse, while Simo was in the cabin, still working on the Memor papers. Cassius hadn't told him about the events of the previous evening.

As he crossed the deck, Indavara kept his eyes on the abacus. Cassius leant back against the side-rail next to him and folded his arms across his chest. For a moment, he wondered if he really needed to go through with it. An apology always made one seem weak and he had been provoked. But Annia had been the one playing games; Indavara had done nothing but speak to her.

In truth, Cassius knew these minor considerations were irrelevant simply because of the debt he owed the man. Indavara was paid to protect him, yes, but risking one's life to save another was not a matter to be taken lightly, or ever to be forgotten. And whatever disputes might arise between them, no matter how awkward or naive or downright stupid Indavara could be, nothing would change that. He had been wrong to humiliate him.

'I think I owe you an apology.'

Silence.

'Last night. It was uncalled for and . . . unpleasant. I had drunk a lot, but I know that's no excuse. So – I apologise.' Cassius gazed across at the island as he spoke. 'You deserve better from me.'

Silence.

After a while, Indavara tilted his head back against the timbers. 'I don't see why we should pretend any more that we're friends. I get paid to do my job. You get paid to do yours. That's all it has to be.'

'Indavara, I know that what I said upset you, but it's that damned girl, she will insist—'

Indavara held up a hand. 'Don't.'

Cassius wondered, did he just want to hear no more, or did

he want to hear nothing said against Annia? Was it possible he really thought he stood a chance with her? If the girl was encouraging it, Cassius thought she was being far crueller than he'd been.

'Well, I've said what I wanted to,' he replied, rubbing the back of his neck. 'I did my sword exercises this morning, by the way. Went very well. Will you still help me?'

'I said I would.'

Cassius pushed himself off the side-rail.

'Corbulo.'

'What?'

'In future, if you laugh at me or make me look a fool, I'll leave. I've enough money. I'll just go.'

Cassius doubted that, because he was pretty sure Indavara had nothing – and no one – to go to. But he nodded anyway.

—◆8◆—

As midday approached, the mist seemed to roll out from the island, shrouding the coast and enveloping the ship; by the time they were nearing Cnossus, visibility was down to less than a hundred yards. The wind had dropped too, and the *Fortuna* slipped gently through the water, barely making way. While the sailors went about their work, the five passengers stood by the deckhouse, gazing into the white nothingness.

'Thank the gods they've still got that lighthouse working,' said Asdribar.

The orange dot off the port bow was quite clear; firelight magnified by burnished bronze mirrors.

'Our luck had to run out some time,' said Squint, who was back on the helm. 'At least we know where we are. When's the turn?'

Asdribar consulted the small leather-bound book he had earlier retrieved from the deckhouse. Cassius was standing behind him and he'd deduced that each page referred to some anchorage or approach. Scrawled notes, figures and diagrams covered every inch of the paper. 'When the light's five points off the bow.'

Though there was so little breeze that the mainsail was barely filling, the mist seemed to have chilled the air and Cassius was glad he'd told Simo to bring up his scarlet officer's cloak. It really was remarkably warm – hardly surprising given the wool was a third of an inch thick.

'Net in the water! Port side,' came the cry from the bow.

'Stay as you are,' Asdribar told Squint.

Something scraped along the hull. Cassius looked over the side and saw a ragged old fishing net drifting towards the port rudder housing. Attached to it were several green glass marker buoys. Without an order, Desenna grabbed a boathook, leant out over the side-rail and flicked the net out of the way so that it didn't foul the housing.

'Clear, Captain.'

'Well done.'

At first Cassius thought he was imagining the sound of voices drifting across the water, but he saw that the others could hear them too.

'Sure we're not in too close?' queried Squint.

'That's why I don't let you navigate, old man,' replied Asdribar. 'Never sure of yourself.'

'What would you do if there was no lighthouse?' Cassius asked.

Asdribar smiled and tapped his nose.

The mist closed even tighter around the *Fortuna*, until there was little more than a hundred feet of the calm, dark sea visible in any direction. Apart from the odd word from the sailors, and the creaking of the *Fortuna*'s hull, all was quiet. Then an unseen flock of squawking birds flew overhead. When the silence returned it seemed doubly oppressive.

'Down to about fifty feet, Captain!'

The mainsail now hung limply from the yard. Cassius looked down at the water and decided they were almost stationary.

'Opilio!' Asdribar yelled.

'Captain?' came the voice from the hatch.

'Those oars ready?'

'Ready.'

'How's your rowing, Officer?' Asdribar asked over his shoulder.

'Not bad,' Cassius answered.

'Good, because I'm light a few oarsmen.'

Cassius grinned as Asdribar turned round.

'I'm serious,' said the Carthaginian. 'We can't afford to drift out here for long. If the wind doesn't pick up, it'll be all hands to the oars.'

Cassius's smile had disappeared; the situation would have to be dire indeed before he played galley slave. He looked at the others. Simo and Indavara were still peering out at the mist. Clara was hanging on to her mistress's arm, eyes wide. To her credit, Annia looked the most composed.

'Desenna, lower the weight,' ordered Asdribar.

The sailor reached into an alcove built into the starboard side-rail and pulled out a coil of rope with knots at regular intervals. Attached to the end was a hefty iron cylinder. Once the rope was uncoiled, he lowered the weight into the water.

'Tarkel,' yelled Asdribar. 'Anything?'

The lad had earlier climbed up the series of little poles affixed to the mast and now sat on top of the yard. Cassius had completely forgotten about him and – when he looked up – found he could barely make him out through the swirling mist.

'I think it's even worse up here, Captain!'

'Neptune's beard, I've not seen a fog like this for a while,' observed Squint.

'You've not seen anything properly for longer than a while,' said Asdribar.

Some of the crew exchanged a few words, then pointed to the women and said something to Asdribar in Punic. The captain silenced them instantly.

'They're blaming us,' Annia said quietly. 'They think it's bad luck to have women aboard.'

'Don't you worry about them, miss,' said Asdribar.

'Thirty feet,' Desenna announced, before bringing up the weight.

Squint whistled. 'There are shoals west of the harbour, remember?'

Asdribar didn't answer him. He was studying his notes.

Cassius tried not to imagine jagged rocks slicing through the timbers of the hull, water flooding into the hold, filling the cabins, coming up through the hatch . . .

'That's it,' said Asdribar. 'Sail hands – get ready to bring your lines in. Squint – come to port until the light's dead ahead.'

The veteran eased the tillers to the right and the bow of the *Fortuna* slowly swung round. The sail hands looked up as they made their adjustments to the huge square of cloth above them.

'We're in the approach channel now,' Asdribar said, turning to face his passengers. 'Not far to the harbour.'

'Will we be able to dock in this fog?' asked Annia.

'Not a chance, miss. Nor will anyone see us coming. No, once we're inside the breakwaters, we'll drop the anchor. Excuse me.'

As the captain made his way forward, Korinth came back to check on the mainsail. It took a good deal of hauling on various ropes to change the angle of the yard, but by the time it was done the wind seemed to have picked up. Cassius felt a slight breeze on the back of his neck. He looked over the stern; the *Fortuna* was again leaving a thin wake.

'Officer Corbulo,' said Annia, 'Might I ask what you plan to do when we reach the port?'

Cassius retreated to the side-rail, so that he could address Annia and still see what was going on at the bow. Asdribar was on his knees under the bottom of the foresail, gazing into the mist.

'That rather depends on what we find there, miss.'

'You are aware of the size of the island?'

'Indeed I am.' Cassius gave her a cordial smile. 'As you now know, philosophy is not a strength of mine but my geography, and my eyesight, are really quite reasonable.'

'I meant only that it could be difficult – to find one man.'

'Very difficult. And as I mentioned before, this affair may not end here.'

Squint spoke up: 'Don't mind me sticking my nose in, but we might not be going anywhere if this fog keeps up or the weather closes in. Couple of years back we were stuck on Crete for half the winter.'

'Sir, a mast!' came a cry from above. 'Just off the port bow.'

Asdribar held his hand out to the right. Squint altered his course, only straightening up when the captain put his hand down again.

'Fifty yards!' added Tarkel.

The other passengers filed past Squint to join Cassius at the port side-rail.

'Coming towards us!'

Cassius couldn't see anything yet.

'There!' said Annia.

Cassius followed the line of her outstretched arm. The bow of another ship was emerging from the mist.

'Thirty yards!' announced Tarkel.

Now they could see figures on the foredeck. They heard shouting.

'Punic?' said Annia.

'Yes,' confirmed Cassius.

Suddenly there was a roar of laughter from the bow.

'It's the *Rusucurru*!' yelled Asdribar.

'The what?' asked Cassius. He and the others turned to Squint for an explanation. The old sailor was beaming, showing more holes in his mouth than teeth.

'Don't look so worried,' he said. 'Friends.'

━━◄8►━━

After a brief conversation with Asdribar, the captain of the *Rusucurru* – a tall, grey-bearded fellow who also seemed to be Carthaginian – brought his ship alongside the *Fortuna*. The freighter, a longer and bulkier vessel, was under oar power and covered the distance swiftly. Asdribar ordered his hands to ease their lines and soon the ships were just ten yards apart, drifting off the still-invisible harbour.

The twenty men on the *Rusucurru*'s deck were, if anything, a

183

rougher-looking bunch than the *Fortuna*'s crew, and the moment they saw the women a shout went up. Asdribar laughed as the sailors waved and blew kisses, but he swiftly got control of himself and spoke a few words to the captain, who eventually quietened his men. The leering continued, however, with even the rowers peering out through the oar holes.

'Come, Clara,' said Annia, leading her maid over to the deck-house as several jovial exchanges broke out across the water between the sailors. Asdribar and the other captain were talking in Punic, occasionally pointing along the channel towards Cnossus.

Cassius walked over to him and waited for a break in the conversation. 'Will you ask about the *Cartenna*?'

'Of course.'

When the captain relayed Asdribar's query to his crew, several men spoke up. Asdribar translated for Cassius. 'The *Cartenna* came in yesterday – it was moored not far from them.'

'And the passenger? Dio. He is a small man, hooded cloak, carrying a—'

'Yes, I know. I asked. Apparently he was going from ship to ship, trying to find passage off the island. Two of Valtava's men spoke to him.'

Captain Valtava shouted across the water again. He pointed to a bare-chested crewman, who took up the tale.

'What's he saying?' Cassius asked impatiently.

Asdribar was too busy listening to reply.

Braving the attentions of the sailors, Annia returned to the side-rail.

When the sailor finished, Asdribar continued: 'That fellow was drinking with a friend of his last night – navigator on an Egyptian merchantman called the *Isis*. His captain agreed to take Dio.'

'Where?'

'That's the thing,' said Asdribar. 'The captain was paid a considerable sum but on condition that only he could know where they were going. The crew weren't to find out until they were at sea. This navigator and some of the others weren't happy about it, but the captain was offering double pay.'

'When did they leave?'

'A couple of hours ago.'

'The ship we saw,' said Annia.

'Yes, miss.'

'By the gods,' said Cassius, smacking the side-rail. 'We almost had the son of a bitch.'

'We could not have got here sooner,' said Asdribar.

'We must go after them,' insisted Annia.

Cassius stared down at the water. He had expected to be in Cnossus harbour within the hour. The thought of heading out to sea again – after a ship that might be headed anywhere – was a deeply unpleasant prospect.

'Yes,' he said. 'I suppose we must.'

Valtava spoke again to Asdribar.

'He says the *Isis* is a grain freighter. She's bigger than the *Fortuna*. Quicker too.'

'You told me your ship was fast, Captain,' said Annia.

'She's the fastest there is, for her size. But the *Isis* has forty or fifty feet on us, perhaps double the sail area.'

'Then we should not delay,' Annia replied.

Asdribar rubbed his brow. 'Miss, the *Isis* was heading west towards the other end of the island. If they're not headed for Greece, they could be bound for anywhere, even—'

'Africa,' said Annia flatly. 'Yes. I know.'

Asdribar came closer, so that the rest of the crew wouldn't hear. 'Miss, that's two hundred miles of open sea. I've done the journey many times in the season, but if the weather turns bad there are no islands, no ports or anchorages. Nowhere to go.'

'We know where we are going,' countered Annia. 'We are following the *Isis*. Captain, I didn't secure your services with the expectation that you would baulk at the first sign of difficulty. More days at sea mean a very full bag of gold coins.'

Asdribar looked up at the mast. 'There is almost no wind.'

Annia pointed across at the *Rusucurru*. 'The *Fortuna* also has oars, does it not?'

185

'Miss, I did explain that I don't have a full crew. We might only make three knots.'

'That's three knots more than we're making now.'

Cassius had listened to the whole conversation and conceded to himself that Annia was undeniably impressive when she got the bit between her teeth.

Asdribar spoke again to his fellow captain, then reported back once more.

'Valtava knows these waters well. He says the mist won't have spread out much further than a mile. They are heading north and will give us a tow while we get the yard down and ready the oars.'

'Excellent,' said Annia. 'Thank you, Captain.'

Valtava's local knowledge and the ability of his crew were soon proved beyond doubt. The well-drilled oarsmen of the *Rusucurru* seemed barely troubled by the additional burden of the *Fortuna Redux*; soon both ships were cutting across the pond-like sea, beyond the last wreaths of the Cretan mist and out into the watery midday sunshine. Tarkel, still at the top of the mast, had just sighted the *Isis*.

'How far?' yelled Asdribar.

'Ten miles, give or take.'

'At what distance will we lose sight of it?' Cassius asked.

'Twelve or thirteen.'

Belatedly realising he hadn't got a description from the two crewmen who'd been approached by Dio, Cassius then spent a fairly surreal half-hour sitting at the *Fortuna*'s bow, conducting a shouted interview with them as they stood on either side of the *Rusucurru*'s sternpost.

He soon concluded that the assassin was well suited to his work. His lack of height seemed to be his only notable physical feature and the two men could offer little more than Drusus Viator had on Rhodes. The sailors did at least remember – after repeated questioning – that he was clean-shaven, with short, black hair; not particularly handsome or ugly; not particularly dark-skinned or light-skinned; and spoke good Greek with no discernible accent.

Just as Cassius finished questioning them, Asdribar came forward to oversee the detaching of the tow rope. The *Rusucurru* slowed, then was stopped dead by the oarsmen, and as the *Fortuna* drifted up behind her, the rope was hauled in by Korinth.

Asdribar was carrying one of the barrels of cinnamon wine, around which he had wrapped a length of rope. Seeing it, Valtava grinned, then held up a little cloth package tied with twine. With a mighty heave, Asdribar sent the barrel into the water a couple of yards from the *Rusucurru*'s broad stern. One of the crew grabbed a boathook and retrieved it. Valtava waited until the still-drifting *Fortuna* was only four or five yards away, then threw the package to Asdribar, who snatched it out of the air with ease. Once Valtava had ordered the oarsmen back to work, the freighter began to pull away. The two Carthaginians kept up their conversation as sailors from both vessels shouted farewells.

Without thinking about it, Cassius waved. Valtava returned the gesture and shouted in Greek: 'Good luck, Roman! Make sure you pay him what he's due!'

'Not my problem,' Cassius said quietly, before turning to Asdribar. 'Why the exchange of gifts?'

'It's traditional for a meeting at sea,' said Asdribar, examining the contents of the package.

'What's in there?'

'Dried camel meat. Carthaginian speciality. You can try some later.'

'Mmm.'

As they walked back along the deck, the five long oars poking out of each side of the *Fortuna*'s hull began to move. Opilio was in charge of the rowing team, which was in fact every member of the crew apart from Squint and Asdribar. Even young Tarkel had been drafted – he was to beat the timing drum. As the ship picked up speed, Asdribar cast a concerned glance at the hatch.

'They've not done a lot of oar-work recently. I shall have to go easy on them. I usually just wait for a wind, unless time is of the essence.'

'A hard taskmaster, young Annia,' Cassius replied.

Asdribar grinned. 'I thought Roman girls were supposed to be seen and not heard.'

'They are.'

⟨8⟩

To the relief of all aboard, the breeze increased steadily throughout the afternoon and, after only three hours under oars, the sails were back up again, filling well and driving the *Fortuna* westward.

They lost sight of the *Isis* just before sunset and Asdribar called in later to tell Cassius there was no sign of a light. Like the other passengers and the crew, he would have to wait until dawn to find out if their prey had disappeared.

XV

At the fifth hour of the following day, with another bout of mist finally clearing, the *Fortuna Redux* rounded the western cape of Crete. The only sign of life on the bleak, undulating headland were five tall flagpoles. There were flags on only two of them – nothing more than shredded bits of cloth, sapped long ago of any trace of colour.

Every passing hour seemed to add strength to the wind blasting from the north, propelling the *Fortuna* across the white-topped waves at close to her maximum speed. The only disadvantage was the constant strain on the mast, the yard and the rest of the rig. Most of the crew were needed to keep the mainsail correctly aligned; Korinth and Squint patrolled anxiously across the deck, checking blocks and lines, rings and knots. The little tender was thumping around on the waves and taking on water – it had already been bailed out twice.

A mile to the south-east were two small vessels that Asdribar had already dismissed as local fishing boats. Ahead was only a vast swathe of sea. Cassius recalled a phrase of Squint's that had stayed with him: *A huge, grey swell that rolls on forever.*

'Hurry then!' shouted Korinth to Tarkel, who was halfway up the mast.

'Leave the lad be,' said Asdribar. 'Poor little sod's been up and down there like a monkey. Do you want him to fall?'

Cassius licked salt off his lips and tried not to watch Tarkel's perilous progress upward. The boy had a rope around him but the pitching of the ship made his climb doubly difficult. Indavara and Annia were to Cassius's left, like him leaning against the deckhouse with one hand on the wooden bar that ran around it.

Annia was wrapped up in a cloak and gazing contemplatively at the bow as it dipped and rose with the waves.

Cassius considered what might happen if the lad couldn't see the *Isis*. If the *Fortuna* turned round, the wind would be against them. How long back to Rhodes? Four, five days? Could easily be a week or longer. And what then?

He wondered how it had all come down to this. Was there more he could have done? All things considered, he doubted it. In fact, he was pretty sure the assassin would have got clean away if he hadn't been there to take charge. Surely the gods had had a hand in that; and it wasn't the first time he'd found himself unceremoniously thrust to the centre of some important affair. Perhaps it was time for him to take his duties less seriously, allow himself to fail – at least that way he might avoid such assignments in future.

Cassius could almost see his father's face, as if the old man could hear his thoughts. The furrowed brow, the interrogative glare; that awful combination of disappointment and anger. Not do one's duty? Heresy in the Corbulo household.

Cassius imagined what would be happening there, half a world away. Late morning. Father would be finishing up his work for the day, sending out a last few messages, listening to reports from his numerous employees, looking forward to an hour or two at the baths. Mother would be overseeing things at the house: doling out instructions to the gardeners, discussing dinner with the cooks. Perhaps one of Cassius's sisters would bring some of the grandchildren over after school?

A thin arc of spray struck the deckhouse, breaking his reverie. Wiping water from his eyes, he watched Annia picking wet strands of hair off her face. She and Indavara were still looking up. Tarkel clambered on to the yard, wrapped his arms around the mast, and looked south.

'Watch your lines!' Asdribar told the crew, half of whom were gazing up at the lookout. So much depended on what the lad could or could not see.

Tarkel turned and yelled something, but Cassius and the others at the stern couldn't make out a single word. Desenna was much closer. He cupped his hands and relayed the message back to them.

'A mast! Two points west of south. Eight or nine miles away.'

'The *Isis*?' asked Asdribar.

'He can't tell for sure. Tall mast though.'

'It's probably them,' said Asdribar. He turned round. 'Miss?'

Annia nodded solemnly, then opened the deckhouse door and went inside.

'South it is!' shouted the captain. 'Squint – hold her steady. Korinth – ready the hands to shift the yard.'

The deck-chief's expression of grudging acceptance was mirrored by the rest of the crew.

Indavara looked at Cassius. 'Africa?'

'Africa.'

The more the wind blew, the more the ship rolled, and the sicker Cassius felt. Having refused Simo's offer of lunch, he took a sip of heavily watered wine and looked at the completed list of names in his hand. Thirty-two men with cause to harbour a grudge against Augustus Marius Memor. He knew the odds were against the list proving useful but at least it was finished.

With that done, and nothing but dark ruminations on what lay ahead to occupy him, Cassius thought of Annia. Clearly he had done himself few favours two nights previously, but he'd spoken to her that morning and she'd been friendly and polite. Wondering how far relations might thaw, he finally admitted to himself that he wanted to win her over. Not that there was any chance of a long-term union; his own situation made that impossible and she was far from an ideal choice. But – putting the objectionable aspects of her personality to one side – she was spirited, bright and undeniably attractive.

There were two barriers to any kind of advance. Firstly, the girl was in mourning, which hardly lent itself to a romantic frame of mind. Then again, she would be feeling vulnerable and uncertain of the future; perhaps in need of a confident, guiding hand.

Secondly, there was Indavara. Ridiculous though the prospect of a romance between him and Annia remained, it was clear the girl was rather taken with him, though Cassius suspected she had exaggerated her interest for his benefit. Taking the pragmatic view, it didn't seem worth driving a wedge between him and Indavara just for a girl. Regardless of how they got on, for as long as Cassius was with the Service, he wanted Indavara with him. When it came to the rough stuff, the man was a beast, pure and simple, and he offered a level of protection that simply couldn't be acquired elsewhere. It would be a mistake to risk losing him.

Still, Cassius didn't have anything serious in mind. He would be happy simply to draw the girl to him (after all, that was where the fun lay) and there would be something very satisfying about bending her to his will, perhaps even getting his hands on her. Indavara need never know. And if she couldn't be tamed, so be it. Hardly the end of the world. Possessed with a sudden desire to see her, Cassius realised he had a perfect pretext for a visit literally in his hands.

Simo returned to the cabin with some towels he'd been drying in the galley. 'Now we're finished with the documents, are you going to work on your project, sir?'

'Not today, Simo.'

Cassius had only done ten pages so far – he was translating a fairly obscure Greek text on military strategy into Latin. When it was finished he hoped to get it published in Rome. One of his uncles had completed three similar works and enjoyed considerable acclaim for his efforts. Such a success might also help with Cassius's aborted legal career.

'I think I shall go and see Miss Annia. She might recognise some of these names.'

'Ah. Good idea, sir.'

──■8■──

Having passed Indavara – who was sitting on his makeshift bed doing something to an arrow – Cassius hurried up to the deck-house. Annia let him in and, upon seeing the list, immediately sat down at Asdribar's table to examine it. Cassius stood behind her and looked down at her breasts as they squeezed against the table. The ship pitched suddenly and he fell against the door.

'Perhaps you should take a seat, Officer,' Annia said without looking up.

Cassius sat down on the bed. Clara was sitting at the other table, preparing some food. Mainly out of boredom, Cassius stared at her until she finally looked up, then blew her a kiss. The maid blushed and glanced anxiously over at her mistress, but Annia hadn't noticed. With the tiniest of smiles, Clara returned to her work.

Annia read through the list again and turned to Cassius. 'I recognise only one name: Albanus Sebastianus.'

'What do you remember of the case?' Cassius asked, straightening the hem of his tunic over his knees.

'I think it was about a year ago. My father needed to write a number of identical letters, so he had Trogus and me make some copies for him. This Sebastianus was an army officer. He was suspected of having ties to an outlawed religious sect. I believe it was in Mauretania Tingitana.'

'Mauretania Caesarinsis, I think you'll find.'

Annia considered this for a moment. 'Yes. You're right.'

'Sebastianus was a tribune,' Cassius continued. 'Had an affair with a local girl who turned out to be a priestess of this sect. I believe your father wrote personally to those in the province who knew him best. I don't recall coming across any documentation regarding the outcome.'

'The case went on for some time. I pressed my father to let me know what happened and he eventually relented. This Sebastianus was dismissed from the army. He would have faced stricter sanctions but he had some associate on the general staff who saw to it that no further harm – physical or financial – came to him.'

'You recall nothing else?'

'No.'

'Please, miss, indulge me. Check the list one last time.'

As Annia did so, Cassius gazed at Clara again but she stubbornly refused to look at him.

'No. Just that one,' Annia said when she'd finished. 'Do you think what I told you might be of any use, Officer?'

Cassius was about to ask her to use his first name but then realised he rather liked hearing her say 'Officer'.

'Possibly.'

'You recalled the details of that one case from amongst that huge stack of papers?'

'I have an orator's memory, miss. It does come in rather useful at times.'

'I imagine it does.'

The ship was really beginning to roll now. A mug on the table slid towards Annia. She caught it but other objects fell to the floor. Clara set about picking them up while Annia looked around for anything else that might come free.

Cassius was feeling worse by the moment but he didn't want to pass up this opportunity. As the ship settled again, he considered asking the girl about her travels but then remembered she'd been with her father. He also doubted she would want to discuss the rest of her family, and mention of her interests had previously led to an argument. What was left?

'I do wish I'd had more time to see Rhodes,' he said. 'If I ever get the chance to return what would you suggest I visit, miss, apart from the Helios?'

Annia's face brightened. 'Well there are the temples, of course. We've some wonderful galleries too. The most incredible work on show is a painting – you know of the *Satyr of Protogenes*?'

'Only the name.'

Actually Cassius knew a good deal about it but he wanted Annia to speak.

'The skill of the artist is unparalleled, the realism of the creatures depicted almost beyond belief. They say he painted out a partridge in one corner because birds would attack the image, believing it to be real.'

The *Fortuna* slipped down the side of a wave, heeling dramatically before righting herself. Annia didn't seem at all concerned but Clara sat down again, bracing herself on the chair. The hollow feeling in Cassius' stomach was growing, as was the bitter taste in his throat.

'Remarkable,' he replied.

'Are you all right, Officer? You look rather pale.'

'I'm fine, miss. I was about to ask you—'

Cassius knew with a sudden certainty that he was going to throw up. He got to his feet, staggered to the door and wrenched it open. With a garbled 'Excuse me,' he stepped outside. As the door shut behind him, he blundered towards the side-rail.

He didn't make it. Squint was on the helm and watched implacably as Cassius vomited onto the deck. As his guts burned, Cassius doubled over, then fell to his knees. Two more heaves and everything was out. Despite the wind and the spray he could smell the contents of his stomach. He retched a final time.

Tarkel was nearby. He found a bucket, dunked it over the side, then threw the water across the deck, sloshing the vomit towards a drain-hole.

'Shall I fetch your servant for you, sir?' he asked.

'No,' said Cassius, hauling himself to his feet. 'No, I'm fine.'

Arms out wide to keep his balance, he made for the hatch. Reaching the first step, he gripped the handrail. Above the noise of the wind in his ears he heard something else and glanced to his right.

Korinth was standing there, laughing at him.

XVI

Sunlight sparks off a blade before it slices through cloth, flesh and bone. An arm falls to the ground. The blade swings again, hacking off the other limb. Blood gushes from the wounds and seeps into the sand. The body spasms and shakes. *The soldier is still alive.*

A red glow illuminates a swollen, mutilated corpse. The sword tip prods at the skin. Black-shelled insects tumble out. *They have burrowed inside.*

Darkness. A faceless warrior leaps at his foe, club swinging. The weapon strikes the head, tearing a gaping rent in the neck. As his enemy falls, the warrior stands over him. *He laughs.*

'Sir!'

Cassius awoke to see Simo leaning over him.

'I thought it best to wake you, sir. You were crying out.'

Cassius pawed at his eyes and propped himself up against a pillow. He was glad to be free of the dreams. Until he remembered how sick he was.

Simo knelt by the bed and put a hand to his forehead. 'You're almost feverish.'

The Gaul took a wet cloth and placed it on his master's brow. The *Fortuna* was being thrown around on the swell, every impact shaking the timbers of the hull. Cassius looked up at the ominous black beyond the porthole.

'By the gods, this is torture,' he groaned. 'What time is it?'

'Four hours after sunset, sir.'

Cassius's condition had deteriorated along with the weather. He had spent the afternoon and evening slipping in and out of a restless sleep. Having thrown up twice more, he couldn't even think of ingesting anything solid.

'What's it like out there?'

Simo pointed at the low roof. Water was dripping into the cabin in more places than Cassius could count. 'The rain hasn't stopped, sir. And the wind's got up too.'

'The *Isis*?'

'We lost sight of her again at dusk. Captain Asdribar has decided to keep us heading directly south. He also told me to pass on his advice, sir. He said you'd be better up on deck – where you can get some air.'

'He doesn't know how I feel. Only someone afflicted as badly as I am can comprehend this kind of suffering.'

'I don't think anyone would know much more about seasickness than him, sir.'

'I've no strength in me, Simo.'

Cassius did however find sufficient energy to strike the bed with his fist. 'Damn this weak gut of mine. I must be the laughing stock of the entire ship.'

'Not at all, sir. Even a couple of the sailors have had some trouble.'

'Indavara?'

'He seems to be faring rather well, sir.'

'Is that right? Where is he now?'

'Up in the deckhouse. He said he wants to keep an eye on the young women.'

'Yes,' Cassius said sourly as he turned on to his side. 'I bet he does.'

———◄8►———

Asdribar had been in to tie down all the furniture, so the only place to sit was on the beds. Clara had also been sick and was now asleep in hers, covers drawn up to her neck. Indavara sat next to Annia on her bed.

He had made sure she was to his right, unable to see his

disfigured ear. He hadn't noticed her looking at it yet but people often did, even though he tried to cover it with his hair. Above them, a lantern swung from a hook on the roof, throwing a shifting pool of golden light across the room.

Indavara looked down as the light illuminated the bed. Annia's hand was inches away from his. He could just reach out and touch her. But he hadn't, and he couldn't – because he didn't know what she'd do.

They'd been talking for at least an hour. Thankfully she hadn't asked him anything about his past; they'd mostly discussed nature and the creatures of the sea. Annia knew a lot; and had told him more about dolphins and turtles and seabirds and sharks. She had a drawing book back on Rhodes with hundreds of pictures in. Her sister's drawings were better, so she said. Indavara told her he'd like to see it.

After that, she'd spoken about her father. How kind he had been, how intelligent, how well respected, how she'd been in bed when she heard the maid scream. Then she'd stopped talking and now she was looking out of the nearest porthole, the plump beads of water rolling down the glass.

Indavara wondered, should he take her hand? Did she want him to?

He would have given every coin he owned to wrap her up in his arms and kiss her.

Still looking away, Annia reached out and put her hand over his. Her fingers were cold yet somehow still sent warmth into his body. Then she glanced at him and pulled her hand away.

A terrible moment of silence, then: 'You should go.'

She had whispered it, to make sure Clara didn't hear.

Indavara reached for her but she put her hands on her lap.

'You should go.'

Indavara felt like he'd been hit. He couldn't think straight. Did she like him or not? Corbulo always said women needed to be told what to do: a man needed to be strong, take the lead, that was how they liked it.

Annia pointed at the door.

Indavara didn't want to upset her. That was the last thing he wanted. He stood up and walked across the deckhouse, then looked back as he reached the door. Her face was in shadow.

———◆———

Later that night, Cassius had a visit from Asdribar. Although the captain's tunic and boots were sodden, he seemed utterly unaffected by the violent motions of the ship.

'Enough of this lying in your pit, young man. It just won't do.'

Cassius waved a hand at him. 'I am exhausted, Captain. I doubt I could even raise myself from the bed. How are we progressing?'

'Quickly. I reckon we've covered a hundred miles – half the distance to the African coast.'

Asdribar beckoned Cassius upwards. 'Come now, I insist. I've seen this before. You'll throw up all the water inside you, then you'll have no strength left at all. Come up on deck and do as I tell you. If you're not feeling better within an hour, you can return to bed.' Asdribar offered his hand. 'Deal?'

Cassius glanced at Simo.

'Can't hurt to try, sir.'

Cassius lifted his hand. The Carthaginian held it, then pulled him up off the bed. Cassius felt like falling straight back down again but Simo took his other arm and steadied him. He was wearing only his vomit-stained sleeping tunic.

Asdribar gripped him by his shoulders. 'Now, it's damned wet up there so bring that oiled cloak I saw you with. Once you're dressed, I want you on deck immediately. Understood?'

'Yes,' Cassius replied.

'See you shortly.'

As Asdribar departed, Simo went looking for a clean tunic. Left to stand alone for a moment, Cassius drew in some long, deep breaths and managed to pull the dirty tunic off himself. He drank some water and, as Simo helped him dress, began to feel marginally better. The Gaul secured the hooded cloak by putting a belt around the outside and once his boots were on, Cassius was ready. Almost.

'Simo, I know my hair's in a terrible state but you can at least run a comb through it.'

'Of course, sir.'

Upon reaching the steps, Cassius had to wait for Opilio to come down. The hold-chief was carrying a tray loaded with mugs and somehow keeping them all upright. The big man flicked his neck back to drop his hood. Water dripped from his flattened nose.

'Someone's upset the gods,' he said with a grim smile. 'Good weather couldn't last for ever, I suppose.'

'Feels to me like this storm's lasted for ever,' replied Cassius, pulling his own hood over his head.

'This is no storm, sir. This here is a gale. You'll know the difference if it becomes a storm.'

Taking a tight grip on both handrails, Cassius made his way carefully up the slippery steps. He was startled by the depth of the darkness that greeted him up top. The only visible light was the lantern hanging from the sternpost. Between the tillers was the hulking figure of Korinth.

Asdribar emerged out of the gloom behind him. Like the other sailors, he was now attired in his own cloak and a wide-brimmed leather hat to shield him from the rain. He took Cassius's arm and helped him up onto the deck.

Cassius narrowed his eyes as salty spray lashed his face.

'Follow me! Use the rope to help you if you need it!'

Asdribar pointed to a newly installed line that ran from a ring by the hatch to the deckhouse. Cassius kept low as he followed, one hand on the rope as water sloshed over his boots. When he reached the deckhouse, Asdribar helped him up and guided him to the handrail. Two other men were there but because of their hats and the darkness, Cassius couldn't work out who they were.

'I'll tie you on!'

Several lengths of rope had been affixed to the handrail and Asdribar ran one of them through the back of Cassius's belt. As he tied it off, Cassius looked forward. The lantern on the bow was lurching up and down alarmingly.

Asdribar spoke directly into his ear. 'That'll keep you steady. Now listen, I've just appointed you ship's navigator. I was doing it but I need to go and check the sails. Move along to the corner there.'

Asdribar followed Cassius to the right-hand corner of the deckhouse, then moved past him and pointed at the sky above the stern. 'There's a lot of cloud so we've a limited choice but up there is what we call Poseidon's Trident. See the three bright stars in a row?'

Cassius couldn't; until he followed the exact direction of Asdribar's outstretched arm. 'Yes. I see.'

'Mark them, and tell me or Korinth if their position changes.'

Cassius raised his arm and used it to measure the approximate location of the stars relative to the edge of the deckhouse.

'That's it,' said Asdribar. 'Good thinking. Remember to call out if we drift off course. And we probably will. Korinth's a decent helmsman but he's no Squint.'

With that, Asdribar made his way forward.

By placing his feet well apart and leaning back, Cassius found he could brace himself against the rope. Facing away from the bow, he was spared the spray and able to fill his lungs with the cold, clean air. And despite the plunging and pitching of the ship, he made sure he kept his eyes fixed on the three stars.

Focused entirely on the task Asdribar had given him, Cassius eventually realised he had completely lost track of time. He couldn't have cared less. He was up, he was out of that accursed cabin and he was feeling better.

XVII

When the storm came, it came quickly. Just after the sixth hour of night, when Simo had struggled on deck to deliver him a welcome mug of hot wine, Cassius saw the first signs that the weather was worsening.

First, the wind began to shift. Though it remained roughly from the north, the sudden gusts and changes in direction left Asdribar and the crew struggling to compensate. Even with every man on deck, altering the position of the yard was a complicated, laborious job. They had just completed a third big adjustment when the wind veered again and blew even harder.

Asdribar had two of the ship's longest, thickest ropes run out from the stern in an elongated U. This 'sea anchor' would apparently help the ship maintain its course. As the men tied off the ropes, Cassius noticed that the tender had disappeared. He asked Squint about it; apparently the little boat had broken free hours earlier.

Though the *Fortuna* was making excellent speed as she coursed up and down the swell, it soon became evident that both crew and vessel were under tremendous pressure. Asdribar's sojourns forward became increasingly regular; one man blundered back to the hatch with blood pouring from a wounded hand; and the noise of the howling wind became so great that Cassius caught only fragments of shouted conversations. Worse still were the crashing thuds and thumps that seemed to presage the holing of the *Fortuna*'s hull or the collapse of the entire rig.

'You all right there, lad?' yelled Squint, who was steering once more.

'Will she hold together?'

'This old girl? Of course.'

'Old? How old is she?'

'A lot older than you. But don't worry. Ships are the opposite of women – they get better with age!'

Cassius tried to rein in his most pessimistic imaginings but what frightened him more than anything was the change in Asdribar. Usually so serene, the Carthaginian now prowled the deck spitting curses, his face dark with worry. After stopping for a brief discussion with Squint, he beckoned Cassius forward. Cassius's fingers were so cold and the knot so tight that it took him a while to untie the rope. Once free, he used the deck-line to get himself over to the captain.

'We've too much sail up,' said Asdribar. 'Got to lower the yard. Get your men from below and send them up to the mast. Then you come back here!'

If this rather impolite demand hadn't done enough to alert Cassius to the gravity of the situation, Asdribar's next action did. Before he could reach down for the deck-line, the captain smacked him on the shoulder and yelled 'Hurry!'

Cassius's shout of protest was lost in the wind. As the stern of the ship rose, he was sent flying towards the hatch. Realising he was in danger of falling straight down it, he dropped on to his side and slid across the water-soaked deck. The thick cloak protected him well and he came to a stop with a yard to spare. Stumbling down the steps, he tried not to touch the bloody streaks left on the handrail by the injured crewman. Arriving at the bottom, he found the upper hold submerged beneath several inches of seawater.

He glanced along the empty passageway and called out to Indavara and Simo. They and the injured sailor came out of the cabin, the crewman with a bandage wrapped round his hand. He hurried past Cassius and up the steps.

'You two are needed on deck. They have to lower the mainsail.'

'Should we put some more clothes on, sir?' asked Simo.

'Forget that, you won't be up there long. Come on!'

Cassius waited until they were behind him, then led the way on all fours. Once back on deck, he saw that Asdribar had taken up the tillers.

Showing remarkable agility for one so aged, Squint came forward and dropped down by the hatch. His thick beard now hung from his chin in waterlogged clumps. 'Keep low and use the lines. Follow me.'

Indavara and Simo clambered past Cassius and towards the mast.

Still trying to find a solid stance for steering, Asdribar kicked his leg free of a rope, one of many now snaking across the deck.

'Corbulo!' he roared. 'Clear these lines out of my way!'

Somewhat perturbed that he seemed to have been relegated to the role of second ship's boy, Cassius nonetheless did as he was told. With the *Fortuna* so seriously undermanned, there was no choice but to help Asdribar and his crew get through the storm. He pulled up his hood and crawled across the deck.

━━8━━

As the *Fortuna* crested another mighty wave, Simo lost his footing and slid forward, knocking Indavara's legs away. The two of them landed in a heap close to the mast behind Squint, who didn't even notice. Indavara helped Simo up and they squatted there, hands flat against the deck. He looked around and realised that most of the crew were close by, several of them handling the mainsail and looking anxiously up at the yard.

Indavara's tunic was already soaked through. The entire deck was covered in water and the icy spray seemed to be striking them from all sides. He glanced at Simo. The Gaul's hair was plastered across his face and he looked very much as though he wanted to be back in the cabin.

Korinth arrived and ordered the men to gather around him, with only those holding the lines staying in position. The burly deck-chief crouched with his back to the mast, hands cupped around his mouth.

Indavara turned his good ear towards him.

'We're bringing the yard halfway down. I'll take the halyard with five men.' He pointed at three of the larger crewmen plus Indavara and Simo. 'The rest of you help with the lines and watch for any snags.'

Squint moved aside while Korinth and his three helpers hunched in front of the mast.

Indavara knew that the halyard was the three-inch-thick rope used to raise and lower the yard; it was the strongest line on the ship.

Desenna was one of those helping Korinth. The curly-haired sailor turned round, coils of the rope in his hands. 'Out the way!'

Indavara and Simo obeyed, watching as Desenna tied the end of the rope around the biggest cleat on the ship. 'Take hold. We'll tell you when the weight's coming on. See the grips on the deck?'

Indavara had wondered about the little squares of wood nailed into the deck behind the mast.

'They're for your feet,' continued Desenna. 'Tubby, you're on the tail.'

Simo took up his position next to the cleat, with Indavara ahead of him, both to the left of the rope. Indavara closed his fingers around the sodden hemp and found the grips with his feet. He shook water off his hair and face.

'Weight on!' yelled Desenna.

Indavara squeezed his fingers tight and leant back. Despite the grips and the efforts of the other four men, he could feel the immense load held by the rope.

'Slowly now! Hand over hand!'

Blocks squealed as they let the rope out inch by inch, lowering the yard and sail. Squint was bawling at the men on the other lines, trying to keep the whole arrangement as straight as possible for Korinth's crew.

Another shift of the deck under them; Indavara felt his body swinging dangerously to the left. Not daring to adjust his feet, he was relieved when the ship pitched back the other way.

'Snagged!' someone shouted.

'Weight on!' added Korinth.

Indavara squeezed the rope tight once more.

Squint appeared from the left, nipped deftly past Korinth, then looked up at the right side of the yard. He took charge of young Tarkel's line and moved it about.

'Well?' asked Korinth.

'One of the lifts is caught,' answered the veteran.

As Indavara sat there – legs and backside in freezing water, chills running up and down his spine – he reminded himself not to slacken his grip.

'Squint! Korinth!'

Asdribar peered forward, trying to work out what was going on. Cassius – down on one knee just ahead of him – looked too, but all he could make out were the dim outlines of the men huddled close to the mast. Asdribar unleashed more bitter curses in Punic as the *Fortuna* slammed down into another trough.

As far as Cassius could tell, all he could really do was keep the ship in something approaching a straight line as it was tossed about on the swell. Enough cloud had now cleared to allow a little moonlight onto the water and Cassius almost wished it hadn't; all around them white horses bubbled at the crest of surging, rolling waves.

The *Fortuna Redux*, all ninety-five feet of her, suddenly seemed like a rowing dinghy. Cassius had hoped never to experience the rage of the gods that held sway over the sea, but now found himself witnessing the brutal power of the elements first-hand. There seemed a very real possibility that some divine power wanted the ship crippled or sunk.

'What are you doing?' cried Asdribar suddenly. Cassius looked over his shoulder and saw that the deckhouse door was open. Annia stood there, a dim light behind her. She shouted something to Asdribar but Cassius heard only his enraged reply: 'Get back inside and shut that bloody door!'

206

The captain turned back towards the mast. 'By the gods,' he said. 'Someone's going up.'

━━■8■━━

Indavara had seen some impressive acts of courage in his time, but nothing that compared to the selfless tenacity of young Tarkel. Moments earlier, his skinny frame had appeared out of the gloom. Crouching down between Korinth and Squint, he'd instantly pointed upward. The two men debated the matter for a moment but swiftly seemed to realise there was no alternative. Squint produced a short length of rope from somewhere and tied it around Tarkel's belt. The lad cast off his cloak, scraped his hair from his face, then set off up the mast to clear the snag. Despite the pummelling the ship was taking, he remained calm and sure-footed and kept up a remarkable pace. Before long, Indavara lost sight of him.

The tension in the rope seemed to slacken. Word came back from Desenna. 'We've tied it off, but keep your grip tight.'

'He there yet?' cried Squint, gazing up at the yard.

'Can't see,' replied Korinth.

'My line's moving,' someone shouted.

'I think he's there!' yelled another.

The *Fortuna* rode up the side of another huge wave that then seemed to disappear, dropping the hull down at the steepest of angles. Indavara braced his feet as the bow struck the water. He saw one man fly across the deck and heard a jarring impact from above.

'Korinth, the halyard.'

The deck-chief scrambled forward.

'It's fraying!'

'Get another line on,' yelled Squint. 'Tarkel! Down!'

'It's coming down!'

'Tarkel!'

Korinth turned away from the mast, grabbed the crewman behind him and shoved him towards the stern. 'Back! All of you back!'

Just as Indavara glimpsed one man being buried under an avalanche of sailcloth, someone ran into him.

He was knocked backwards on to the deck. Head half submerged in water, he heard a colossal crash and felt the timbers of the ship shudder beneath him.

———8———

Cassius saw the whole thing. The sky was even clearer now, clear enough for him and Asdribar to behold in horror the moment the yard plunged forty feet and struck the deck. The huge timber now lay on the crumpled sail, extending far beyond both side-rails. Thankfully, most of the men seemed to have got out of the way in time and some were already moving. Cassius could also see the lantern mounted at the bow and, crucially, the light at the top of the rig. The mast was still standing.

The wind eased for a moment. He turned from his kneeling position, one hand still on the deck-line, and looked up at Asdribar. The Carthaginian seemed to have only a loose grip on the tillers. He was staring ahead, mouth hanging open.

Then he looked down at Cassius. 'Corbulo, take the helm.'

'What?'

'You heard me.'

'I don't know—'

Asdribar let go of the tillers, grabbed Cassius and pulled him to his feet. 'Shall I call the girl?'

'All right,' Cassius yelled back at him. 'What do I do?'

Asdribar undid the line running from his belt to the deckhouse, then dragged Cassius into position and retied it on his belt. 'This'll help you. Just do what you can to keep her from turning. You must keep the wind to the stern.'

'Why?'

'Because otherwise we'll capsize!'

Cassius was struck on the leg by one of the tillers, which were shearing about all over the place. Asdribar grabbed them and wrestled them into submission. As Cassius took over, he was stunned by the force coming through the shafts of wood, as if he could feel every churning movement of the sea beneath the ship.

'Just hold her steady.'

Asdribar turned away, bowed his head into the wind and set off towards the mast.

— ☙8☙ —

Indavara was one of the first up. He helped Simo to his feet, then saw the scene of utter chaos around them. In amongst the mass of bodies, bits of wood and endless yards of rope, one man was lying on his side, hands clawing at his leg. Another hauled himself out from under the sail and turned back to help a compatriot who was pinned. Korinth and Squint were looking over the side at the water.

'Where is he?' someone shouted.

Then Indavara remembered. The boy.

He reached the side-rail and saw that it had probably saved the ship. The yard had ploughed its way through several inches of solid wood and was now wedged. Most of the sailcloth had piled up on the deck with only a small section hanging in the water.

'There! There he is!'

The end of the yard was at least five yards away. Trailing from it by the rope attached to his belt was Tarkel. The wind and the swell were still pushing the ship along and the lad was struggling to stay above the water. He raised a hand for a moment but then his white, contorted face was lost beneath the waves.

'Grapple hook!' shouted Korinth. Desenna ran past the others towards the stern.

'Maybe I can get out to him,' volunteered another of the crew. Indavara looked at the soaking, circular timber and reckoned there wasn't a chance he would make it more than a yard or two.

'Don't be an idiot,' cried Korinth, dragging the man back by his tunic. 'We're not losing you too.'

Like the others, Indavara's eyes were fixed on Tarkel as his flailing hands broke the surface. He seemed to be reaching forward, trying to grab the rope.

'Everyone on the yard!' ordered Squint. By now the trapped sailors had dragged themselves clear and Simo was attending to the injured man. Squint, Korinth, Indavara and the others clutched whatever they could get their hands on and tried to pull the yard in.

It shifted a few inches through the hole in the side-rail but then stopped. In amongst the tangle of rope and sailcloth, something was stuck fast.

'He's gone under again,' someone yelled.

Desenna returned with Asdribar. The captain was holding a length of thin line attached to a triple-headed iron hook. He already had the rope coiled and didn't hesitate in choosing Korinth for the throw. 'Stand clear!'

Despite their captain's words, the crewmen stayed as close as they could to the side-rail. Several had dropped to their knees and raised their hands to the heavens in prayer.

———◦8◦———

Cassius blinked to try to clear the stinging water from his eyes. He wasn't even sure if his efforts were making any difference, though a glance back at the stars confirmed the ship was at least maintaining her course.

But now the wind seemed to have caught the right side of the *Fortuna* and the stern was sliding left. Setting his feet, Cassius hauled both tillers to the right and watched the lantern at the other end of the ship.

Slowly, the bow came round.

———◦8◦———

Indavara saw instantly that the effort would fail. Korinth loosed the hook with an arcing throw, trying to land it on Tarkel's line. Despite the weight of the iron head, by the time it neared its target, the fierce wind had blown the rope off course. The hook landed closer to the yard than the boy.

'No!' came Squint's despairing shout.

Indavara was already on the move. Having sat against the side-rails for much of the trip, he knew exactly where to find what he needed. As he shouldered his way past Opilio and plucked the nearest boathook from its mount, the men cried out:

'Tarkel!'

'Stay up, boy!'

'Hold on! We're coming for you!'

Indavara ran back and held the boathook up in front of Asdribar and Korinth. 'Get a line on this.'

'Yes,' said Asdribar. Korinth reached for the nearest piece of long rope and wrenched it free.

Squint turned from the side-rail. 'I can't see him!'

With blinding speed, Korinth tied the rope to the iron ring at the butt end of the boathook. Indavara still had his hand on the wooden shaft. 'Let me?'

'Go,' said the deck-chief. He grabbed the other end of the rope, ran to the side-rail and squatted down. Indavara raised the boat-hook over his shoulder. Though a lot more unwieldy, he reckoned it weighed about the same as a throwing javelin.

'Now!' roared Squint.

Indavara looked out at the dark sea. He saw where the trailing line disappeared under the water. There was no sign of the boy. He fixed his eyes on the rope, took a single step and let fly.

The boathook arrowed across the waves and plunged into the water a foot beyond the line. Korinth was already backing up, pulling the rope with him.

'Think you got it,' yelled Desenna.

As Korinth kept pulling, the trailing rope bent. A hand emerged from the waves, then a head.

Indavara took hold of the line too and the others cleared a path as he and Korinth retreated along the side-rail, pulling the rope – and the lad – towards the ship.

211

The ever-enterprising Desenna had located an even longer boathook, which he now dropped over the side and hooked around Tarkel's belt. He was able to keep his head above the water as the others manoeuvred him over to the yard.

Asdribar ordered two men to grab his legs, then he lay on the timber and reached down. At the third attempt he grabbed Tarkel under one arm and pulled him from the water.

Indavara, Simo and the sailors gathered round as Asdribar deposited the lad face down on the deck. They could see the ugly red welts on his hands where he'd wrestled with the rope to keep his head up. As Korinth detached the line, Asdribar pulled Tarkel up by his belt and repeatedly slapped him hard on the back. Tarkel's body spasmed, then water began to pour from his mouth. His head turned to the side and his eyes opened.

A cheer went up from the men and Indavara felt several hands strike his own back.

As if to remind them of their situation, the *Fortuna* pitched sharply, sending two men sliding into the mass of sailcloth.

With one hand still on the boy, Asdribar addressed his crew. 'Korinth, take Desenna and rig the foresail. The rest of you clear this mess. Check the hull for any damage and get the yard inboard.'

He looked down at Tarkel. The lad's tongue was hanging out and he was staring up at the sky. Asdribar turned to Indavara and Simo. 'Get him below and into a bed.'

—◆8◆—

Cassius heard the cheer, but it barely registered. Ignoring the sailors scurrying around by the mast, he kept his gaze locked on the bow lantern. Emitting a steady stream of curses, he struggled on. Every time he thought he was making progress, one or both of the tillers would pull in an apparently random direction. He was terrified that the boat would turn side-on to the wind and capsize. Commanding a century of legionaries suddenly seemed like a comparatively easy job.

'Where is he?' Cassius yelled, only to be answered by the welcome sight of Asdribar striding towards him.

The Carthaginian untied the safety line and shouted 'Well done!' as he took over the tillers. 'Now help them with the boy,' he added.

Cassius met Simo and Indavara at the hatch. He went down first and took Tarkel's feet, then the three of them carried him below.

'To your bed, sir?' asked Simo.

'Of course,' Cassius replied, leading the way. He propped open the cabin door as Simo and Indavara took Tarkel inside and deposited him gently on the bed. Simo grabbed a towel and some blankets.

Once back at the steps, Cassius and Indavara had to wait for Squint and a limping sailor to come down. Cassius pointed along the passageway. 'Simo will have a look at you when he has a moment.'

Squint left the injured man and hurried into the hold, sloshing through the water to where the timber and tools were kept. He suddenly stopped and turned. 'What are you two doing just standing around? Lend a hand!'

XVIII

By dawn the storm had blown itself out. Cassius and Indavara remained on deck throughout the night, and were as grateful as the crew for every decrease in the strength of the wind and the size of the waves. It was the first clear morning for several days and the sight of the new sun lifted the spirits of everyone aboard.

With Squint back on the helm, Asdribar came up to the fore-deck to take charge. His first order was to replace the current foresail with a bigger sail stored below. While Korinth and Desenna dealt with this, Asdribar told the others to take a break. One man knelt to offer a quiet prayer, but most – Cassius and Indavara included – just sat or lay down while Asdribar surveyed his ship.

Aside from a couple of small holes, the deck was remarkably undamaged. All the rope, tackle and sailcloth had been gathered up and stowed. But even a cursory glance at the yard showed the most serious problem: a huge crack running half the length of the timber.

'I assume that's beyond repair,' said Cassius.

'Far beyond,' said Asdribar. 'We have a spare but it's two-thirds the size. We'll have to brail the mainsail – make it smaller – but we should be able to maintain a decent speed.'

'That's something, I suppose.'

'As long as the wind stays to the north we should strike land tomorrow.'

Cassius heard sandals slapping on the deck and saw Annia and Clara walking towards them, the young lady lugging a pail, her maid carrying a tray of food. He observed the reaction of the men. Despite their exhaustion, most of the sailors were smiling.

The sight of the two young women, with their fair faces and long hair shining in the sun, was the greatest fillip imaginable. The prospect of something to eat and drink probably didn't hurt either.

Annia looked at the damaged yard, then at the men. The weary faces and bruised, battered bodies told the story of the night better than any description.

'Thank you,' she said quietly. 'Thank you all.'

Floating in the pail full of water were wooden mugs, which the men filled up and drank from. Piled high on Clara's tray were slices of bread smeared with olive oil and chunks of crumbly white cheese.

'Don't be too nice to them, miss,' remarked Asdribar. 'I don't want them going soft on me.'

'They deserve it, Captain,' Annia replied.

'I won't argue with you there.'

The Carthaginian sat down on the yard and grabbed a piece of bread. He found a grin for Clara. 'All right, girl?'

'Poseidon's anger has passed, sir. We might reach the land now, mightn't we?'

'I'll see to it. Don't you worry.'

When Annia had delivered water to every man, she returned to Asdribar. 'You were right about the *Fortuna*, Captain. She got us through.'

'Her and the crew, miss, yes.'

Asdribar tipped his mug at Cassius and Indavara, who were sitting next to each other. 'And not forgetting our auxiliaries of course.'

Annia looked down at Cassius and Indavara as they took food from Clara's tray. Though he suspected the travails of the night might have skewed his thinking somewhat, Cassius had to admit she did look lovely; those chestnut tresses framing her delicate features. But there was something about the girl Clara too, with that generous figure and naive vulnerability. Cassius had always had a weakness for maids.

'Sure you've no Thracian blood in you, Indavara?' asked

Asdribar. 'I've not seen harpooning skills like that since I was in the Cyclades.'

'What's this?' asked Annia.

Asdribar related the details of Tarkel's rescue, ably assisted by enthusiastic contributions from Desenna and Opilio. Cassius had heard the crew talking about Indavara's quick thinking and skill for much of the night. Embarrassed, the bodyguard concentrated on his food. Cassius watched Annia as she listened and – try as she might – she just couldn't hide her admiration. Was there anything a woman loved more than a modest hero?

When he'd finished his tale, Asdribar got to his feet and gestured to Cassius. 'And don't forget Officer Corbulo here – helmed the ship on his own during the worst of the storm.'

Cassius reckoned his efforts deserved rather more recognition than that but he did his best to appear magnanimous.

'You did well,' Asdribar added. 'Sorry if I was a little rough with my orders.'

'Not at all. Happy to help.'

Annia put the pail down. 'Captain—'

Asdribar seemed to know exactly what she was going to ask. 'No sign from the bow, miss, but visibility is excellent. I'll send someone up the mast later.'

'Thank you.'

Annia began a second round with the pail.

Cassius turned to Indavara. 'Not to going to volunteer yourself for lookout duty, hero?'

Indavara glowered at him as he shoved some bread into his mouth.

'Oh come on,' added Cassius. 'Just a jest. Cheer up, man. We should all be smiling after surviving last night.'

The expression on Indavara's face hadn't changed. He lowered his voice. 'The storm. Do you think it was because of what I did at that temple?'

'It's November. There are a lot of storms in November. Let's just hope we can make it to shore before there's another one.'

———◆8◆———

Cassius was already working on a plan, but when the crew asked for more food a little later, he realised an immediate opportunity had presented itself. He hurried to the hatch and down the steps, relieved to note that everyone else was occupied: Asdribar was steering, deep in conversation with Annia; Simo was hanging wet clothes on the side-rail; and Indavara was helping the sailors.

In the end, no one had put themselves forward for lookout duty, but Desenna had volunteered to check the integrity of the mast and make the few minor repairs needed before they could raise the spare yard. Once at the top, he had seen a ship to the south, though it was no more than a speck on the horizon. They couldn't be sure it was the *Isis*, but Asdribar had changed course, commenting that there were unlikely to be many other vessels at sea. They would just have to follow as best they could.

Down below, some of the crew were still clearing water. Just beyond the steps, Opilio and another man were pushing the excess into the sluices with wide brushes, while another team could be heard singing lustily as they cleared the lower hold.

Cassius hurried along the passageway, also glad that young Tarkel had been moved into Squint's quarters. Apparently the lad had said a few words and even managed a bit of breakfast. The crew had all insisted on checking on him and Simo had eventually been forced to ask Asdribar to ban visitors.

Cassius stuck his head into the galley and checked it was empty, then went inside the cabin. He wedged the door open with his foot, ran a hand through his hair and waited.

Clara came along not long after, carrying the empty tray.

'Hello,' said Cassius. 'As you're on your way to the galley, perhaps you'd collect my dirty crockery for me?'

He pointed to the single mug on the table by the bed.

Clara looked at the mug, then glanced back along the empty passageway.

'Won't take a moment,' Cassius assured her.

Keeping her expression neutral, she walked past him into the cabin. Cassius pulled his foot away and the door slammed shut. He took the tray from her and put it on the bed.

Clara looked up at him. He watched her running her eyes over the features of his face. They came to rest on his mouth.

'Do you think I'm handsome, Clara?'

'Yes, sir.'

'You can call me Cassius. Do you think I'm handsome?'

'I think you're very handsome, Cassius.'

He had asked that question of a lot of women, numerous maids amongst them; often enough to know the difference between a real yes and a fake yes.

He ran a finger softly up her neck. 'You won't tell your mistress about this, will you, Clara? I don't think that would be helpful for anybody.'

She shook her head.

Cassius bent forward and kissed her on the lips. Clara opened her mouth wide and drew in his tongue, licking at it with her own. He pulled her to him and ran his hand across her bottom, squeezing the soft flesh. Clara sighed.

Cassius turned her around, grabbed her waist and pulled her in close again. His cupped her heavy breasts in his hands and kissed her lightly on the neck.

'You like that, don't you, Clara?'

She nodded, mouth open.

'Cassius,' he whispered.

'I like it, Cassius.'

Just as he found her nipples with his fingers, someone came striding down the passageway. They both froze as the interloper reached the door, but the footsteps went on into the galley. Clara tried to free herself but Cassius held on tight, one arm round her waist, one across her chest. Whoever it was came out of the galley and hurried back along the passageway.

'I should go, sir,' Clara breathed.

Cassius agreed; no sense pushing his luck. He turned her round again and took one last kiss, then let go and opened the cabin door. 'I do hope that we can find a time and place for another such meeting, Clara. Do you?'

She rearranged her hair and picked up the tray before replying. 'I do, sir.'

'I told you to call me Cassius. We are after all quite well acquainted now.'

The pink flush of the girl's cheeks made Cassius grin. Clara walked out into the passageway and he shut the door behind her. Still smiling, he leant back against the wall.

He felt good. The nausea was gone, the ship had survived the night, and, for the briefest moment, all thoughts of Africa and what awaited them there had been forgotten.

If the dark times he'd faced over the last few years had taught him anything, it was that you took your pleasures when and where you could find them, and as far as he was concerned, there was no greater pleasure than getting one's hands on a compliant young woman.

He wandered over to the table, took a swig of wine straight from the bottle and whispered to himself: 'Who needs ladies?'

By midday the spare yard was up and – other than the broken spar lashed to the deck – there were few visible signs of what the *Fortuna* had endured. Once the hold was clear of water, Asdribar rotated duties so that his exhausted crew could get some rest.

And when Desenna scaled the mast again just before sundown, and announced that he could not only still see what they hoped was the *Isis* but also a distant coastline, relief spread swiftly through the ship. Even those who had been sleeping roused themselves and – while Asdribar finally allowed himself a break – Squint led a ceremony of thanks to the gods. Annia, Clara and Indavara all attended, gathering by the altars with the sailors. Before leaving them to it and taking himself off to the bow, Cassius noted two things. The first was Indavara showing particular reverence whenever Poseidon's name was mentioned, the second that he was standing next to Korinth. The night's events had evidently brought an end to any remaining antagonism.

As he wandered past the hatch, Cassius ruminated on why he hadn't stayed to give thanks. It seemed he was experiencing yet another change of heart concerning matters divine. So, apparently the gods had spared them. The others wanted to show their gratitude, ensure they reached land unharmed. Perhaps they were also considering their return journey (Cassius didn't even want to think about that). For him, the ceremony seemed rather pointless.

They were after all engaged in a just and noble mission – the investigation of a brutal murder. Yet the gods had chosen to hinder rather than help. In such circumstances, who could assume that a gesture to the heavens would produce any effect whatsoever?

When this latest assignment was over, Cassius decided, he would either embark on a consistent and genuine programme of worship or forgo such efforts for ever. To do neither one nor the other seemed foolish, and he castigated himself for not confronting the issue earlier. He suspected he would opt for the former, though the latter remained an option taken by a few. His now deceased grandfather had been one, though after the old man passed away, his wife had revealed that he'd continued to make offerings to the gods in private.

Shaking his head at the frustration of it all, Cassius ducked under the bottom of the mainsail and passed the two men left in charge of it. There was only a slight chop on the sea and the *Fortuna* was cutting along quite smoothly; he could walk along the deck with his hands tucked into his belt. He stopped close to the bow and gazed at the horizon. If that was the *Isis* ahead of them, where was she headed?

He had spent some of the afternoon with Asdribar, examining his navigation book and a few well-worn maps. Directly south of the western cape of Crete was the African province of

Cyrenaica, a region dominated by the Five Cities – the Pentapolis. Served by the port of Apollonia, Cyrene itself was the biggest. This was the *Isis's* most likely destination; there were no other major ports for hundreds of miles either east or west along the coast.

Cassius considered what little he knew of Cyrenaica. The territory had belonged to Rome for more than three centuries and – like much of Africa – enjoyed relative peace and prosperity. One local product in particular, the medicinal herb silphium – which was also purported to have aphrodisiac qualities – had contributed to the early prosperity of the city. Recent history had been less kind. Cassius reckoned the earthquake had been about ten years ago and he recalled one of his teachers discussing how much of Cyrene itself had been devastated. The scholar had suggested that, as a consequence, the city's best days were now well behind it.

Was this forgotten province the lair of whoever had struck out at Memor from afar? Sent Dio to kill a man who had done him harm? Cassius thought again of the assassin, still with that rotting head in his hand; not standing in a sea cave now, but walking away into the yellow haze of the desert.

XIX

Cassius intended to sleep for most of the next morning, so was somewhat annoyed to be woken at the second hour. Reaching for his mug of water – which Simo duly passed to him – he sat up and yawned.

'What's going on?'

'I assumed you'd want to be told, sir.'

'Told what?'

'The ship isn't headed to Apollonia, sir.'

'What? Where else is there?'

'Apparently a town to the east named Darnis. We should arrive there this afternoon. The ship is approaching the coast now.'

Despite this development, Cassius fell instantly back into sleep and when he eventually rose at the sixth hour, he wondered if he had imagined the conversation with Simo. The Gaul confirmed he hadn't.

Once he was up, Cassius felt as well rested and strong as he had in days. Despite the uncertainty that lay ahead, his relief that land was close verged on the euphoric. He completed Indavara's blade exercises, washed, then downed a large, tasty lunch of dried sardines and stewed vegetables. Stepping up out of the hatch, he found the Fortuna bathed in brilliant sunshine. Gulls were wheeling and squawking high above the stern.

'Where is everyone?'

Squint, who was steering, thrust his jaw towards the bow. 'That ship's come back out again. Looks like the *Isis*.'

Cassius hurried forward and took his place at the starboard side-rail with Asdribar, Annia, Korinth and Indavara. Young Tarkel was there too, wrapped up in a blanket. All five were examining the ship now heading east towards Egypt. Her light brown sails were full and the wind at her flank was causing her to heel over at a steep angle.

Dead ahead – no more than four or five miles away – lay Africa. The coastline was a mix of white beaches and rocky headlands. Beyond Darnis's small harbour lay the town: a cluster of pale buildings surrounded by fields of gold, yellow and innumerable shades of green.

'Broad stern. Egyptian rig on the headsail,' said Asdribar. 'That's her.'

Annia looked despairingly to the heavens. 'Again we arrive just in time to see a ship leave.'

'Yes,' said Cassius. 'But it was hired by a man who seemed to know exactly where he wanted to go. I'll wager our friend Dio got off.'

'Might have stopped for repairs after the storm,' offered Korinth.

'Possibly,' replied Cassius. 'But if that's so, they completed them remarkably quickly. What do we know about Darnis?'

'Not much,' said Asdribar. 'Other than the harbour's a useful spot if you get caught in bad weather. Remote and isolated. Cyrene is the closest city – fifty miles to the west.'

'Army presence?'

'No idea.'

Annia tapped the side-rail with her hand and turned to face Cassius. 'Should we make for the harbour?'

'We don't have a lot of choice, miss,' said Asdribar. 'The spare yard is a temporary measure. It wouldn't stand up to a battering half as bad as that storm.'

'Captain, if we stop here and my father's killer is aboard that ship, all is lost.'

Cassius glanced at the *Isis* again. 'What are the chances they know we followed them from Crete?'

'They may have seen us on the first day,' replied Asdribar, 'but from then they were only visible from the masthead.'

'So the same would be true for us?' Cassius asked.

'Exactly.'

'We've no chance of catching them?' interjected Indavara.

Asdribar shook his head. 'Not even with a full rig. We've done well to keep pace.'

'Could we signal them?' Cassius asked.

'Yes,' said the captain, 'it's a clear day. But they might not see it. And they probably wouldn't stop even if they did.'

Cassius looked back at Darnis. 'On the balance of probability, I think Dio has left the ship. The town sounds like an ideal place to lose oneself and he may not even be aware of our pursuit. It would make sense for the captain of the *Isis* to head for his next destination while the weather holds.'

'And if Dio didn't get off?' asked Annia.

'Then we'll have to see about finding stables and a local guide, miss, for we shall require overland transport to Egypt.'

━━■8■►━━

Darnis's harbour was even smaller than it looked from the sea and was enclosed by two breakwaters, each about a hundred yards long. They were in the shape of a broken bow, with five straight sections within the curve. The breakwaters were built of grey marine concrete striped with weed and scarred by cracks and holes. There were no other large ships docked, just a couple of small fishing boats. Running along the edge of the harbour was a row of brick-built warehouses, one of which had lost its roof. Between them and the town was a strip of marsh perhaps a quarter-mile wide that could be traversed via a stone causeway.

The *Fortuna*'s sails had been taken down half an hour earlier and the freighter passed through the narrow entrance with only a few feet to spare on either side of the oars. Asdribar ordered Squint to steer the ship towards the east side of the harbour and one of the more solid-looking sections of the breakwater, which was at least equipped with a few mooring rings.

Cassius stood with Indavara and Simo close to the mast, surveying the town – or what was left of it. Evidently Cyrene

224

hadn't been the only settlement in the area to suffer from the earthquake; hardly anything higher than two storeys had been left standing and there were as many ruined buildings as intact ones. The only remaining structures of any height were the thick columns of a roofless temple on the eastern side of the town.

Like all Roman settlements, Darnis had been constructed around a central crossroads. Between the two wide avenues running north–south and east–west was a paved square. Several hundred people had gathered there.

'Wonder what's going on,' said Indavara.

'Who knows?' replied Cassius. 'But with that crowd, news of our arrival will travel fast.'

Cassius had concocted a simple cover story: he and Annia were cousins who had chartered the *Fortuna* for a journey to Cyrene, where they were to attend his sister's marriage the following month. The ship had run into difficulties and put into Darnis for repairs. Cassius had asked Asdribar to explain to the crew the importance of maintaining this pretence. He had also asked Annia to stay aboard, at least for the moment. To his surprise, she had agreed.

'So who am I supposed to be?' Indavara enquired as Asdribar shouted instructions down to Opilio and the oarsmen. 'Why would a man on his way to a wedding have a bodyguard?'

'I am clearly a gentleman,' replied Cassius. 'Gentlemen are usually rich. Rich men usually have bodyguards.'

'So if I'm a bodyguard, why can't I carry a sword?'

'Were you listening? Because I want to draw as little attention to us as possible. Come, you two, we're not going to wait for the gangplank.'

Cassius had opted for his anonymous brown cloak and plain tunic and, like Indavara, was armed only with his dagger.

As they neared the breakwater, the crew tied fenders to the port side of the ship to protect the hull from the concrete. With a few more shouts from Asdribar, the oars were retracted and the *Fortuna* drifted gently to a stop. Desenna was first off with the bow line, closely followed by Cassius and Indavara. The top of the breakwater was two yards above the side-rail and, without a helping hand from Indavara, Simo would have struggled to make it up, especially as he was weighed down with Cassius's satchel.

Once they'd taken a moment to let their unsteady legs adjust, Cassius set off and found considerable concentration was required to avoid the fissures and hollows underfoot. The quite remarkable volume of black-and-white gull shit didn't help matters; scores of the birds flapped into the sky as the interlopers leapt and stumbled their way towards the shore.

The impression of neglect and decay was reinforced by the rest of the harbour. The western side seemed to have silted up completely and a wooden dock that had once joined the two breakwaters had partially collapsed into the water. Behind the dock was a section of gravelled road that broke up the row of warehouses. The door of the closest building was swinging back and forth in the breeze.

As they crunched across the gravel, Cassius looked inside the shadowy interior and saw nothing but a pile of sand. 'Something tells me we're not going to find a harbour master here.'

They reached the causeway. It was built upon a sloping platform of pebbles, constructed of hardy hexagonal flagstones and wide enough for two carts to pass. The strip of marsh was a collage of muddy soil, dark puddles and clumps of high, green reeds. A sweet, fetid smell hung in the air.

'I thought Africa would be dry,' said Indavara.

'Me too,' replied Cassius. 'Notably warmer than Rhodes, though.'

As they walked on, he looked at the distant crowd. They were congregating on the western side of the square, facing some kind of platform on which several figures had appeared.

At the end of the causeway, what had once been a grand arch marked the official boundary of the town. Only the left side of the arch remained – a column perhaps twelve feet high. Cassius perused the still-visible inscriptions. The arch was just twenty years old and listed below the date were the names of the wealthy patrons who had funded the structure. Cassius wondered how many of those families remained.

Running along the northern edge of Darnis on either side of the arch was an old wall composed of huge, deeply weathered blocks of stone. There were several gaps, and no more than two blocks placed on top of each other at any point. Cassius knew that many of the settlements on the North African coast were originally Phoenician and reckoned the wall might even date back that far.

The road continued on through the middle of a sprawling, abandoned dye works. To the right of the road were scores of wide clay bowls sunk into the earth. Here and there were traces of opulent dyes, now diluted by stagnant rainwater. To the left was a large courtyard filled with countless amphorae, some still standing in neat rows.

The townspeople were gathered to the right of a marketplace made up of wooden stalls and stone-built booths for municipal officials. Cassius's sense of foreboding grew as they approached the crowd. He estimated there were about four hundred people gazing at the platform, which was located on the corner of the avenues leading south and west. Now he was closer, Cassius realised what the platform had once been: the pyramidal front section of Darnis's forum. It had inverted during the collapse of the building and now lay atop a pile of rubble and the remains of several columns. Close to the rear of the platform was a dented silver statue of the she-wolf nursing Romulus and Remus.

Standing in front of it were four legionaries clad in full armour with their swords drawn. On his knees between them was a man wearing only a torn tunic. His wrists had been tied together behind him and his head was bowed. The soldiers seemed to be waiting for something.

Some of the townspeople had by now noticed the three new arrivals. They alerted their friends and soon half the crowd were gazing at Cassius, Indavara and Simo, or beyond them – at the *Fortuna*'s mast. But the curiosity faded quickly, and in moments all but a few had turned back towards the platform.

227

Now Cassius examined them. A broader mix was hard to imagine, and they had gathered in distinct groups amongst the throng. There were the poor; brown-skinned and barefoot, some of the children clad in animal skins. Then there were the richer locals, who wore long, baggy-sleeved tunics of red, purple and yellow edged with exotic patterns. The men wore their wealth on their fingers and some of the women were very striking with their long, curly black hair and gleaming bangles on their wrists. And of course the proud Romans, who – even though their families might have been in the region for centuries – made no concession to local fashion. With their leather sandals, well-cut tunics and pale capes and cloaks, they would have looked entirely at home on the streets of the capital. Worryingly, there wasn't a single man in a toga – no one who looked like a local politician or administrator.

Appearances aside, the individuals gathered in front of the ruined forum had two things in common: none were talking loud enough to draw attention to themselves and none looked particularly happy.

'What's going on here?' Indavara murmured.

'Nothing good,' Cassius replied. 'But keep your eyes open. You too, Simo. I know the description's vague but our man might be here.'

Milling around the edge of the crowd in pairs and threes were two dozen more legionaries. They also appeared ready for action and several were brandishing long wooden coshes.

Another soldier made his way up the pile of rubble and on to the platform. He was older than the others, forty at least, with a bowl-shaped head of sandy hair and a drawn face matched by his spare frame. He was wearing no armour, just a tunic split by the diagonal stripe of his bright red sword belt. In his hand was a tatty sheet of paper.

'I think most of you know me. If you don't, I'm Optio Procyon. This here's Optio Mutilus.'

A paunchy soldier of about the same age followed Procyon on to the platform and stood beside him. He too was wearing a red sword belt and a patch over his left eye. Procyon continued, speaking with the low-born accent and weary delivery of a street vendor.

'By order of the Administration, this man . . .'

The optio's voice tailed off as he consulted the others about the prisoner's name. The soldiers all shook their heads. Procyon shrugged.

'. . . this man has been found guilty of both withholding taxable income and slandering officers of the Roman Army. For the first he shall lose a finger, for the second he shall lose his tongue. Let all those present observe the cost of such criminal behaviour and disloyalty to the Empire.'

'Oh, Lord,' whispered Simo.

'Nice,' added Indavara.

Cassius had suspected something of the sort. He could see the hostility towards the soldiers in the eyes of the townspeople, yet no one dared speak. Two local women, hand in hand, tried to leave but one of the legionaries barred their way with his cosh. The women silently retreated. Some of the men glanced warily at the soldiers, who were in turn watching them, studying their charges for any overt sign of disapproval.

Up on the platform, Optio Mutilus untied the captive's hands and shoved him in the back, sending him sprawling on to the grimy white stone. On the edge of the market was a small pen with a dozen goats inside. Apparently sensing the crowd's disquiet, they herded together and circled the pen, knocking against the wicker fence.

Cassius looked beyond the animals. An army officer of about thirty – identifiable by his red tunic and wide belt – was leaning against one of the market stalls, observing proceedings, unnoticed by most of the crowd. He was tall and remarkably well built, with the colouring and tightly curled black hair of a local.

'Wonder why he's just watching?' Cassius said. 'Looks like a native himself.'

'How can you tell from here?' asked Indavara.

'Look at—'

Cassius then realised they were talking about two different people. Beyond the forum, some way up the avenue running south, a single horseman had appeared. He had brought his mount to a halt in the shadow of a building but the silhouette of his crested helmet was clear. He was slouched back in his saddle, watching.

Some of the crowd had noticed the horseman too but attention swiftly returned to the platform. The captive had begun to plead quietly in Latin. Mutilus came forward and planted a boot on the man's wrist, then knelt down beside him.

Simo turned away and walked towards the market. One of the soldiers watched him but did nothing.

'You're just going to let this happen?' Indavara asked Cassius.

'What do you suggest I do?'

'You outrank those two. It's not right.'

'Think for once in your life,' Cassius whispered. 'You want me to announce to what looks like most of the town that I'm with the army? If he's here, I think our friend Dio might just be able to put two and two together, don't you?'

'Talk to one of the officers then.'

Optio Mutilus drew his dagger. The other soldiers held the captive.

'We are here to find a murderer,' said Cassius, 'not stick our noses in where they don't belong. We don't know the situation here. Sometimes it's necessary to make an example of someone.'

Indavara shook his head. 'I'll leave you to enjoy the show then.'

He took himself off to join Simo, who was facing away from the crowd, standing behind a stall not far from the big officer. Cassius saw one of the soldiers attempt to eyeball Indavara. He tried his luck for a couple of moments then gave up, relieved his fellow legionaries hadn't noticed.

Optio Mutilus wielded the long army-issue dagger like a cleaver. As it struck the stone with a metallic whine, many of the people looked away. Others put their hands to their mouths. One man vomited noisily.

The captive didn't cry out. He simply gripped his mutilated hand with the good one, trying to staunch the flow of blood.

Cassius felt something cold twist in his gut. It was all horribly reminiscent of one particularly gruesome evening in Palmyra, but he repeated to himself what he'd told Indavara: there could be no question of intervening.

With a level of organisation that suggested this was not their first time, Optio Mutilus and the men then set about taking off the captive's tongue. Cassius spied one young man in the crowd barely able to contain his rage and two women pleading with him to calm down. Thankfully, none of the soldiers noticed.

One of their compatriots took up a position behind the captive and gripped both sides of his head to keep it straight. Two others stationed on either side hooked their fingers into the man's mouth to keep it open. One flicked some spittle off his hand, pulled a face, then replaced his fingers.

The goats were charging around the pen now, the noise of their hooves drowned out by their high, desperate bleats.

As Mutilus reached for his face, the captive somehow shut his mouth. One of the men pinched his nose but Mutilus waved the effort away. His solution was to jab his dagger handle between the captive's eyes. As the man's head lolled backwards, Mutilus reached inside his mouth and pulled out the tongue, gripping it between finger and thumb. He took aim, then slashed downward, hacking off a good two inches.

Cassius had already looked away but the garbled scream crackled icily down his spine. He glanced back in time to see Mutilus holding the bloodied piece of flesh up to the crowd.

'Think on it, all of you,' said Procyon. 'Speak ill of us, or the centurion, and you might never speak again.'

Mutilus threw the tongue to the ground in front of the platform. To the soldiers' amusement, a dog appeared from somewhere, snatched it up in its jaws and ran off with it. Mutilus took his canteen from his belt and used the water to clean his blade and hands. He then sheathed his dagger and walked down the pile of rubble with Procyon. By now the soldiers had gathered

231

around them. The optios gave a few orders then sauntered along the avenue that led west.

Just in front of Cassius, two young boys came running through the crowd. One was chopping his hand down in the motion of a knife. The other was covering his mouth. They seemed to be enjoying themselves. The captive lay on his side on the platform, motionless. Once the soldiers were gone, several people went to help him. As the crowd began to break up, Cassius looked to the south, at the mounted officer. He turned his horse round and rode away.

Indavara was also on the move, pursuing the other officer, who was heading across the square to the east. Cassius jogged after them and caught up with Indavara just as he spoke.

'Enjoy that, did you?'

The big man turned round. He was armed with a dagger.

'Excuse my bodyguard, sir,' said Cassius, darting between them. 'He used to be a gladiator – rather takes exception to violence as spectacle.'

The officer looked them both over, and Cassius noted that he seemed slightly unsteady on his feet. Even so, he was an impressive character; not just imposing, but even-featured and handsome. He stared hard at Indavara and marched back towards him.

Cassius got out of the way.

The officer stopped a yard from Indavara. He was as tall as Cassius though far broader, and looked down his nose at the bodyguard.

Indavara matched the stare, hands by his belt, ready to move.

Cassius recalled what he'd told him on Rhodes after the incident at the temple, about him becoming a bit of a liability. More like a major liability.

'I asked you if you enjoyed that?' said Indavara.

The officer bent his head towards him until their faces were inches apart. 'Do I look as if I enjoyed it?'

With that, he turned round and strode away.

Indavara watched him until Cassius spoke.

'What in Hades do you think you're doing? You go against me like that again and I'll make damned sure Abascantius hears about it. And if he finds out you put this investigation at risk, I wouldn't expect any more silver ingots, or even a single bloody coin for that matter.'

Indavara looked at him but said nothing.

'Or of course I could tell Annia,' Cassius continued. 'I doubt she'd be particularly impressed either.'

Simo arrived. 'Sir, if you could do without me for a few moments, I could go and help that poor man.'

'By all the gods,' spat Cassius, trying to keep his voice down, 'you two are as bad as each other. I suggest you both remind yourselves why we are here.'

Cassius looked at the people. He needed information, quickly. Approaching the optios or the soldiers was a rather unappealing prospect, particularly with Indavara alongside him. He could try to find the governor's office but that would take time and attract a lot of attention.

A portly man passed by. 'Welcome to Darnis,' he said sourly. 'Sorry you had the misfortune to come ashore here.'

'Our ship needs repairs,' said Cassius, seeing an opportunity. 'Apparently there was another vessel here this morning.'

The man shrugged.

Cassius glanced at the platform. 'That sort of thing a common occurrence?'

The man looked around to check there were no soldiers close by. 'Increasingly.'

Cassius gestured towards the big centurion, who had reached the edge of the square and the road that ran east. 'Strange. He didn't seem to approve.'

'Eborius? Didn't do anything about it though, did he? It's a shame. He was a good man.'

'I take it the optios follow the orders of the other officer – the one on the horse?'

The man looked down at the ground.

'Good luck with the repairs,' he said before hurrying away.

Cassius turned to the east again. Eborius had just disappeared down a side street.

'Come on.'

'Where are we going?' asked Indavara.

'I need to talk to that officer. Can I rely on you to keep your mouth shut?'

Now Indavara glanced at the platform.

Cassius took a step closer to him. 'Back on the ship I thought we'd agreed to each do our own jobs. How about you leave the decision-making to me?'

'I don't want to see things like that,' Indavara said quietly.

'Nor Simo. Nor I. But the affairs of this town are not our concern. Dio is. And we don't have time to waste.'

XX

Eborius passed a tavern, apparently the only occupied building on the street. Lounging around on benches outside were about twenty legionaries, though only a few of them were drinking. They implored the officer to join them but he waved a dismissive hand and continued purposefully on his way.

'Slow down,' Cassius murmured to the others.

Though they inevitably drew the attention of the soldiers, nothing was said as the trio walked by.

This was an area of two- or three-room villas divided by low walls, most of them with a stone-built cistern at the front or rear. Though every dwelling seemed abandoned, the signs of habitation remained: potted plants, either dead or wildly overgrown; small vegetable plots in a similar condition; and, mounted above the doorways, carvings of deities entrusted to guard the home.

Eborius kept his head down as he walked and – despite the considerable amount of drink Cassius guessed he'd imbibed – kept up quite a pace. So by the time he turned right into an alley, they were well past the tavern and away from any prying eyes.

'Eborius!'

The officer stopped and waited as Cassius hurried over to him, Simo and Indavara a few paces behind.

'How do you know my name?' he asked irritably. 'What do you want?'

Cassius now noted that the impressive physique and strong face masked a rather dishevelled individual. He smelt of sweat and wine, his tunic was stained, and the metal of his belt buckle was greasy and dull.

'To talk to you.'

Cassius gestured to Simo, who took the spearhead from the satchel and passed it to him. Cassius unwrapped the top half and showed it to Eborius. 'Imperial Security. I need your help.'

'I'm not in charge here.'

'That doesn't matter. I need information.'

'About what?'

'Is there somewhere we can talk?'

Eborius rubbed his eyes, then sighed. 'This way.'

Cassius returned the spearhead to Simo and they followed the officer along the alley and across the next street. To the left, it ran down as far as the old wall; beyond lay the marsh and a broad expanse of beach. Halfway along the next alley they came to a low, arched doorway and Cassius followed Eborius into what had clearly once been a small temple. Lying in one corner was the top half of a statue carved from some inferior stone. It was identifiable only by the owl cupped in one scarred hand – the goddess Minerva. In the opposite corner was the base of an altar, upon which Eborius sat. As Simo and Indavara followed him inside, Cassius offered his forearm. 'Officer Cassius Quintius Corbulo.'

The older man looked up at him, then took his arm. 'Manius Eborius.'

'Centurion?'

Eborius gave a weary nod.

Cassius took his canteen from his belt. 'Water?'

Eborius drank most of the contents then gave it back. Everything about him was big. Big head, big face, big shoulders, big arms and legs, but every part well formed and in proportion.

Cassius leant back against an ivy-covered wall. 'I'm after a man who calls himself Dio. Short, left-handed. Ring any bells?'

'No.'

'I believe he arrived this morning aboard that ship the *Isis*.'

'I heard she came in. Unless it's a supply ship, no one takes much notice these days.'

'I need to find him quickly,' said Cassius. 'If he did get off, he may have left the town. What about the governor's office? Does anyone there keep track of new arrivals?'

Eborius snorted. 'Did anyone come and meet you?'

'I take it that order has rather broken down here.'

'You could say that. Though I suppose there is order. Of a kind.'

'That other officer's kind? Who is he?'

'Centurion Valgus Carnifex.'

'I may need his help. Can you take me to him?'

'That would be difficult. He and I are not on the best of terms.'

'I see. It seems I shall just have to start asking around then.'

Eborius frowned. 'I would advise against that.'

'I don't seem to have a great deal of choice. Somebody might have seen the man, might know him. Every hour counts. He may already be gone.'

'Gone? Gone where? Travel more than ten miles in any direction and you're liable to find yourself face to face with a band of Maseene.'

'Maseene?'

'Local tribesmen. They've recently taken to attacking anyone they come across who doesn't speak and look like them.'

'The army has lost control of the area?'

'Not Darnis and its immediate surroundings. But beyond that . . . let's just say your short friend is unlikely to have set off for anywhere, unless he's anxious to meet his end at the point of a javelin.'

'I haven't heard of any uprisings in this area.'

'I'm fairly sure nobody on the other side of the Green Sea has heard anything from Darnis in a while.' Eborius kicked a lump of rock into the wall. 'Which is exactly how certain people want it to stay.'

'If you're so convinced he wouldn't have left, then there's all the more reason to think someone here will know something. Where do you suggest I start?'

'Have you been listening to me? The situation here is complicated and you are a stranger. You could easily run into trouble

237

blundering around unescorted. And Carnifex would soon hear of it.'

'So? He is bound by law to assist me.'

Eborius almost laughed at this. 'He is bound by nothing but his one and only interest: maintaining and protecting the profitable little empire he has carved out for himself here. I suggest you keep quiet about your true identity and leave in the morning.'

'That's not possible.'

'What has he done anyway, this man you seek?'

'He is an assassin.'

'Who did he kill?'

Cassius wondered if he hadn't already told Eborius too much. But the centurion had in turn revealed plenty himself, and it seemed unlikely he would cooperate unless he knew the true importance of the investigation.

'The Deputy Commander of the Service. On Rhodes, a week ago. Now do you understand why I cannot just turn round and leave?'

Eborius considered this for a moment. 'How many men do you have with you?'

Cassius gestured to Indavara and Simo.

'Why so few? If you're engaged in such an important mission.'

'Let's just say it was all rather rushed. In any case, if I'd arrived with a squad of men in tow, we'd never find Dio, would we? From what you've said I doubt this Carnifex will allow me to requisition his troops, so I appear to have only one source of help.'

Eborius's face tightened and he scratched the back of his neck.

'His name was Augustus Marius Memor,' Cassius continued. 'He was beheaded. In his study. He had a wife and two daughters. The oldest girl is on the ship.'

Eborius said nothing, but Cassius didn't mind that. The centurion seemed to have accepted he was duty-bound to assist, and judging by his face, the emotive tugs had done their job.

'What about your century – your men?' asked Cassius.

'If you followed me from the square you would have seen most of them. At the tavern.'

'What?'

'Long story.'

Eborius glanced at the elongated shadows on the cracked tiled floor of the temple. 'We haven't much light left. Let me make a few enquiries.'

'And then?'

'I'll come down to the causeway at the third hour of night. Wait for me by the arch. Is there any other information on the man?'

Eborius actually seemed to have sobered up during the conversation, but Cassius repeated all the details he knew twice. He also told him about the cover story and the damage to the *Fortuna*.

'Will the captain be able to make his repairs here?'

Eborius held up a hand. 'One thing at a time. That can wait until tomorrow. Keep all the men on the ship for now.'

'As you wish. Thank you for your help.'

'My pleasure,' said Eborius unconvincingly. 'What was your name again?'

———8———

They arrived back at the *Fortuna* to find the ceremony of arrival had just concluded. The crew were gathered on the deck in good spirits, readying themselves for a night in Darnis. Cassius found Asdribar at the stern, gazing out to sea. One altar was still slick with blood from one of the cockerels, and feathers littered the deck. Smoke was rising from the galley and drifting out over the harbour.

'Captain, you need to speak with your men. I'm afraid they can't visit the town tonight.'

'I hope that's a joke.'

Asdribar only relented once Cassius told him what he'd seen and heard.

'Gods,' said the Carthaginian. 'I'll need another sacrifice to keep the boys happy – a barrel of the Rhodian stuff.'

'Aside from the dangers of the town, it's essential that our real purpose here not be revealed. I know you've briefed your men but we both know how drink can loosen tongues.'

'We'll have to go in at some point,' said Asdribar. 'We need timber for the new yard. This centurion – perhaps I might speak with him too?'

'I don't see why not.'

Asdribar sighed. 'I'll go and break the news then. If you hear a splash, grab a boathook – because they might just throw me over the side.'

———◆8◆———

In fact, the crew's voluble protests lasted about as long as it took Asdribar to open the barrel of cinnamon wine. They swiftly relocated to the smoky warmth of the galley and were soon throwing insults at each other and bellowing songs.

'By Jupiter,' said Cassius as Simo draped his cloak over his shoulders, 'I hope this doesn't go on all night.'

'Would you like me to come along to this meeting, sir?'

'No, you can stay here.'

'Me too?' asked Indavara, leaning against the door frame.

'Yes. I shan't be long and Asdribar's accompanying me.'

Korinth wove his way out of the galley with a jug in his hand. 'There you are!' he bawled. 'Come and have a drink with the lads.'

Before Indavara could protest, Korinth had grabbed him and dragged him into the galley. For a moment Cassius thought Indavara might take exception to this but a cheer went up when the others saw him. Cassius walked into the passageway and looked on; Indavara was grinning as the sailors made space for him by the hearth.

Korinth turned round, eyes struggling to focus. 'And you, sir?'

'A tempting invitation but no thanks.'

Korinth turned his attentions to Simo. The Gaul tried to retreat into the cabin but the big sailor came after him too. 'Come on, lad!'

'No, thank you, I really would—'

Cassius laughed as Korinth hauled Simo out of the cabin by his belt, then pushed him into the galley.

'Go on, Simo! It'll do you good.'

Asdribar was waiting up on deck. He too had his cloak wrapped round him and was carrying a lantern. Cassius gestured towards the gangplank. As he followed the captain, the deckhouse door opened.

'Officer Corbulo?' said Annia with an appeasing smile.

'Yes?'

Cassius had already given her a brief – and judiciously edited – report of the afternoon's events.

'You will let me know if you learn anything more?'

'I said I would, miss.'

'Thank you.'

Cassius looked for a glimpse of Clara, but Annia closed the door.

'Bloody girl,' Cassius muttered as he crossed the gangplank and joined Asdribar on the breakwater.

Apart from the fact that he had plenty else to occupy him, he had decided to forgo any further pursuit of Annia, and not only because of his new-found interest in Clara. He had simply reached the conclusion that she didn't find him attractive. This didn't happen often – and was initially rather frustrating – but he now found he hardly cared. Cassius had never understood those fellows who pursued unrequited interest. If a woman didn't like him, he found he soon ceased to like her. Let Indavara try his hand if he wished. Good luck to him.

'I've seen some shithole harbours in my time,' said Asdribar, 'but this one barely deserves the name.'

Even with the powerful lantern, negotiating the ageing break-water in the dark was quite a challenge.

'The rest of the town's no better,' replied Cassius. 'Ruins and empty buildings everywhere. It seems the earthquake pretty much killed the place off but it looks like a long, slow death.'

As they crossed the causeway, a light rain began to fall, pattering against the stone and the drier patches of the marsh. Asdribar pulled up his hood but Cassius kept his down – he didn't want to restrict either his hearing or his vision. There was no sign of Eborius at the arch. They looked along the road towards the town; there were only a few smudges of light and not a sound to be heard.

'It really is dead,' observed Asdribar. Just as he was about to sit down on the wall, they heard the rustling of feet moving through grass. A big shape appeared from behind the standing side of the arch.

'It's me,' came the rich, deep voice. Eborius scowled as Asdribar held the lantern up to his face. 'Who are you?'

'This is Asdribar,' replied Cassius, 'captain of the ship. He wanted to speak with you too.'

The scowl remained.

'How did you get on?' asked Cassius.

'A few people saw the *Isis* come in. A few people saw the crew walk into town and buy some supplies. And a few people saw them cast off again two hours later. No one saw or heard anything about a passenger.'

Cassius blew out his cheeks. 'Wonderful.'

'Of course that doesn't mean nobody else came ashore. It wouldn't be difficult to slip into town unnoticed if you were trying to avoid attention.'

The rain was getting harder. Eborius and Cassius pulled up their hoods.

'Tell me,' said Cassius. 'I've seen the state of the forum, but what about the rest of the administrative buildings? Is there anywhere with records on the population?'

'I think documents like that were moved to the library, though I doubt anyone's looked at them in a while.'

'Could you get me access to them?'

'Probably. I—'

'Gentlemen,' interjected Asdribar as water dripped from his hood past his face. 'There is a dry and warm ship just a few moments' walk away. Can I suggest we adjourn there?'

Cassius turned to Eborius. 'Well?'

The big centurion shrugged.

'Tell me, sir,' said Asdribar warmly. 'Have you ever sampled the delights of Rhodian cinnamon wine?'

While Asdribar escorted Eborius below, Cassius called in on Annia. She would inevitably find out about the centurion's visit, so he thought he might as well invite her along. Clara opened the deckhouse door but Cassius only had time to smile before Annia appeared. She snatched a shawl from Clara and followed Cassius to the hatch.

'So we're still not even sure if Dio got off here?' she asked.

'No. But all the crew of the *Isis* did was buy some provisions – only three days after leaving Crete, which is suspicious in itself. I've nothing definitive yet but I'm sure this man can help us.'

With the raucous goings-on in the galley, Asdribar had placed four stools in a circle just beyond the steps. Just as Cassius and Annia arrived, Opilio appeared carrying a small brazier. Behind him came Tarkel and Desenna, who placed some bricks on the floor for Opilio to mount the brazier on. Inside was a pile of glowing coals giving off plenty of heat. As the galley crew left, Asdribar issued more orders. 'Opilio – those Syrian glasses, and bring us something to eat.'

Centurion Eborius seemed rather surprised to be in the presence of a young lady and nodded shyly when Cassius introduced Annia. Asdribar encouraged them all to sit down, then poured three good measures from a jug of the cinnamon wine when Opilio returned with the glasses. Annia refused the offer of a drink. Opilio had also brought two bowls, one full of dates, one full of almonds.

'There, Centurion,' said Asdribar. 'A bit of *Fortuna* hospitality for you.'

Eborius raised his glass. 'That's her name?'

'*Fortuna Redux.*'

'I hope that proves prophetic.'

'These records at the library you mentioned,' said Cassius. 'Any idea what's there?'

'Perhaps tax documentation. Although that might be kept at the mansion now.'

'The mansion?'

'Big villa overlooking the plain just south of Darnis. Used to belong to the Gratus family but when they left Carnifex took it over.'

'There's no barracks in the town?'

'There is. My century – the Second – uses it.'

'Is Carnifex's century as undermanned as yours?'

Eborius gave a grim smile. 'Oh no. The First now has about a hundred and forty men.'

'But you have—'

'Thirty-seven.' Eborius shook his head. 'Gods, it all sounds so bizarre now I hear myself speak of it. I suppose I've become used to the way things are here.' He looked around at the others. 'Perhaps I should explain. It will all seem even stranger if I don't.'

'Please,' said Cassius.

Eborius took a long swig of wine before beginning. 'You know about the earthquake, of course.'

'Ten years back, wasn't it?' said Asdribar.

'That was to the west. Hit the Five Cities badly. We felt it here, but no, the one that struck close to Darnis was just five years ago. Knocked all the big buildings down, ruined the aqueduct, killed several hundred. Things had been good here before. There have always been two centuries: the First and the Second. Theoretically, they're attached to the Third Augustan Legion, but they've been stationed here for decades – to protect the coast

244

road and the estates. The centurion of the First was always considered the senior man. His name was Donicus – he'd been here almost twenty years. He was overseeing a detachment working on the sewers when the earthquake hit. He was killed. Crushed. A few weeks later his replacement arrived.'

'Carnifex?' said Cassius.

'Carnifex.'

Resting his elbows on his knees, Eborius hunched over, staring at the glowing coals of the brazier. 'The main problem was the aqueduct – it runs fifty miles from the interior into the west side of Darnis. There are no rivers here, so the water that supplied the whole area came from a system of barrages and cisterns. The Maseene are nomads – they move with the season, with their animals. When Rome first settled this territory centuries ago, they lost much of their best grazing land. Initially there were conflicts but eventually a compromise emerged; the building of the aqueduct allowed the creation of a series of wells and reservoirs to help them water their animals.'

'But without the aqueduct . . .' said Cassius.

'Even then the situation could have been salvaged – if Carnifex had put all our manpower into the works and the governor had secured the engineers and money we needed. His name was Mordanticus – ineffective and corrupt but Donicus had always kept his worst excesses in check. Mordanticus and Carnifex together were a disastrous combination. With the water supply gone, it was only a matter of time.'

Eborius shook his head and took a breath. 'I tried to arbitrate between the Maseene elders and Mordanticus, but he wasn't interested in helping them. Carnifex told him he didn't have to; said *he* could take care of them. Then, about two years ago, the raids started. There'd always been the odd problem – stolen livestock and so on – but all pretty small in scale. Then one estate lost a whole herd of goats and the landowner retaliated by fouling the nearest tribe's well. From there things escalated. Again, if Carnifex and Mordanticus had been minded to negotiate, some sort of agreement might have been possible, but they always just

245

backed the landowners. The raids got worse. Some of the richer families – those with the biggest estates – had left after the earthquake. And once it became obvious they weren't safe, the rest began to leave too. Then Mordanticus and Carnifex realised they could actually benefit from the situation. There was no hope for the southern estates, all that territory is in Maseene hands now, but those that border Darnis – those could be protected. So Mordanticus and Carnifex began buying them up. Now each estate is nominally run by retired men from the First Century. All done in the name of Rome of course. It's incredibly inefficient – I doubt the whole territory produces a tenth of what it once did – but Carnifex controls thousands of acres and creams off the profits for himself.'

'Himself?' interjected Cassius. 'What about this Mordanticus?'

'Died a while back. Kicked in the head by his horse. Carnifex decided the chief collector of taxes – a man named Lafrenius Leon – should replace him. Leon is governor in name only; he is quite happy to stay in his villa and leave Carnifex in charge. Mordanticus only maintained a small staff anyway, and most of them have gone now too.'

'What a mess,' said Cassius.

'The local peasants have never had it easy, but they at least used to be able to make some money from their own little bits of land. The tax rate on produce was a quarter for more than two centuries. Mordanticus raised it to a third and now Carnifex has made it one half. So as if it wasn't bad enough to turn the Maseene against us, now the peasants hate Rome too. I've tried to tell him how it will end but he never listens to me. He never did, actually. He said I'd always side with them because I'm one of them.'

Eborius looked around the group as if he was confessing something. 'I come from a village in the mountains to the south. My mother was Maseene.'

He paused for another swig of wine.

'Do you know we once had one of the best-functioning assemblies in the province? People used to vote. We had a strong court too. And the Maseene worked on the estates in the summer months. Gods, it seems like another world now.'

'Surely someone could have gone over Carnifex's head?' said Cassius. 'To the provincial administration in Cyrene?'

'They have their own problems to deal with. You must have heard what the Great Earthquake did to the rest of Cyrenaica. In any case, I've written to anyone and everyone, the governor and the prefect of the Third Augustan included. Six months ago the prefect assigned a tribune to investigate. Carnifex sent him back a week later with a bulging bag of gold coins and a slave girl. As long as our esteemed centurion keeps order – and enough money flowing up to the right people – nobody cares.'

Cassius noted how taken aback Asdribar and Annia were by this. Hearing how Carnifex had established this personal fiefdom had shocked him; revelations of corruption in the army were less of a surprise.

'And this situation with the two centuries?' he said. 'Presumably Carnifex forced the men to join him?'

Eborius smiled bitterly. 'He didn't have to. My legionaries get a regular wage –– when Leon sees fit to pass on the money, that is – but Carnifex's soldiers collect the taxes and he allows them all manner of kickbacks. The delightful Optio Procyon, for example, doesn't take coin. He prefers an hour or two with a man's daughter, and he's none too picky about her age. Carnifex is a master at finding money, even in an area run as chaotically as Darnis. On top of what he takes off the taxes there is a constant flow of 'gifts' to the mansion. He even claims pay for three full centuries from the coffers in Cyrene.'

'And this afternoon, in the square?'

As he spoke, Cassius saw the curious look on Annia's face; he'd chosen not to tell her the gruesome details.

'Cutting out tongues is his latest tactic,' Eborius replied. 'That man was a peasant. I expect one of his own overheard him and sold him out. It's one of the few ways they can still make money.'

Annia decided she would have a drink after all. Asdribar topped up the other glasses.

Eborius continued: 'That was nothing, by the way – today. You should see what he does with the Maseene he has taken to the mansion.'

He glanced at Annia.

'Don't halt on my account, Centurion,' she said.

'Let's put it this way – crucifixion is the best they can hope for.'

'By all the gods,' said Cassius. 'If money's all this man is interested in, can't we just bribe him to secure his cooperation?'

'Possibly. But if Carnifex finds out you're with the Service, he'll be a lot more interested in you than this man Dio. Sure you want that kind of attention?'

'Point taken.'

'I will give you what help I can. But if you want my advice, you'll leave as soon as the ship is ready.' He addressed Asdribar: 'Captain, I'll send someone down to you at the first hour. He'll take you to a man who can help with your repairs.'

Eborius put down his glass. He looked ready to leave.

'Centurion,' said Annia. 'Do you think this man Dio is here?'

'I don't know, miss, but we have always had our share of unsavoury characters here in Darnis. Amongst those that have stayed on, many have no choice. They are exiles.'

'There are exiles *here*?' asked Cassius.

'Of course. Because Darnis is so remote, it has always been used as a destination for those banished from Rome.'

'I didn't know that,' said Cassius.

Annia had noticed the gleam in his eye. 'You mean—'

'Yes. The Service might have investigated some of these people – the issues that led to their exile. Your father may have been involved.'

Cassius turned to Eborius. 'Thank you, Centurion. You have been most helpful.'

XXI

Eborius was true to his word. One of his legionaries arrived at the harbour not long after dawn to collect Asdribar, and was also carrying a message for Cassius. The centurion had arranged a meeting with someone who could help them gain access to the local records; the legionary would take Cassius there before escorting Asdribar to Darnis's sole remaining supplier of timber.

Cassius decided he would need both Simo and Indavara and took considerable pleasure in rousing them. The sailors had shown little mercy the previous night and it was hard to tell who was in the worse state. Indavara's eyes seemed to be glued shut, while Simo – for the first time Cassius could recall – had failed to get up before his master.

'Look at you two,' said Cassius as they walked past the dye works into the town. 'A lot of use you'll be to me today.'

'I really can't apologise enough, sir,' said Simo.

'They just wouldn't stop,' mumbled Indavara, head down.

'They certainly didn't stop singing,' added Annia. To allow her and Clara some time off the ship, Cassius had agreed that the pair of them could accompany Asdribar, who'd also brought Korinth along.

'Never drink with sailors,' advised Cassius. 'They down even more than soldiers.'

'Bloody right,' said Korinth.

'No chance, sir,' retorted Noster, the friendly legionary from the Second Century. Though he was at least forty and had lost most of his wispy brown hair, his face had a keen, youthful quality. Given the circumstances, Cassius imagined the few soldiers who'd remained loyal to Eborius were probably as virtuous a group as one might find in the army.

'There's only one way to find out for sure,' said Asdribar. 'A competition. What's the local stuff like, Noster?'

'A bit sharp but good and strong.'

'Can't we talk about something else?' pleaded Indavara.

—■8■—

The centre of Darnis was almost deserted. Just two of the market stalls were occupied and the only other people in view were an old woman brushing her courtyard and a pair of legionaries with another man on the far side of the square.

'They with your lot?' Cassius asked Noster. He didn't know what Eborius had disclosed to the legionary, but had decided to stick strictly to the cover story while with the others. It wasn't too hard to act the curious visitor.

'That's right, sir, they're with the Second. Generally we look after the town; the First patrol the countryside. We usually keep ourselves to ourselves.'

'But not yesterday.'

'No,' replied Noster gravely. 'Things have been difficult these last few months. We don't all approve of the tactics certain people use.'

Noster had a figure 'II' sewn on to the sleeve of his tunic in yellow thread. He was one of the least muscular soldiers Cassius had ever seen but walked with the effortless stride of a man who could march all day without breaking a sweat. He looked across the square at the other fellow with the legionaries: a lean, balding individual in a white cloak edged with purple.

'And that's our so-called governor.'

'Lafrenius Leon,' said Cassius.

'None other.'

'Was that the forum?' asked Annia as Noster led them along the avenue to the west. Cassius now noted from a bronze sign that it was the Via Cyrenaica.

250

'Indeed, miss,' replied the legionary. 'I remember when it was rare to find fewer than two hundred people gathered there of a morning: councillors, clerks, priests, patrons and their retinues. They used to post announcements on the message board every day. I enjoyed that duty. Saved me going to the temple to see family and friends.'

'You still have family here now?' Annia asked him.

'Just me and my wife.'

'What's that smell?' asked Korinth.

'See the aqueduct?' The legionary pointed to an area of higher ground three or four miles to the south-west. The pale, arched structure stretched away south towards the interior. 'Looks all right from here but no water flows. Sewers are clogged up. Be grateful it's not summer.'

The section of the Via Cyrenaica closest to the square had clearly once been porticoed, but every last column now lay on the ground, poking out on to the street from under broken roof slabs.

'That's new,' observed Noster. Scrawled on one of the columns in red paint was a line of Latin: *THE GODS WILL PUNISH THEM.*

Beyond the fallen portico, about twenty people were gathered around half a dozen stores housed in small, stone-built villas. Here again was a mix of those in typical Roman attire and locals in their colourful garb.

The new arrivals attracted quite a bit of interest.

'Let's try and blend in,' Cassius told the others quietly as he took his satchel from Simo.

The group broke up, drifting away to investigate the goods on offer. One of the vendors asked Asdribar if he was from the ship while Annia and Clara were soon being set upon by a merchant selling jewellery. Indavara and Simo wandered over to a butcher's. Hanging from a hook under an awning was the skinned carcass of what appeared to be a giant rabbit. Indavara eyed it curiously.

'Gazelle,' said Noster. 'Not bad if you cook it long enough.'

Cassius followed the legionary to the store furthest from the square. Here, a middle-aged woman presided over a selection of dried fruit and nuts laid out on wooden trays. She had just finished serving a young girl, who departed with an amphora full to the brim with raisins. Cassius saw something moving on the floor and realised there was a little black-haired monkey sitting next to a flat piece of stone. It was wearing a miniature tunic and was attached to the woman's chair by a collar and chain. She put down a bowl of nuts. The monkey took one, smashed it against the stone, threw the shell to one side, then gave the kernel back to its mistress.

'Remarkable,' said Cassius.

The woman looked up. 'Morning, sirs.'

Recognising Noster, she lowered her voice. 'Ah. Go ahead. He's already here.'

As they walked round the stall, she offered another nut to the monkey but this time it kept its hands down and looked away. Cursing, the woman threw the nut at the little creature, who shook his head at her, then scratched his nether regions.

'What's wrong with Adrianus?' asked Noster.

The woman tutted. 'One of his moods.'

Behind the stall were stone steps leading down to a structure built entirely underground.

'A cellar without a house,' said Cassius.

'Actually it was a house. A local technique – cool in the summer, easy to heat in winter. They use it to store their stock.'

Noster took a wary look around before hurrying down the steps.

'Is all this secrecy really necessary?' Cassius asked as he followed. 'I can't see any soldiers around.'

'They're not the only ones who report to Carnifex,' explained Noster.

At the bottom of the steps, a middle-aged man was transferring bunches of herbs from a barrel into wooden trays like those from the stall. He nodded to Noster and aimed a thumb over his shoulder. Behind him were passageways to three rooms, all lined with brick and lit by square glass skylights in dire need of cleaning.

'In here,' came the sonorous tones of Eborius from the room to the right. They found the big centurion leaning against a wall beside a woman of about sixty who was sitting on a chair. She was wearing faded red robes and her arms were weighed down with dozens of bangles. She had a pinched, narrow face and a healthy head of greying hair tied up with a band the same colour as her robes.

'Morning,' said Cassius.

'Morning,' said Eborius. 'This is Hamman. She works at the library. Apparently most of the records are kept in two storerooms. They're locked but she thinks she can get to the key. At certain times of the week – tomorrow afternoon for example – only she and the clerk are there. He's one of Leon's men, lazy and stupid; usually takes a long sleep after lunch. We can probably get you into the storerooms for an hour or two.'

Cassius spoke clearly to make sure the elderly woman understood him. 'Thank you for helping us.'

'It doesn't come free,' she said in faultless Latin.

'Ah.'

'An aurei now. One afterwards.'

Cassius looked at Eborius, who shrugged.

'Best I can do.'

'These records. What exactly is in there?'

'It's a mess,' said Hamman. 'Leon's only interested in keeping an eye on who's paid what at the end of every month. Most of it was recovered from the forum. There's definitely some tax documentation, probably some electoral records too.'

'Will I be able to take anything out?'

'I'd prefer it if you didn't but no one's been in there in months, so I doubt anything would be missed. But you cannot get caught. You *must* not.'

'I'll be careful.'

The old woman stuck out her hand.

'In a moment.' Cassius reached inside the satchel and took out the list he and Simo had completed on the *Fortuna*. 'Would you also have a look at this for me? Tell me if you recognise any of those names.'

The old woman snatched the list, then stood up so she could read it below the skylight. Cassius took a gold coin from his money bag and waited for her to finish. Eborius paced round the chamber, sipping from his canteen. Judging by the smell, there was as much wine in there as water.

Hamman shook her head briskly, then handed back the list.

Cassius dropped the gold aureus into her open palm. 'Tomorrow then?'

'I'll make the arrangements,' said Eborius.

Hamman ambled away towards the stairs.

'You want me to check that as well, I presume?' asked the centurion.

'Please. I should have asked you last night.'

Eborius hung his canteen from his belt and examined the sheet. Cassius wandered over to the steps and watched Hamman disappear from view. The stall owner and his trays were gone too. In one of the amphorae were shiny, freshly washed black olives. Cassius was considering trying one when Eborius spoke.

'Helvetius Cornix. I know that name. I believe he's still here.'

Cassius hurried over to him and looked at the list. 'Helvetius Cornix. Some kind of a scandal, I think. I can't remember the details of it, nor the outcome.'

'He is a small man, not particularly distinctive.'

'Do you know where he lives?'

'No, but I can find out.'

Cassius took the sheet and started towards the steps.

Eborius didn't move. 'Corbulo. Leave it to me. We can't be seen together asking questions in town. I'll come down to the ship at midday – let you know if I've made any progress.'

'And until then?'

'You'll just have to be patient. If Carnifex hears we're up to something, we'll both be in the shit.'

The thought of idly waiting around while Memor's murderer

might be freely roaming the streets of Darnis didn't sit well with Cassius, but he didn't seem to have a great deal of choice.

'Very well,' he said, heading for the steps once more. 'Midday, then.'

'Midday.'

——◆8◆——

The timber yard was on the Via Roma – the avenue that ran south from the square, perpendicular to the Via Cyrenaica. Once past yet more fallen porticoes and horizontal columns, they came to what had once been the baths. Only a few bits of wall were left standing. The roof had fallen straight into the main pool and blocks of sundered stone lay atop each other in the filthy water.

'Twenty people died in there,' said Noster as they passed by.

'Where were you when it happened?' asked Annia.

'Out on manoeuvres with Eborius,' replied the legionary.

'What time of day was it?' asked Asdribar.

'The sixth hour. Eborius tried to keep us together but all the men just dropped their shields and weapons and ran back to the town.'

'For their families,' said Annia.

Noster nodded. 'I was lucky. My wife was outside, in the garden. She watched the house come down. The first night was the worst. You could hear people all over, stuck under the rubble. There weren't enough of us to help them all, so Eborius decided we should concentrate on those that sounded youngest. But some we just couldn't find. The second night was quiet. Sometimes the ruins shift and another body turns up. Usually they're just bones now.'

The next section of the avenue turned out to be the busiest part of the town they'd seen. Beyond two large, fallen apartment buildings were a series of inhabited villas with washing hanging from lines and children playing outside. Some of the villas were newly built, and even a cursory glance showed they'd been constructed with durability in mind.

Not far past the last of them was a fenced yard containing a broad warehouse, which also looked new. Close to the front of the property, surrounded by the only patch of grass, was a tall gum tree. At the base of the pale, mottled trunk sat a young girl playing with carved wooden toys. Seeing the group arrive, she ran over and opened the gate for them.

'Thank you,' said Noster.

In front of the warehouse was a cart. A man appeared from behind it and waved. 'Morning, Noster.'

'Morning, Maro. I've got some clients for you.'

Noster introduced Asdribar and Korinth, then the timber merchant led the three of them back towards the warehouse.

The little girl grabbed Annia's hand. 'Do you want to see my toys?'

'No, thank you.'

'You can show me if you want,' said Clara, trying to coax the girl away from her mistress.

'I want to show *her*!'

'Oh, very well,' said Annia, and the two women followed the girl towards the tree.

Despite the predominance of blue in the sky, cloud had arrived overhead and released a light rain. Cassius glanced at the warehouse. 'Come, Simo, I need to discuss something with you.'

Indavara walked under the tree. 'I'm going to lie down.'

Cassius and Simo set off across the yard as drops of rain darkened the dusty ground.

'One of the names on that list we made is Helvetius Cornix. Do you remember anything of the case?'

'I do recall the name, sir. I think it was from the documents I dealt with.'

'Obviously, or I would be able to remember more. I must have reviewed it though.'

'Er . . .'

They walked around the cart, which was stacked with freshly cut timber complete with branches and leaves, and sheltered from the rain under the warehouse roof. The others were sitting at a table. Maro was making notes with a piece of charcoal.

'Come on, Simo. Think.'

'Sorry, sir, I—'

'Yes, yes, I know. The wine's still clouding your mind. Perhaps I should remind you of the time I got home from an all-nighter at the second hour and was delivering an extended oration on the works of Marcus Antistius Labeo by the fourth.' Cassius looked up at the white, bulbous cloud. 'Helvetius Cornix . . . Helvetius Cornix.'

'Would you like me to run back to the *Fortuna* to fetch the documentation, sir?'

Cassius didn't answer; he was looking at a long-legged spider descending upside down from one of the branches sticking out of the cart.

'Helvetius Cornix, Helvetius Cornix . . .'

He was vaguely aware of a horse galloping along the Via Roma.

———8———

Indavara heard the horse too but was happy to stay where he was, eyes shut, lying flat on his back under the tree. Thankfully, the ache at the front of his head was at last starting to recede. The little girl was describing her toys to Annia and Clara. Simply by listening, he was able to picture each one.

As the horseman came closer her voice was lost in the pounding of hooves. The first voice Indavara heard when the rider had passed was Clara's.

'Oh,' the maid said thoughtfully.

'What?' asked Annia.

'That man. I think I've seen him somewhere before.'

'Where?'

Indavara sat up.

'I'm not sure,' said Clara.

Annia turned to Indavara. 'She's never left Rhodes.'

Indavara scrambled to his feet, ran to the gate and vaulted over it. He looked along the Via Roma. The rider was thirty yards away already but still close enough to see he was not the largest of men.

'Get Corbulo!'

He set off down the road.

——◆8◆——

'Helvetius Cornix, Helvetius—'

'Officer! Officer Corbulo!'

Cassius darted round the side of the cart and saw Annia, holding up her stola as she ran across the yard.

He came out to meet her, Noster and the others not far behind. 'What is it?'

'A man rode past. Clara recognised his face. It could be him.'

Cassius looked past her through the fence and saw Indavara sprinting along the road. 'Noster, with me!'

Clara watched Cassius speed past. She had her hands on the shoulders of the little girl, who looked like she was about to cry.

Once over the gate, Cassius and Noster bolted after Indavara, who had just reached the inhabited villas. The rider – whose mount was tall and dark – was already a long way away.

'Recognise him?' asked Cassius between breaths.

'Not from here,' answered Noster.

As they ran past the houses, several dozen of the townspeople now sheltering from the rain looked on.

'Caesar's balls,' said Cassius. 'So much for blending in.'

——◆8◆——

Indavara had already given up his attempts to look casual; it wasn't easy while sprinting along a wet road trying to keep up with a horse. The rider slowed his mount to a trot as he crossed the town square heading east. He now had a hood up and hadn't looked back once.

By the time Indavara reached the market, the rider was well on his way along the Via Cyrenaica. With no way of knowing how far he was going, Indavara tried to slow his breathing, prepare for a long haul. But once on the road, he could see that the buildings petered out after a mile or so. Assuming the rider wasn't leaving the town, he would at least be able to see where he turned off.

Indavara felt himself slowing; it was a while since he'd run like this and the slippery paving stones and his sodden tunic didn't help. Just as he lengthened his stride, the rider veered towards the right side of the road.

———8———

Attracting more stares from a couple of market vendors, Cassius and Noster cut across the square. They'd been close enough to see Indavara turn east and Cassius reckoned they hadn't lost much ground. Despite Noster's disadvantage in years and height, the sprightly legionary had easily kept pace. When they reached the road, however, both the rider and Indavara had disappeared.

But the Via Cyrenaica wasn't empty. Six soldiers on horseback trotted out from a side street to the left, every man clad in helmet and armour. They came to a halt in the middle of the road and stared at the villas on the other side.

'Yours?' asked Cassius as they slowed to a walk.

Noster shook his head. 'First Century. Wonder what they're doing in town.'

———8———

Indavara knelt by the corner of a low stone wall and peered round the edge. The soldiers were about fifty feet away, half the group obscured behind a villa. He pulled back his head as one of them glanced in his direction.

'Shit.'

The rider had turned off about a hundred yards ahead of him. He'd been considering whether to continue up the road or try to find a short-cut when the first of the legionaries had appeared, making the decision for him. He'd sprinted into the nearest side street, then turned down an alley.

Cassius had briefed him earlier about what Eborius had disclosed, but Indavara had no idea which century the soldiers were from or what they would do if they saw him. He peered round the corner again. One of the legionaries was pointing to the east and the two others he could see were also looking that way.

He stood up and ran across the street into the next alley. There was no shout or clatter of hooves. He ran on.

— 8 —

'Shit,' said Cassius.

'That's not good,' added Noster as the soldiers urged the horses off the avenue into the maze of villas. He and Cassius were standing still, trying not to look as if they were watching the legionaries.

'Hope they don't run into your friend,' Noster continued. 'Carnifex's men aren't known for their restraint.'

'Neither's my friend.'

— 8 —

'Got you.'

Indavara looked across the street. Twenty yards away, the rider had just led his horse into a high-walled courtyard. He was indeed short, his head lower than his mount's saddle. He returned to the street for a moment, took a brief look around, then pulled the gate shut behind him. The courtyard and the villa to which it belonged seemed to be in good condition compared to the other houses nearby.

Indavara retreated into the shadows next to one end of what looked like a sanctuary. There were gaps in the front wall that he thought might provide a good view of the villa. He smiled. He liked it when he was leading the way, getting things done. He reckoned it reminded Corbulo how much he needed him.

The arched gateway into the sanctuary had lost a lot of bricks

260

and looked as if might collapse at any moment. As he passed warily underneath it, Indavara's wet legs brushed against the knee-high weeds that carpeted the interior. Once inside, he realised the structure wasn't a sanctuary; there were no flower beds or benches or fountains.

Ahead of him, arranged in pairs, were six large cubes of a pink-tinged marble, each five feet across. Well-rendered faces and lines of text had been etched on each one, though much was now obscured by moss and grime. At the far end was another arched entrance. This one still had a gate, which had been left ajar.

Indavara heard the legionaries calling out to one another. They were getting closer.

He walked on, between the first pair of what he'd now decided were probably tombs. The black and white tiles beneath his feet were barely visible through the grass and a dense tangle of weed. He passed the second pair of tombs and looked for a suitable gap in the wall to his left; there were a couple of missing bricks but both were too high to look through. Approaching the last pair of tombs, he looked straight at the gate. Or rather the wet ground in the alley beyond it.

The marks in the mud looked fresh.

The faint sound of breathing seemed to be coming from ahead of him. He turned his good ear towards it.

The flash of movement came from the tomb to his right.

Indavara turned; and had time to register only three things. A lithe, dark figure springing at him; a pair of wide, bright eyes; and a narrow blade coming at his neck.

He swung his left arm into the man's wrist, smashing it into the tomb, but the assailant's impetus kept him moving forward. Indavara reached out with his right hand and grabbed whatever he could, which turned out to be the diagonal belt across the man's chest.

He heard boots scuff the ground behind him.

Second man. Moving in.

Gripping the belt tight, Indavara spun round and launched

the first attacker towards the second. To his surprise, the man came right off his feet.

A moment after he let go, he heard two simultaneous yelps. Unbalanced, he fell on to his backside and reached for his dagger but when he saw his assailants he realised he wouldn't be needing it. He got up and drew it anyway.

They couldn't have been more than fourteen or fifteen, and one was lying on top of the other. Their skin was dark, their long black hair tied into tails with twine. Despite the rain, they were barefoot and wore only baggy, roughly made tunics. Each carried a small, circular shield of hide on a strap over his back. They had both dropped their daggers and Indavara could see the identical leather sheaths fixed to the inside of their left forearms. Surely these were two of the local tribesmen Eborius had spoken of. The Maseene.

The youth lying on top rubbed his head, then rolled off his compatriot. The other warrior was still on his back. Wincing, he pushed himself up off the ground and stared at Indavara. Then he glanced down at the weeds where one of their daggers lay. Indavara retrieved it and tucked it into his belt. Spotting the other one, he grabbed that too.

The pair got to their feet.

'Down there!' cried one of the legionaries. He sounded very close.

The bulkier of the two youths also looked to be the youngest.

'Soldier?' he asked quietly in Latin.

The accent was like nothing Indavara had ever heard but the word was clear. He shook his head. Even though he'd been close to taking a blade in the neck, he couldn't help admiring the young warriors for taking him on. But though there could be no doubting their bravery, their fear was equally evident as they stood there, narrow chests rising up and down, rain soaking their faces.

He waved the youths towards the tomb – so they'd be out of sight. Once they'd hesitantly complied, the three of them just stood there in silence, listening to the legionaries moving through the streets and alleys around them. Indavara didn't know what he'd do if they were discovered, only that there was no way he was going to give up the tribesmen to the legionaries – not after what he'd heard and seen in the square.

Thankfully, it seemed the soldiers were reluctant to dismount and search every hiding place, and before long their voices and the clip-clop of hooves moved away.

Indavara approached the young warrior who had spoken. He held up his spare hand in what he hoped the youth would recognise as a signal of peaceful intent, then pointed at his left forearm. The Maseene exchanged a confused look with his friend but eventually realised what Indavara intended. He offered his arm.

Indavara took one of the daggers from his belt and slipped it into the sheath. The warrior pushed it into place, then dropped his arm. Indavara returned the other dagger to the second warrior in the same manner, then stepped away from them. He aimed his blade towards the gate.

The pair retreated, eyeing Indavara all the way. Their smooth, measured movements reminded him of the hunters he'd seen at work in the arena. As the older lad disappeared behind the tomb, the younger one gave a respectful nod and then a cheeky grin. Indavara walked forward and watched them slip silently into the alley.

———◆———

'At least they're moving away,' said Noster, looking down the side street from the Via Cyrenaica.

'But where's Indavara?' said Cassius. 'We don't even know if he came off to the left or right. That bloody rider could be anywhere by now.'

'There he is,' said Noster as Indavara suddenly appeared on the street.

Cassius and Noster ran over to him.

Indavara grinned. 'What kept you?'

———◆———

'Know the place?' asked Cassius as the three of them squeezed together in a corner of the mausoleum, all looking at the villa through a hole in the wall.

'No,' replied Noster. 'I didn't even know anyone still lived round here.'

'Indavara, did you check the perimeter to see if there are any other gates?'

Indavara glared at Cassius. 'When was I supposed to fit that in?'

'It's strange,' said Noster thoughtfully, leaning back against the wall. 'Maseene hardly ever come into the town in daylight.'

'Just children, messing around,' said Cassius.

'You're lucky they didn't "mess around" with you,' replied Indavara.

'Children or not, it's still unusual,' said Noster.

'You must go and find Eborius,' Cassius told him. 'Bring him here, tell him he can forget everything else. But be damned careful. We can't afford for our friend over there to know anything's amiss.'

'Yes, sir.'

Noster left and Cassius took his first proper look at the building. The villa was modest but well maintained, the only unusual features the high wall and shuttered windows.

'I think it's him,' said Indavara. 'Looked pretty small.'

'Well, we're due a bit of luck. Gods, I never even questioned the female staff at Memor's place about Dio. But remember that servant Cimber? He saw the son of a bitch heading for the village earlier in the day. Looks like Clara saw him too.'

'Someone's coming,' replied Indavara, looking left along the street.

They heard a bell chiming and a voice cry out in Latin: 'Water! Nice clean water!'

An elderly man appeared from the direction of the Via Cyrenaica, trudging along towing a mule. Tied to a yoke over the saddle were two large barrels. 'Get your water here!'

The gate of the villa swung open and the resident walked out on to the street holding a water skin.

'That's him,' said Indavara.

Little could be gleaned from the man's nondescript attire. He was wearing a well-cut beige tunic and a pair of sandals.

'Just the one, sir.' The vendor stopped and began filling the skin from one of the barrels.

'Short and slight,' whispered Cassius. 'Dark hair. Not very light-skinned, not very dark; not particularly handsome, not particularly ugly.'

Once the skin was full, the vendor rested it against the gate while the man reached into a money bag and paid him.

'And left-handed,' added Cassius.

'Dio,' said Indavara.

Now came Cassius's turn to grin. 'Dio.'

XXII

Once Noster and Eborius returned, the legionary was posted as a lookout while the other three gathered at the far end of the mausoleum. Cassius estimated an hour had passed since the assassin had emerged from the villa. There had been no further sign of either him or Carnifex's men.

'You don't know the place either?' he asked.

Eborius shook his head. 'I thought this area was empty. We do see the odd new face from time to time, but I try to keep track of who arrives and leaves. He can't have been here that long.'

'Or he's purposefully kept a low profile,' said Cassius. 'He seems rather good at that.'

Eborius tapped the pommel of his sword. 'So, are we going in? Before he has another chance to get away.'

'He can't,' said Cassius. 'I just checked. The gate's the only way in or out. How did you fare with this Helvetius?'

'My mistake,' Eborius said sheepishly, running a hand through the tight curls of his hair. 'The man's name is Helvetius Cordus, not Corvix.'

'Ah,' said Cassius.

The centurion still smelt of wine. There was no way to tell if his mistake was an honest error or a result of the drink. What had the fellow at the marketplace said? *He was a good man.*

'So – *are* we going in?' demanded Indavara. 'Is there time for me to go back and get my sword?'

'It's four against one,' said Cassius.

'Assuming he's alone,' replied Indavara.

'How do you want to do this?' Cassius asked Eborius.

'Someone should go to the rear. Just in case.'

266

'Agreed,' said Cassius. He turned to Indavara. 'You can get over that wall?'

'Easy.'

Cassius continued: 'At the back there are only two high windows – very small. You should be able to approach unseen.'

'So what are you three going to do?' asked Indavara. 'Just walk up to the gate?'

The centurion gestured at his belt. 'He'll see Noster and I are soldiers. May even know our faces.'

Eborius and Indavara looked at Cassius.

'Looks like you're ringing the bell,' said Indavara.

Cassius wasn't overly enamoured with the prospect of facing the assassin alone, even if only for a moment.

'It's best you go,' added Indavara. 'You won't scare him.'

'Also true,' said Eborius. 'No offence.'

'None taken,' Cassius replied. 'Very well. But you and Noster must be quick.'

'We'll watch from here,' said Eborius. 'As soon as that gate opens we'll charge straight in.'

'Just make sure you do,' said Cassius, recalling the foul-up on Rhodes when they'd tried to apprehend Drusus Viator.

'I'll brief Noster,' said Eborius, walking away through the weeds.

Cassius took a moment to check his boots were well tied. He tightened his belt a notch and took a deep breath.

'Don't worry,' said Indavara. 'I'll be over that rear wall in no time.'

'I'm not worried.'

'He's a small man.'

'He's a small man who slits throats and cuts heads off.'

Cassius took a moment to consider what they were doing; he didn't want to be rushed into a wrong move.

'Perhaps we're being rather hasty.'

Indavara frowned. 'We've followed this bastard hundreds of miles across the sea. Now we've got him.'

'But I'm sure he's not working alone. Maybe we should just watch the villa – see who he makes contact with. Remember what Eborius said about all the exiles here?'

'You want to wait? What if that gate suddenly opens and he rides out? We might not get this chance again.'

Cassius knew he could always rely on Indavara to favour the direct approach, but his thinking was correct. 'Good point.'

Eborius returned. 'Ready?'

Indavara ran his knife in and out of the sheath a few times. 'I'll get going.'

'Take a wide route round,' Cassius advised him. 'Watch those windows.'

'What are we going to do with this Dio anyway?' asked Eborius once Indavara had left.

'I'm not sure. We'll have to search the place. Then perhaps wait until nightfall and get him back to the ship.'

'You need to make him talk, I suppose.'

That particularly dark line of thought was a bit too much for Cassius's nerves.

Eborius noticed. 'You really aren't like the other grain men I've met, Corbulo.'

'I hear that a lot. I've come to consider it a compliment.'

'And so it is,' replied the centurion with a ready grin.

Cassius pointed towards the Via Cyrenaica. 'I'll walk back towards the road, then come down the street from a distance. Just in case.'

'Good idea. See you shortly.'

Cassius waited for Eborius to reach the other end of the mausoleum, then walked out under the arch and turned left into the next street along. Once there, he made for the road, moving slowly to give Indavara time to get in position. Only when he was close to the Via Cyrenaica did he cut back and head down the street towards the villa.

With every step the cold hollow in his stomach grew larger. What should he say when Dio came to the gate? Did he even need to say anything? Not if the others were quick enough.

Thirty yards. Even walking suddenly seemed difficult; the tension had spread to his legs. He tried to saunter. He tapped his fingers against his belt; just a curious visitor taking a nice stroll. Twenty yards. No sound from the villa. He was almost level with the end of the mausoleum. No sign of Eborius and Noster. Would they get across the street quickly enough? Ten yards. Had he allowed enough time? What if Indavara wasn't ready? Why hadn't he waited longer?

The boy came tearing on to the street from an alley to the right and ran straight towards the villa. He looked about nine or ten. Over his shoulder was a leather pouch just like the young letter-carriers wore in towns and cities across the Empire. A messenger.

Cassius kept walking. With only a brief glance at him, the boy stopped at the gate and rang the bell. Cassius was well past when it opened.

'Where have you been, you little shit?' asked a voice in Latin. 'I said the third hour.'

The Carthaginian sailors had been right. No obvious accent, nothing distinctive.

'Sorry, sir. The goats got loose, I had to—'

'Just come inside!'

A pause. A silence. Cassius imagined Dio staring at his back and again tried to affect the casual stride of a wandering visitor.

'Do I have far to go, sir? Grandfather said I must be back by midday.'

'You will be.'

The gate clanged shut.

Cassius intended to keep walking, circle back and tell the others what he'd heard. Then he realised: Indavara.

He darted left into the next alley and sprinted to the end, then looked round the corner towards the villa. 'Thank the gods.'

Indavara was standing there, back pressed against the wall, listening.

Staying well hidden, Cassius waved at him.

After a few moments Indavara spotted him and ran over, crouching low.

'By Jupiter, what a relief,' said Cassius. 'I thought you might have heard the bell and gone straight in.'

'I was about to jump but then I heard him. Didn't seem very likely he'd call you a "little shit".'

'A letter-carrier. And it sounds like Dio's got something for him. Might be going to his employer.'

'What are you thinking?'

'We wait. Then grab the boy.'

——8——

The young messenger left a quarter of an hour later. It turned out Eborius knew him and the plan was to let him get well away from the villa before intercepting him. Indavara and Noster would remain behind, with orders to apprehend the assassin if he tried to leave.

Cassius and Eborius were already poised at the far end of the mausoleum. They heard the gate shut once more and Noster relayed a signal from Indavara, pointing back the way the boy had come – towards the Via Roma.

Eborius sprang away along the alley, Cassius close on his heels. The two officers kept their eyes trained to the south as they ran but it wasn't until they crossed the fourth street that they saw the lad – disappearing into an alley thirty yards away.

Now nearing the Via Roma, they put in a burst and turned left down the next street. The lad emerged from the alley and stopped dead when he saw Eborius charging towards him. Barely out of breath, he glanced anxiously up at the two tall men.

'Hello,' said Eborius with a creditable attempt at warmth.

'Hello, sir.'

'You're Baro's grandson, aren't you?'

'Yes, sir.'

'What's the name?'

'Lucius, sir.'

The lad was skinny and dirty, wearing an unbelted tunic several sizes too big for him. He was evidently not of local stock, with skin as light as Cassius's, straw-coloured hair and even a few freckles.

'Well, Lucius, I'm on army business. I need to have a look in that bag of yours.'

270

Cassius had circled round to stand behind the boy.

'Master said I shouldn't stop, sir. I don't think he'd like it.'

'What's his name?' asked Cassius.

'Don't know, sir,' the lad answered, glancing nervously over his shoulder. 'Said I was to just call him "Master".'

'You're a good boy, Lucius,' said Eborius. 'You know what I am, don't you?'

'A soldier.'

'Just a soldier? Haven't seen my crest or—'

'A centurion.'

'That's right. You do know that the army is very important? If I tell you to do something, you have to do it. I promise we'll give the bag back. Master won't even know we've seen it.'

'Grandfather said you're not really a proper centurion, sir. He said Carnifex is the only one that counts.'

Eborius forced another smile. 'Quite right. Centurion Carnifex is the one that counts. You wouldn't want me to tell *him* that you went against the army, would you?'

Lucius took the bag off his shoulder and handed it over. As soon as Eborius had it in his hands, the lad tried to run. Cassius had seen it coming and stuck out a leg. As Lucius tripped and fell to the ground, Cassius grabbed his belt and held on to him. He kicked out, catching Cassius on the leg.

'Ow! Little bastard.'

Eborius lifted Lucius up, planted him on his feet and held him by the shoulders. Tears were now streaming down the lad's face.

'Listen, Lucius. You've not done anything wrong. A few moments and you can be on your way.'

'Just wanted to get a few coins for my grandfather, sir.'

'I know.'

Cassius did his best to ignore his aching leg and pulled a golden aureus from his money bag. 'All yours. If you do what we tell you.'

Lucius gazed longingly at the coin.

'Come on.'

271

With a hand still on Lucius's shoulder, Eborius directed him towards the nearest intact villa. The big centurion ducked under the low doorway and guided the boy over to an empty hearth, then sat him down on a stool. Cassius dragged a rickety bench over for himself and Eborius, which had the additional benefit of corralling the boy into a corner.

'Now let's see what's in here.'

Eborius reached into the bag and pulled out three rolled-up sheets, each tied with a piece of twine. It was customary for names and addresses to be written in a corner or on a separate label but there was nothing.

'Who are these for?' Eborius asked as he passed the sheets to Cassius.

Lucius wiped his wet cheeks with his sleeve. 'Don't know, sir.'

'Then how can you deliver them?'

'I know where they're to go.'

'Which house?'

'Three different houses. And I'm not to ask who lives there. Master tells me the directions five times so I don't forget. He says he uses me because I always remember it right.'

'How long have you worked for him?' Cassius asked.

'Not long. Last time was a few weeks ago. I didn't know he was back until he came to get me this morning.'

Turning to Cassius, Eborius switched to Greek. 'Lad lives with his grandfather – who can barely hear or see.'

'Master chose his messenger well,' observed Cassius.

'Have you delivered anything else today?' he asked Lucius, switching back to Latin.

The lad shook his head.

'But you've delivered to those houses before?'

'Two of them.'

'How many times?'

'Three or four.'

Cassius undid the twine and examined the first sheet. The paper was new and unmarked. He checked his fingers were clean before handling it.

Eborius leaned over and looked at it. 'Looks like a shopping list.'

'Precisely as intended, I imagine.'

Cassius opened the other two. Exact copies.

'Can I go soon?' asked Lucius. 'I'm supposed to go back and tell Master I delivered them safely.'

Cassius and Eborius exchanged grimaces.

'Can you get the addresses from him?' Cassius asked the centurion. 'I need to look at this.'

'Of course.'

As Eborius asked Lucius about the first house, Cassius took one of the letters and walked past the hearth into the villa's only other room. He stood close to the rear door; out of sight, but with enough light to examine the sheet.

The list detailed twelve separate foodstuffs and was split into three sections: a single line at the top, then a space, then five lines, then another space, then six lines.

Cassius gazed at it. What could be hidden in such a short, uncomplicated note? A time and a place perhaps? Dio had only been back a day; if the three recipients were involved in the Memor plot, was he now arranging a meeting?

The solitary first line suggested a key for the code.

Three pounds of millet.

Three. Wishing he had his satchel with the charcoal and paper, Cassius looked at the third letter of each food but could come up with nothing. Then he tried the third letter from the end but again the letters didn't seem to form words. He looked at the first letter of the third word in each line, then the first letter of the third word from the end of the line. Nothing.

Perhaps the first line was intended to mislead?

Cassius decided to ignore it and focus on each line in turn. Place and time; he felt sure they were in there somewhere. But still he could see no pattern.

Eborius walked into the room. 'Got the addresses, but he needs to go soon. How are you doing?'

Cassius held up a hand and didn't take his eyes off the sheet. 'Please.'

Was there a pre-existing key? If so, it might prove impossible to break the code.

He looked again at the second group of foods. The pattern of the words at the end of each line was unusual; as if it had been rearranged to accommodate the cipher. Cassius tried taking the last letter of the first line, then the penultimate letter of the second line and continuing from there. It wasn't difficult to rearrange the letters from the first group into a word. *Fifth*.

Fifth hour. Considering the time, presumably that night. But where?

He tried the same approach with the second block of lines but got nowhere. Then he realised it was continuous – he needed the sixth letter from the end of the sixth line, the seventh from the end of the seventh and so on.

Cassius repeated the six new letters to himself but couldn't find the word. Then he turned the sheet over and imagined them on the blank page, pictured moving them around to form new words.

In moments he was smiling. Hurrying into the other room, he beckoned Eborius over and whispered to him. 'Is there a quarry here?'

'Two miles west up the coast. Not been used in years.'

'Then we have what we need. It seems our friend Dio is a better killer than he is a spy.'

They returned to the hearth. Cassius retied the twine on the sheets and Eborius placed them carefully back in the bag. The lad had at last stopped crying.

'I told Lucius we'll give him the aureus once he's delivered the notes and told his master all's well,' announced Eborius.

'Absolutely,' said Cassius, taking the coin from his purse and giving the lad another good look at it before handing it to Eborius.

'I also told him our men will be watching him every step of the way, and that as long as he does as he's told, everything will be fine.'

274

'Quite right.'

Lucius stood and gave his face a last wipe.

Eborius placed the bag over his shoulder. 'Off you go then, lad.'

Lucius ran out of the dwelling.

'Poor little sod,' said the centurion.

'That poor little sod might just have led us to the people who hired Dio. What about these addresses?'

'The first is at the far eastern end of town. There's only one occupied house around there and it belongs to Galenus Frugi.'

'Know him?'

'Yes. We don't get many new arrivals and he's only been with us a year or so. As I understand it, Frugi was in a position of some authority in the province of Pontus. During the struggle for power after Claudius's death, he was a supporter of Quintillus. When Aurelian ended up as emperor—'

'He was out of favour. Not the first to pay the price for backing the wrong side.'

'Indeed. I believe he never speaks of it, but everyone knows he was exiled here.'

'Pontus was one of the provinces Memor dealt with. Now we're getting somewhere. Number two?'

'I know the house well. Dilius Nepos. He's been here rather longer – three or four years. Again, nothing was said publicly, but when he arrived I was still party to such information. He was a magistrate in Cappadocia. Apparently got himself involved with some whore who turned out to be a Goth spy.'

'Cappadocia. Another of Memor's provinces. Looks like we can cancel our trip to the library. The pieces are slotting into place.'

'I'm afraid there's still a big piece missing. The third address is a farmhouse on the edge of town. Not been inhabited for years. Lucius says his master told him to just leave the note inside the door. He's never been sent there before. One of the three notes always goes to a different place. Always somewhere quiet.'

'So our third man takes even more precautions than the others,' said Cassius. 'Might be the leader.'

'That farmhouse is in the middle of nowhere, surrounded by open ground. It would be almost impossible for us to get close.'

'Then we shan't bother. Neither shall we attempt to monitor the other two. The more we expose ourselves, the more chance there is of alerting one of them and there's no need now. We know exactly when and where they're going to be.'

'But this third man. Could be anyone.'

'We'll find out soon enough.'

Cassius looked out of the doorway, at the empty, silent street. 'Up to this point, I'd thought one man had hired Dio. But three? I suppose if it was to happen anywhere, it would be Darnis or somewhere like it – one of the far shores where those discarded by the Empire wash up. I wonder how it started.'

'Maybe they just got talking one day,' said Eborius. 'Found out they had something in common.'

'It might just have been that simple. I imagine they thought they were safely out of reach here. Listen, there'll be four of them at the quarry at least. Do you have five reliable men?'

'All my men are reliable, but five's a good number if you intend to spring a trap. What do you have in mind?'

'I haven't thought that far ahead yet. Come, let's get back to the others. We can talk on the way.'

XXIII

The *Fortuna Redux* was quiet. Asdribar had made arrangements with Eborius to take the crew to the tavern where the men of the Second Century drank – apparently the only functioning hostelry in the whole of Darnis. The centurion had sent two of his men along to supervise, but Asdribar had given assurances there wouldn't be any trouble. Of the sailors, only the eldest and youngest were still aboard – eating dinner together in the galley.

It was the first hour of night and Cassius stood alone at the side-rail, hands cold beneath his cloak, gazing down at the reflected crescent moon. He couldn't decide if a clear night was helpful or not, considering what lay ahead.

Simo and Indavara were below too, also eating. Cassius couldn't face a thing, though he planned a fortifying swig of wine before leaving the ship. What he needed was a few moments alone to run over the plan; ensure no crucial detail had been overlooked.

He and Indavara were to meet Eborius and his squad at the arch at the second hour, then set off for the quarry. The site was very close to the sea and a covert approach could be made from a path that ran along the shore. Eborius felt certain that Dio and his associates would arrive via one of the access roads that connected the quarry to the Via Cyrenaica west of Darnis. The centurion had also suggested that all armour be left behind and the men wear dark, hooded cloaks.

They would arrive well before the fifth hour, find a suitable location from which to observe the meeting then – at Cassius's signal – intervene and arrest the conspirators. He'd been concerned that perhaps there weren't enough of them but Eborius reminded him that – whoever the third man turned out to be – both Galenus Frugi and Dilius Nepos were the wrong side of fifty.

Noster and another legionary were still stationed opposite Dio's villa. They would wait for the assassin to leave, then meet the others at an arranged point close to the quarry. Assuming the arrest went to plan, the conspirators would be brought back to the ship and kept captive below decks.

That afternoon, Asdribar had taken delivery of the length of timber that would become the new yard. The crew had been labouring all afternoon but the captain estimated it would take them another full day to complete the work. He'd promised Cassius the *Fortuna* would be ready to leave by dawn the day after that.

Eborius, meanwhile, seemed almost as impatient as Cassius to see the affair swiftly concluded. The troubling uncertainty of the mysterious third man remained, and they still knew very little about Dio. Frugi and Nepos both had young wives and hired staff. Once they were declared missing, suspicion might easily fall on the visitors, not to mention the only seagoing ship in the harbour.

Eborius was above all concerned that Lafrenius Leon and Centurion Carnifex might become involved. Fortunately, they had their own concerns to deal with: Indavara's encounter with the young warriors hadn't been an isolated incident. It seemed the Maseene were becoming more brazen by the day; there had been several skirmishes close to the town and there were rumours that the previously disunited tribal clans were now coming together to take on Carnifex and his men. Cassius guessed this was the other reason why Eborius wanted the matter resolved and the *Fortuna* gone.

He turned and looked at the town. The sight of a settlement was usually a reassuring one: the warmth, the light, the noise – the sense of an ordered community forged from barren, primitive lands. But there was no comfort to be found here; Darnis was a place of shadow and ruin, where the normal rules of civilised society didn't seem to apply.

The deckhouse door opened. Cassius hoped whichever of the

women it was wouldn't notice him; he didn't need such distractions.

'Officer.'

Cassius cursed quietly to himself before he turned. 'Miss.'

Earlier that evening, he'd been to see Annia to keep her apprised of developments, though he'd been purposefully vague regarding the conspirators and the night-time operation. With so much still unknown, he didn't want to raise her hopes that a resolution was close.

She walked across the darkened deck and stood next to him. 'I thought you might be gone by now.'

'Soon, miss.'

Annia looked out across the harbour. 'I've been thinking about them. These men who ordered the killing. How they must have despised him.'

'All enemies of Rome in their way,' said Cassius. 'To some, exile is considered a kind of death. They blamed your father for it.'

'Why can't you tell me their names?'

'I believe I explained myself earlier, miss. We have moved forward but I know very little for certain.'

'If you do arrest them, if you bring them aboard – I want to see them.'

'Miss Annia, please. I cannot concern myself with this now. You did assure me you would remain in the deckhouse until morning.'

'Very well.'

She took two paces, then stopped.

'I have a right to know who they are. Without me we wouldn't even be here – we wouldn't even have found them. I just want to see them. Their faces. That's all.'

8

Cassius found Indavara with Simo in the cabin. He too had his cloak on and a pack ready by his feet.

'Got the rope?'

Indavara pointed at the pack. 'In there. Squint cut it up for me. I put in some cloth for gags too. Don't want them calling out, do we?'

'Good thinking.'

Cassius spied his canteen. 'Throw that in too, would you, Simo? Don't want it knocking against my sword.'

'Yes, sir.'

Cassius picked up the sword belt from the bed where Simo had laid it out.

'Sure you want to bother?' said Indavara. 'Might be best to travel light.'

Cassius hung the belt over his shoulder. 'Wouldn't make a very good impression with our friends from the Second Century, would it?'

'You think they care? Their officer is a drunk.'

Cassius said nothing as Simo helped him adjust the belt so that the eagle's head hung just over his hip.

'You hadn't noticed?' Indavara continued.

'A man who likes a drink isn't necessarily a drunk.'

'Korinth spoke to some other people in the town. They said Eborius's men didn't leave him because of money. They left him because he's weak. Because he couldn't do the job.'

'I told you what's gone on here since the earthquake. If I was in his situation, I'd probably have been driven to drink too.'

'The way I heard it he was like that when he got here.'

'What do you mean, "when he got here"? I got the impression he'd lived here all his life.'

'No. He was born close to here and he joined the army here, but he ended up with a big job with some legion in La . . . La-something.'

'Lambaesis. The headquarters of the Third Augustan Legion.'

'That's it. He was sent back here because he couldn't cut it.'

'What's your point?'

'These men we're going after – people who were put here as a punishment. What do you call them again?'

'Exiles.'

'If Eborius was sent back here, doesn't that make him an exile too?'

—■8■—

The path ran along the old Phoenician wall to the western edge of town before turning towards the shore. The next half-mile meandered through low, undulating dunes topped by thorny bushes. The path then sloped up above a small cove and the sand beneath their feet became solid rock. Despite the relative calm of the sea, booming echoes sounded in unseen caverns below.

The group of eight walked on in silence, hoods up. Cassius kept his eyes on the murky ground ahead of him – there were only a couple of yards between the path and a sheer drop to the right. Leading the way ahead of him was Eborius. What Indavara had found out hardly inspired confidence; clearly the man had been through a difficult few years. The centurion's past was not Cassius's concern, however, the investigation was, and the progress made since arriving in Darnis would have been impossible without him. For that reason alone, Cassius was prepared to trust him – not that there was any workable alternative.

Eborius had introduced the five legionaries to Cassius and Indavara by name and told them that the men they might soon be arresting were responsible for the murder of what he called a 'very high-ranking army officer'. Cassius appreciated the fact that he hadn't mentioned Memor had been deputy commander of the Service; most legionaries might even have viewed such a killing as a public service. Cassius had also given each of the legionaries an aureus – 'special payment', he'd called it.

Eborius kept up his customary swift pace. The moon was shrouded now but the cloud was thin, and he clearly wanted everyone in place well before there was any chance of the conspirators arriving. The path turned inland and became steeper, zigzagging through sharp rocky outcrops until they were a hundred feet above the sea.

281

The big centurion stopped and waited until Cassius, Indavara and the soldiers were gathered behind him. 'We're close,' came the deep voice. 'There is grass for cover but we must keep low or anyone looking up will see us.'

The last section of the path was even steeper, and Cassius had to grab the gnarled rock on either side to stop himself sliding back with every step. He was out of breath by the time he reached the top and took his place beside the crouching Eborius. Again, the centurion waited for the others before speaking.

'Twenty yards in, then we stop. Don't go past me. The sides of the quarry are vertical.'

Cassius followed Eborius inland. The grass was so thick that he had to hold the long scabbard up to stop it getting caught. Eborius paused once, then continued on a few yards and stopped. They knelt down.

The edge of the quarry was no more than five yards in front of them. Cassius could see nothing of its interior, just an inky bowl carved out of the rock, perhaps a hundred yards wide. He gazed out beyond the quarry, at the scattered lights of Darnis to the east, and the handful dotted along the Via Cyrenaica.

Eborius shuffled closer. 'The entrance is directly opposite us. Narrow and high-sided.'

Indavara moved up to listen in.

'We could skirt around to there but the view will be poor. I suggest stationing my men there, hidden but close to the path. The only other way in or out is a steep cut just around to the right from here. We can stay here where we can see everything, then come down via the cut when you give the shout. My men can block off any attempted escape.'

Cassius couldn't fault the plan; and he was also relieved not to detect any trace of wine on Eborius's breath. 'Agreed.'

'We should still have an hour or two. I'll get the men in position. Keep your eyes to the rear. Noster will come up from the shore.'

Eborius spoke to his men and the six of them moved quickly away to the left around the edge of the quarry.

'Has your faith been restored?' Cassius asked Indavara. 'I'd say he's doing rather well.'

'So far. I'm going to check on this cut. Make sure we know where it is when we move.'

'Very well.'

As Indavara disappeared into the gloom, Cassius pulled the edge of his cloak under him and sat down. Rearranging the sword belt until he was comfortable, he stared into the quarry but still couldn't make out a single feature or shape. Glancing over at Darnis, he pictured Dio's villa. Was the assassin already on his way? And the others – Nepos and Frugi? Would they come alone or with attendants, bodyguards? And most important of all – what of the third man?

Indavara returned. He sat down and lowered his hood. 'It's steep but safe enough. We should be able to get down there pretty quick.'

'Good.'

Indavara took the canteen from the pack and drank, then passed it to Cassius. Now there was nothing to do but wait, the grass swaying around them, the sea rumbling far below.

———⬥———

An hour passed and still Eborius hadn't returned.

'Where in Hades is he?' said Cassius.

'Perhaps they ran into—'

Indavara's head snapped round.

'What is it?'

Indavara slid out his sword and got to his feet.

Cassius turned towards the sea. He could hear something too. 'It's probably Noster.'

'Let's hope so.'

Indavara moved away through the grass, staying low. Leaving the pack as a marker, Cassius drew his own sword and followed him back to the cliff where the moonlit water beyond helped them see the path. Indavara stationed himself in front of it and directed Cassius to the side.

There was definitely more than one man approaching, though how many more Cassius couldn't tell. Boots scraped on rock.

Indavara eased his sword back, ready to swing if he had to.

The whisper was barely audible above the wind and the rustling grass. 'Noster coming up.'

Indavara lowered the sword.

'Go ahead,' said Cassius.

The veteran came up the path, breathing hard. With a glance at Indavara, he crouched down in front of Cassius. The second legionary – despite being about a decade younger than Noster – sat at the edge of the path, panting like a dog.

'When did Dio leave?' asked Cassius.

'About three-quarters of an hour ago. Alone, on horseback, one pack on his saddle, heading west out of town. I thought he'd be here by now. Where's Eborius?'

'Good question,' said Indavara.

'He went off to place the rest of the men near the entrance,' Cassius explained. 'But that was more than an hour ago. Come on.'

Sheathing his blade, he led the others back to the pack. While the second legionary lay out on the grass, still recovering, the other three sat there, eyes fixed on the shadowy depths of the quarry.

'What do you think might have happened?' Cassius asked Noster. 'Might they have run into Maseene?'

'Unlikely, but I've given up counting things out in Darnis.'

Cassius kept quiet, preoccupied with all the possible scenarios that might have unfolded in the darkness below. After a while, Noster rose up on his knees and turned his head to one side.

'Horse,' whispered Indavara.

'Horses,' added Noster.

The second legionary sat up behind them.

Whoever was riding them, the mounts were moving slowly, but the noise of the hooves striking the ground rolled into the cavernous quarry and drifted up to the watchers above. Cassius glimpsed the flicker of eyes and moonlight glinting off metal.

'Two or more,' said Noster.

They heard voices, low and urgent.

'Where is he?' said Cassius. 'The whole idea was to get set before anybody arrived.'

'Don't worry, sir,' said Noster. 'Eborius knows this area like the back of his hand. He'll be here.'

From below, the unmistakable clink of a fire-striker hitting a flint. A speck of orange in the darkness, then another, then a torch burst into flame – so quickly that the man holding it had to stretch out his arm. Laughter from a second man, who held out his own torch to be lit. The pair then walked over to the quarry wall, and each found a crevice in which to place his torch.

'Frugi and Nepos,' said Noster. 'Frugi's the fat one.'

Frugi was indeed fat, with a large gut that sat unpleasantly over a tight belt, pushing aside his cloak. He waddled over to his horse and retrieved a bottle from a saddlebag. He took a long swig, belched, then offered the bottle to Nepos.

The taller man shook his head and rubbed his arms to keep warm.

Both men suddenly turned towards the entrance.

'Here comes someone else,' said Noster.

The rider approached slowly. Frugi and Nepos drew closer to each other. Even after he had stopped and dismounted, the new arrival stayed in the shadows, beyond the reach of the torchlight. Frugi and Nepos listened to him, nodding as he spoke. Cassius could hear them but couldn't quite make out the words. Frugi and Nepos collected the torches from the wall and took up their horses' reins. The other man led them further into the gloom. The three of them came to a stop after fifty feet or so, still on the right side of the quarry.

'Closer to the cut,' Noster whispered to Cassius. 'Easier for us.'

'Only if your centurion ever gets back here. This could all be over soon.'

Once the horses were tied to a rock and the torches set, the new arrival showed himself. Unlike the others, Dio wasn't wearing a cloak, just a long-sleeved tunic. He was armed with a sword and holding a small sack in one hand. He remained utterly unremarkable.

'Is that it?' asked Frugi, pointing at the sack. Now that they were closer, the words were quite clear. Dio ignored him. He leant back against the quarry wall close to one of the torches and dropped the sack.

'Is that what?' Noster asked Cassius.

'I have a fairly good idea.'

Nepos spoke up: 'All went to plan?'

Dio cast a tired look at him before replying. 'Let's not talk until we're all here.'

As the silent moments passed, Cassius gazed down at the assassin. He imagined him striding up the path through the peach trees to the villa on Rhodes, greeting the doorman, cutting his throat as he turned, walking into the study, creeping up behind Memor, pulling his chin up, drawing the blade across his neck . . .

Indavara came close to Cassius. 'What if the soldiers aren't covering the way out? We might not get a better chance at this.'

'We have to wait. The third man.'

'And then what? Watch as they ride back out? We don't even have mounts.'

'We wait.'

Down in the quarry, Frugi returned to his saddle to take another swig of wine.

Dio glanced to the right and pushed himself off the wall.

'Can't hear a horse,' said Noster. 'Might be on foot.'

Cassius watched Dio's hand drift towards his sword. Frugi and Nepos gazed into the darkness.

A cloaked figure walked into the pool of light cast by the torches. Dio relaxed and returned to the wall.

'No horse?' asked Frugi.

'Too loud,' came the reply as the hood was pulled down.

The woman was hard to age; her hair was still fair but her face was heavily lined. She walked over to the others and looked down at the sack next to Dio.

Cassius was so transfixed by the scene below that he barely noticed Indavara drawing his sword again. But when the bodyguard turned to his left, Cassius did too. The grass was moving, and not solely because of the wind.

'It's me,' came the deep voice, and Eborius emerged from the dark a moment later.

'Thank the gods,' said Cassius. 'Where have you been?'

The centurion clapped a hand on Noster's shoulder and knelt next to Cassius. 'Sorry, Corbulo. Cervidus almost snapped his ankle on the way down, not a hundred paces from here. Couldn't even walk. I had to get him and Atrabates back to the shore path, then find a position for the other three. Then this lot started turning up.'

'Seen the latest arrival?'

'Yes. Didn't expect the third man to be a woman.'

'You know her?'

'The face. Can't remember the name.'

'Justina Trebantius,' interjected Noster.

'That's it,' said Eborius. 'Lives out on the south side of town. Not far from that farmhouse Lucius was to deliver to.'

'What do you know of her?'

'Widow,' continued Noster. 'Husband was a procurator in Bithynia. Killed himself after some kind of scandal.'

'I think I can probably guess who led that investigation,' said Cassius.

He looked down into the quarry. Justina Trebantius was still staring at the sack. Nobody was talking.

'Now?' asked Indavara.

'No,' said Cassius. 'Look at them. They're still waiting. Someone else is coming.'

XXIV

The flaming torches appeared in quick succession. One, then three, then six; bobbing up and down, casting flickering streaks of light on to the narrow gully that formed the entrance to the quarry. The soldiers slowed their mounts to a walk as they neared the four conspirators.

'This just got a lot more complicated,' said Noster. Optio Procyon was first off his horse, closely followed by Optio Mutilus. Procyon nodded to Dio, then looked at the other three. Once the rest of the legionaries had dismounted, Mutilus ordered them into a line, penning the three men and one woman against the wall. Cassius counted the soldiers, some of whom weren't carrying torches. Twelve. They all turned, waiting for the last rider to dismount.

'Shit, shit, shit,' whispered Noster.

The last man walked out of the darkness then stopped, surveying the scene in front of him.

Cassius turned to Eborius, whose head was bowed. 'Carnifex?'

'Carnifex.'

The centurion removed his helmet, the crest of which had been chopped down to half its normal height. Beneath was a close-cropped head of grey hair almost white at the temples. His armour was an archaic bronze muscle cuirass, his armament a similarly old-fashioned short sword. Carnifex was bull-necked and squat, with long, powerful arms and thick-fingered hands, which he rubbed together as he approached Dio. He had a slight limp.

'Welcome back,' he said, as they shook forearms. The assassin looked like a child next to Carnifex.

Cassius noticed that one of the men resembled a local more than a legionary. 'Who's that with the long hair?'

'Sulli,' replied Noster. 'Carnifex's local guide. He's Maseene.'

Carnifex threw his helmet to Procyon, then gestured for Dio to pick up the sack. As the assassin did so, the old centurion turned to Mutilus. 'Pilum.'

Mutilus took a long spear from his saddle, walked past the watching conspirators and handed it to his superior. Dio proffered the open bag. With a lopsided grin, Carnifex reached inside and pulled out Memor's head by the hair. The skin was a strange dark grey and the face seemed to have collapsed in on itself. Carnifex held it up to Nepos and Frugi. Nepos simply gave a satisfied smirk, while Frugi took a celebratory drink from his bottle. Carnifex showed the head to his men, then finally to Justina Trebantius. She stepped forward and spat at it.

Chuckling, Carnifex jammed the head down on to the blade of the pilum, twisting it for good measure. At the bottom of the pilum was a butt-spike, which he drove into the ground next to the quarry wall.

He stepped back for a moment to admire his handiwork. 'You got what was coming to you, friend. I've waited a long time for this.'

Carnifex took Procyon's torch and held the flames under the head. It took a while to catch light, until the fat began to seep out of the skin. Carnifex seemed to particularly enjoy lighting each eye – watching the flaming jelly slip down over what remained of Memor's face. For his final flourish, he waited for the flames to die, pulled the spear out of the ground, then swung it hard against the quarry wall. The head exploded, leaving fragments of skull and charred flesh on the ground.

Carnifex threw the pilum back to Mutilus, then snatched Frugi's bottle from his hand. He took a long swig and gave it back to him.

'Now,' said the centurion, 'to business.'

Within a few moments, Frugi, Nepos and Justina Trebantius had all produced heavy-looking bags of coins. Carnifex waved

289

Procyon forward to collect them; the bony optio could only just carry them all. The centurion pointed at Dio.

'Don't worry,' he told the other conspirators, 'I'll make sure our friend here gets his share. Reckon he deserves it. My own contribution – bringing in such an accomplished professional. That arrangement still all right with you three?'

Carnifex possessed the harsh accent and belligerent tone of those from the roughest, poorest quarters of Rome. Cassius despised him already.

'Absolutely,' said Frugi.

'Of course,' added Nepos.

'I'd pay the same again if we could have Memor killed twice,' said Justina Trebantius, drawing another chuckle from the centurion.

The last of Carnifex's men arrived – a driver on a cart towed by two horses.

'What's that for?' asked Frugi, bottle still in hand.

'Your bodies,' Carnifex replied flatly. He gestured to his men and stepped backwards. Four of the legionaries without torches drew their swords and advanced on the conspirators. Frugi's bottle fell to the ground as he and Nepos retreated towards the quarry wall.

'Carnifex, we had an agreement!'

'Why, man?' pleaded Nepos. 'You know you can trust us.'

Justina Trebantius made a pathetic attempt to flee, only to be grabbed by Carnifex. He pulled her to him and held her, one arm round her neck, one arm round her waist.

'We're just going to sit and watch this?' asked Indavara.

Cassius didn't reply. Even if they could have got down there in time, they were heavily outnumbered.

The legionaries paired off and stabbed their swords into the cornered men. Nepos crumpled to the ground in an instant. Frugi died noisily, choking and flailing at his wounds as he slid down the quarry wall. Carnifex pushed Justina Trebantius towards Mutilus. The optio took a moment to line up his blade with his spare hand, then drove the blade straight into the woman's heart. Her head shot up in a paroxysm of agony, teeth sparkling in the torchlight. There was an awful sucking sound as the legionary retracted his blade. Justina Trebantius staggered backwards. Carnifex caught her again, and turned her face towards him.

'By the great gods,' whispered Eborius.

The woman gazed at Carnifex with unblinking eyes. He gripped her chin and kissed her full on the lips. Procyon giggled. The centurion let go and shoved her towards the wall. She fell to the ground between Nepos and Frugi. Not one of them was moving.

'Nice touch,' said Dio.

Carnifex put his arm over the assassin's shoulder and led him away from the bodies. 'You did well, lad, very well indeed. Now what about this ship? Nothing to worry about?'

Cassius felt an icy chill wash over him.

Dio shook his head. 'Just some rich idiot and a couple of women.'

Carnifex turned to Procyon, who nodded.

'Like I said, covered my tracks all the way,' continued the assassin. 'Reached Rhodes via Paphos, changed ships on Crete.'

'Very good,' said the centurion. 'What did I tell you, Procyon? You want a job done right, you've got to hire the best. And you know something else about assassins? Travel around a lot. Not many friends, not many ties. A lonely life. But it's helpful in a way. Because it means no one will ever come looking for them.'

The arm that had been over Dio's shoulder now dropped under the assassin's chin. Carnifex squeezed his forearm, crushing Dio's neck against his bronze cuirass.

'Cent—'

Carnifex squeezed tighter. The assassin struggled, lashing out with his hands and feet, but Carnifex didn't move an inch. In fact he didn't even bother to use his other arm. The centurion looked around at his men and shrugged as Dio's head shuddered and spittle bubbled from his mouth. Only when he had finally stopped moving did Carnifex let go. The small, limp form dropped to the ground at his feet.

'What are you waiting for?' he told Procyon after a moment. 'I want them back in the villa in an hour and you lot out of town before dawn.'

'Yes, sir.'

The optio returned Carnifex's helmet.

The old centurion walked away past his men. One of them handed him his horse's reins and he disappeared into the shadows.

———8——

For a long time, nobody said anything. Cassius, Indavara, Eborius and the two legionaries looked on as the men of the First Century went efficiently about their work. They put the bodies inside big sacks and loaded them on to the cart. Mutilus even took a moment to scatter gravel and dirt over the bloodstains. He and Procyon then mounted up and led the others out of the quarry.

When all the torches had finally disappeared, Noster spoke first. 'Sir, shall I go and get the others?'

'No,' answered Eborius. 'I'll do it. You'll never find them.'

He stood up and seemed to be about to say something, but then walked away through the grass. The others got to their feet too. Cassius reached into the pack, took a drink from his canteen and wished he'd brought something stronger.

———8——

The barracks were on the east side of Darnis, close to the old wall. Anxious to avoid any risk of contact with Carnifex's men, Eborius retraced their route along the shore, then past the harbour – where all was quiet – before turning up into the town. Cassius recognised the area from when they'd followed him the previous day.

The building looked barely large enough for a century and was housed in a low-walled compound with a small parade ground at the front. Ignoring the main gate, Eborius led them round to the rear, where a sentry let them in. Some of the other men came out to meet their fellow soldiers but Eborius ordered them back to their rooms and instructed the squad to head directly to his quarters. He gave Noster a key and left him to open up, then went to check on the injured man.

The officers' quarters were divided into two small rooms: an office at the front with a bedroom to the rear. For Cassius, it was hauntingly reminiscent of the fort at Alauran and his first assignment in Syria. As he, Indavara and the legionaries filed in, Noster fetched an oil lamp, then lit a lantern hanging over a large table. There were only two chairs so nobody sat down. Little had been said during the journey back and the silence continued until Eborius returned. The centurion shut the door behind him, took off his cloak and sword belt and hung them from hooks on the wall.

'How is he?' asked Cassius.

'Ankle's badly swollen but I don't think there's a break.' Eborius gestured to one of the chairs. 'Please.'

Cassius sat down; he was grateful to take the weight off his feet.

Eborius addressed his men. 'First things first. None of you can speak of what you saw tonight. Not amongst yourselves, to the other men, nor to anyone else. I don't think I need to explain why.'

Cassius caught the centurion's eye. 'I'll need a signed and dated account from all those who can write. Evidence.'

'They can all write. I'll get the accounts to you later.'

Eborius turned to the legionaries again. 'I need a pledge from each of you. This goes no further.'

Noster began. 'You have my word, sir.'

'And mine, sir,' said the next man.

Each in turn gave his promise.

'Now,' said Eborius, 'I need to talk to the officer here. I'm sure you could all use some shut-eye.'

He opened the door and the men trooped out. Noster hung back but Eborius gestured towards the door and gave the veteran another clap on the shoulder. Once they were gone, Eborius grabbed a chair from the bedroom for Indavara, then located three wooden mugs and a jug. He filled up the mugs with wine, sat down and drank.

Cassius stared down at the lamp, the little wick floating on a sea of golden oil. 'I don't hold with much of what Simo rambles on about, but the Christians believe their god is engaged in an eternal battle with his nemesis, a dark lord named Satan. They think this Satan has unleashed demons into the world in the form of men. After what we saw tonight, I find myself rather more accepting of such a concept.'

Eborius looked at his wine as he swilled it around the mug. 'I should have known there couldn't be any sort of underhand activity going on in Darnis without Carnifex being involved somehow. Any idea what he might have had against Memor?'

Cassius shook his head. 'Just another in a long line of vengeful enemies, I expect.'

'What about his orders – "I want them back in the villa"?'

'Dio's place, perhaps,' said Cassius. 'They might try and make it look as if he killed them, or that they were all killed together by someone else.'

'Very neat.'

'Enough to fool the locals perhaps, but in the grand scheme of things it won't matter. Your testimony and mine and the men's accounts will be enough for a court in Rome. That's if the Service would want to handle it in so public a manner, which I doubt.'

Eborius looked up. 'What are you saying?'

Cassius hadn't spoken during the trip back but he had been thinking, and the alternatives were remarkably simple.

'There are really only three choices. First, we could get help from the Service, which probably means Egypt – I know of a man there my superior mentioned. Second, we could go to the governor in Cyrene, present him with the facts and invoke the full authority of the Service. He might at least place Carnifex under arrest. But both of those would take time. Weeks in fact.'

Eborius leant back in the chair. 'Or?'

'Asdribar tells me the *Fortuna* will be ready to sail within a day.' Cassius paused; he could hardly believe what he was about to suggest. 'What if we grab Carnifex and take him with us?'

Eborius gave an ironic smile, then stared up at the ceiling.

'Well?' Cassius asked after a few moments. 'Darnis could be rid of him for good. You could take over here, try and get things back to how they were. The Service would be grateful. Very grateful. I'd see to it that you were well—'

'Don't,' said the big centurion. 'Don't bother.'

Cassius decided to keep quiet; there was no point trying to make Eborius's decision for him.

The centurion hunched forward, arms on the table. 'If you take that man on, you need to be prepared to go to war with him.'

'I've got no problem with that,' said Indavara.

'There'll be no war,' said Cassius. 'If we do this right, there needn't even be a drop more blood spilt. Carnifex thinks his plan worked to perfection. He doesn't know we're here. He's vulnerable. So we have to do this now. Will you help?'

Eborius's chair screeched on the stone floor as he pushed it away and stood. 'He's clever. And he can sniff out a trap a mile off.'

'I don't doubt it. So we shall have to be clever too.'

'He keep anyone close?' asked Indavara. 'Bodyguard?'

'Did it look to you like he needs one?'

Eborius let out a long breath and walked away from the table.

Cassius looked up at him. 'Listen, I'm not one for reckless heroism, but to have that man ruling this place under the scarlet and gold is an affront to the entire Empire. Someone has to stop him sooner or later. You were wise not to take him on alone – I certainly wouldn't have – but the three of us, together . . .'

Indavara was nodding. 'Bloody right.'

He raised his mug.

Cassius did the same and tapped it against Indavara's.

Eborius came forward, knocked his mug against theirs and downed the rest of the wine.

'It will be light soon,' he warned.

'Well then,' said Cassius. 'We'd better get started.'

XXV

Cassius awoke to the sounds of hammering and shouting. While Simo went to fetch some hot water, he got up, looked out of the porthole and saw the entire crew gathered on the breakwater. The length of timber that would become the yard was laid out on three X-shaped stands. The sailors were working on different sections, some wielding saws, planes or drills, others affixing iron rings and wooden blocks. Asdribar stood with Squint, examining a sheet of paper.

Cassius sat down on the bed. Surprisingly, the plan he, Eborius and Indavara had concocted in the darkest hours of the night still seemed feasible. It was, however, worryingly dependent on the big centurion, who had raised concern after concern before finally agreeing to go ahead. Some of his contributions had been valid but the impression remained that he was struggling with the very thought of taking on Carnifex. Hardly surprising; he had lived in the man's shadow for so long.

A brisk knock on the door and Indavara walked in, looking remarkably fresh-faced.

'Get any sleep?' he asked.

'Just dozed a bit really. Had I slept properly I might have assumed I'd had the most horrific of nightmares.'

Indavara shut the door behind him. 'I've been thinking. Carnifex.'

'Yes?'

'It's too risky – leaving it to Eborius.'

'He'll come through.'

'You've seen his hands? They shake.'

'He'll come through,' Cassius repeated. 'In any case, Eborius is the only one with a chance of drawing Carnifex away from his men. We stick to the plan and wait for him to contact us.'

'There is another choice. Let me kill him.'

Cassius took a moment to reply. 'Indavara, no one respects your abilities more than I, but you wouldn't stand a chance. He has over a hundred men at this mansion. You don't know him and you don't know the territory.'

'Eborius can get me close. I can do the rest.'

'No. We take him alive. Despite everything we saw last night, he is still a serving centurion. He must face the authorities; the decision doesn't lie with us.'

'Like you said, he doesn't know we're coming. We have one chance at this. A man like that doesn't give second chances.'

'We have to take him alive.'

Indavara looked out through the porthole. 'If this goes wrong, everyone who came here on this ship will be in danger, the women included.'

'It won't come to that. Consider your view duly noted. I've made my decision.'

———◄8►———

Once he'd washed and taken a little breakfast, Cassius went to find Annia. It had been too late to call in at the deckhouse during the night and he'd wanted some time to consider what to tell her. Coming up through the hatch, he saw her standing alone at the end of the breakwater, well away from the sailors. Asdribar was in his chair, watching the crew.

'You two were late back last night,' said the Carthaginian. 'Any progress?'

'Of a sort,' Cassius replied. 'We'll definitely be ready to leave first thing tomorrow?'

'I said we would. Where are we bound?'

'Apollonia. What is it, fifty miles or so?'

'About that. Miss is in agreement, I take it?'

'Leave her to me. But we have to depart at dawn, whatever the weather.'

'Whatever the weather? You have a short memory.'

'It will be impossible for us to stay here. Can't we just hug the coast? Stay as close as possible to the land?'

'Being close to land doesn't make a lot of difference if there's another storm like the one that brought down my rig. In fact it makes it even more dangerous. I'm not going to risk my men and my ship like that again.'

Cassius didn't want to get into an argument. He glanced at the sea, which was as calm as a millpond. 'Looks set fair for now. Just please make sure we're ready.'

Cassius crossed the gangplank on to the breakwater. Once past the busy crewmen, he disturbed a group of gulls who flapped into the air to join the multitude circling above. Annia was gazing out to sea, arms wrapped around her. She didn't notice Cassius until he was close.

'Morning, miss. Apologies for not coming to see you sooner.'

'I lay awake all night, and I watched you come aboard. Why was there no one with you?'

'Things have changed.'

'What do you mean? What about these men?'

Cassius regretted telling her even that; now she expected to know the rest.

'The situation is even more precarious and dangerous than I had imagined. I must simply ask you to trust me. We'll be leaving in the morning, of that I'm sure.'

'And what about Dio?' Annia demanded. 'What are you waiting for?' She jabbed a finger at the *Fortuna*. 'I want him on the ship in chains. I want him taken back to Rhodes, or to Rome.'

'Miss, please, try to calm down.'

'You're enjoying this. Having this power over me.'

'That is ridiculous.'

For the briefest of moments, Cassius considered telling her – Dio, the quarry, Carnifex, everything. But he, Indavara and Eborius had agreed that what they'd planned must remain between the three of them. Annia was simply too volatile and unpredictable to trust with such information.

'Miss, you asked me to begin this investigation back on Rhodes and we are now hours from a resolution. Tomorrow I will be able to tell you everything. You must trust me.'

'Why should I?' she said without looking at him. 'When you so clearly do not trust *me*.'

With that, she hurried back to the ship as fast as the uneven surface beneath her feet would allow.

Cassius couldn't summon the energy to be concerned about the girl; there was too much else to worry about. He turned and looked west along the shore. There, about a mile away, was a tiny fisherman's hut between the old wall and the water. If all went to plan, he would be spending the night there.

—◆8◆—

The day passed as painfully slowly as Cassius knew it would, but he at least had a little work to occupy him. First, he recorded the three dead conspirators' names, along with a physical description and the personal information Eborius had passed on. He then wrote out his account of the night's events, filling four sheets with ink. This he read to Indavara, who agreed it was accurate and added his signature. Cassius commended him on his effort – even though the single word was barely legible – and resisted the temptation to ask again why he had no family name.

Just after midday, one of Eborius's men delivered the signed statements from the centurion and the legionaries. Cassius checked through them all and was pleased to find they were clearly written and corroborative, aside from the inevitable minor inconsistencies that occur when several people are asked to describe the same event.

Carnifex's arrogance and penchant for brutality had condemned him. Not only had he admitted to organising the assassination, he had committed one murder – albeit of the assassin – with his bare hands and presided over three others. If the issue was ever

299

presented to a court, which Cassius still thought unlikely, the man had little chance of escaping justice. If the evidence was used simply to convince Abascantius and Chief Pulcher of the rogue centurion's guilt, his fate was sealed. Cassius tucked all the documents into the satchel and placed it under the bed.

Noster came down to the harbour at the ninth hour with a simple message from Eborius: all was proceeding as intended and they should go ahead as planned. Cassius felt a mixture of relief and anxiety; Indavara seemed almost happy. Noster also had some other news, which he related as the three of them stood at the *Fortuna*'s bow.

'The bodies were "discovered" this morning, by men of the First Century. Carnifex pinned it on two Maseene picked up just outside town yesterday. Procyon and Mutilus crucified them this morning. They're hanging in the square.'

Indavara came closer. 'Two warriors? Young men?'

'Little more than boys. Some of the braver locals have protested to Governor Leon but he won't do a damn thing.'

'The two that attacked you?' Cassius asked Indavara.

Indavara wandered over to the side-rail without a word.

'Even neater than I thought,' said Cassius.

'The townspeople have swallowed it hook, line and sinker,' said Noster. 'They think they need Carnifex to protect them more than ever now.'

Indavara spat into the water.

'Eborius hasn't told me what you're going to do,' said Noster, 'but whatever it is, I'll be praying to Jupiter that it works.'

—◼8▶—

The crosses had been put up close to the ruined forum. One boy's head had settled to the left, the other to the right. Cassius was thankful that their eyes were closed. He guessed they might have been dead before they were nailed up; their tunics were riven with holes, their lean frames covered with gashes and gouges. The blood from the nail-wounds in their palms had dried in dark

300

streaks upon their skin and the wood. Splintered bone splayed out from the large nail that had been driven through one boy's ankles.

'By the gods, how foul.'

Indavara looked at Cassius. 'Is that all you can say? The poor bastards were running round the streets this time yesterday. Can't you offer a prayer or something?'

'Considering what we're about to do, I'd concentrate on your own fate. Come on.'

Indavara didn't move. 'Corbulo.'

Cassius stopped. 'You don't even share a god.'

'Just say something. You're good with words.'

Cassius let out a long breath before speaking.

'These warriors died young. Too young. May their gods honour their memories and . . . watch over their families.'

Indavara clasped his hands together and nodded at the dead youths in turn.

'Didn't they try to kill you?' asked Cassius.

Indavara looked at a trio of legionaries on the other side of the square. 'Only because they thought I was one of *them*.'

Cassius didn't recognise any of the men and concluded they were with the First Century. 'We should go.'

'Lead on,' said Indavara. 'I'm looking forward to this.'

———8———

The last person they saw in Darnis was Maro, working alone at the timber yard. They took care to stay away from the gate; the fewer people who saw them the better. After a mile or so, the slabs of stone underfoot came to an end and the Via Roma became a wide track of compacted mud. They saw no one at work in the fields, only a distant goatherd watching over his charges as they grazed across a water meadow.

According to Eborius, the road led eventually to Carnifex's headquarters. Cassius had a story ready if they did encounter any of his legionaries, but even being seen in the area might prove costly considering what they were about to attempt. Eborius felt it was worth the risk of venturing beyond the town; Carnifex would be less wary close to his home ground.

'What if he's not alone?' asked Indavara.

'He will be.'

Indavara scowled. 'Last night didn't exactly go as planned, did it? Who do I have to back me up? You and a drunk.'

'Just do your job and take the son of a bitch down quickly. He'll never know what hit him.'

'My pleasure.'

A mile further down the road they came to a bridge.

'Not far now,' said Cassius.

'I thought there were no rivers here,' said Indavara.

'There aren't. Look – it's just a gorge. According to Noster the hole at the bottom widened during the earthquake.'

The bridge was about thirty yards wide: a single arch composed of large blocks of a reddish stone. The surface seemed to be in good condition but there was a painted sign next to the road: BEWARE: BRIDGE DAMAGED. Close by was a stack of timber, a pile of rusting nails and some coils of rope.

As they started across, Cassius moved close to the left-hand wall and looked down at the gorge. The slope was shallow close to the top but then angled sharply down before reaching a dark fissure ten feet wide. 'Gods, it looks as though it leads down to Hades itself.'

A piercing cry was his only reply and he watched a pair of large black birds swoop out from under the bridge, monitoring the series of burrows close to the top of the gorge. Cassius noted the forked tails and the grey flecks on their wings.

'Eagles?' asked Indavara.

'Black kites. Like an eagle, but they'll take anything – food from your hand, fish from the water.'

As they neared the far side of the bridge, Cassius looked back and belatedly understood the need for the sign. Much of the supporting brickwork under the arch on the northern side had been lost, and the structure was reinforced by a flimsy-looking lattice of timber. This formed a frame under the stone, which was in turn supported by six large wooden posts embedded in the slope. Whatever had been used to keep the timbers together evidently hadn't been deemed sufficient; each joint was also held together by thick lengths of rope. Cassius quickened his pace.

Beyond the gorge the Via Roma followed an incline up to a ridge. Just before the top – and exactly as Eborius had described – was a track running at right angles to the road. They turned left and followed the track through a dense grove of olive trees.

Apart from the scuffing of their boots on the ground, and the constant buzzing of unseen insects, all was quiet. The track eventually curved to the right and reached a small clearing, in the middle of which was a long-dead tree stump, charred and grey. On the other side of the clearing, facing north, was a barn with two arched doorways.

'There it is,' said Cassius. He led the way across the clearing and into the building. The interior was dominated by a wide stone oil press. At either end were shelves occupied only by a few broken amphorae. Shrunken, bitter-smelling olives littered the floor.

Indavara pointed at the doorways in turn. 'One of us here, one of us there?'

'Makes sense.'

Cassius removed his canteen from his belt and took a long drink of water mixed with Asdribar's strongest wine, then put it down on the ground out of the way – he didn't want it clinking against something at the wrong moment. Indavara took off his pack and leant his stave against the wall next to it. Cassius walked outside and around to the rear of the barn. Standing there was a small cart with a pack similar to Indavara's in the back. Cassius returned to the building to find Indavara checking the view through various gaps in the masonry.

'It's there?' asked the bodyguard.

'It is.'

Taking care to remain in the shadows, Cassius tucked his thumbs into his belt and looked out at the track.

—8—

The red sun was low in the sky and the olive grove shrouded in shadow when Eborius arrived. He dismounted, tied his horse to the tree stump and hurried into the barn, not saying a word until he was inside.

'He's early. Coming now. I saw him on the road.'

'Alone?' asked Indavara.

'Yes.'

Eborius's face was clammy and pale.

'Good,' said Cassius. 'This won't take long. Stay close to the building to give us the best chance.'

'I can see him,' said Indavara.

'You better go,' said Cassius. 'We're with you.'

Eborius took a deep breath, then walked outside. Indavara was positioned by the right-hand doorway. Cassius moved carefully to the left and found himself a decent spyhole. Eborius ventured only a few yards from the barn.

Centurion Carnifex guided his horse – a big, sturdy black stallion – into the clearing at a trot. Sitting back in the saddle, he brought it expertly to a stop five yards from Eborius. He was again clad in the bronze muscle cuirass and Cassius noted that even his helmet was of an old-fashioned design, also bronze, with angular panels to protect the cheeks and neck. The cut-off crest was a bizarre touch, especially as his entire kit was in pristine condition. He glared down at Eborius.

'Got your message. What's this bullshit about Procyon and Mutilus?'

'It's complicated. We need to talk.'

'Reckon I said all I needed to say to you three months back. Thought you were seeing sense at last – staying out of my way.'

'Believe me, I'd prefer not to talk to you, but what I heard today couldn't wait.'

'You really think I'm going to take your word over theirs? They've been with me since before you popped out your mother's hole.'

'They were overheard discussing these murders. Seemed to know a lot more about it than they should.'

This piqued Carnifex's interest sufficiently to get him out of his saddle. With a grunt, he slid to the ground and tied his horse to the tree stump.

Cassius turned to Indavara. The bodyguard reached for his stave. Cassius put one hand on his sword handle, even though he wasn't planning to use it. Face pressed against the cold stone, he watched the centurion flick his reins back over the saddle then approach Eborius. Though the younger officer was four or five inches taller, the breadth of Carnifex's chest, shoulders and neck made him seem the bigger man.

Much to Cassius's relief, Carnifex took off the helmet, wiping the sweat from his brow with one big paw. In the middle of his forehead was a deep, yellowish, circular scar; it looked like an arrow wound. There was a lumpen solidity to Carnifex's face and his eyes shone with the contemptuous arrogance of a man with nothing to fear. Cassius now noted the cause of his limp: a messy pink scar running from his left knee down the side of his leg.

'What are you saying?' he growled.

'It seems to me that if Procyon and Mutilus know something about these killings, maybe you do too.'

Carnifex took a step towards Eborius.

Sweat was running freely down Cassius's flanks as he turned to Indavara again. He told himself that the bodyguard could handle the old centurion and walked out of the doorway.

Carnifex spun round to face him, his frown deepening.

Cassius surprised himself by managing to get some words out. 'Good evening, Centurion.'

He forced himself to look at Carnifex, not Indavara, who was creeping up behind him.

'Who—'

Sensing danger, Carnifex turned just as Indavara swung the stave at his head. He still had the helmet in his hand and threw his arm up. The stave glanced off the helmet but caught him on the back of the head with a solid crack.

Cassius was in no doubt that the blow would have been enough to knock most men into unconsciousness or worse. But even as the skin opened up and blood ran down the cropped grey hair, Carnifex stayed upright. He staggered, shot a fiery glare at Eborius and threw his helmet at him. The weighty lump of bronze struck the younger officer on the side of the head. He stumbled back into the barn then slumped to the ground.

Still reeling, Carnifex turned to face Indavara, who had the stave up high, ready to swing once more. The centurion mumbled something, then reached for his sword.

'Hit him again!' yelled Cassius.

Indavara moved to his right and swung a second time. This blow caught Carnifex on the base of his neck, just above the rim of his armour.

The centurion lurched forward, then back, and seemed about to topple over, but he somehow remained on his feet. Blinking and gulping in air, he reached for his blade once more.

'Again!' yelled Cassius.

Indavara launched a full-blooded swing at the centurion's chest. The stave struck the armour but the sheer impetus of the blow knocked Carnifex clean off his feet. The old soldier crashed to the ground at last, arms and legs splayed wide. His eyelids fluttered for a moment, then shut.

'Shit me,' said Indavara. 'What a beast.'

'Get the ropes. Quickly,' said Cassius as he ran over and knelt by Eborius. There was a nasty inch-long gash on the centurion's cheek, but his eyes were open and alert.

'Bad?' he asked.

'Don't worry,' said Cassius, 'the ladies love a scar.' He grabbed Eborius under one arm and helped him up. 'All right?'

'Think so.'

Cassius watched him carefully before letting him stand alone.

Eborius gazed down at Carnifex, then put his hand to his cheek and looked at the blood on his fingers. He took his canteen off his belt and sloshed water over the gash.

Indavara returned from the barn with the pack, several lengths of rope already in his hand.

'He is breathing, I take it?' Cassius asked.

Indavara dropped the rope next to Carnifex and bent over him, ear by his mouth. 'Yes.' He pulled the centurion's dagger from the sheath and took off his sword belt. 'Let's turn him over.'

By grabbing his main belt and his right arm, they manoeuvred Carnifex on to his front. Even taking the armour into account, Cassius couldn't believe the weight of the man. Indavara pulled his wrists together and placed one on top of the other.

Eborius came forward and looked thoughtfully down at Carnifex again.

'You did well,' said Cassius. 'The worst of it's over now. Can you bring the cart round?'

Eborius was still staring. Only the blood that trickled from his cheek on to his tunic broke his reverie. 'What?'

'The cart.'

Eborius nodded and walked round to the back of the barn.

By now Indavara had Carnifex's wrists well tied. He moved on to the feet, lashing them together at the ankle. 'We gagging him too?'

'Not right now,' replied Cassius. 'He might choke while he's out.'

'That would be a shame.'

Eborius hauled the cart into the clearing, then set about removing the saddle from his horse.

'What about Carnifex's mount?' Cassius asked when he was done.

Eborius reached into the back of the cart. 'One of my men was killed by the Maseene a few weeks ago. I found these close to the body.'

He dropped three wooden javelins on the ground.

'Ah,' said Cassius. 'Good idea.'

'Can you yoke my horse?'

'No, go ahead,' replied Cassius, not feeling it necessary to explain that he didn't know how. 'I see what you have in mind.'

While the others worked, Cassius jabbed the javelins into Carnifex's saddle. The horse didn't like it much but soon there were several notable indentations in the leather. One javelin actually became stuck, so he left it there.

'Nice job,' observed Eborius as he threw his own saddle up into the cart. 'We'll set it loose here,' he added, walking over and untying the stallion's reins. 'It'll probably find its way back to the mansion.'

Eborius led the horse over to the track and gave it a slap on the rump. Whinnying, it charged away towards the Via Roma.

'Think they'll search the town?' asked Cassius, flinging the other javelins into the grass.

'They'll search everywhere, probably including the ship, but I'll try and make sure they leave the north end of town to us. That old hut is as good a place as any, and it's close if you have to leave suddenly.'

'I presume we'll take the bridge back across the gorge?'

'No, we'll cross the Via Roma and head west. The other bridge is five miles away but we can come around the town, then cut across the Via Cyrenaica and down to the shore. I doubt we'll see anyone given the hour. We better hurry or we'll need torches to light our way.'

Cassius collected up Carnifex's weapons and also threw them into the high grass.

'Don't think he'll be getting free in a hurry,' said Indavara, tapping Carnifex on the shoulder.

Cassius walked over and inspected the wound on the back of the centurion's head. The stave had taken off a big lump of skin.

'Something tells me he's going to be in a fairly bad mood when he wakes up,' added Indavara.

'Let's put him in,' said Cassius. Indavara took the legs and with the other two grabbing the straps of his armour they hauled

Carnifex's dead weight up into the cart. Eborius took the blanket he had left there and draped it over the inert centurion.

'You watch him,' Cassius told Indavara. 'Any noise . . .'

'I hit him with the stave again?'

'No. Just gag him.'

Indavara climbed into the cart. Eborius and Cassius jumped up on to the narrow bench at the front.

'Good idea – that story about the optios,' said the centurion. 'Those two usually go with him everywhere.'

With a gentle tug on the reins, the horse set off and the cart trundled out of the clearing.

XXVI

In fact they saw five people during the journey, the first of them at the second bridge. The gorge was narrower here, and the bridge – though composed entirely of timber – was still in good repair. As they reached the northern side, they passed an elderly peasant with two dead birds in his hand and a bow over his shoulder. He looked down as the cart came near and continued on his way without a word.

Then, as they crossed the Via Cyrenaica outside Darnis, they spied four riders, also traversing the road a mile to the west.

Even at that distance, Eborius could see enough to identify them. 'Maseene. Gods, they come and go as they please now.'

Beyond the tribesmen, and partly obscured by trees, was a damaged section of the aqueduct – an arch with its middle missing.

Cassius glanced over his shoulder at the still-unconscious Carnifex.

'With that bastard gone, perhaps you'll have a chance of improving things here.'

'If it's not already too late.'

Eborius whipped the reins at his horse's back, sending the cart bumping down the side of the road and on to a narrow track that ran between fields of swaying, golden wheat.

'Why has no one harvested this?' asked Cassius.

'Not enough workers,' replied Eborius.

No one spoke again until they were approaching the marsh.

'I assume there's a way through to the hut?' asked Cassius.

'A path. But it's not wide enough for the cart.'

'I think he's coming round,' said Indavara.

'Might be better if he does wake up,' said Cassius. 'At least we won't have to carry him.'

Eborius pulled up his horse and halted the cart. The marsh was thick with low, sprawling trees, twisted branches hanging close to the mud. The path was indeed narrow but clear, made of gravel and sand. Cassius waved away a pair of persistent flies, jumped down and joined Eborius at the rear of the cart.

Indavara removed the blanket and dragged Carnifex back by his legs. The centurion was stirring; grunting and moving his hands. With Indavara holding his armour straps, Cassius his belt and Eborius his feet, they lowered him to the ground, then propped him up against one of the cart wheels. Cassius took the top off his canteen and poured the contents on to Carnifex's face.

As Carnifex blinked and sniffed, Indavara examined the old wound on his forehead. Cassius didn't want to get any closer but also couldn't take his eyes off the hole; it was at least half an inch deep.

'Did an arrow do that?' Indavara asked Eborius.

'The way Procyon tells it, it was a stray bolt that came over a shield wall. Apparently he left it in, kept fighting, then pulled it out later.'

Indavara whistled as he pulled the stave from over his shoulder. Eborius put a hand on his sword hilt.

Cassius took a step backwards. 'How old is he anyway?'

'No one knows. Old. He was at the Battle of Carthage.'

'By Mars,' said Cassius, 'that was almost forty years ago.'

Carnifex's chin was against his chest. Eyelids flickering, he slowly raised his head. He flexed his arms, then realised his hands were tied behind him. Glancing at the trio in turn, he settled his gaze on Eborius.

'Not bad for a barefoot. How long you been planning this?'

'It wasn't his plan, Centurion,' said Cassius. 'I trust you're going to cooperate? If you try anything, I'll have to have my friend here hit you again.'

'Who are you, boy?'

'I'm with Imperial Security. I'm taking you into custody because of your involvement in the death of Augustus Marius Memor. Once we're in Cyrene, my superiors will decide what to do with you.'

When Carnifex frowned, the scar became oval. 'Guess you were on that ship. Looks like I overrated Nicasias.'

'Is that Dio's real name?'

Carnifex let his head drop back against the wheel.

'Get on your feet,' Cassius told him.

'What d'you like, grain man? Gold? Sapphires? Girls?'

'Don't waste your breath.'

'Boys?'

'Get on your feet or we'll knock you out and carry you.'

The old centurion looked up at the sky. 'It's almost dark. If you're putting me on that ship, you won't be leaving till morning. My lads'll find me.'

'The man told you to get up,' said Indavara, stepping closer.

'You got my blood on that stick of yours, One Ear,' replied Carnifex. 'I'll get me a lot more of yours. Count on it.'

Indavara held the stave one-handed and tapped it against the side of Carnifex's head. 'Not going to say it again, old man.'

Carnifex butted the stave aside, then nodded at his feet. 'What about the rope? Unless you want me to hop?'

Nobody moved.

'What? No one wants to get too close to old Carn?'

Indavara drew his sword and put the tip of the blade under Carnifex's chin.

'You so much as twitch and I'll give you a nice new scar for your collection.'

The centurion stared back at Indavara, then gave a lopsided smile. 'I like you. I'll get me that blood of yours, but I do like you.'

Carnifex turned his attention to Eborius as he drew his dagger, knelt down and cut through the rope. 'Got to say, didn't think you had the balls for this, Manius. Don't reckon you could have managed it on your own, though. And you still can't look me in the eye even now, can you?'

'All right, that's enough,' said Cassius.

Eborius finished. He stood up and grabbed Carnifex under the left arm. Indavara grabbed him under the right and they hauled him up.

Carnifex inspected Cassius. 'You really a grain man, boy? Good disguise – 'cause you look like a useless streak of piss.'

'Appearances can be deceptive,' countered Cassius. 'You look like a centurion.'

Carnifex snarled his reply: 'I was a centurion an age before your piece-of-shit father shot his load into whatever bitch you call Mother.'

'Well,' replied Cassius, 'as much as I'd like to continue this stimulating exchange, we don't have time to waste.'

Indavara sheathed his sword and aimed the stave towards the path. 'Move.'

With another grin, Carnifex set off, Indavara close behind him.

'You'll get rid of the cart?' Cassius asked Eborius.

'Later.'

Eborius hurried ahead of the others and led them into the marsh. Cassius took the pack from the cart – and a final glance along the track – then jogged over to take his place behind Indavara.

As they walked on, the smell of mud and decaying vegetation grew stronger. Tiny birds flitted about above them in the higher boughs of the trees, greeting the dusk with their merry chirruping. Twice Indavara told Carnifex to slow down when he got too close to Eborius; the younger centurion turned round regularly to check on the captive. For his part, Carnifex didn't seem overly concerned by his predicament, and even took to whistling a tune that Cassius recognised as an old marching song.

By the time they reached a wide gap in the Phoenician wall, there was barely enough light for them to see their way. Fortunately the hut was close. It had been built only a few yards above the high-water mark, on sandy soil surrounded by pebbles and weed. Atop the uneven stone walls was a sloping timber roof. The two doors – one facing east, the other west – were stained green at the bottom and hinged by lengths of rotting rope. Eborius pulled the west-facing door open and stood to one side.

'In you go,' he told Carnifex.

With a prod from Indavara, the centurion shuffled through the doorway. Eborius stayed outside and took a fire-starting kit from his pack. Cassius walked past him into the hut. It smelt of salt and fish.

'Far corner. Against the wall,' he said.

Cassius and Indavara kept their distance as Carnifex got down on his knees, then sat on the thin reed matting that constituted the hut's floor. Eborius struck the flint with the fire-striker four times before he got a flame. He lit a tiny clay oil lamp and put it in the middle of the hut, then went back outside.

Carnifex calmly watched his captors. 'So you followed Nicasias, eh, grain man?'

'That's right.'

'How'd you connect him to me?'

'We were at the quarry. We saw it all.'

Carnifex failed to hide his surprise at this, but recovered swiftly. 'Reckon you two should go outside with your new friend and take a look at the sun. Might be the last one you ever get.'

'I'm not listening to his shit all night,' said Indavara. 'May as well gag him now.'

'Agreed.'

'Can't see the lamplight from outside,' said Eborius as he returned.

'Good,' replied Cassius, taking a length of cloth from the pack. 'Indavara, if you can again persuade the centurion that he would be wise to cooperate.'

Indavara leant the stave against the wall, then drew his sword and held the tip close to Carnifex's throat.

'Head forward,' instructed Cassius.

'You forgot to say "sir", grain man.'

'Head forward,' Indavara repeated, pressing the metal into Carnifex's skin.

'You ain't going to kill me, One Ear.'

314

'Who says I have to kill you? Maybe I'll just cut out your tongue – see how you like it.'

'Head forward,' Cassius repeated. Still grinning at Indavara, Carnifex finally complied. Cassius bent over him and placed the strip of material in his mouth.

The centurion managed a final taunt. 'Be easier if your hands weren't shaking.'

Cassius pulled the gag tight and tied it off. Indavara sheathed his blade, reclaimed the stave and stood over Carnifex.

Cassius followed Eborius outside. 'What'll you do once you've got rid of the cart?'

'Get back to the barracks. Needs to look like a normal night when the men of the Second turn up – which might be fairly soon. I'll be back before dawn.'

The very mention of the word reminded Cassius just how interminable the night would be. Twelve hours. And at this time of the year – when almost three-fifths of the day was spent in darkness – they were long hours.

Eborius gripped Cassius's arm. 'Corbulo. Watch him. Every single moment.'

'I think he's asleep,' whispered Indavara. 'Either that or he's choked on the gag.'

Cassius took three steps across the hut and peered at the slumped shape next to the lamp. He could just about make out Carnifex's chest moving up and down. He walked back to Indavara. 'No. He's still breathing.'

'Pity.'

'What do you think? Two hours gone? Seems like an eternity already.'

Indavara didn't reply. Cassius knew that he sometimes struggled to keep track of time, which – on occasions like this – seemed almost a skill. Cassius had also noted his remarkable powers of concentration – he could easily spend three or four hours on a single task, a consequence of his training perhaps. It didn't hurt, of course, if one lacked the intellect to consider wider matters or the grand scheme of things.

Cassius could seldom avoid doing so. His mind had a tendency to wander and he constantly had to remind himself to stay alert, focus on the job in hand. But as he stared at the dark shape on the other side of the hut, he felt his eyelids getting heavier by the moment. He and Indavara had been checking outside at regular intervals, so he decided to take his turn.

'Won't be a moment.'

The chill wind woke him up soon enough. He brushed his hair out of his eyes and looked west along the shore. He thought of those black kites from the gorge; imagined them flying high past beaches and coves and cliffs before finally reaching the harbour at Apollonia and the sprawl of Cyrene. Fifty miles – they might be there in two days.

It wasn't until he turned east towards the town that he saw the torches. Some were close to the warehouses but another group were moving along the breakwater towards the *Fortuna*. Cassius had expected as much. But who were they? Men of the First Century or the Second? They'd find no trace of Carnifex on the ship, but what if they realised Cassius and Indavara weren't aboard?

There was, however, a more pressing concern: the group in the harbour had split in two, one heading east, the other heading west along the shore path.

'Shit.'

Keeping his eyes fixed on Carnifex, Indavara backed up to the door.

'What is it?'

'Looks like a search party. Coming our way.'

'Here. Swap.'

As Cassius took his turn to guard the sleeping centurion, more questions assailed him. Would the legionaries remember the hut? Would they see it from the path?

All they could do was wait. Every few moments Cassius would

stick his head out of the door to see how much closer the torches were. At one point he heard – or imagined he heard – Carnifex say something. He walked over to the lamp and looked down; the centurion was asleep but mumbling into the gag.

'They're coming off the path, straight towards us,' said Indavara.

Cassius retreated to the doorway. 'All of them?'

'No. Some are continuing along the shore. One torch. Looks like two men.'

Cassius felt a tap on his arm.

'Hold this.' Indavara offered him the stave. 'If he stirs, hit him again.'

Sliding his blade out of its scabbard, Indavara continued: 'What do I do if they're Carnifex's men?'

Cassius took the stave. 'Whatever you have to.'

Now he could hear the soldiers' boots striking pebbles as they strode across the sand. He snatched a glimpse of the shadowy figures below the torch. They were no more than five yards away when one of them spoke.

'It's Noster. We're coming in. Stay out of sight.'

Indavara hurried inside and stood by Cassius, who wiped sweat away from above his mouth.

Noster walked in, the sizzling torch in his hand. The second soldier was another of the men who'd been at the quarry. They spied Carnifex in the corner and stared at him. The centurion's eyes opened. He squinted up at the torch, then grunted as he struggled to free himself, teeth bared over the gag.

Indavara moved closer to him and waved his sword in Carnifex's face.

'Calm yourself, old man.'

'Some of the First Century are with us,' explained Noster, still unable to take his eyes off Carnifex. 'We volunteered to check in here – all part of the show.'

'What about the ship?'

'Don't worry. Eborius and some men from the First. Bunch of idiots – they don't even know who was on there to start with, let alone who might be missing.' Noster grinned, his uneven teeth lit red by the flames. 'Procyon and Mutilus aren't coping well. They're panicking.'

'You should go,' said Cassius.

'Good luck, sir,' replied Noster.

He pushed the other man out of the door and they set off for the shore path at a run.

Indavara let out a long breath as he sheathed his blade. Cassius returned his stave and glanced over at Carnifex. The centurion's head was between his knees. He looked like a beaten man.

XXVII

Once the soldiers' torches were gone, the only remaining lights were the lanterns aboard the *Fortuna*. When it was his turn to be outside, Cassius would gaze at them and occupy himself by imagining each person aboard. He left Clara until last and devoted at least an hour to various possible scenarios they might enjoy together. He was surprised to be able to think of such things, but the mind-numbing boredom and sapping tension of their night-long vigil demanded the occasional distraction. Apart from a few shouts from the town, all they heard was the gentle lapping of the sea and the occasional snore from Carnifex. Remarkably, the centurion slept on until dawn, only waking when Eborius returned.

'All clear?' asked Cassius.

'Not quite,' replied Eborius, who looked as weary and unkempt as Cassius felt. 'There are still a few of the First Century hanging around. I'll try and keep them out of your way. Give it half an hour, then make your move.'

'What's happening? Noster said Procyon and Mutilus are panicking.'

Eborius came further inside the hut. 'With good cause. Two of their search parties ran into Maseene during the night. They've four dead, twice that wounded.'

He stared at Carnifex. 'The soldiers are starting to think he's dead too. And some of the Roman townspeople are talking about leaving. If you don't go soon they'll be piling onto the *Fortuna*.'

'What will you do?'

Eborius pressed a knuckle against his brow. 'If Procyon and Mutilus will listen to me, I'll withdraw the First Century to the town, then try and find someone to act as an intermediary. See if we can negotiate, restore some sort of order, some sort of peace.'

'You can do it. I'm sure of it. And once I've contacted the governor in Cyrene you'll get some help.'

Eborius didn't look convinced. 'I have to go.'

'My thanks for all you've done,' said Cassius as they gripped forearms.

'Farewell,' said Eborius to Indavara.

'Farewell.'

Carnifex strained at the ropes, bulging eyes locked on the younger centurion. Eborius took one last look at him, then loped back to the shore path where he'd left his horse. Carnifex slumped back against the wall and stamped down hard on the floor. Indavara kicked over the oil lamp and joined Cassius at the doorway. They watched Eborius hoist himself on to his mount, then set off at a gallop towards the causeway.

'Is this him?'

It took a moment for Cassius to register that he'd heard Annia's voice.

Indavara turned first. 'Get away from him!'

Cassius spun round. She was just inside the other door, standing over Carnifex.

The centurion twisted and swept his right boot into her, knocking both her legs away. She cried out as she landed on the ground beside him.

Indavara charged across the hut, ready to swing the stave at Carnifex. He halted with the weapon a yard from the centurion's face. Cassius stopped too.

Carnifex's right boot was hovering just above Annia's neck. The front two hobnails on the sole were unusually long and had been sharpened to a lethal point. Winded by the fall, Annia coughed and spluttered as she stared up at the spikes. Carnifex nodded towards the doorway.

Indavara lowered the stave. He and Cassius retreated.

Carnifex put his left boot on Annia's jaw, pressing her face into the floor. She was whimpering, spittle running down her chin. Careful to keep both boots in position, Carnifex bent his head towards her and moved his mouth.

Cassius had seen the look on Annia's face before: on sacrificial animals before the priest's blade slit their throat.

'You hurt her, I will knock your head off,' Indavara told Carnifex, who moved his mouth again and nodded at Annia.

'Annia,' said Cassius gently. 'Annia, look at me.'

She did so, though her hair half covered her eyes.

'He wants you to take the gag out of his mouth. His hands are tied; he can't do it himself. Can you pull the gag down?'

Carnifex kept his eyes on Indavara but bent his head closer to Annia. She managed to reach up with her left hand.

'That's it,' said Cassius.

Annia gripped the top of the gag and pulled it out of Carnifex's mouth. He sucked in three deep, rasping breaths before speaking. 'You two do anything I don't like and I'm going to make a big hole in that little neck. Weapons on the ground, One Ear. Back to the door.'

Indavara stayed where he was.

Carnifex pushed his left boot down on Annia, distorting the lines of her face.

'You son of a bitch!' snarled Indavara.

Cassius grabbed him by the arm and hauled him backwards. 'What's wrong with you? Do as he says.'

Indavara's face was flushed, his muscles tense. He put down his stave.

'Blades too,' said Carnifex.

Indavara threw his dagger to the floor, then pulled his sword belt off and dropped it. He withdrew to the doorway.

'Sword next to One Ear's,' Carnifex told Cassius. 'Then take out your knife and throw it over here close to my hands.'

Cassius complied. The dagger clattered on to the floor but Carnifex left it where it was, instead pushing a section of the reed matting aside. He then reached down and shifted a couple of the bricks below. When he was satisfied with the arrangement he picked up the dagger handle and jammed it between the two bricks. Then he began to move the ropes tying his wrists up and down the blade.

'You boys were doing all right, but I reckon you didn't count on Beautiful here. Who is she?'

Cassius said nothing. Indavara shifted his feet.

'Don't even think about it, One Ear,' said Carnifex, still working the ropes along the blade. 'Might not kill her straight off, my special studs, but I don't reckon you'll stop her bleeding. Ask yourself – you really want to see that?'

Carnifex was by now through enough of the ropes to free himself. He picked up the dagger, sliced through the gag, then pulled it away. With a smug grin, he shook off the last of the rope.

'How you feeling there, Beautiful?'

Annia was coughing. Carnifex put the blade to her throat and encircled her neck with his other hand. He pulled her up off the floor with him, his eyes not once leaving Indavara.

'What's the name?'

Annia's whole head was shaking, her unblinking eyes unnaturally wide.

Carnifex pressed the metal into her skin. 'Come on now, don't be shy.'

'A-A-Annia. Annia Augusta Memorus.'

'Memorus, eh? Well, well. Looks like you know these two, but let's complete the introductions. I'm Valgus Carnifex. And yes – I'm him. The one who had your father killed. But don't take it personal. I'm sure it won't stop us getting along fine.'

Carnifex pushed Annia in front of him, locking his knife hand around her neck. 'Time for a little walk, boys, and I reckon we best stay away from your mates on that ship. You know the route – we did it yesterday. You first, Streak. One Ear next. And best do as you're told – there's plenty I can cut before I get to her throat.'

As Cassius walked out of the hut towards the path, he heard Carnifex pick up a sword up from the floor. He glanced over at the harbour. Eborius was long gone and there was no sign of anyone on the deck of the *Fortuna*.

'Eyes front, Streak,' snapped Carnifex.

After that, all Cassius heard from behind him was Annia, quietly weeping.

━●8●━

By the time they emerged from the other side of the marsh, Indavara had been through a dozen different plans, none of which stood any real chance of success. As long as Carnifex kept his distance and that blade at Annia's neck there was nothing he could do except bide his time, look for an opportunity.

Corbulo should have let me kill him.

Indavara barely noticed the sky lightening around him or the track ahead; all he could see was Annia on the floor of the hut, squirming under Carnifex's boot. He imagined that blade sliding into her neck; life draining out of her.

Indavara was certain of one thing: he would keep her alive, or die trying.

━●8●━

Cassius's hands formed fists as he walked. They had been so close. What had she done? Watched Eborius from the ship? Followed him to the hut, just to see the man responsible for her father's death?

Stupid, arrogant, headstrong little bitch.

All three of them would pay for it; he was sure of that. What had Indavara said? You can't give a man like that a second chance. Now he had it; and when Cassius thought of what the savage centurion might do to them, his throat dried and his legs almost buckled.

I should have let Indavara kill him.

━●8●━

Carnifex kept them moving and kept them in front of him: Cassius ten paces ahead, Indavara five. They walked on towards the Via

323

Cyrenaica in silence, apart from an occasional whimper from Annia or a grunted order from Carnifex. Once she hissed a curse at him, but whatever he did by way of response kept her quiet for the remainder of the journey.

When they reached the road, Carnifex directed them east towards the town until they came to an old wall at the edge of a field. He ordered Cassius and Indavara to kneel down behind it, facing the road. Cassius turned and watched him position himself behind a nearby tree, with Annia sitting beside him.

'I told you eyes front, Streak!'

Cassius could see part of the road through a hole in the wall. The first people to pass were two middle-aged local men whose horses galloped by, heading west out of town. A quarter of an hour later, six legionaries appeared from the opposite direction. They looked exhausted, trudging along in silence with their heads down.

'Ha!' cried Carnifex.

The men stopped and looked at the tree.

'It's him!'

'It's the centurion!'

'Over here,' ordered Carnifex.

Cassius heard the men scrabbling over the wall, then watched them drop to the ground close by.

'Belletor, Salonius, run into town and find me some horses and a cart.'

'Sir!'

Two of the men sprinted away.

'Marius, take hold of this one for me. Streak, One Ear – stand up. Keep facing the wall.'

Cassius and Indavara got to their feet.

Cassius heard a rush of movement behind him. Something thumped into his back and he was thrown forward. He cried out as his thighs and groin struck the sharp edges of the wall. Thick fingers gripped his neck and smacked his head down on to the cold rock. He heard a hollow thump and lights burst in his eyes.

Cassius thought he might faint but the brightness faded away.

He was left lying on the wall, watching as Carnifex moved on to Indavara, who had turned round to face him.

'Got to get me some of your blood, remember, boy? You know what bleeds a lot?'

Indavara brought his hands up but the centurion caught him cold.

He drove his forehead down into Indavara's, knocking the smaller man backwards into the wall.

'The head.'

Some of the men laughed. Cassius blinked away the sweat in his eyes. Indavara was lying flat, stretched out on the top of the wall. The blood came quickly, running down over his brow, his cheek, then on to the pale grey rock below.

The irony of their reversal of fortune was not lost on Cassius as he lay on his side under a blanket, hands bound, staring down at the muddy contours of the road. It hadn't taken long for the soldiers to return with a cart and now they were on the Via Roma, already well past the gorge and presumably headed for the mansion. Cassius wedged his foot against the other side of the cart to stay as still as possible. The pain from his head had lessened but every bump seemed to rattle through his skull. Indavara was in a worse state, he knew, but when Cassius had turned to check on him and Annia, the legionary guarding them had poked him with his sword.

He thought about rolling out of the back of the cart. Assuming he could even get back up on his feet, with his hands tied he wouldn't be going anywhere fast. And even if he could get away, they were far from Eborius and the men of the Second Century. In any case, he could hardly leave Indavara and Annia; the three of them would share the same fate now.

The road ran up and down a series of short, steep ridges. At the peak of one, Cassius got a good look at Darnis and esti- mated they were at least five miles from the town. They had passed scores of fields (the vast majority untended and

325

overgrown), several empty hamlets, even a handful of roadside inns, yet he hadn't seen a single person.

The cart turned right off the road and under an arch. On either side of it was a high wall running hundreds of feet in both directions. Just after Cassius heard the horses' hooves clatter on stone, they came to a halt in a courtyard.

The blanket was pulled away and a foul-breathed legionary grabbed him by the tunic and hauled him out of the cart. If Cassius hadn't quickly swung his legs down he would have fallen flat on his back. Another legionary pulled him upright and held on to him as two more of them dragged Indavara out. The skin had opened up nastily on his forehead and matted, blood-soaked hair stuck to his brow, but – to Cassius's immense relief – the green eyes were still bright and alert.

'Careful with her,' said Carnifex, striding over as the men lowered a wriggling Annia to the ground. 'We don't get tender white meat like that very often.'

The men laughed along with him.

'To the barn. Salonius, go and get one of the girls to rustle me up some wine and a bit to eat.'

'Sir.'

'Where are Procyon and Mutilus?'

'Not back yet, sir.'

'Send them to me when they are.'

With two men to guard Cassius and four surrounding Indavara, Carnifex took hold of Annia himself and led them into a stable, past a series of empty but well-maintained stalls. They passed through another courtyard and into a barn.

'What's that stench?' said the centurion. Ahead was a wide door, the bottom of which was obscured by the straw that covered much of the barn's floor. The wall to the right was adorned with every type of metallic tool imaginable: rakes, knives, spikes, saws, scythes. To the left, hanging by chains from one of the five large nails hammered into the wall, was a man, or rather what had once been a man.

The face was a sagging, rotten horror. Further down, bits of

326

bone and stringy muscle could be seen beneath the greying flesh and torn tunic. Below the body, the straw was covered with a green-brown sludge.

'Who was that?' asked Carnifex.

'The, er, barley farmer, sir,' said one of the men. 'Didn't pay his pasture dues. What was the name again?'

The other legionaries shrugged or shook their heads.

'Well whoever he was, he stinks,' said Carnifex. 'Get that bloody door open.'

One of the men gestured towards the body. 'Should we put it in the pit, sir?'

'You want to poison him, you prick? No, we'll have something fresh for him before long. Bury it.'

Two soldiers set about removing the body.

Carnifex pointed at Cassius and Indavara. 'Hang 'em up.'

They were led over to the wall.

'Bring me those chairs.'

Once a legionary had done his bidding, Carnifex sat Annia down facing the wall, her bound hands in her lap.

Not for the first time in his life, Cassius was grateful for being tall. He reckoned the nails were about seven feet off the floor. The men had stretched his arms high and dropped the rope tying his wrists over the nail, but he could easily touch the floor. Carnifex shook his head as he watched his legionaries struggle to get Indavara up high enough. Three of them eventually managed it, though the toes of Indavara's boots were barely supporting his weight. He'd made no attempt to resist or even curse at them. Cassius hoped he was saving his strength.

'You lot – disappear,' ordered Carnifex.

The legionaries helped the other two with the body and left through the newly opened door. Beyond was a sunlit section of grass enclosed by a cactus hedge.

Carnifex sat down and leant back in the chair, arms crossed. He turned and looked at Annia. Her hair had come loose and hung down over her face. She had lost her stola and her pert breasts were visible through her tunic.

327

'Mmm,' said the old centurion. 'There's women, then there's girls.'

A soldier arrived with a jug of wine and a plate of bread and cheese. Carnifex pointed at the floor next to his chair. Once the soldier had put the food and drink down, he left. After a few more moments spent staring at his captives, Carnifex picked up the jug and drank noisily.

'Sore throat,' he said, standing up when he'd swallowed half of it. 'That's what comes of having some stinking rag in your mouth for twelve hours.' He took another mouthful of wine and spat it at Indavara.

'How you doing, One Ear?'

As the wine ran down over the still-drying blood, Indavara looked at him.

Carnifex grinned. 'I'm guessing knocking me about with that stave is starting to seem like a pretty bad decision, eh?'

'Yes,' said Indavara. 'I should have stuck you with a blade and had done with it.'

Carnifex laughed, and turned to Cassius. 'I do like him.'

He sat back down, grabbed a hunk of bread and started chewing his way through it.

'I'm so sorry,' Annia said quietly, head bowed.

'You should be, Beautiful,' said Carnifex. 'Otherwise these two might just have got away with it. What were you doing on Rhodes, Streak? The truth – or Beautiful here won't keep her name for long. I'm not a big face man.'

Carnifex reached over and tweaked Annia's left breast. She let out a little cry and managed to drag the chair a few inches away.

Cassius cursed Carnifex, then the girl, then himself, for ever allowing her to set foot on the *Fortuna Redux*.

'I was there to meet Memor,' he said. 'I arrived at the house the day after Nicasias killed him.'

'Lucky.'

'That's not the word I'd use.'

Carnifex tucked in to the lump of cheese.

Cassius doubted he would get another chance to reason with

328

him, though he knew his chances of success were negligible.

'Centurion, I'm a realist. I'm not going to pretend my position is a strong one. But neither is yours. The Service know I'm here. If they don't hear from me soon they will come here and they will retaliate. You may think you're untouchable, but I can assure you, you're not.'

Carnifex didn't bother to finish his mouthful of cheese before replying. 'Streak, no one gets post out from here. Which means if you did contact your masters, you sent a letter from Rhodes. You telling me you already knew then that Nicasias was on his way back to Darnis?'

Cassius was ready for that one. 'Your assassin friend talked too much. To a thief named Drusus Viator – on the ship that brought them to Rhodes from Paphos. My superior is named Aulus Celatus Abascantius. He was friends with Memor, as was Chief Pulcher – I'm sure you know that name – and when they find out the girl's missing too, I think there'll be a ship full of troops arriving here pretty soon.'

'Careful, Streak. I'm starting to think maybe you're threatening me.'

'Not at all. Just making sure you understand the consequences of your actions.'

'Thing is,' replied Carnifex. 'I've known Nicasias since he was your age. One of my best men till he was discharged and took up a new career. When he arrived here needing to lie low for a bit I was happy to look after him – in return for a favour for some associates and me. He sat in the mansion garden yesterday and swore with his hand on his heart that he hadn't spoken to anyone about me *or* Darnis. Reckon I'll take his word over yours any day.'

Cassius thought suddenly of the timber yard. Nicasias had ridden in from the south, probably returning from the mansion. The exchange of greetings between him and Carnifex at the quarry had been purely for the benefit of the three conspirators.

'Course we'll have to do something about your friends at the

329

harbour,' Carnifex continued. 'I could use a ship. But all things considered, probably better to just kill them all and sink it.'

Cassius's head dropped. He had no leverage over the old centurion and Carnifex knew it. He'd been a fool not to listen to Eborius that night at the barracks. They could have already escaped Darnis on the *Fortuna* and left Abascantius to deal with Carnifex later. How many lives would have been saved?

'You should have stayed on Rhodes, Streak. You already know what I do to grain men who get in my way.'

'I didn't know what I would find here. I was just doing my job.'

Carnifex stood up again. He walked over to Cassius, then glanced back at Annia.

'Reckon that's what her old man said when he had me sent here. Took me twenty-five years to reach legion quartermaster of the Fifth Macedonian. Prefect was a useless arse-stabber with a pretty face and a palace accent just like yours, Streak. I led them men. All five thousand of them. Up into the mountains of Dacia to root out mercenaries, north to see off the Goths, even against other legions when them usurpers tried their hand.'

Carnifex stepped closer. 'You know, I'm in the history books, me. First man to win four medals in one battle. All for chopping the heads off Carpi tribesmen no brighter than the barefoots round here. Was one of them gave me this.'

Carnifex pushed a finger into the hole in the middle of his forehead. His stinking bulk had blocked out all the light.

'Then one day the prefect gets a letter from that cocksucker Memor and it's marching orders for old Carn. And for what? Taking a few little extras here and there. So here I am, and I reckon that as Rome don't need me no more, I don't need Rome.'

'I didn't start this,' Cassius said quietly. 'You did – when you sent Nicasias to kill Memor.'

'He'd still be alive if he'd kept out of my affairs. Same goes for you, Streak, but you just had to stick your snout in.'

Carnifex gripped Cassius's nose between his thumb and forefinger. Cassius shut his eyes as the centurion pinched harder. He could feel his teeth grinding together.

Carnifex twisted his fingers in an instant, snapping Cassius's nose.

He felt bone splinter and pierce his skin. As blood ran down into his mouth and his eyes filled with water, he heard himself scream. Forgetting his hands were tied, he tried to bring them down and ended up spasming against the wall, boots scraping the floor.

But the pain had peaked. And as it subsided he heard a voice: 'Corbulo, put your head back.'

'Cassius,' Indavara continued. 'Put your head back.'

Cassius did it, and after a time the flow of blood began to slow.

'Keep it up,' advised Indavara calmly. 'Deep breaths.'

Cassius blinked away salty tears and spat out blood.

Procyon and Mutilus walked into the barn. With only a passing glance at the three captives, they stopped beside Carnifex and bowed their heads.

'Sir.'

Carnifex sat down again and spoke while he chewed through the last of the bread. 'Twelve hours I was gone. You had a hundred and thirty men and you didn't manage to send one of them to a hut less than a mile from the harbour. If not for this' – he nodded at Annia – 'I'd probably be on my way back to Rome by now.'

'I'm truly sorry, Centurion,' said Procyon.

'Me too, sir,' added Mutilus.

'Who's still out?'

'Couple of squads on horseback,' replied Procyon. 'Everyone else is here.'

Carnifex continued to speak without looking at them. 'Gather the men by the barracks. We're going to have some fun with these two.'

'Sir,' said Procyon. 'We lost four men in skirmishes with the Maseene overnight and there have been several sightings of a large band of them gathering on the plain.'

'How big?'

'Around a hundred.'

Carnifex snorted. 'I'm shaking.'

'Sir, even some of our people in the town are talking about leaving. And the locals – this talk of the clans coming together—'

'Talk. How much bloody talk have we heard in the last year? What does Sulli say?'

'He says the clans haven't come together in a century and they're not about to start now.'

'Exactly. And he knows them better than anyone.'

'We've also seen more of them close to the town, sir,' added Procyon. 'More than ever.'

Carnifex sighed. 'All right. Standing order – every man to carry full weaponry, armour and shield at all times. Now do as I said and gather them at the barracks.'

'Yes, sir.'

Procyon and Mutilus left.

Cassius decided he had nothing to lose. 'Carnifex.'

His voice sounded strange: muted and low. 'It's not only the Service you have to worry about. Another of my patrons is Prefect Oppius Julius Venator of the Fourth Legion. I have powerful friends. They will avenge me.'

Carnifex took a last swig of wine.

'What'll they know, Streak, these friends? That you, your mate, a girl and a bunch of sailors headed south from Rhodes after some ship? Could easily have been lost in a storm. There won't be a trace of you – I'll make sure of it. All except Beautiful that is. I've got me a maid, but I've done her every way I can think of – and you know what, it's getting a little stale. Think the magic's gone.' Carnifex ran a finger down Annia's tear-stained cheek. 'A year or two of fun with me then I'll hand her down to Procyon and Mutilus. When they've had their fill, she can join the other serving girls and double as a barracks whore.'

Carnifex stood and lifted Annia up off the chair, his thick, filthy fingers around her pale throat once more.

Indavara strained against the ropes, his face colouring as veins bulged on his arms and neck.

Carnifex laughed. 'Reckon you boys'll be thinking on that – and how there was nothing you could do about it – just before your eyes close for the last time.'

XXVIII

Simo and Asdribar hurried past the dye works, anxious to see what had drawn so many of the townspeople into the square. Cassius had told neither of them about the plan to capture Carnifex, only that he and Indavara would be returning at dawn. And so when a tearful, desperate Clara reported that Annia was also missing, Asdribar didn't wait long before deciding they should head into Darnis to investigate.

As they got closer to the crowd, Simo realised the townspeople were gathered around a group of legionaries. Behind them, lined up on the Via Cyrenaica, were a dozen carts loaded with belongings. There were many women there, a few children too.

Simo kept close to Asdribar as the Carthaginian pushed his way through the locals. Noster and the other soldiers had formed a protective cordon around two injured comrades, one of whom had a bandaged thigh, the other a wounded wrist. All the soldiers had the 'II' sewn on to their tunic sleeves. Centurion Eborius was kneeling between them, trying to talk to his men, but the locals were firing questions at him.

'Where were they attacked?'

'What about the First Century?'

'Why isn't Carnifex taking action?'

'Why aren't you doing anything?'

Eborius stood and held up his hands. 'One at a time. Give me a chance to speak.'

As the crowd quietened, he noticed Simo and Asdribar. 'Why are you still here?'

'They didn't come back,' said Asdribar. 'And we can't find the girl.'

'Noster, with me.'

The veteran followed Eborius as the centurion ushered Simo and Asdribar away through the crowd, some of whom groaned and shouted protests. Only when he was out of earshot did Eborius speak again.

'Noster, go and check the hut. Quickly!'

The legionary ran over to a group of horses tied to a vacant market stall.

'When did the girl go missing?'

'Dawn,' replied Asdribar. 'Her maid said she went out on deck and never came back inside.'

'She knew what Corbulo was doing?'

'No, sir,' answered Simo. 'He didn't even tell us.'

'She must have been waiting for them,' said Eborius. He gazed towards the harbour. 'Perhaps she saw me – where I went.'

'She was desperate to know what was going on,' said Simo.

'So am I,' said Asdribar. 'What's this about a hut?'

'Just down the coast there,' answered Eborius. 'That's where they were keeping him.'

'Keeping who? And what about last night? Why were you and those others searching my ship?'

Eborius lowered his voice. 'All right, listen. We wanted to keep it between us but you may as well know now. It was Carnifex – he was behind the murder of Annia's father. We grabbed him yesterday. Corbulo and Indavara were holding him in the hut. I had to go along with the search, pretend I was helping his men.'

'So what do you think happened?' asked Asdribar.

'I don't know. It's only been an hour or so. Let's see what Noster finds.'

Two men ran over to them. Simo expected them to address Eborius, but it was Asdribar they were interested in.

'That your ship?' asked one.

'It is.'

'How much to take us and our families?'

'My vessel's not available for hire.'

Simo was relieved to hear that. From what he'd seen over the past week, the captain was a good, fair-minded man. But sitting somewhere in his deckhouse was a stash of gold coins, and if Master Cassius, Indavara and Annia really were missing, surely he might be tempted to leave – especially as the situation in Darnis seemed to be worsening by the hour.

'We have money,' said the man.

'Plenty of money,' added the other.

'You heard the man,' said Eborius. 'Back over there. I'll speak to you all in a moment.'

The pair grudgingly left.

Asdribar glanced at Eborius's soldiers. 'What's going on?'

'More attacks by the Maseene last night,' explained the centurion. 'Killed a farmer and his sons. My men were hurt after running into another lot. Some of the townspeople have already gone. The Maseene won't harm the locals, but the settler families have a lot more to fear. They're thinking about forming a column and heading west to the Five Cities. They want me and my men to provide an escort. Wait here.'

Eborius ran back to the crowd and quietened them down. Simo and Asdribar listened as he tried to reassure the people but it seemed minds had already been made up. As he spoke, a man wearing a purple-edged cloak approached the crowd.

'That the governor?' asked Asdribar.

'I think so,' said Simo.

Lafrenius Leon stopped at the edge of the crowd and waited for people to turn and notice him. He was lean almost to the point of emaciation, his thinning hair forming a V atop his head. When the noise died down, he clasped his hands behind him and spoke with an affected gravitas. 'People, these are difficult times. But we must put our trust in Centurion Carnifex and the men of the First Century. They have protected our lands for years—'

'They can't protect a damn thing any more!'

'Where is Carnifex anyway?'

'I heard he's missing – that's who they were out looking for last night. I heard the Maseene got him!'

Leon blanched and didn't say another word. As the discussion descended once more into a shouting match, Noster's mount came charging back into the square. When Simo saw what the legionary was carrying, he knew something had gone dreadfully wrong. Eborius shouldered his way back through the crowd and ran over to them.

'The hut's empty, sir,' Noster said as he dismounted. 'All I found were these . . .'

He showed Eborius Indavara's stave and dagger and Cassius's sword.

'. . . and this,' he added, passing his centurion a few strands of rope.

'Cut,' said Eborius. 'By the gods, he's free.'

He glanced around the square.

'Where could Master Cassius and the others be?' asked Simo.

'Look," said Eborius, "I did all I could to help. My first obligation is to these people.'

Another of the legionaries jogged over to the centurion. 'Sir, they want to leave now. They say they're going with or without us.'

Eborius looked despairingly up at the sky before responding. 'Take the men back to the barracks and saddle the horses. I want everyone in full armour and ready to leave within the hour.'

'Yes, sir.'

The legionary hurried away.

'You'll do nothing?' Simo asked quietly.

'Remember your place, servant,' snapped Eborius. 'Carnifex lives in a fortified compound and has one hundred and thirty men. I have thirty-seven. Thirty-five that can walk.'

'And the girl?' said Asdribar.

'There are women *here*. And children. I suggest you return to your ship and cast off. I'm sorry.'

Eborius looked at the weapons Noster was still holding and pointed at Simo. 'You might as well return those.'

He walked back towards the crowd.

'You won't leave them, will you, Captain?' asked Simo.

Asdribar nodded at the departing Eborius. 'If he won't help, what can I do?'

'Can't we even look for them?'

'My men are sailors, not soldiers. I've asked enough of them over the last week as it is.'

'We cannot leave.'

Asdribar looked at the crowd. 'Everyone else is.'

He strode away towards the harbour.

Noster handed Simo the three weapons, then gripped his arm.

"Don't give up. I'll work on the centurion – bring him round. He won't just leave them to die, I know it. But you must do your part.' He pointed at Asdribar. 'Persuade him to stay – until sundown at least. If your friends aren't back by then, they aren't coming back.'

━■8►

The legionaries of the First Century were horribly impressive. Cassius had expected an ill-disciplined mob of misfits and criminals, but Carnifex's men were orderly and well turned out, with only the thick beards and excessive number of tattoos suggesting an unconventional regime. Many of them wore sleeveless tunics to better display the single 'I' etched in green ink on their upper arms. The emblem of the Third Augustan was Pegasus, so winged horses were also popular; the ever-present eagle too. Of the phrases detailed on the leather shield-covers in yellow or white paint, as many honoured Carnifex as the gods.

The soldiers looked on as the three prisoners were taken out through the mansion gate and across the road. There were mocking smiles and muttered jokes and an air of jubilation about them; they were glad to have their centurion back.

The Via Roma ran right through the centre of Carnifex's headquarters. Cassius took a brief glance back over his shoulder at the mansion. It was a huge, luxurious villa flanked by towers and surrounded by a ten-foot wall. The building and grounds appeared well maintained and Cassius spied a dozen local servants – men and women – gathered by the main door.

To the south the Via Roma ran down to a plain several hundred

338

feet below. A thin haze hung over the yellow expanse; mile after mile of barren ground interrupted only by a few scattered pockets of date palms. In the distance was an unending sea of low, rolling hills.

Opposite the mansion were the barracks: a low, red-brick building built at ninety degrees to the road. The legionaries were lined up outside, holding spears and helmets as well as their shields. Cassius was near the front, behind Procyon; and when he didn't keep up, he got a spear-point in his back from the man guarding him. He glanced at some of the more amenable-looking legionaries (they were few and far between) and briefly considered appealing to them, telling them who he was. But – apart from the thought of the spear point slicing into his flesh instead of pricking it – he was certain he would be wasting his breath. Carnifex had had a long time to make the First Century his own.

Though his hands were still tied, Cassius was able to reach up and touch his nose. He felt the drying blood beneath his nostrils, then dared to reach higher. But as soon as he felt bone moving under the skin, he cried out, provoking chuckles from the men.

Then there were whistles and jeers as the legionaries turned their attention to Annia. Cassius was surprised to find he could barely summon any anger towards the girl now, even though her actions had probably cost him his life. His guts churned as he thought of what awaited her. Death would be better.

Procyon led the way past a smaller building and a deep hollow in the ground filled with refuse. Cassius looked back again. The legionaries were all following and he noticed the long-haired Maseene guide, Sulli, amongst them. Indavara was walking with his head down, Mutilus right behind him. Annia was further back, with Carnifex.

The well-trodden path traversed a low ridge, then ran along the right side of another, far larger hollow thirty feet across and ten deep. This, Cassius presumed, was 'the pit' Carnifex had mentioned. At the far end, behind a hefty iron gate, was the dark mouth of a cave. Chains ran up from the gate to a joist mounted at the pit's edge.

Procyon turned and held up a hand. Cassius stopped. The pain from his nose was tolerable now but he felt bereft, utterly drained of physical and mental strength. The day was bright, the sun warm on his face, but he was shivering. He couldn't think straight, couldn't connect one thought to another. He wished he was closer to Indavara.

Procyon turned him round so that his back was to the pit.

'On your knees,' ordered the bowl-haired optio.

The soldiers filed round the edge of the pit. Mutilus pushed Indavara down next to Cassius and stationed the guard with the spear behind them. Indavara's bloodstained brow and eyelids seemed almost pink in the sunlight. Cassius was glad to be beside him again. He looked at his face, desperate for some sign of hope, but Indavara just gazed blankly down at the muddy ground.

'I'm sorry,' said Cassius. 'You were right.'

The bodyguard didn't seem to hear him. He looked up as another soldier brought Annia towards them.

The men parted to let Carnifex through.

'Spread out there!' he ordered. 'Right the way around.'

The centurion still had his muscle cuirass on and was now armed once more with dagger and sword. His sturdy bronze helmet hung from a strap on his shoulder. Ignoring the captives, he looked on, arms crossed, as the men swiftly followed his instructions. He then raised a hand. Every last man became silent.

'Morning, First,' he growled.

'Morning, sir,' came the rumbling reply.

'You've had a long night thanks to these two. Mercenaries – paid to kidnap me by an old enemy.'

'That is a lie!' blurted Cassius. 'I am an—'

Procyon was quick. His boot caught Cassius in the chest; a weak blow, but enough to send him backwards into the mud.

Carnifex continued: 'But luckily old Carn got the better of them.'

He turned to Annia. 'Grabbed this bitch too. A keeper, don't you reckon?'

Shouts and grunts from the men. Carnifex picked strands of

hair away from Annia's face, gently tucking them behind her ears. She wiped her eyes.

The guard let Indavara help Cassius back on to his knees.

'Now,' said Carnifex, 'I'm thinking it's about time Chief had himself another meal. There's slim pickings on Streak, but One Ear here's got plenty of beef on him. Time for a wager or two, boys.'

Carnifex waved at the men standing above the cave. The chains rattled as they hauled the gate upward. Someone began a chant.

'Chief! Chief! Chief!'

Cassius and Indavara turned in time to see the soldiers tie the chains off. The men closest to the cave cheered and the noise grew.

'Chief! Chief! Chief! Chief!'

Two orange eyes glinted in the shadows, then the lion padded out into the light. It was a lean, long-legged beast, with a jagged scar down its left haunch and a heavy, golden mane that turned to black at its shoulders. The lion yawned – exposing two long, curved, yellowing incisors – and looked around at the soldiers, blinking. Then it licked its lips.

The men cheered again.

Cassius had just about recovered himself. He turned to Indavara. 'You did say you'd always wanted to see one.'

'I think I changed my mind.'

'Took him a while to get used to man flesh,' Carnifex told them, scratching at the arrow hole in his forehead as he spoke, 'but once he realised that was all he'd be getting he got to like it well enough.'

He held up a hand again and the chant ended. 'First Century, make your bets!'

There was a flurry of activity as opinions and coins were exchanged and wagers made. From what Cassius could gather, most of them seemed to centre on how long they would survive and which part of them 'Chief' would eat first.

He forced himself to block out the noise and looked at the man kneeling next to him. How long since he'd come to his aid at that inn at Palmyra? No more than three months. It seemed like years.

Indavara was once more staring down at the ground. Even he couldn't do anything now. They were going to die here, and what a sordid, terrible death it would be.

'You might as well tell me now.'

Indavara looked at him.

'Who you are,' continued Cassius. 'Where you come from.'

Indavara hardly seemed to think about it.

'I took a blow to the head somehow. I was still delirious when the slave trader sold me for the contests in Pietas Julia. The only man who knew me was killed in the arena the next day. All they could tell me was my name. I remember only the last six years of my life. I don't know who I am.'

Before Cassius could even absorb what he'd heard, Annia dropped to her knees. Too far away to hear their hushed conversation, she was just looking at them, her contorted, tear-streaked face a reflection of the suffering within. She fell forward, arms covering her head.

Carnifex hauled her back to her feet. 'No, no, Beautiful. You're going to watch every last moment. That way you'll be nice and obedient from the start.'

Indavara was glad to have said it. Even though he knew death was close, it felt good to have told Corbulo the truth.

He also knew there was no way he was going to let Carnifex live. He scraped dried blood out of his eyes and looked up. The centurion was directly ahead of him, Annia to the right. The closest soldier was Mutilus, a couple of yards to the left.

'All right,' shouted Carnifex. 'Finish up now, lads.'

He tilted his head towards the pit. 'Put 'em in.'

Procyon unsheathed his knife and came towards Indavara, who had bowed his head again.

'Don't worry,' added Carnifex. 'We won't leave you completely defenceless – we'll let you use your hands.'

'Why don't you try punching him?' suggested Procyon, giggling as he cut through the ropes.

Indavara let his hands drop by his sides, then rubbed his wrists to get the blood flowing.

'Hands,' said Procyon.

As Cassius offered them, he sliced the blade down, cutting the ropes. The optio turned away and replaced his dagger in the sheath on his belt.

'Now then,' said Carnifex. 'Who's first?'

Before the last word was out of his mouth, Indavara had already sprung to his feet. He plucked the dagger from Procyon's belt and charged at Carnifex. Some enterprising legionary got his shield up and drove it at him, but managed only a glancing blow to the shoulder.

Mutilus was also moving. With no time to go for his sword, the one-eyed optio came out swinging. Indavara was already under the punch when he drove his left elbow into Mutilus's chin. Bone struck bone. Mutilus's head snapped up and he tottered backwards. Ignoring the pain shooting up his arm, Indavara raised the dagger as he bore down on Carnifex. But Carnifex was ready for him.

The centurion slammed one hand into Indavara's chest, stopping him dead. The other huge paw clamped around his fingers and the dagger handle. Indavara felt one of his fingers slide across the other, then heard a crack. The pain came a moment later. Carnifex let go. The dagger fell to the ground.

Carnifex spat in Indavara's face and gripped his tunic. He stomped three steps forward and drove him bodily into the air, flinging him straight over the still-kneeling Cassius.

Indavara hit the ground hard and slid towards the lip of the pit. Only by turning at the last moment did he ensure he fell feet first. His boot caught the side on the way down, breaking his fall, and he rolled to a stop, covered in mud. The roar from the legionaries was so loud that he got to his feet in an instant, fearful that the lion might already be coming at him. But for the moment it was just watching, eyes half-lidded, tail idly swinging.

Indavara looked down at his right hand. The shattered little finger was hanging at an unnaturally acute angle.

Carnifex came up to the edge of the pit and glowered down at him with a triumphant grin. 'You think you're the first to try and do for old Carn, One Ear? You ain't even the hundred and first!'

The men were in raptures, jumping and whooping at the old centurion's every word.

'Looks like you're first up. Don't reckon this'll take too long.'

'Chief! Chief! Chief! Chief!'

The lion was prowling from side to side now, head low, eyes fixed on its prey.

Cassius glanced back at Annia. She was standing completely still, hands over her eyes, mouthing something to herself.

Indavara watched the lion; the dead eyes, the open, expectant mouth. He fought off an image of the broad paws pinning him to the ground, the huge head blocking out the sky as the teeth tore at his neck . . .

It's just an animal.

Though he'd never seen one, gladiators talked a lot: about tricks, methods, techniques. He'd only ever heard one piece of advice when it came to lions. *Don't take a single step backwards.* He didn't have a lot else to work with.

Indavara took off his belt and slid the buckle up to one end.

It's just an animal. It's just an animal.

He took a long breath, then marched across the pit towards the lion, the belt in his left hand.

'Is he insane?' said one of the men.

'By Mars,' said another.

Cassius looked up at Carnifex, who was standing next to him, brow now heavily furrowed. 'Bet you never saw that before, did you?'

The lion was still shifting from side to side, swinging its head and pawing the ground. Indavara kept his feet well apart and stretched his arms high to make himself big. When he was ten feet away, the lion shifted again – a couple of inches backwards.

Indavara accelerated into a run. The lion held its ground. When he was just two yards away, Indavara whipped the belt down at the beast's head. The buckle caught it right on the nose, ripping out a sliver of black flesh.

The lion jumped back with a yelp.

'By all the gods,' said another of the soldiers.

Cassius wiped his wet face with his sleeve and yelled at the men around him. 'See that, you miserable whoresons? He's survived worse than this and he's a better man than every last stinking, criminal, bloody one of you!'

This time Procyon's boot struck Cassius between his shoulder blades, sending him sprawling face first on to the ground. He lay there at the edge of the pit.

Indavara whipped the belt from the left this time, narrowly missing the lion's head. The beast roared and Indavara caught a whiff of rotten breath. It sunk its front paws into the ground and lowered its head, ready to leap.

Thud. Thud. Thud. Thud.

The four arrows embedded themselves in the lion's flank in quick succession. The animal's back legs gave way first, then it keeled over on to its side. Clawing at the mud, it let out a weak moan. Indavara watched the pink stomach expand only three times more before it became still. He turned to where the arrows had come from.

So did Cassius, Carnifex and the men of the First Century. They had been so intently focused on the action below that no one had noticed the twenty or so figures now getting to their feet on the ridge separating the pit from the barracks. A deep voice rolled towards them, clear even over the legionaries' shouts and the drawing of swords.

'The games are over, Carnifex,' said Eborius, whose sheer size would have identified him even without the crested helmet. He was flanked by his men, Noster included. At least half were wielding bows and every one was now aimed at the old centurion.

Carnifex took a sour look at the fallen lion but was quick with his reply. 'Seems to me they've just begun.'

Eborius addressed the men: 'First Century, I don't want any trouble. I ask only that you hear me out.'

345

'Manius,' replied Carnifex smoothly, 'let's discuss this like officers.'

'No. Your men will know the truth, Carnifex. I don't want a fight, but be in no doubt. If you try anything, I'll give the order. One of the bolts will hit you.'

'And then you'll all die.'

'We'll see. Legionaries, I don't know what the centurion's told you, but that man next to him is named Corbulo, and he is an agent of the Imperial Security Service.'

Cassius glanced up again at Carnifex, who was looking less sure of himself by the moment.

Eborius pointed at Indavara. 'That man is his bodyguard and the girl is the daughter of Augustus Marius Memor, deputy commander of the Service. Carnifex had him assassinated. The four people found dead yesterday were his accomplices and he killed them too, at the quarry last night. I saw it with my own eyes.'

'You won't have any eyes when we're done with you!' shouted one of Carnifex's men. There were a few cheers, but only a few. Cassius looked around; some of the legionaries seemed concerned by what they'd heard.

'How many jugs of wine today, Manius?' said Carnifex calmly. 'Your imagination's running wild.'

Eborius continued: 'I know some of you won't care what he's done, but know this: if they don't return to their ship, the captain will sail to Egypt and Corbulo's man will make contact with the Service there. It might take weeks or even months, but Carnifex's rule will come to an end. All I can offer you is a choice. I know that most of you weren't party to these crimes. Side with me, and you might still have a future with the army.'

'Anyone who takes a single step towards that lying son of a bitch will have me to deal with!' yelled Mutilus.

'You'll hang alongside your master, Mutilus,' replied Eborius. 'But the rest of you have a way out.'

Some of the legionaries were talking, especially those well away from Carnifex and the optios.

But beyond the low hum of their voices was a distant thrumming Cassius knew well: horses on the move.

346

Procyon suddenly looked around him, examining the faces of the men. 'Where's Sulli?'

Carnifex looked around too.

Cassius glanced up at the ridge. Some of Eborius's men had turned to the south.

'Maseene!' shouted one.

Without waiting for an order, several of them ran back down the ridge, away from the pit and towards the road. Eborius looked south. Despite the distance, Cassius saw his features freeze. The centurion hesitated for a moment, then waved the rest of his men after the others.

'First, to the mansion!' ordered Carnifex, his voice steady. He slipped his dagger from its sheath and held it under Cassius's chin. 'Up, grain man.'

Cassius got to his feet.

'And you over here, One Ear!' added Carnifex. 'You ain't going anywhere.'

With a despairing glance at Eborius, Indavara ran back to the edge of the pit, tying his belt on the way. As the rest of the First Century flooded past them, Mutilus and another man reached down and pulled him up.

Carnifex pushed Annia into Procyon's arms. 'Those two try anything, slit her throat. All of you, move!'

As he ran, Cassius looked up at the ridge. Eborius had disappeared.

XXIX

Cassius almost collided with a legionary. In avoiding him, he somehow tripped over his own feet but a steadying hand grabbed his arm. Indavara came up beside him as they bolted along the side of the barracks.

Despite the weight of their shields and armour, the quickest of Carnifex's men were already crossing the road. Suddenly, the mansion gate swung shut in front of them. Cassius saw the long-haired Sulli lock it, then hold up the key, mocking the legionaries as he withdrew. He escaped through the grounds, accompanied by some of the male servants.

The thunder of the horses seemed to envelop the trapped Romans, echoing off the walls of the mansion and barracks. Hundreds of Maseene surged up from the plain, their ranks spread far beyond the width of the road. Their unsaddled mounts were small and lithe, galloping across the ground at tremendous speed. Most of the barefoot warriors had circular shields strapped to their right arms and daggers on their left wrists. They hunched forward on their mounts, one hand on their reins, one gripping their javelins, long black hair streaming out behind them.

As he and Indavara passed the end of the barracks, Cassius found himself in the middle of Carnifex's men. Some were still trying to force the gate open, while others looked around desperately for another way out. Cassius was surprised to see Eborius's men retreating south along the road towards them. Beyond were dozens more Maseene, urging their horses forward at a trot, corralling the Romans towards the main force.

Cassius listened in to Carnifex.

'Trying to run us down while we're strung out. They won't be half so keen on a stand-up fight.'

Cassius felt a hand grip his tunic and pull him to a halt. Mutilus took hold of Indavara, sword already drawn.

'Barracks?' said Procyon.

'Too late for that,' replied Carnifex as he stopped in the middle of the road.

'First!' he bellowed. 'Gather here!'

Even the legionaries pressed up against the gate instantly ran back to the centurion. Carnifex grabbed the nearest man, turned him towards the advancing tribesmen and slammed his shield into the ground. 'Form the line here between the mansion wall and the barracks.'

He then looked north up the road, seemingly unconcerned about Eborius and his men. 'A third of you take ten paces that way and do the same there. Go!'

Carnifex turned to Mutilus and pointed at the wall. 'Dump those two there. Procyon, keep that girl close.'

Mutilus waited for the soldiers to pass, then pushed Cassius and Indavara across the road.

The first row of men in Carnifex's southern rank planted their shields and shuffled sideways to form an even line. Despite the onrushing Maseene, they moved calmly and efficiently and communicated with quiet words and gestures. One last legionary nipped between the end of the shield wall and the mansion wall, then the gap was closed.

'Interlock!' ordered Carnifex. 'Anyone with a spear, get it over the top and ready.'

Carnifex pulled on his helmet as he stalked up the road across the ten-yard square formed by the two lines of troops and the walls of the mansion and barracks.

Eborius's retreating men were now mixed in with those of the First Century. One man took exception to this, pushing a legionary from the Second Century away with his shield, but Eborius aimed his sword at the aggressor. 'You got a problem, you can settle it with me when this is done.'

'Couldn't have said it better myself,' interjected Carnifex. 'Take command of your line, Centurion. Let's see if you really have finally grown a pair of balls.'

Eborius snatched another look at the advancing tribesmen and gave a grim nod.

'Oh, and watch your back,' added Carnifex.

'Anyone with a bow, second rank,' ordered Eborius. 'Everyone else behind a shield.'

Procyon crouched down with Annia, close to the southern line. Mutilus coaxed Cassius and Indavara further to the right and shoved them down on the ground by the mansion wall.

'Remember who's got your girlfriend,' he said, pointing at Procyon. When he saw they were watching, the other optio tapped his dagger blade against Annia's cheek. Mutilus hurried back to join Carnifex.

Cassius got up on his knees and watched as the Maseene on both sides slowed their mounts. With the Romans spread out and disorganised they would easily have held the advantage, but Carnifex had taken only a few moments to give Darnis's divided garrison a fighting chance. Eborius had fewer men on his side, fifty at the most, but he faced the lesser force – no more than a hundred.

Cassius put a hand on Indavara's shoulder. 'Fortuna must be on your side. Surely not even you could kill a lion with a belt buckle.'

Instead of replying, Indavara grabbed Cassius's tunic and dragged him back against the wall. A long javelin landed in the muddy ground where Cassius's legs had been.

'Gods. Thanks.'

The weapon's shaft was still wobbling when Indavara pulled it out. He looked along the wall but Procyon had already seen him. The optio shook his head like a parent admonishing a child. Indavara threw the javelin away. 'We have to get her away from him.'

Two more javelins landed close by. Another struck the wall above them and fell harmlessly into Cassius's lap. He put it down by his side where Procyon couldn't see it. The Maseene weapons were different to the army's shorter, metal javelins; the shaft was wood, and they were as tall as a man, with a broad-bladed iron head.

Soon dozens of the javelins were raining down on the Romans. Most of them thudded into the hide covers and planking of the shields, but a few found their way through. Two cries went up from the northern line and one legionary without a helmet staggered backwards, hand gripping his face. Cassius squeezed back against the wall and followed Indavara's example, bowing his head and covering it with his arms.

'Second rank!' shouted Carnifex, now crouching behind his men. 'Turn and put your shields up. Now they'll hit us in the back.'

Having made little impact on the first rank, the Maseene lengthened their range precisely as Carnifex had predicted. There were far fewer shields on Eborius's side and three men at the rear were struck immediately.

One unfortunate fell just yards from Cassius. The javelin had somehow found its way through the panels of his plate armour and into his flank. Lying on his side, he bit down so hard that his teeth sank deep into his bottom lip.

Javelins now littered the section of road between the Roman lines.

'Steady there, lads,' shouted Carnifex as he buckled his chin-strap. 'There won't be many more. They usually carry three to a man and they'll keep one in hand for later.'

Moments later, the hail of javelins petered out.

'Coming forward, sir!' another man told the centurion. 'Still on horseback.'

'I can hear that. Don't fret – those desert nags'll start getting nervous soon.'

Carnifex checked on the situation to the north, where the horsemen were also closing in. The legionaries on both sides were virtually silent. Maseene voices yelled what sounded like a mixture of instruction and encouragement.

'Still coming forward, sir,' said Mutilus. 'Hundred feet.'

'Yes, yes,' said Carnifex. He pulled a man out of the line and ordered him to collect up some of the javelins.

'Dismounting, sir,' said Mutilus.

'Archers to the north,' shouted Carnifex. 'Wait until they're good and close.'

Eborius – keeping his big frame hidden behind two shields – turned and looked at Carnifex. The old centurion gave him a wolfish grin.

Cassius and Indavara got up on their knees again. The Maseene were forming a dense attacking line, leaving perhaps a fifth of their number at the rear to take charge of the mounts. At a shouted signal the tribesmen on both sides jabbed their javelins into the air three times. At a second shout they unleashed a long, piercing war cry. Their march towards the Romans became a run.

'You got a spear or a sword, protect your shield-man,' ordered Carnifex.

Closer to Cassius and Indavara, Noster drew his bow and aimed it over the crouching men who formed the first line. 'Sir?'

'Wait.'

Eborius watched the advancing warriors, his dark face slick with sweat beneath his helmet.

'Sir?' repeated Noster.

When Eborius's order finally came, it was a full-blooded shout. 'Loose!'

Twenty bowstrings snapped tight and as many screams went up from the Maseene line. Noster and the others reached for their next arrow.

'Keep those shields together!' ordered Carnifex, making adjustments where the row of legionaries curved slightly to join up with the corner of the barracks.

The Maseene slowed as they reached the shield walls. Though some had swords strapped to their belts or the little daggers ready at their forearms, almost all attacked with javelins, jabbing over the tops of the shields. The legionaries behind them stayed low,

352

solely occupied with keeping the barrier in place. The second rank did as Carnifex had instructed, hacking at any well-aimed javelins with their swords.

Despite the numbing din of grunts and shouts and the clash of metal and wood, Cassius saw that the southern line was swiftly settling into a stalemate. The outnumbered Romans couldn't advance but the lightly armed Maseene couldn't break through Carnifex's immaculate line. The two sides would keep at each other until fatigue set in or a breach was made.

Eborius's men were faring better. With a smaller force attacking them – and no more thrown javelins to worry about – the archers were able to pick their targets. Without a single piece of armour between them, Maseene were falling one after the other.

'They should withdraw,' said Cassius.

'Not likely,' replied Indavara. 'Look at their faces.'

Cassius had seen such wild-eyed fury before and he knew these men had more reason to despise Rome than any Palmyran warrior.

Eborius swung his long blade and chopped the end off a Maseene javelin, then ducked down to survey his line. Satisfied that they were more than holding their own, he turned and looked at Carnifex, who had stopped next to the pile of javelins collected by the legionary. Bent almost double, Eborius then moved left along the line to Noster, who was drawing an arrow from his quiver. He spoke a few words into the veteran's ear, then returned to the fray, discouraging the Maseene with more broad sweeps of his sword.

'Centurion!' came a desperate shout from the First Century. A group of Maseene three or four deep had clustered close to the centre of the southern line and some of the massed javelin thrusts were starting to tell. Two legionaries were already on the ground and in moments two more fell back. Others moved quickly to take up their shields but the line was looking vulnerable.

Carnifex, still with sword undrawn, picked up two of the Maseene javelins and ordered the legionary to follow with the rest. Crouching low, he ran to the over-pressed section. Weighing

353

one of the weapons in his hand, he suddenly stood up straight and flung the javelin over the top of a shield. Cassius saw two arms fly up and heard an agonised shriek. Carnifex crouched over once more and took five steps to his left. He popped up again and let fly, this time hitting another unprotected warrior in the face. The legionary passed him more javelins and on he went, never appearing in the same place twice, always finding a target. In moments, he had taken out ten of the enemy and the pressure on the shield wall had been relieved. Carnifex pulled a canteen off Mutilus's belt and took a drink.

With a nudge from Indavara, Cassius turned to see Noster kneeling close by. The legionary faced away from them as he spoke, towards the barracks. 'See the window? If you can get inside you can get away. Make for the bridge. We'll follow if we can.'

Noster dropped the bow and quiver close to Indavara. Drawing his sword, he nodded subtly at Procyon. 'For him.'

Procyon hadn't noticed the conversation. He was watching the southern line.

As Noster returned to the battle, Cassius looked across at the barracks – the window was big enough and low enough. He leaned back to cover Indavara as the bodyguard took an arrow from the quiver and set it against the string. He pulled it halfway back, then looked over Cassius's shoulder along the wall.

'She's in front of him.'

Annia was indeed blocking the optio, staring at the ground as if she couldn't bear to even acknowledge what was going on around her. Procyon still had his left arm round her neck but was preoccupied with the fighting.

'Over here, over here,' Cassius said, though he knew she couldn't hear him over the noise.

'Corbulo – someone's going to see.'

'I know.'

Over here, over here.

She looked at him.

Cassius checked that Carnifex and Mutilus weren't watching, then motioned towards the ground. Annia seemed confused, but

Cassius leant forward and she saw what they intended. Covering her eyes again, she bowed her head.

'Forward a little more,' said Indavara, bringing the bow up behind Cassius's back.

'If I hit him, grab her and run for the window,' he added. 'I'll be right behind you.'

Cassius felt Indavara tense as he drew the bowstring.

Procyon's head snapped forward as the bolt punched into the back of his skull. Annia took her hands from her eyes and bumped her head on the shaft of the arrow. Cassius looked across at Carnifex again. He had just unleashed his next javelin.

Indavara slapped him on the shoulder. 'Now.'

Cassius hauled himself to his feet and ran along the wall. Annia was already up but staring at the arrow sticking out of the inert Procyon. Cassius grabbed her hand.

'Go!' hissed Indavara, just a few paces behind.

Cassius sprinted towards the barracks, Annia in tow. They passed within yards of Carnifex's back, but like all the others in the line, he was completely focused on the enemy. Once past him, Cassius didn't dare look back. It seemed to take an age to reach the window – and at every pace he expected some cry from behind them – but finally they were there.

'Inside!'

Without any help from Cassius, Annia climbed up on to the ledge and dropped adroitly into the barracks. Cassius turned and saw Indavara jogging backwards towards him, another arrow at the ready. Cassius got his hands on the ledge and hoisted a leg up. Annia was lying on the floor directly below, so he leapt past her and landed in the cool, murky interior. The two of them looked around; they were surrounded by bunk beds.

Indavara never knew what made Carnifex turn from the line but he was glad he hadn't taken his eyes off him. Seeing his dead optio, Carnifex spun round to face the barracks. Indavara already had the bow up and drawn. He aimed at Carnifex's throat. The old centurion saw him just as he let fly.

Carnifex bent his head to protect his face but the arrow

was six inches low anyway. It hit the bronze cuirass with a dull crack and dropped to the ground. Carnifex's head came back up. He took two steps forward and picked up the nearest javelin.

'Shit.'

Indavara turned and threw himself through the window, dropping to the floor between Annia and Cassius.

The javelin landed between Cassius's thighs, tearing through his tunic and pinning him to the floor. Indavara yanked it out and handed it to him. 'What are you waiting for?'

With the bow still in one hand and the quiver over his shoulder, he dragged Annia to her feet and bolted out of the little room. By the time they reached the other end of the barracks, the sounds of the battle had faded.

'Anyone following?' asked Indavara.

Cassius looked back. 'No.'

He joined Indavara at a doorway. To the right was the ridge that bordered the pit; directly ahead was a meadow of high grass.

'Horses,' said Indavara. 'Eborius and his men must have tethered theirs close by.'

'No,' said Cassius. 'Mounts will draw too much attention. We get in that grass and we're as safe as we'll be anywhere. We can work our way north towards the bridge.'

Annia, who had been crouching low, suddenly dropped down on her backside.

Indavara still had hold of her hand. 'Get up.'

Cassius knelt down beside her.

Indavara let go, retreated into the barracks and looked back down the corridor. 'Corbulo, we have moments if we're lucky—'

'I know.'

Cassius tipped Annia's chin up. Her eyes were glassy, vacant. 'Annia, we have to go. You need to get up. Can you do that?'

Another chilling shriek from the battle.

Annia squeezed her eyes together.

'Corbulo—'

Cassius put his hands under her arms and helped her to her feet.

Indavara moved back to the doorway. He checked left, then right.

'We're clear. You first.'

Cassius took Annia's hand and ran out of the barracks towards the meadow.

XXX

Simo, Clara and the sailors watched it all. First, the crowd that had gathered in the square dispersed. Then, over the next two hours, most of the townspeople returned, driving carts or on horseback, tripling the size of the column. And when some soldiers also joined the group, they finally set off west along the Via Cyrenaica. Simo was relieved to note there were only a dozen or so legionaries. He felt sure Noster had managed to change the centurion's mind; that Eborius and the rest of his men were searching for Cassius and the others.

Once the column had gone, they saw nothing more of the residents, but by midday half a dozen fires were alight across the town and scores of Maseene warriors rode unchallenged through the streets. One band stopped long enough to pull down the statue of Romulus and Remus, but now they and the rest of the tribesmen had disappeared too. Darnis was silent and empty.

The *Fortuna* was ready to leave at a moment's notice: the oars on the starboard side were in the rowlocks, and the foresail shackled to the halyard. A light rain had been falling for about an hour. Simo stood just in front of the mast, his arm round Clara's shoulder. The poor girl had been praying most of the morning. Despite a double tunic and one of her mistresss's cloaks, she was shivering. Simo gazed out across the causeway at the square, hoping for some sight of the missing trio.

Asdribar came up next to him and wiped rainwater off his hairless head.

'I asked for signs from my gods,' the captain told Simo quietly. 'They told me I was wrong. They told me we should have gone to find them.'

358

With plenty of time to consider Asdribar's decision, Simo had in fact now decided it was the right one. Given how quickly the situation had deteriorated, with no one to guide them they would undoubtedly have run into trouble.

'It is enough that you stayed, sir. All we can do now is wait.'

'And pray.' Asdribar kept his voice barely above a whisper. 'I've seen your books. You are a Christian.'

'I am, sir.'

Clara heard this, but – to Simo's relief – said nothing. The girl was conventional in her beliefs, and he'd found it was rarely possible to predict how different individuals would react.

'What does your one god tell you?' asked Asdribar.

'Only that I must not lose hope. My master and Indavara have faced great danger before. I must believe they are still alive.'

'If those warriors come down to the harbour, we will have to cast off.'

'I understand, sir.'

'And I cannot do so at night, not with that narrow entrance. At least the wind and the waves are still calm.'

Clara spoke up: 'You will wait as long as you can, won't you, sir?'

'I will, girl.'

Squint walked over to them and pointed over the bow. 'Captain.'

A line of people had appeared from an alley in front of the dye works. Leading the way were half a dozen armed men with perhaps twenty women and children behind them. The men were all weighed down with heavy packs and most of the women were carrying woven baskets.

'Ready the lines, Korinth,' ordered Asdribar.

The big sailor and his constant companion Desenna hurried over to the port side-rail.

Asdribar turned to Opilio, who was sitting against the mast, hood drawn over his head. 'Take three others and get ready with the oars. We just need enough to make way.'

'Sir.'

More armed men were bringing up the rear of the group,

looking warily at the square as the others started across the causeway.

'I doubt they wish to cause us any harm, sir,' said Simo.

'They look desperate,' replied Asdribar. 'You'd be surprised what desperate people will do.'

Squint caught his captain's eye and pointed at a barrel he and Korinth had earlier brought up from the hold. It was stuffed with weapons.

'Go ahead,' said Asdribar.

The veteran handed out spears and swords to the other sailors and took a bow for himself. Tarkel surreptitiously tried to grab a blade.

'Back to the stern, you,' said Asdribar. The lad slunk away empty-handed.

'Ready to cast off, Captain,' said Korinth.

As the group continued across the causeway, Simo looked at the fires burning in the town. He had even more reason than the others to be depressed by what he'd witnessed. Africa was a stronghold of the Church, a land that had produced glorious martyrs and influential thinkers. Yet Darnis seemed to him the most forsaken of places, where cruelty and hate had triumphed.

The group stopped when they reached the warehouses. A man close to the front spoke briefly with the others, then lowered his pack and sheathed his sword. He ran past the collapsed dock and started along the breakwater.

'Captain?' said Squint, an arrow at the ready.

'You spoiling for a fight, old man? Calm yourself – and don't point that thing anywhere near me.'

Asdribar went up to the bow to talk to the man, who was clad in the nondescript tunic and cloak of a middling Roman. He was perhaps fifty, with slate-grey hair and craggy features.

'Is this your vessel, sir?' he asked, stopping opposite Asdribar.

'It is. Sorry, no space for extra passengers.'

'Why are you still here?'

'Not your concern, friend.'

Clara nudged Simo and pointed at the group. 'Do you remember her?'

The daughter of Maro the timber-mechant was standing there with a woman. In her hand was one of her wooden toys. There was no sign of her father.

'We can pay you,' the man told Asdribar.

'I'm already being paid. Well.'

Clara walked past Simo and approached Asdribar. 'If she were here, Miss Annia would ask you to take them aboard, sir.'

Asdribar looked down at her with a half-smile that suggested both surprise and admiration. 'I'm not sure she would, Clara, though I'm sure it's what *you* want me to do.'

Simo took his opportunity. 'It is the right course of action, Captain.'

'The Christian course?' asked Asdribar rhetorically.

He turned back to the man. 'What's your name?'

'Vivius Reberrus.'

'It's November, Reberrus. What makes you think you'll be any safer at sea?'

'What I've seen in the last few hours. The Maseene are killing our people. Where are you headed?'

'Apollonia.'

'That's good for us.'

'What if I let you aboard, then another group turn up?'

'There is no one else left, Captain. The locals have returned to their villages. The others left today.'

'How much will you pay?' asked Asdribar.

'Twenty denarii each.'

'That's funny.'

'Thirty,' said Reberrus.

'Fifty,' said Asdribar. 'Twenty for the children.'

'Sir,' said Simo. 'You cannot put a price on—'

Asdribar raised a hand. Simo kept quiet.

'Sir,' implored Clara. 'Look at the sweet young girl there. Her name is—'

'Remember your place, Clara,' said Asdribar.

'We can't pay that,' insisted Reberrus.

'Then I can't help you,' replied Asdribar. 'Korinth, ready with the ropes.'

'All right,' replied Reberrus. 'All right. We'll pay.'

'Then we have a deal,' said Asdribar. 'One more thing – your blades stay behind.'

Reberrus glanced at Squint, who was still holding an arrow close to his bowstring. 'But we will be at your mercy.'

'It's not my mercy you have to worry about,' said Asdribar, gesturing at the sea. 'It's the gods of the deep.'

Simo came forward. 'The captain is an honourable man, sir. You have no cause to fear him and his crew.'

'Why do you speak for us?' asked Reberrus.

'I . . .' Simo turned to Clara. '*We* wish to see you and your people safe.'

'How touching,' said Asdribar.

'I will go and tell them,' said Reberrus.

'You can also tell them to have their money ready at the gang-plank,' added Asdribar as Reberrus hurried away.

The Carthaginian turned and winked at Clara. 'I would have taken them for twenty.'

'I think you would have taken them for nothing, sir,' said Clara. 'You're a good man.'

Asdribar leaned close to her and whispered: 'Maybe. But don't tell anyone, especially the crew.'

'How long to sunset, sir?' asked Simo.

'Three or four hours.'

Simo looked back at the town.

Asdribar nodded skyward. 'Better keep at those prayers.'

The grass was rough against the skin and six feet of it would have been better than five, but Cassius thanked the gods for the stuff; as long as they kept low, they could stay hidden.

Indavara had a fair sense of direction but Cassius knew his

was better, so he took the lead as they crossed the meadow. He reckoned they were at least a mile from the mansion now and by keeping the sun in roughly the same position over his left shoulder, he could ensure they kept heading north. He was still carrying the Maseene javelin. It was a light, well-balanced weapon and – for Cassius – highly preferable to a sword. He'd always been half decent at the throwing disciplines and adhered to the theory that enemies were best dealt with from a distance.

They came eventually to a large tree beside a ditch that ran at right angles to the Via Roma. Cassius squatted next to the tree and Annia sat down on the lip of the ditch, puffing hard. Her arms were laced with little cuts from the grass and bruises where she'd been manhandled by Carnifex and Procyon.

'Sorry, miss, but we must cover as much ground as we can.'

Cassius took his canteen from his belt, unscrewed the lid and handed it to her. Indavara leant against the tree and looked back at the mansion. While Annia drank, Cassius joined him.

At that distance it was hard to make out much detail, but both shield walls seemed to be intact. The Maseene were fighting on but scores of dead warriors lay on the ground. The tribesmen to the rear were struggling to keep control of all the riderless mounts, several of which had broken loose.

'I can hardly believe we made it out of there,' said Cassius, resting his head against the rough bark of the tree. 'Thank the gods for Eborius and his men.'

'I just hope they make it out of there too,' said Indavara. 'If the Maseene don't get them, Carnifex will.'

'We must keep moving.'

Cassius surveyed the flat expanse of land to the north. The only structure close by was the barn where they'd confronted Carnifex.

'We'll stay in the grass,' he added, 'parallel with the road, then cut towards the bridge when we can.'

They heard a metallic rattle – the canteen lid shaking against the container as Annia tried to screw it back. She didn't seem to have noticed the blood that had splattered her neck when Procyon was killed.

'I can do that, miss,' Cassius said, taking the canteen.

Annia looked at him for a moment, then stared down at the weeds and nettles that carpeted the bottom of the ditch. She hadn't said a word since collapsing at the pit. Cassius knelt beside her and tried to take one of her shaking hands, but she recoiled and turned away.

Cassius looked over at Indavara, who was examining his broken finger. 'Bad?'

'Need to strap it.'

'With what?'

Cassius felt a hand on his shoulder.

Annia was pointing at the shredded hem of her long tunic. She tried to tear it but her hands were still shaking too much.

'I'll do it, miss. If you don't mind.'

Cassius picked up the javelin and used the blade to cut off a section of the cloth.

'Thank you, Miss Annia,' said Indavara as Cassius waved him over.

'This might hurt.'

Indavara didn't make a sound as Cassius pushed the broken little finger next to the adjacent one and tied them together. Cassius then inspected the broken skin on Indavara's forehead. 'And how's that?'

'Sore. How's the nose?'

'Very sore. How does it look?'

The expression on Indavara's face told Cassius all he needed to know.

'Wonderful. Come on.'

This time Annia took his hand. He helped her to her feet and across the ditch. Indavara retrieved the bow and quiver and fell in behind them.

As they got further from the battle, it became even harder to tell what was going on and soon they could see no more than the scattered Maseene horses and sparks of glinting metal between the barracks and the mansion.

As they approached the track they'd used the previous day,

Cassius heard a rustling sound up ahead. Leaving Annia, he took a few steps forward and stopped. The grass in front of him was moving. Something was coming towards him.

The plump brown bird took off at a low trajectory and missed his head by inches. It flapped away to the south, leaving Cassius on his bottom. He blew feathers away from his face. 'Caesar's balls.' He turned to the others. 'Sorry.'

'Quiet,' said Indavara, ten paces behind him. He ducked down and jabbed one end of the bow towards the Via Roma. Cassius peered over the grass and saw three Maseene warriors on horseback. One pointed at their position and the trio guided their mounts off the road. Cassius wondered why they weren't fighting. Had they fled, or had the Romans broken up the attack? It hardly mattered; they were coming their way.

Cassius and Annia crawled back to where Indavara was kneeling. Cassius looked down at the broad-bladed head of the javelin in his hand. Whichever warrior it had belonged to had looked after it well; the gleaming iron had been tapered to a lethal point.

Considering their horses were walking, the tribesmen seemed to cover the ground quickly. They were in a line, five paces between them, now less than a hundred feet away.

Indavara still hadn't put an arrow against the bowstring.

'What are you waiting for?' asked Cassius.

Indavara grimaced and looked thoughtfully down at the ground.

'You think they'll hesitate to kill us?' continued Cassius. 'Because unless you've suddenly developed the ability to speak their language, that's exactly what they'll do.'

Indavara gave a brief shake of his head, then fitted the arrow against the string. 'We wait until they're almost on us. The one to the right is yours. Aim for the chest.' He glanced at the javelin. 'Know what you're doing with that thing?'

'Of course. I was fifteenth in my class with these.'

'Out of fifteen?'

'Thirty-two actually.'

Cassius tightened his grip on the javelin and tried to swallow the lump in his throat.

Annia was lying on the ground between them, eyes shut once more.

'Just listen and keep your head down,' Indavara told Cassius. 'We'll know when they're close enough.'

Cassius turned himself side-on to make the throw easier. Before long he could hear the horses' legs brushing through the grass, see dark shapes through the swaying, bright green stalks.

Indavara brought the bow up level with his shoulder and drew the string halfway.

Cassius looked at the point of the javelin, imagined it slicing into the bare skin of the warrior's chest.

Him or me.

He could see the riders now: their dark, wiry frames; their lean, striking faces.

'Wait,' Indavara breathed.

Cassius shifted slightly towards the man to the right. The warrior's hands were on the reins. Cassius drew back his arm.

'Ready,' said Indavara, tightening his fingers on the bowstring.

Him or me. Him or me.

The three Maseene suddenly looked to their left. Cassius realised he could hear horses somewhere behind him. The tribesmen urged their mounts towards the track at a trot.

'Down,' Indavara whispered.

Cassius was already down and he watched the closest horse slip through the grass not ten feet away. Had the warrior looked to his right he would have seen all three of them.

Once he was past, Cassius and Indavara lifted their heads and spied four more tribesmen coming along the track from the east. After a brief discussion, the seven of them set off back towards the Via Roma. Cassius lowered the javelin and sat down. 'I can't take much more of this.'

'Could have been a lot, lot worse,' replied Indavara, at last letting the bowstring go slack. 'What hour do you think it is?'

Cassius glanced up at the sky. 'Seventh or eighth.'

'It'll be hard to reach the harbour before nightfall.' Indavara pointed towards Darnis. Five plumes of smoke were rising from the town. 'What do you think that means?'

'Nothing good. Let's just get to the bridge and hope Eborius can make it there too.'

'C-Cassius. Indavara.'

Annia, still sitting on the ground, pushed her lank hair away from her face and looked up at them.

'I – I'm sorry. Truly. I – I should never have left the ship.'

'What's done is done, miss,' Indavara said after a while.

'Quite,' said Cassius. 'We know you didn't set out to do any harm, miss. We're all still in one piece. And once we're over that track, it's only a mile or two to the bridge. Mostly olive grove as I recall, which unfortunately won't hide us half as well as this grass.'

'Miss, you should take those off,' said Indavara, pointing at the two silver bangles on each wrist.

'They'll catch the sun, miss,' added Cassius.

Annia set about removing them. Her hands were shaking less now.

'You *can* call me Annia, you know.'

'Yes, miss,' they said.

Once across the track and into the olive grove, their progress slowed. Without the reassuring shelter of the grass, Cassius felt terribly exposed (especially as he was leading the way), but he soon developed a workable routine: they would stop beside one of the larger trees, check the Via Roma and the surrounding countryside for signs of movement, then dash to the next piece of cover. Five times they had to wait for danger to pass; on each occasion groups of Maseene horsemen. Cassius decided he couldn't glean much from the direction of their movements; two groups had been on the road heading north, another heading south, and the last two cross-country.

He reckoned an hour and a half had elapsed since their escape when they finally reached a high date palm thirty yards from the bridge. Crouching in welcome shadow, the three of them caught their breath and looked out at the empty Via Roma – the sloping section that ran north from the ridge down to the gorge. The only sound was the shrill cries of the black kites.

'We cannot wait,' Cassius said, gazing across at the patchy scrub on the other side of the gorge. 'We must cross while we have the chance.'

There was virtually no cover between the bridge and the edge of Darnis. The nearest hiding place was a cactus hedge on the east side of the road, but even that was half a mile away. Cassius pointed at it.

'Straight over, then on to the hedge. Ready?'

'Ready,' answered Indavara and Annia.

They ran out into the sunlight and towards the bridge.

XXXI

'Corbulo!'

Cassius and Annia had almost reached the other side. They turned to see Indavara readying his bow.

Two horses had just appeared at the top of the ridge. The riders were thrashing at their mounts, driving them down the road.

Cassius grabbed Annia's hand again. 'Here.'

They ran to the end of the stone wall on the eastern side of the bridge and crouched behind it, close to the warning sign and the stack of unused timber. Indavara wasn't far behind. He knelt beside Cassius and raised the bow. The speeding riders had already covered half the distance to the bridge. Their helmets and mail shirts were clear. Legionaries. But from the First Century or the Second?

Cassius covered his eyes with his hand. 'Can't tell who they are. This damned sun.'

Indavara drew back the bowstring.

The riders reached the bridge. Cassius was expecting them to slow down but they came across at a gallop. One – a slight individual – took off his helmet. Beneath was a head of thinning brown hair.

'It's Noster!' said Cassius.

Indavara lowered the bow as he and Cassius stood up.

Noster reined in his horse just yards from them. The second man was Lentellus, one of the younger legionaries who'd been with them at the quarry. Noster's face was dripping with sweat and his words came between panting breaths. 'The battle's over but it's chaos back there. Eborius and a few of us got away but Carnifex was seen leading the remainder of his men towards the stables.'

'How many?'

'Thirty or more. Eborius isn't far behind. He sent me ahead to get you. We must go now, sir.'

'Come on,' said Indavara, ready to run.

Cassius looked back along the bridge, then up at the legionaries. 'Dismount. I need your horses.'

'What?' said Noster.

'That's an order. Get off!'

Noster was quicker to comply than Lentellus but both men looked as bemused as Indavara as they dropped to the ground. Cassius caught the younger soldier's eye. 'Come.'

Annia was still behind the wall. Cassius pulled her up, turned to Lentellus and pointed at the distant cactus hedge. 'Go with her and wait there.'

Annia shook her head. 'I want to stay with you two.'

'We'll be along soon.' He took her hand and placed it in Lentellus's. 'Go.'

The legionary looked to Noster for guidance.

Cassius wasn't in the mood to tarry. He gripped Lentellus by the tunic and pulled him close. 'I am an officer. You are not. Go!'

The two of them set off along the road.

'Corbulo, what are you doing?' demanded Indavara.

Cassius ignored him. 'Noster, tie both saddles on as tight as you can.'

Cassius ran around the wall to the sandy slope beside the bridge, Indavara close on his heels. He pointed at a thick coil of rope next to the stack of timber. 'Bring that.'

'What—'

'Just do as you're bloody told for once, man!'

Cassius half ran, half skidded down the slope. Forcing himself to ignore the sheer angles and the dark fissure below, he scrambled across to the supporting timbers. The six vertical posts formed a triangle, with three close to the side, a second rank of two, and the final one only a yard from where the slope abruptly steepened.

'Anyone coming?' Cassius yelled, his voice echoing along the gorge.

'Not yet,' cried Noster from above.

'Then we still have time.'

Indavara arrived next to him. 'To do what?'

Cassius took the rope. 'Judging by those fires, the Maseene are in control of the town. If we get caught between them and Carnifex's men on open ground in daylight, we're as good as dead. This might buy us some time.'

With a series of leaping steps, Cassius made his way down past the second rank of posts, then slid on his side until his leading boot landed on the final support. Sandy earth and clumps of weed fell over the edge of the almost vertical slope just ahead. He tied the end of the rope around the support with a strong knot he'd seen the sailors use, then pushed the rope as high as he could using the javelin. The top of the post was twenty feet above him, at the apex of the network of timbers beneath the stone base of the bridge.

Cassius headed back up the slope on all fours, uncoiling the rope as he went. He gave the javelin to Indavara and pointed up at the rope wrapped around the timbers. 'See the lines? Cut as many as you can.'

Indavara made his way into the shadows under the northern end of the structure. 'What if it falls?'

Cassius pointed at the fissure. 'Then I'll see you down there.'

'Here comes Eborius,' yelled Noster from above.

'Carnifex?' asked Cassius.

'No sign yet.'

Pumping his aching legs, Cassius ploughed up the slope until he reached Noster and the horses. He ran the rope around the horns of each saddle twice, then brought it back and tied it off about ten feet behind the mounts.

'Your dagger.'

Noster handed it over and watched as Cassius cut off the remainder of the rope. This he cut in two before returning the dagger to the legionary.

Only then did he allow himself to look across the gorge. Another man was riding alongside Eborius. They were almost at the bridge.

Cassius looked north. Annia and Lentellus were halfway to the hedge.

Indavara emerged from the other side of the bridge and sprinted across the road.

Eborius and the other man brought their speeding horses to a halt so abruptly that the legionary almost fell out of his saddle.

'Corbulo, what are you doing?' yelled the centurion, his face streaked with blood and grime.

'We're going to bring the bridge down.'

Before the stunned centurion could summon a reply, Indavara pointed at the ridge. 'There they are.'

The men of the First Century were riding hard, three or four abreast across the road.

'Indavara – here!'

Cassius ducked down behind the wall.

'Eborius, there's no time to argue,' he said as Indavara crouched beside him. 'You're my bait. Look as if you stopped to pick up Noster, then ride.'

Eborius stared at the rope leading to the two horses.

Cassius pointed at Annia and Lentellus, who were snatching glances over their shoulders as they ran. 'If we don't make it, get her back to the ship.'

Eborius turned towards the distant figures.

'Did you hear me, Centurion?' demanded Cassius.

Finally, Eborius nodded. 'Yes.'

Noster hurried over to the other soldier, who helped him up on to the horse behind him.

'They're a quarter-mile away,' said Eborius. 'Forty or more.'

'Go now!' Cassius yelled.

Eborius wheeled his horse around and led the way at a gallop.

Cassius could hear the rumble of the approaching riders. Indavara glanced anxiously at him from beneath his dark fringe. 'Is this going to work?'

'It might.'

Cassius looked around the wall. The legionaries slowed their mounts and narrowed the column into pairs as they approached the bridge. Close to the back was a splash of red amongst the iron and bronze. Carnifex.

Cassius looked at the horses and the rope. He saw with a sudden clarity what they were about to attempt and suddenly it was his turn to hesitate.

'I can't do this. They're Roman soldiers.'

Indavara spoke straight into his ear. 'Who'll kill us in an instant given a chance. Annia and the others too.'

Assailed by a dozen thoughts at once, Cassius was paralysed by indecision.

'This was your idea!' shouted Indavara, his voice drowned out by pounding hooves as the first of the horses clattered on to the bridge.

Cassius gave him one of the lengths of rope. 'Now!'

The two horses were already agitated and when Cassius whipped the line across the nearest one's rump, it charged away. Indavara struck the second horse. Both animals were brought up short by the rope but Cassius and Indavara lashed them again and their flailing hooves dug into the ground.

Cassius turned. The rope was taut but the post wasn't moving. The first of the legionaries were almost halfway across; close enough for him to see their frowning faces.

'Come on!' Cassius yelled. Indavara still had the javelin. He sliced the blade across the backside of one horse, then the other. Maddened by pain, the struggling animals strained against the rope, kicking earth back at their tormentors.

Cassius watched the post wobble, then come flying away from the bridge. As soon as the timber hit the ground, the sheer power of the enraged horses hauled it up the slope. Cassius and Indavara threw themselves towards the wall as the animals sped away, dragging the post along the ground behind them.

Seeing this bizarre sight, the leading legionaries raised their hands and came to a halt. About two-thirds of the force were on the bridge.

Cassius and Indavara looked down at the supports. The other five posts were still intact.

373

Then some of the men started shouting.

Two planks of wood came free, rolled down the slope and disappeared into the fissure.

Carnifex and a few of the others had pulled up to one side of the road.

'Get off!' he bellowed. 'Get off there!'

A large block of red stone fell from the northern end of the bridge. It careened down the slope and struck one of the second rank of supports, knocking it away. The entire structure began to shake.

'It's going,' said Indavara.

The yelling legionaries were bunched together. Panic-stricken, they turned their horses in different directions and rode into each other. Three riders somehow got free of the crush and drove their mounts back to the southern side.

Just as they reached safety, more of the stones fell. Then came a series of loud, splintering cracks and the entire wooden structure collapsed. Timbers tumbled down the slope in a cloud of dust. Ropes scythed through the air.

The northern side of the bridge gave way first. The great arch seemed to collapse yard by yard, block by block.

Men and horses loosed high-pitched screams, and suddenly everything was falling.

Cassius saw one rider slip from his saddle, clutch at thin air, then fall beside his horse, spinning over and over before striking the side of the gorge. He bounced off it like a straw doll and fell straight into the fissure.

His horse struck the ground yards away, the impact splitting its belly. Innards fountained into the air and thick gouts of scarlet blood splattered across the pale earth. The sundered body fell into the darkness.

The cries and booming impacts of falling blocks and timbers faded almost as quickly as they had begun. The fissure seemed to greedily suck men, horses, stone and wood into it and in moments only a single horse and a single man remained. The horse was close to the top of the southern side, where the slope was less steep. Far below, the legionary hung to the sheer side of the gorge, just yards from the chasm.

Terrified by the noise, some of the remaining horses had become unbiddable, and several of Carnifex's men had been thrown. Only he and a few others had kept control of their mounts.

'Pull it clear!' he ordered, pointing at the horse.

Two men ran towards the edge of the gorge but they were too late.

The horse lost its grip and slithered down, carving lines in the sand with its hooves. Its head struck the edge of the fissure with a sickening thud, then it too was gone.

'Help me!' pleaded the legionary. 'Centurion!'

The soldier's mail shirt and most of his tunic had somehow been torn from his body. Scrabbling with his hands, he tried to dig his feet into the earth but one boot slipped, then the other. 'Centurion!'

With that final, echoing cry, he disappeared into the black maw.

Aside from a few intact blocks of stone on either side, the bridge seemed to have disappeared. Strewn across the northern slope were timber and rope; pieces of saddle and armour; swords, shields and spears. The silence didn't last long. Four of the black kites soared along the gorge, straight through where the bridge had been. Their crowing sounded like mockery.

Cassius and Indavara were sitting side by side, their hands planted on the sand.

'By the great gods,' whispered Cassius. 'What have I done?'

'Given us a chance,' replied Indavara. He got to his feet and pulled Cassius up beside him.

The other legionaries still on their horses continued to gaze at the fissure in stunned disbelief. Carnifex dismounted and walked to the edge. He took off his helmet and stared across at Cassius and Indavara. He brought up a hand and drew a single finger sideways across his throat.

XXXII

They let the horses go and continued north on foot, not straying too far from the Via Roma. The first shelter they came to was an isolated shack about a mile and a half from the gorge. Most of the building was taken up by a mound of grey flints laced with cobwebs.

Once the seven of them had filed inside, Cassius glanced around the group: Eborius, Noster, Lentellus and the other legionary, plus Indavara and Annia. Not one of them looked anything less than exhausted.

'Where are the rest of your men?' he asked Eborius, who was scraping dirt off his scabbard.

'The Roman townspeople decided to leave, so I gave them a dozen of my legionaries as an escort. Hopefully the Maseene have been too occupied here to worry about them.'

'I meant from the battle.'

Eborius paused, then looked at the three soldiers. 'Did anyone else get away?'

Lentellus and the other man shook their heads. Noster seemed unwilling or unable to meet the centurion's gaze.

'Still sure we made the right decision?' Eborius asked him.

The veteran didn't reply. Eborius leaned against the door and looked out towards the road.

'What now?' asked Cassius.

'Assuming your captain friend hasn't left – make for the ship. Unless you have any better suggestions.'

'Might we be there by nightfall?'

'Perhaps. Depends how many Maseene are between us and the harbour.'

'And how quickly Carnifex gets round to the west bridge,' said Lentellus.

'He's down to twelve men now,' said Indavara. 'Fifteen at most.'

'But he knows where we're going,' countered Lentellus.

'We must rely on stealth,' said Cassius.

'Agreed,' said Eborius. 'Let Carnifex mix it with the Maseene again if he wants.'

'What happened back there anyway?' asked Cassius.

'I thought the Maseene would fold but more of them came up from the plain. I lost most of my men. Carnifex too. Our lines collapsed. They had us pinned back against the mansion wall but then a dozen of the First Century turned up on horseback and cut a hole through them. Only the gods know how we got out.' Eborius turned from the doorway. 'And you? The girl followed me, correct?'

'Yes,' replied Cassius. 'Carnifex grabbed her and turned the tables on us. Met up with some of his men and took us to the mansion.'

Eborius cast a cold glare at Annia, who was sitting on the floor.

'Centurion,' said Cassius. 'My profound thanks.'

'You said it yourself: somebody had to stop him sooner or later.'

Eborius addressed the group. 'There's a well on the way. We'll refill our canteens there, then it's across the old Tadius property and into the town. Noster, you bring up the rear.'

'Yes, sir.'

'How's your arm?' Eborius asked, inspecting a gash just below the sleeve of the veteran's armour.

Cassius gazed enviously at the mail shirt. His was of far better quality but – as always seemed to happen – was tucked up in a bag somewhere, not over his tunic where it could actually do him some good.

'Just a slice, sir. I'll take care of it later.'

With that, the tension between Eborius and Noster seemed to dissipate.

Eborius spoke to the other legionary. 'Did I see you limping?'

'It's nothing, sir.'

Cassius caught the soldier's eye. 'What's the name?'

'Adranos, sir.'

Like Lentellus, Adranos was short but sturdily built. They were two of Eborius's younger men but both had a couple of years on Cassius.

'I'm Officer Cassius Corbulo. That's Indavara and the young lady is Miss Annia.'

Adranos pointed at the floor. 'Your feet are bleeding, miss.'

'Gods, so they are,' said Cassius.

She was wearing a pair of light sandals and running across the hard ground had torn them – and Annia's feet – to pieces. Her skin was latticed with scratches and the soles of the sandals were red with blood.

'We'll try and find you some other shoes,' offered Indavara. 'Or perhaps wrap them up.'

'Are you in pain, miss?' asked Cassius.

With a helping hand from Indavara, Annia stood. 'I was trying not to think about it.'

'She'll live,' said Eborius gruffly. He moved back to the door and took a long look at the road. 'We'll stay in cover as much as we can. And just because you're not at the front or back, that doesn't mean you don't keep your eyes open. Let's go.'

———◆———

The Tadius property turned out to be a sprawling farm divided into dozens of fields and orchards. Their route took them right through the cluster of buildings in the middle of the plot. They had already filled up with water and, while the others waited inside a stable, Eborius and Noster checked the main house to see if they could forage some food. While they were gone, Cassius and Indavara used an old cotton sheet they found on a washing line to bind Annia's feet. In normal circumstances such close contact with a young lady would have been unthinkable but necessity demanded it; aside from the pain, they couldn't allow her to slow them down. With Annia sitting on the ground between them, they took a foot each, cutting the cloth with the javelin blade and securing the whole arrangement with knots around her ankles.

Eborius and Noster returned empty-handed; it seemed the Maseene or other opportunists had beaten them to it. But as the centurion led the group north again they passed through an orchard of fig trees. The few figs left were well past their best but everyone took a handful to eat – all except Annia, who shook her head when Indavara offered her the fruit.

As they pressed on, Cassius found he was struggling to follow Eborius's request that they all stay alert. In fact he was struggling to do anything other than put one foot in front of the other and keep up. He reckoned it was now well over thirty hours since he'd last slept. His nose was still throbbing, his arms and legs felt leaden, and the light Maseene javelin now seemed as heavy as a cavalry lance. There was, however, one advantage to such utter exhaustion; it stopped him thinking about the horrors of the last few hours and the dangers yet to come.

———8———

The sound of horses on the Via Roma reached them before the riders came into view. Though he knew the Maseene might prove as deadly as the legionaries of the First Century, Cassius was relieved it wasn't Carnifex and his men. Not one of the twenty or so tribesmen took their eyes off the road as they sped south.

Eborius waited for an all-clear signal from Noster then set off. They passed the line of date palms that bordered the southern edge of Darnis and through the gate of a small villa.

'How long before sundown?' Cassius asked Eborius, picking his way through a pile of broken roof tiles.

'Perhaps an hour.'

The centurion, who was carrying his helmet, waited until everyone was inside the villa before speaking again.

'It gets harder now. We must watch every alley and window

and door. And we must move fast if we want to reach the harbour by nightfall.'

'What if Asdribar has left?' asked Indavara.

This was an eventuality Cassius had tried not to even entertain.

'You three will have to make your own choices,' replied Eborius. 'But we can wait until dark, then slip away to the west. I have family in a village not ten miles from here. They'll protect us.'

Eborius looked around at the glum expressions that greeted this prospect. 'Hopefully it won't come to that. Noster, you take your bow back. I might need you to clear the way ahead of us.'

The legionary glanced at Indavara. 'Why not let him keep it, sir? Then I can stay at the rear. I reckon he's a better shot than me anyhow.'

———◆———

Indavara knew it would be impossible to move as quickly as he needed to with an arrow drawn, so he kept one alongside the bow in his left hand. Noster's weaponry was in excellent condition and – apart from the thin twine around the bow's middle to improve grip – not dissimilar to his own.

Even though it always took time to get used to a new bow, moments such as this made all the hours of practice worthwhile. There had been no real call for archery while he was a gladiator but he'd always been fascinated by the weapons. His long-distance shooting was still developing, but at short range he considered himself passable, and short range was all that would be needed now. The broken little finger wasn't a problem.

Indavara found the streets of Darnis confusing, but Eborius seemed to know every last corner of the place. Considering his size, the centurion moved with great speed and agility as he led the group towards the Via Cyrenaica. He never covered more than twenty yards of ground in one burst, always found cover for the seven of them, and only ever stopped long enough to check the area immediately ahead.

Indavara's view of the man had already changed. Whatever his past failures, he had saved them from certain death at that pit and was doing his best to help them reach the harbour. The past day and night had been a dizzying series of reversals and trials, but to Indavara they were already distant memories. He, Annia and Corbulo were alive and his thoughts had narrowed to a single aim: they just had to get to the *Fortuna*.

'Now,' said Eborius quietly.

They scuttled across a courtyard and inside another villa. Eborius stopped a couple of yards beyond the doorway. Indavara passed him so that the others could enter, then saw what had halted the centurion. Lying on the floor were a middle-aged man and woman surrounded by scattered clothes and other belongings. Close to the man was a small, empty iron box. He and the woman had been killed by multiple slashes to their necks.

Eborius – who couldn't stand up straight in the low-ceilinged room – knelt between the dead pair and gently closed the woman's eyelids.

'Oh no,' said Noster when he saw them. 'Crotila and Helvia.'

He bent down and picked up a broken javelin-head. 'This man worked alongside the Maseene for years. Gave jobs to scores of them. Helvia even made him arrange his harvest around their festival days.'

Indavara glanced at Annia and Corbulo, who were still staring down at the bodies.

'There is no way back from this,' said Eborius. 'Not now.'

'*He* has been a curse on this town,' said Noster.

The legionary laid the man's arms by his side and put a blanket over him and his wife.

'There's a little food here,' said Adranos as he picked up a wicker basket.

'Take it,' Eborius told him. 'Crotila was a generous man.'

The centurion walked into an adjacent room. 'This way.'

Indavara followed him through to a narrow doorway and waited as Eborius checked the alley between this villa and the next. Over his shoulder, Indavara spied a small (and broken) glass window he recognised. They weren't far from the mausoleum and Dio's house, which meant the Via Cyrenaica was close.

Like many of the villas, the dwelling next door was surrounded by a low wall. Eborius held up a hand to indicate Indavara should stay put, then ducked down, crossed the alley and skirted along the wall to the right. Indavara came up to the doorway and heard the others lining up behind him. Eborius crouched at the corner of the wall and looked north, then motioned for Indavara to follow.

Indavara was already moving when Lentellus tugged the back of his tunic.

'Wait,' whispered the legionary. 'Look there – to the left.'

The four tribesmen were on foot, heading south behind the row of villas. Eborius was still looking up the street. Indavara stepped back into the darkened room and waved the others back too, then put an arrow against the bowstring and peered round the doorway.

The Maseene were carrying firewood and seemed to be looking for more. Two were wearing what looked like recently appropriated cloaks and another had an army-issue helmet on his head. Not one was carrying a javelin, though all four were equipped with arm daggers. They stopped at the end of the alley, talking loudly. The warrior with the helmet was older than the others and his matted black hair fell almost to his waist. He nodded along the alley towards where Eborius had been.

Indavara guessed the centurion must have seen the tribesmen and somehow hidden himself.

One of the other Maseene seemed to disagree with the older warrior, who responded by raising his voice and setting off down the alley. Indavara heard the dull scrape of swords being drawn behind him. The other tribesmen relented and followed their compatriot.

Indavara withdrew another step and tightened his grip on the bowstring, wishing he had a sword in his hand.

The four Maseene walked right past the door, two of them laughing about something. Indavara couldn't hear their bare feet on the ground, but when the voices faded he moved forward.

After a time, Eborius reappeared at the corner, hand still on his undrawn sword.

'All clear.'

Indavara followed him out of the alley, then left along the front of the villas. The Via Cyrenaica was just up ahead. Indavara looked around; despite the ever-darkening sky, their position seemed dangerously exposed. As if to confirm this, two horsemen trotted into view on the road.

Eborius, Indavara and the others crouched down and pressed themselves against a wall. In a moment the riders were gone but then came the shouts of more Maseene, sounding alarmingly close. Eborius turned left through the next entrance and lifted a timber that had fallen across the villa doorway. Indavara covered the street and was last in behind Noster.

'By Mars, they're bloody everywhere,' said Adranos.

Eborius undid his chinstrap and took off his helmet. 'I'll go forward and check the road, see if there's any way across. I could use someone to watch my back.'

Indavara almost volunteered but knew he should stay with Annia.

'I'll come, sir,' offered Noster.

'No,' said Corbulo. 'Allow me. I want to see the road for myself.'

'As you wish,' said Eborius. 'I think I know where we can get a good view. The rest of you sit tight. We'll be back soon.'

⟶◼8◂⟶

At the first sight of the Maseene, Asdribar gave the order. Simo had been down below with Clara – helping the townspeople as they settled into the now very cramped hold – but once he heard the shouts from above he hurried up to the deck, arriving just as the sailors cast off.

Korinth, Desenna and two other men gave the *Fortuna* a final push, then jumped aboard. Asdribar waited until she was clear, then instructed the four men manning the port side to put out their oars and turn the ship round. Even as he shouted orders,

383

the captain kept his eyes on the tribesmen – they had just reached the end of the causeway.

There were perhaps twenty of them, all barefoot and clad in their pale, baggy tunics. A few were wielding javelins; all were carrying bottles or jars, presumably filled with wine. When they saw the *Fortuna* on the move, half a dozen left the main group and ran past the collapsed dock on to the eastern breakwater. But Asdribar had made his calculations; he knew he could get his ship out of the harbour before the tribesmen reached them.

That didn't stop the small group of warriors trying, and they didn't seem overly concerned by the uneven concrete beneath their unprotected feet. Korinth and Desenna each took a bow from the barrel of weapons and positioned themselves by the starboard side-rail.

Once the *Fortuna* had been turned round, swift, deep strokes from the eight oarsmen sent her cutting through the water towards the entrance. With Squint on the helm, Asdribar moved up to the mast and silently directed the veteran with his hands. As the bow came level with the breakwaters, he shouted down to Opilio and the oars were retracted.

One of the local women and a teenage boy came up the steps to look out of the hatch, but a shout from Asdribar sent them straight back down. As the oars were run out again and the ship picked up speed once more, the Maseene reached the end of the breakwater. Korinth and Desenna drew their bows and aimed their arrows but the warriors had already settled for triumphant jeering. The javelins stayed in their hands and the only object thrown was a wine bottle that plopped into the middle of the *Fortuna*'s wake. Korinth and Desenna lowered the bows.

Simo looked back over the stern at the town. He had kept up with his prayers but now dark thoughts overwhelmed him. Were they still alive, perhaps even watching the ship depart? Or were they lying somewhere, injured or dead, victims of the Maseene or Carnifex and his men?

'Keep her heading north,' Asdribar told Squint before walking over to Simo. 'You better get below again and make yourself useful – keep those people away from my oarsmen.'

Without a word, the Gaul walked back towards the hatch.

'Simo,' said Asdribar.

The Gaul halted at the top of the steps.

'I had no choice.'

——•8•——

Cassius had expected Eborius to move directly north towards the road but he headed west. As they edged round one of the stone cisterns, Cassius asked him why.

'I want to see the square too. We're nearly there.'

'What about the ship?'

'You want to make a dash for it without seeing what's in your way? Go ahead.'

It seemed impossible to move more than ten paces without running into Maseene, and without the gloom of twilight to hide them the short journey might have taken hours. But Cassius was relieved to note the sun still hadn't quite set when they reached a large villa that faced the square. As he followed the centurion along the overgrown path that bisected the villa's courtyard, he could hear fires crackling and the victorious cries of the tribesmen.

Eborius paused by the rear door. Cassius rested the butt of the javelin on the ground and took the opportunity to check behind them. For one brief, chilling moment, he thought he could see two men – one with a spear – but he almost laughed when he realised what he was actually looking at. The flames from the square had illuminated a fresco on the courtyard's rear wall: the goddess Venus reclining on a giant seashell. The 'spear carrier' was in fact a nymph holding a fishing rod. Cassius's aunt had the very same picture at her summer villa.

Eborius tapped him on the shoulder and pointed up and to the right. On the other side of the villa was a small tower, complete with miniature battlements and a conical tiled roof. The centurion led Cassius into the pitch-black interior. Fortunately, the noise from the square was more than sufficient to cover their stumbling, curse-ridden progress through the villa. The tower was accessed by a steep staircase and they eventually emerged into a tiny circular space that seemed to have remained untouched since the residents had left. Though everything was covered with a thick layer of dust, there were floor cushions, a miniature brazier, even a shelf stacked with scrolls and books.

Just below the base of the tower roof were two grilled windows, one facing north on to the Via Cyrenaica, the other west. Cassius put down the javelin and knelt next to Eborius, who was gazing out at the square.

'By all the gods,' breathed the centurion.

The fire had been fuelled by the market stalls, of which not a single timber remained. The stack of wood was as tall as two men and just as wide. Thick flowers of flame reached skyward and a heavy pall of smoke drifted high. The tribesmen stood around it in groups of a dozen or so. Cassius estimated there were between a hundred and fifty and two hundred of them. Most were drinking and some were deep in discussion, gesticulating wildly to their fellows. Others idly watched the flames. On the far side of the square, dozens of horses had been tethered, watched over by some of the younger tribesmen.

Cassius thought of the youthful warriors Carnifex had crucified and looked at the southern side of the square. He was surprised to see that the crosses and the bodies remained.

'Cervidus,' whispered Eborius.

The centurion was also looking at the crosses. And when Cassius looked closer, he realised that in fact the two bodies were of fully grown men, not youths. One had a white bandage around his ankle. Cervidus: the legionary who'd injured himself at the quarry.

'You had to leave him behind.'

'Yes.'

Eborius moved away from the window and slumped back against the wall. 'Until today I wouldn't have thought the Maseene capable of such things.'

'The other man?'

'Lafrenius Leon. I bet they had their fun with him.'

Cassius watched as a group of tribesmen walked past the crosses. Every one of them took his turn to spit at the body of the dead governor. Cassius looked out beyond the big blaze to the west, along the Via Cyrenaica. There were smaller fires every fifty yards or so. He moved to the other window and looked east. The situation was the same, and he could see dozens of figures close to every fire.

'Gods, we'll never get across now.'

Cassius peered towards the harbour but it was too dark to see if the *Fortuna* was still there. He turned away and sat below the window, opposite Eborius. After a while, he realised the big centurion was weeping. Cassius reached across and touched him on the arm. 'Manius.'

Eborius wiped his face, so ashamed that he almost seemed to be trying to scrape the tears off his skin. 'My apologies, Corbulo. I have long since acknowledged my part in what's happened here, but it is another thing to see the results of it.'

'You didn't cause this. The blood of all who have died here is on Carnifex's hands, not yours.'

Eborius put his head back against the wall. 'This is not the first time I have failed in my duties.'

'You mean your demotion? Being sent back to Darnis?'

'Even you know.'

'People talk. I imagine it must have been very difficult, but at least you were assigned to a legion in the first place. I barely scraped through training. If not for the Service, I doubt they would have passed me.'

'You are a young man. With chances to prove yourself.'

Cassius saw little point in explaining that he thought he'd already had quite enough chances.

'You have proven much today.'

'When it's already too late.'

Cassius's weary mind couldn't summon a constructive reply to that. Outside, the fire roared and hissed. Occasionally another cry of victory went up from the Maseene.

'Much was always expected of me,' Eborius continued quietly, 'looking as I do. Sometimes I think that was the only reason I was promoted – just because I looked impressive on the parade ground carrying a standard. When I arrived in Lambaesis, everyone told me I would rise up the ranks. They just piled more and more duties on me, thinking I would . . . flourish. In the end I think I did well to hold it together for a year. Then one day I realised I couldn't remember the last time I'd had water in my canteen. Not long after that I was back here.'

'That's history now. You stayed. And you stood up to Carnifex. I don't believe I would have.'

Eborius said nothing, which to Cassius seemed like progress.

He continued: 'I thought I was going to die in that pit. You risked everything in coming after us – you should feel pride, not shame.'

'Pride?' Eborius looked towards the square. 'For that?'

'You're a good officer. I see it, and your men know it.'

'My men are dead.'

'Not all of them. And Noster, Adranos and Lentellus need your help just like we do. No one else is going to get us out of here.'

It took a long time for Eborius to reply. 'You speak well, Corbulo.'

'Better than I fight, so I hope you'll continue to lead us as well as you have so far. What now?'

Eborius got up on his knees and looked out of the window facing north. 'Once it's properly dark, we shall try and find a gap in the lines – get across the road.'

'Let's head back to the others then,' said Cassius, moving towards the steps.

Eborius stayed where he was. 'Must be three hours or so since the bridge. Plenty of time for Carnifex to reach the town. He's out there. Somewhere.'

XXXIII

Even in the time it took them to collect the others and move east, the numbers of Maseene seemed to swell, with warriors converging on Darnis from all directions. Eborius had already identified four different local clans; it seemed the rumoured coming together was no longer a rumour. After another hour of darting from one villa to the next, they finally reached what the centurion had decided was the best place to cross the Via Cyrenaica.

Though the Maseene were in control of the road for at least two miles east of the square, the largest gap in their lines was next to the roofless temple of Jupiter. As Cassius joined him at the corner of the walled sanctuary behind it, Eborius quietly explained why. 'They have always feared the place. It's the only structure above ten feet still standing – testament to the power of the Roman god of gods.'

'Even though the roof came down,' said Cassius.

'It didn't come down. It was never built. They started work when I was a boy. The temple was paid for by a man named Sallustius, the richest man in Darnis at the time. He died before it was completed and his family decided they would rather spend the money on themselves. But Sallustius had insisted that every part was to be made as strong as possible – said he wanted it to still be here in a thousand years.'

Cassius listened to the hurried breaths of the others arriving. He and Indavara had taken it in turns to lead Annia through the maze-like town. Even so, she had fallen several times and had barely uttered a word. She was standing behind Cassius now and he could feel her shivering, even though Indavara had found an old blanket and tied it round her shoulders with twine.

'All here?' asked Eborius.

'All here,' confirmed Noster, who was still guarding the rear.

'Stay close.'

The centurion led them up the broad stone steps and between two of the columns into the half-completed structure. There was one distinct advantage to moving through a temple: they invariably followed a uniform design.

Close to the rear were the staircases leading up to the ante-rooms where religious documents and treasures would be stored. These rooms, however, hadn't actually been built – there was just a section of floor mounted on a set of smaller columns.

They then entered what would have been the temple's central chamber. There was no proper flooring of tiles or mosaics, just slabs of stone underfoot. Neither was there a statue of Jupiter, only a large, unoccupied plinth where Eborius waited for the rest of the group to catch up. When they'd all come to a stop, Cassius realised he could hear the squeaking and scurrying of rats somewhere beneath.

Eborius continued on through a wide doorway to the porticoed, open section at the front of the temple. Ahead was the podium where priests would address the faithful, then another set of steps leading down to the low-walled courtyard next to the road.

The centurion paused by a column, Cassius and the others gathered behind him. The Maseene had kept away from the front of the temple, but had made fires on either side of it. The tribesmen could only be seen when they passed in front of the flames; lean, long-haired silhouettes, swigging wine or raising their javelins. From one group, a melodic song; from the other a burst of gleeful laughter.

Cassius descended the steps as slowly as Eborius, holding the javelin high to stop it striking the stone. They were so close now; once across the road they could easily move along the shore to the harbour. But what of the *Fortuna*? Had Asdribar already left?

Halfway across the courtyard, Eborius stopped next to the temple altar.

'I'll go first,' he whispered. 'Wait a few moments, then Adranos and Lentellus, you come across. Corbulo, you and the girl next. Then Noster. Indavara – will you cover the road?'

Without a word, Indavara headed for the courtyard wall. Eborius and the soldiers moved up to the entrance.

'Are we going to the ship now?' Annia asked, teeth chattering.

'Hopefully, miss,' said Cassius.

'I'm cold. Very cold.'

'I know.'

He took hold of her arm and led her over to the others. Eborius and the legionaries were down on their haunches, checking the road. Cassius could make out Indavara to the right. He was on his knees, head just above the level of the wall.

'See you over there,' said Eborius.

He got to his feet and walked boldly across the road, his broad, mail-clad back soon merging with the darkness.

Lentellus whispered a brief prayer to Jupiter, which Adranos repeated. Cassius closed his eyes and gave a line to the god of gods himself.

'Now?' asked Lentellus.

'Wait, man,' warned Cassius. 'He said to give him a moment.'

'Shit,' said Adranos. 'Look.'

To their right, three Maseene warriors were walking away from the fire towards the square. One was holding a lantern.

The legionaries shuffled backwards. Cassius and Annia followed Noster, who had crawled behind the left side of the wall. Cassius leant back against the cold brick, wincing as the spear blade clinked against the stone floor. The trembling in Annia's fingers seemed to transmit itself to his, but he gritted his teeth and resisted it.

The soft, near-silent footsteps of the Maseene made their proximity hard to gauge. They began talking just yards from the temple entrance, then stopped. The lantern seemed impossibly bright; its glow reached far beyond the altar into the courtyard. Cassius bowed his head.

One of the tribesmen belched.

Noster was to Cassius's right. Cassius felt him reach for his sword, ready to draw it and strike. Cassius moved his hand to a less sweaty section of the javelin. He had to be ready too.

Then came the faint sound of movement and the voices drifted away.

'Go,' whispered Noster, and they all returned to their positions by the entrance.

'You two now,' said Cassius.

Lentellus and Adranos stood, edged away from the shelter of the wall, then they too were lost to the darkness.

'Annia, are you ready?'

'Yes.'

Cassius took a last glance in both directions. All clear.

He gripped her hand tight. They stood, then started across the road. At the first tap of his hobnailed boots, Cassius forced himself to slow down. Not daring to look at the Maseene, he stared straight ahead as they walked. Only when they were almost in the undergrowth on the other side did he spy Eborius. The centurion was squatting between two bushes, waving them forward. Once Cassius and Annia were beside him, he turned to his men.

'There's a path back there somewhere that leads down to the shore. Go and find it.'

'Yes, sir.'

Cassius gazed back across the road but all he could see were the great columns of the temple, black against the dark grey sky. Then two shapes materialised out of the gloom, one considerably bulkier than the other. Indavara and Noster came across side by side and dropped down next to the others.

'Thank the gods,' said Eborius.

'Jupiter in particular,' added Cassius.

'Even if the ship has gone, the shore might be the safest way to get clear of the town,' said Eborius.

'And this village?' asked Cassius. 'We could make it by dawn?'

'Probably. Let's hope we don't need to.'

Noster stood up and peered towards the marsh. 'That Lentellus and Adranos?'

'Back already?' said Eborius, turning round.

Cassius could just about see the two figures coming towards them.

'Get back across the road,' said Indavara, moving in front of Annia.

'What?' said Eborius.

'It's not them,' said Indavara, raising the bow. 'Look.'

Cassius saw it straight away. Of the two figures, one had only a single eye glinting in the dark. Mutilus.

From behind him, a desperate cry: 'Eborius, help us!'

'Lentellus! Adranos!' yelled Noster.

'Hel—' The second cry ended as a groan.

Another rank of men appeared behind Mutilus.

Cassius gripped Annia's hand and ran back across the road with Noster and Eborius not far behind.

Indavara drew the bowstring, aimed at Mutilus and let fly. He heard a metallic whine as the legionaries accelerated, armour jangling, blades held high. Trying to ignore the shouts of the nearby Maseene, he turned and sprinted after the others.

Annia somehow struck the edge of the courtyard wall and Cassius felt her hand slip from his as she tumbled to the ground. Eborius and Noster skidded to a halt behind him as he helped her up.

'Quick,' said Eborius, striking him on the shoulder. 'Back through the temple!'

Cassius and Annia ran on, only stopping when they reached the bottom of the steps. Cassius turned in time to see Eborius and Noster on either side of the altar, blades already drawn.

Indavara paused long enough to shoot another arrow at the legionaries, then dashed through the entrance. One of the soldiers cried out and managed only a couple of stumbling steps before hitting the ground. Mutilus jumped over him and led the others into the courtyard.

'Cassius!'

Annia pointed up the steps. Standing at the top was a large figure flanked by two men on each side. The silhouette of the cut-off crested helmet was unmistakable. Carnifex waved a hand and the four legionaries came charging down the steps.

Hauling Annia along beside him, Cassius made for the eastern side of the temple.

'They're behind us too,' he cried. 'This way!'

Eborius and Noster sped after him.

Indavara was last away. The bow and quiver were now more trouble than they were worth, so he threw them at Mutilus and darted round the altar after the others.

Carnifex's men came down from the podium at an angle, trying to cut him off, and the quickest of them was almost ahead of him. Bounding down the steps, the legionary raised his sword. He was right-handed, so Indavara reckoned his blade was far enough away to risk a pre-emptive strike.

He leapt up two steps, straight into the legionary's path. The shoulder charge knocked the man clean off his feet and sent him crashing into the unforgiving stone. 'Uhhh!'

One of the soldiers behind tripped and came flying over the top of him. A flailing hand caught Indavara's trailing boot. He stumbled and overbalanced so far forward that his hands scraped the steps, but he somehow stayed upright. A few more paces took him to the edge of the temple. He jumped down to the ground then followed the others to the right. More shouts rang out from the road; the Maseene were on the move.

'Go!' yelled Eborius from somewhere ahead.

Cassius didn't doubt Annia's willingness to run but the girl was simply exhausted. She was whimpering at every step and almost fell again as they reached the rear of the temple.

'Annia, come on.'

Eborius and Noster were just a few paces behind and only narrowly avoided running into them.

Indavara had already caught up. He shouldered his way between the two soldiers. 'Javelin!'

Cassius gave it to him.

Eborius took Annia's other hand and they set off round the corner of the temple with Noster.

Indavara drew the javelin back over his shoulder as the first of the legionaries charged into view. This man had evidently overtaken Mutilus, but he paid a heavy price for his enthusiasm. Again Indavara aimed low and again he hit something, because in a moment the soldier careened head first into the ground in front of him. Indavara sprang away once more.

The others had just turned left down the next street, Cassius and Eborius virtually dragging Annia along. Cassius knew it was only a matter of time before she fell again.

'Eborius, she's had it,' he said. 'We have to stop and hide somewhere.'

'All right, do it,' replied the centurion. 'We'll try and draw them off. Noster, this way!'

The two soldiers stopped, then ran back the way they'd come.

Luckily for them, Indavara was unarmed. He had just turned on to the street, and if he'd had a sword in his hands, might well have swung at the two figures speeding towards him out of the gloom.

'Keep going!' yelled Eborius before cutting right into a nearby alley. He and Noster continued shouting to try and attract the legionaries' attention.

Indavara ran on, but soon realised there was no one coming after him. He slowed to a walk and listened. More shouts to the east, but he couldn't tell from whom. And he thought he could hear quieter voices too, close by. Then came pounding footsteps from behind him and the rattle of heavy armour.

'Got one!'

'Over here, sir!'

Knowing he could outpace the legionaries, Indavara bolted down the street and was already pulling away when he heard a familiar voice spitting curses. He spied Cassius to his right, trying to force a door open, Annia beside him. They turned as Indavara vaulted over the villa wall.

'Corbulo, stand clear!'

Cassius pulled Annia out of the way as Indavara sprinted past and leapt at the door. He struck it with his shoulder and knocked it clean out of the frame. Landing right on top of it, he slid into the room beyond.

Cassius hurried past him, Annia in tow. 'They're right behind us!'

Once back on his feet, Indavara reached down, gripped the sides of the door and picked it up. He waited until the first legionary ran into the dwelling, then heaved the door straight into his chest.

'Uufff!'

The wood splintered as it struck the man's plate armour, the impact sending him backwards into the others.

The villa was dark. Cassius blundered forward, determined not to let go of Annia. Pushing a table out of the way, he found himself in front of another door. He tried the latch but it too was locked.

'Move!' yelled Indavara.

The legionaries had recovered quickly.

'I've got it,' said Cassius. He pushed Annia aside, took a run-up and threw himself at the door. To his surprise, it gave way easily and he half fell into the next room, colliding with a chair by the wall to his left.

Vaguely aware that there was light coming from the right, Cassius turned to see Indavara and Annia bundle through the doorway, the broad bulk of Mutilus looming behind them. Lacking any other armament, he picked up the chair.

Him or me.

Summoning a roar, Cassius darted in front of Indavara and Annia and smashed the chair down on Mutilus's helmet. The chair disintegrated in his hands but at least stopped the optio. Head still down, Mutilus struck out wildly. His arm caught Cassius a glancing blow on the face, knocking him back. Cassius hit something and dropped on to his backside. From the tone of the ensuing grunt, he realised the something was Indavara.

Suddenly there was a *lot* of light coming from the other side of the room. Mutilus and his men stopped just beyond the doorway. Cassius, Indavara, Annia and the legionaries all turned at the same time.

Only a few yards away, a youthful Maseene tribesman was holding up a lantern, staring at them open-mouthed. Behind him at least twenty more of the young warriors were gathered round a fire in the middle of the room, where a steaming pan hung from a spit. Most of them were holding wooden mugs and many of them spilled their wine as they overcame their initial shock and jumped up. The biggest of the youths pointed at the interlopers and yelled, then reached for his javelin.

'Out the way!' growled a familiar voice.

Mutilus and the other legionaries parted and Carnifex himself strode into the room, clad in muscle cuirass and helmet once more. Sweat glistened on his broad, scowling face. He aimed the tip of his sword at Cassius and Indavara as they got up. 'I've had about enough of this chasing through the streets shit.'

Cassius looked over his shoulder. Annia was pressed up against the wall beside another door.

A javelin flew across the room and struck the side of Carnifex's helmet. Without even flinching, he turned and glanced curiously at the Maseene. Raising his sword high, he bellowed at them. 'Yaahhhhhh!'

The young tribesman with the lantern stumbled backwards and fell over.

Carnifex chuckled as more of his legionaries piled into the room behind him.

'You know the problem with these barefoots?' he said to Cassius and Indavara. 'Never bothered to understand the value of a good set of armour.'

The big Maseene warrior dropped his javelin, walked to the fire and wrenched the pan off the spit. The other tribesmen dived out of the way as he ran across the room then swung it straight at Carnifex. Cassius and Indavara turned away as the pan struck the centurion's cuirass, sending most of the boiling water straight up into his face.

There was a strange pause, then Carnifex's sword clattered

to the floor. He clutched his cheeks and fell to his knees, steam rising from between his fingers. 'Aaaggghhh!'

Emboldened, the young Maseene warriors advanced, javelins ready.

Mutilus and the legionaries pressed forward to protect Carnifex and within moments a vicious melee had erupted.

Cassius and Indavara got ready to charge the door.

'Let me,' they said simultaneously.

Annia lifted up the latch and pushed the unlocked door open.

The three of them ran out into the darkness. Another party of torch-carrying Maseene were coming down the street towards them, attracted by the sounds of the fight.

'Here.'

Cassius led the other two in the opposite direction and behind one of the stone cisterns as the tribesmen ran into the villa.

'Now what?' asked Indavara once the warriors had disappeared. 'We don't have a weapon between us and Annia's out on her feet. We need somewhere to hide up until dawn.'

Cassius had already given this issue a little thought. 'Follow me.'

——•8•——

'Are you sure about this?' Indavara whispered as they reached the top of the steps, stopping briefly to look out at the Via Cyrenaica. There were fewer Maseene close to the fires, but the scattered torches still seemed to surround them.

'Last place they'd look, isn't it?'

Cassius dragged his eyes away from the road and let them get used to the dark again. Passing the smaller columns, he reached the stairway that led up to the right side of the temple's uncompleted antechambers. Beneath the film of dust, the stone was cold to the touch as he felt his way upwards. He waited for Indavara and Annia to reach the turn, then continued round the corner and up. The bare section of flooring formed a platform about ten yards off the ground. In daylight the position would be dangerously exposed; in darkness its only disadvantage was the lack of an escape route.

Though the slabs of stone felt reassuringly solid, Cassius moved carefully to the middle of the platform. Indavara brought Annia over to him and they sat her down. She had managed to keep hold of the blanket and they wrapped her up in it as best they could, tucking the edges underneath. She managed a mumbled 'Thank you' before lying down between them.

Cassius had lost his canteen somewhere so they didn't even have any water to drink. He and Indavara were wearing only their tunics and the cold of the stone seeped swiftly into their bones.

'Wonder where Eborius and Noster are,' said Cassius.

'I'm more worried about Carnifex,' replied Indavara.

'I doubt he got out of that villa. Thank the gods for quick-thinking young tribesmen.'

'I wouldn't put anything past that old bastard.'

'He knew we would try and cross the road here. They were just waiting for us.'

Cassius looked down at Annia as she turned on to her side. She was still shivering terribly, her bare head against the cold stone.

He unlaced one of his boots and pulled it off. 'Hope she doesn't mind the smell. Gods, I need a wash.' He gently lifted her head and placed the boot underneath. 'Poor girl. What she's been through today.'

'Made a right mess of your plan, didn't she?'

'At least she might lose a little bit of that arrogant streak, assuming we get out of here alive.' Cassius couldn't see much of Indavara's face in the darkness but he could tell he was still looking down at Annia. 'You really do like her, don't you?'

Indavara didn't reply.

'Well,' Cassius continued. 'Stranger things have happened. And she seems to like you too.'

'I'm not so sure. I think it was just a game to her.'

'I did tell you ladies can be difficult. If we ever make it back to Antioch in one piece we'll get ourselves a nice pair of hearth girls to do our bidding and provide our every need. No complications. Sound good?'

Cassius could hear the smile in Indavara's voice. 'It does.'

He looked out towards the harbour, but still couldn't tell if the *Fortuna* was there.

'You think they've already left?' asked Indavara.

'Not if Simo has anything to do with it.'

'And if they have?'

Cassius was still trying not to think about that. They might have stood a chance with Eborius to guide them, but alone, unarmed, and with Annia in such a state?

'Look at it this way, we're in a better position than we were at that accursed pit, so whatever our predicament, I'm going to consider the last few hours progress.'

Indavara lay down.

'You're sleeping?' Cassius asked.

'Resting.'

Cassius sat there in the darkness, knees drawn up to his chin, arms tight around them. He thought again of the pit; of what Indavara had told him when they'd both thought they were about to die. It all made sense now. He never said anything about his family and his past because he didn't know anything. And that almost childlike naivety – he knew so little of life and the world because all he had ever known was the arena.

Cassius actually had his mouth open, ready to say something, but he stopped himself. Now wasn't the time; they needed to rest. He put his head against his knees and closed his eyes.

XXXIV

Only once during the night did the Maseene get close. Dozing fitfully, Cassius woke when he heard their shouts and crawled to the side of the platform. He looked out through the temple's pillars but the tribesmen were moving fast, on their way back to the road. He had no idea of the hour but there were far fewer torches alight and most of the warriors seemed to have gathered around the fire in the square. Once more he looked for the *Fortuna* but he saw nothing, no light, no sign to give him hope. Indavara stirred too but lay down again when he realised nothing was wrong. Like him, Cassius stretched out close to Annia – to try and provide her with a little warmth. She was sleeping soundly now and had at last stopped shivering.

When Cassius closed his eyes there was no comfort or peace, only the blurry noise of what he had seen and endured over the last few hours. Those two seemingly endless journeys: one across the grassy plains, one through the darkened streets. And the terror of that last pursuit, with Carnifex and the murderous men of the First Century right behind them.

And worst of all, the gorge. Soldiers and horses tumbling into that black hole, falling to places only the gods knew. Had some of them survived, only to look back at the light, call out for salvation? Or had they just kept falling, falling, falling . . .

———◆———

He was snatched out of the dream by a hand shaking his arm. Indavara's green eyes were smiling. The sky beyond him was several shades lighter than when Cassius had fallen asleep. As he sat up, Indavara pointed towards the sea.

The *Fortuna Redux* was lying peacefully at anchor not a quarter-mile from the shore, a similar distance east of the harbour. The yard was raised, the oars were out, and several figures could be seen moving around on deck.

'Thank the great gods,' said Cassius.

'It gets better,' said Indavara, glancing down at the road.

Though some of the fires were still alight, the Maseene were lying down by the roadside, covered with blankets and hides. The only man on his feet was relieving himself into a bush. He weaved his way back towards the fire and collapsed onto his makeshift bed.

'The wine,' said Cassius.

'Or maybe they did finish off Carnifex and the others,' replied Indavara. 'Maybe they think there's no one left to fight.'

'What about Eborius and Noster?'

'We have to go while we have the chance.'

Cassius looked down at Annia, who had just woken. Now there was a little light, he could see the blood that had seeped through the wrappings on her feet.

'Agreed. Let's move.'

Cassius pulled the blanket away and helped her sit up.

'Annia, the *Fortuna* is there, see? We have to go now.'

She pushed her hair from her eyes and gripped his arm when she saw the ship. There was even a trace of a smile.

Cassius's throat was horribly dry. Resisting the temptation to cough, he crawled across the platform, his stiff limbs resisting every command. He waited for the others, then they slowly made their way down to the temple floor. He looked around but could see no sign of anyone close. The cold morning air was bitter with smoke from the Maseene fires.

Annia winced as she came down the last few steps.

'One last effort, miss,' said Cassius. 'Simo will look after you as soon as we're back aboard.'

He set off through the half-completed temple towards the road, glancing warily in every direction. The dawn light revealed sights they'd missed in the darkness: the remains of a fire, a pile of brown palm leaves dried almost to dust, and the arm of a statue, hand reaching for the sky. Grass had forced its way up between the floor slabs and the bases of the columns.

Cassius reached the podium and looked left. There were only three Maseene lying by the fire to the west. There were more men – ten at least – surrounding the smoking pile of ash to the east, but they were sleeping just as soundly. He waited for a nod from Indavara then tiptoed down the steps. Aside from the twittering birds announcing the dawn, all he could hear were the snores of the tribesmen. It seemed to take an age to reach the altar.

'We must stay low,' he said. Down on his hands and knees once more, he crawled to the entrance and checked the road. He couldn't see a single warrior on his feet.

'Ready?'

'Go,' whispered Indavara from behind him. 'It's getting lighter every moment.'

Like the previous night, Cassius didn't look along the road as he crossed it. He couldn't have cared less about the dirt and his aching knees – just as long as they made it to the other side.

Once off the paving stones, he navigated his way through the thick, spiny bushes, only stopping when the Maseene were out of sight. As he and the others got to their feet, he had to resist the urge to smile. 'Gods. It almost seems too easy.'

'That's what worries me,' replied Indavara, striding past him. He soon found the path Eborius had mentioned and ten yards along it, they came across the body of Lentellus. The unfortunate legionary was lying face down in thick grass and had been struck at least half a dozen times; one particularly grisly blow had almost severed his arm.

'Oh no,' said Annia.

Indavara went straight for the legionary's sword and had to prise apart the dead man's fingers to free it. As they set off again, Cassius looked around but he could see no trace of Adranos.

The ground was drier here than to the west and the strip of greenery between the Via Cyrenaica and the shore was more of a wood than a marsh. Cassius caught tantalising glimpses of the *Fortuna* through the trees and had to remind himself to keep checking behind them. Indavara soon sped up – with Annia somehow keeping pace – and by the time they reached the sandy beach, the three of them were almost running.

Indavara and Annia immediately began waving at the ship and, once he had checked there was no one else in view, Cassius joined them. He couldn't tell who the three men on deck were; they were close to the bow and seemed to be doing something with the anchor.

'We're here,' urged Annia. 'We're here.'

'Please,' implored Cassius.

It seemed almost as though the sailors were purposefully ignoring them and their waving became so frantic that Cassius could barely stop himself shouting. Suddenly aware that their attention was entirely on the ship, he looked back at the wood, fearful that the Maseene might have seen them. But the path was far from straight and the vegetation thick; he couldn't even make out the temple.

'Ha,' cried Annia.

Cassius spun back round. Two of the sailors were waving and the third was running towards the stern. Within a few moments more men came up through the hatch. Cassius saw splashes: oars dropping into the water.

Again, he had to stop himself smiling. They weren't aboard yet.

'Come on.'

He set off at a brisk walk along the shore towards the harbour. As the others joined him, he heard a rustling from the undergrowth to their left. Indavara cut in front, Lentellus's sword at the ready. Cassius spied a red tunic, then a big arm pushing a branch aside.

Eborius was grinning. So was Noster, who appeared from behind him as they stumbled their way through a particularly dense tangle of shrubbery. Eborius had his helmet in his hand and the right sleeve of his mail shirt had been sliced off, leaving a ragged edge over his shoulder. Noster was in a worse condition. He had a makeshift bandage around his knee and required considerable help from the centurion to reach the sand.

'Thank the gods,' said Cassius as he gripped forearms with his fellow officer.

Eborius was already looking past him at the *Fortuna*. 'Don't suppose there's room for two more on that thing?'

'Absolutely.'

Eborius shook forearms with Indavara too, and took a moment to greet Annia. Cassius clapped Noster on the shoulder and looked down at his knee. 'You wounded?'

'Sort of. Ran into a wall. My kneecap seems to be facing the wrong way.'

Eborius put his arm around Noster's back and helped him as they set off along the shore. 'Come on, old man.'

Indavara moved to the front of the group and kept his gaze to the left as they neared the harbour.

'What happened to you?' Cassius asked Eborius.

'We got away from the first lot but then ran into more Maseene. Ended up spending most of the night hiding in a cistern, then crossed the road an hour or so ago. Knew you'd head this way if you'd made it through the night. What about you?'

By the time Cassius had finished replying, the *Fortuna*'s anchor was up and four sets of oars were in the water. Cassius reckoned the large figure close to the bow looked like Simo.

To the east of the harbour, the warehouses were near the shore, with only a narrow belt of sand between them and the water. Beyond the wide doorway of the first building lay a dark, cavernous interior. The rectangle of light at the other end looked a long way away. Cassius was still looking at it when he heard a voice from up ahead.

'Mornin' all.'

Carnifex stepped out from behind the corner of the warehouse. Still leading the way, Indavara stopped five yards in front of him.

The old centurion was still clad in full armour and helmet. He tapped the triangular tip of his sword against a heavy, circular shield emblazoned with a black phoenix. His face was a blotchy pink mess – the boiling water had stripped skin from his cheeks, nose and forehead.

Annia turned straight into Cassius's arms. She would have run if he hadn't held on to her.

'Shame,' said Indavara. 'I was hoping the Maseene had finished you off.'

'Take more than a bunch of barefoots to do for old Carn. Told you I'd get me some of your blood, didn't I, boy?'

Indavara glanced back at Eborius. Carnifex watched for the younger man's reaction and gave another of his lopsided grins when Eborius came forward and stood beside Indavara. The bodyguard kept his eyes on Carnifex while he spoke to Cassius.

'Corbulo, get Annia to the ship.'

'You too, Noster,' added Eborius, pulling on his helmet.

'Not likely, sir.'

'That's an order.'

For once in his life, Cassius actually wanted to stay and fight. Carnifex deserved death more than any man he'd ever encountered. But he was unarmed, and the truth of it was he'd cause more harm than good.

'I'll come back,' he said, coaxing Annia away from the others.

'I'll be waiting, Streak,' said Carnifex.

'Come on,' Cassius told Noster. He put his spare hand around the limping legionary's shoulder and led him and Annia into the warehouse.

'I been looking forward to this,' said Carnifex as he flexed his shoulders. 'Now who's going to see the ferryman first?'

Indavara was to his right, Eborius to his left. After the briefest of nods they struck out, jabbing their swords straight at him. Carnifex held Eborius off with his shield and traded blows with Indavara, one blade thudding against hide-covered wood, the other clanging, iron against iron.

Given the old soldier's condition, Indavara favoured trying to tire him, but Carnifex had other ideas. Forcing Eborius back with a drive of the shield, he lunged towards Indavara. Their blades screeched and sparked as Carnifex's sword slid past Indavara's handle, missing his thumb by an inch.

'Slow, boy,' gloated Carnifex as he retreated to set himself again. 'Very slow.'

He turned to Eborius. 'Can you do any better, Manius?'

After his failed attack at the pit, Indavara was sure Carnifex would underestimate him. So as the centurion pushed Eborius back once more, Indavara readied himself to spring left and attack his flank.

He saw Carnifex's blade coming at him too late and instantly had to adjust, swerving back to the right. He didn't see the shield coming at all.

The edge slammed into his chest and knocked him off his feet. His back hit the sand but his head hit something a lot harder and as the crack reverberated through his skull he felt the sword fly from his fingers.

When the shimmering light eventually cleared, he was looking up at the grey-blue sky. Hearing scrapes and grunts, he turned towards the sea. The two clashing figures were distant and hazy. He tried to push himself up but when he fell back he realised why his head hurt so much. His neck was against rock. Wet rock.

The battling pair seemed far, far away. *Who are they again?*

Indavara turned on to his side. He could see the glinting metal of the sword but as he reached for it the image shifted and contorted until he had to look away.

Get up. Got to get up.

Sucking in lungfuls of air, he fumbled his way on to his knees. He shook his head to clear the fog but the pain struck him once more and he fell forward onto the sand. When he could see again, the first thing he noticed was the blood. The blood that had collected in a hollow atop the small rock in front of him.

I landed on it. Hit my head.

'Come on, Manius!'

Manius. Manius Eborius.

Indavara got up on his knees again and reached for the back of his head. The hair was sticky, soaked. His fingers found the wound – a half-inch rent in the flesh. He cried out and let go.

You've had worse. Get up.

He reached for the sword. It took a while to make his fingers work but he held it and pressed the tip into the sand to help him stand. Up on one knee, then on both feet. The sky swirled around him. The pain swirled around his head. He staggered but stayed upright.

He looked along the beach. They were coming back towards him, a thrashing tangle of red and bronze, arms and blades. He tried to move towards them but almost fell again.

Stop. Breathe. Long, deep breaths.

'Come on, man! You can do better!'

Carnifex. His name's Carnifex.

Somehow, Indavara found himself on his knees again, though he had kept hold of the sword. The fingers of his left hand were in a pool of icy water. He bent over, cupped his hand and flicked the water on to his face. His vision began to clear again, though he could have sworn someone was still hammering the back of his head with that rock. He looked up.

Eborius was forcing Carnifex – who had somehow lost his shield – back along the shore. The younger centurion launched a prodigious swing over his head. The older man blocked the blow but the impact sent him back several feet.

'That's the way!' roared Carnifex. 'Come on!'

Indavara gripped the sword handle tight. At last his body seemed to be doing what he told it to. Resting his other hand on the rounded pommel, he put the blade in the sand again to help him up. Eyes closed, he waited until he was steady on his feet. Then he opened them. Eborius and Carnifex were even closer.

With his height and a reach perhaps even longer than his foe's, Eborius now seemed to have the advantage. Mouth set in a snarl, both hands on his sword, he swung again. This time Carnifex didn't block, but stepped neatly to his left and watched the tip of the blade fly past his chest. With Eborius momentarily

408

unbalanced, Carnifex plucked his dagger from his belt and jammed it deep into Eborius's right arm where the armour had been cut away.

Carnifex left the knife there and retreated.

Indavara felt thick, warm blood oozing down the back of his neck.

It seemed to take Eborius a moment to realise what had happened. As he stared dumbly at the dagger handle, Carnifex heaved his sword at his head. The helmet absorbed most of the blow but Eborius was reeling.

Indavara started towards them but in the next instant he was down again.

Eborius's sword fell from his hand; the arm was useless now. Carnifex knew he had him and he wasted no time. Three swift hacks made a mess of the mail shirt, and as Eborius tottered backwards, hundreds of the little metal rings rained down on to his boots. He was still looking at them when Carnifex reversed his sword and jabbed the solid bronze handle between his eyes.

Stunned, the big officer fell to his knees.

Carnifex lowered his blade and reached under the younger man's chin to undo the strap. He then wrenched off the helmet and threw it away. Eborius' eyelids were flickering, his head lolling to one side. Carnifex ran a hand though his curly black hair, then gripped it and tilted his head up.

'I killed you, Eborius.'

'I fought you, Carnifex,' Eborius gurgled through the blood running down over his teeth.

Indavara tried to blink away the double vision.

Get up. Move.

A casual swing of Carnifex's blade took two inches out of Eborius's neck. The lifeless frame crashed forward onto the sand.

'That you did, lad,' Carnifex said as he turned. 'That you did.'

Indavara was back on one knee.

Get up or he'll kill you. Get up!

Carnifex wiped his mouth, boots squelching in the sand as he walked towards him. 'Your turn again, One Ear.'

———◼8►———

The broken, crumbling concrete was agony for Annia and Noster. Cassius had to try to help them both and progress was maddeningly slow. He wanted to stop and look back but he forced himself not to turn round.

They were still fifty feet from the end of the breakwater when Asdribar brought the *Fortuna* alongside. Korinth and Desenna made daring leaps up on to the concrete and held the ship in position with two lines. Simo made his way on to the side-rail and clambered up between them. Cassius heard Asdribar shouting at Clara, telling her to stay onboard. Squint was the only other sailor on deck; the others were manning the oars.

'Get them aboard!' Cassius told Simo.

'Lad, take this!' yelled Squint, flinging a short sword up on to the breakwater. Cassius let it land, then picked it up and ran back towards the shore.

———◼8►———

Carnifex was five yards away when Indavara got to his feet. He retreated towards the warehouse, mainly to give his head more time to clear.

The sweat running down Carnifex's face was loosening more of the burnt skin. He touched his brow and a strip of it peeled off in his hand. Indavara ran his eyes over the old centurion for signs that Eborius had caught him but there was little damage to his armour and no marks anywhere else. Only that slight limp and the gnarled left knee.

Grinning, Carnifex forced Indavara back with a few half-hearted but well-aimed thrusts. Indavara found he could barely get his weapon in the way, let alone think about mounting an

410

attack. The throbbing at the back of his head seemed to be seeping forward again.

'Even slower now, boy,' said Carnifex before launching a scything blow that knocked Indavara's blade high and away from him. He followed up with an arrow-straight kick that landed in Indavara's midriff.

The blow sent him flying backwards. His left foot gave way and he fell sideways into the timbers of the warehouse wall. As he slumped to the ground, splintering bolts of pain shot across his left shoulder; he knew instantly he had dislocated his arm.

'Oh,' said Carnifex, observing the strange angle at which the arm now hung. 'That's not going to help. Think it's broke, One Ear. Best get this over with.'

Carnifex thundered forward and heaved the sword down at his head. Indavara brought his weapon up in a horizontal block and set his right arm. The blades connected six inches above him with a shuddering clang.

A moment of silence. Indavara looked down and saw the shattered remains of both blades lying in the sand. He and Carnifex were holding handles with only a few jagged inches of metal attached. The centurion gave a surprised grunt.

Indavara pushed himself up the warehouse wall. He threw the broken sword to the ground, reached over and tucked his left hand into his belt. The arm just hung there, burning. He reckoned if he hadn't had the wall behind him he might have fainted.

I feel no pain. No pain.

He formed a fist with his right hand and took a single step forward.

Carnifex – standing no more than three feet away – glanced at the crippled arm and gave an approving grin. 'Ain't ever seen that before. Always did like you, One Ear. You a soldier?'

Indavara shook his head. 'Gladiator.'

'Well then that explains it. Don't think I ever killed me a gladiator.' Carnifex threw his sword to the ground. 'But I reckon I'll do all right against a man with one arm. Ready for your last fight, boy?'

Indavara answered by darting forward and swinging his leg straight into Carnifex's left knee. He caught it with his shin but the pain barely registered when he saw the old centurion grit his teeth to stop himself crying out. Indavara sidestepped to his right, away from the wall.

Carnifex turned towards him, snarling.

This time Indavara came at him from the left. Ducking under the centurion's swinging right hook, he lashed out a kick and hit the knee with the reinforced front of his boot.

Carnifex's leg almost buckled yet he straightened himself and raised his fists. But it was a show of strength. A show.

'Slow, old man. Very slow.'

Carnifex was ready this time. He reached down to grab Indavara's boot but the kick was a feint and he was struck only by a short punch that caught him on the nose. Not the hardest of blows, it nonetheless froze him for a moment and a moment was all Indavara needed. He shifted right and pounced, smashing another kick into the old centurion's knee.

The thin layer of flesh over Indavara's shin was ablaze but he knew he could take it; knew he could take more than Carnifex. He reckoned Carnifex hadn't been hurt like that for a long time.

Indavara just kept on kicking. The centurion swung wildly at him – a glancing blow that did more damage to his hand than to Indavara's jaw. Then Carnifex tried to lurch clear, but at the sixth blow his knee finally gave way. A final sweep from Indavara into his standing leg and he fell flat on his back.

Carnifex's last attack was a desperate kick of his own, but Indavara stayed clear of the sharpened studs. There was little point striking the cuirass, so he stamped straight down into his groin. That ended any remaining resistance.

Indavara's next swing of his boot hit Carnifex's helmet so hard that he almost fell over. He drove his foot into that horrid pink face again and again, only stopping when there was no sound or movement from below. Then he looked down.

The helmet's angular cheek guards had been pushed deep into Carnifex's face, not that you could really call it a face now. The eyes had disappeared under riven flesh and pooling blood. Indavara spat into the mess.

Ship. Harbour. Walk.

He took three steps and pitched forwards on to the sand.

———8———

As Cassius reached the end of the breakwater, he saw a young Maseene on the other side of the causeway. The tribesman looked in his direction, then ran back under the arch towards the square. Somehow Cassius forgot all the weariness and pain as he sprinted along the side of the warehouses.

All three men were lying on the ground but only Indavara was moving. He opened his eyes as Cassius crouched down next to him.

'By the great gods. Can you move?'

'Left arm's screwed.'

Cassius helped him to his knees. 'We have to go. The Maseene. Can you walk?'

'There's nothing wrong with my legs.'

Cassius didn't think it wise to tell him what state his right shin was in. Once Indavara was on his feet, Cassius glanced over at Eborius. Even though he was lying face down in the sand, motionless, he wanted to go over to him.

Indavara shook his head. 'He's gone.'

There was no need to ask about Carnifex; the old centurion's face resembled something from a butcher's slab.

To Cassius's astonishment, Indavara managed a kind of limping jog. He kept hold of him as they ran, blood leaking from the bodyguard's head on to his arm. By the time they reached the breakwater, dozens of Maseene were coming across the causeway.

Indavara almost fell with his very first step on to the concrete. Throwing the sword aside, Cassius grabbed his belt and kept him upright. In doing so he knocked the dislocated arm, prompting Indavara to unleash a vicious stream of curses.

'Sorry.'

Cassius looked back over his shoulder. The Maseene seemed to be racing each other to reach them first.

'We need to hurry up.'

Indavara turned.

'Don't look back,' advised Cassius.

Indavara ignored him. Seeing the Maseene, he somehow sped up.

The two of them stumbled and scrambled on as best they could until they were close to the *Fortuna*. As Simo came forward to meet them, Indavara caught his left foot and would have gone down if Cassius hadn't grabbed a handful of tunic.

'Indavara, you can do it. Almost there.'

Korinth and Desenna were waving them on and shouting encouragement.

'Oh Lord,' said Simo.

Cassius wasn't sure if he was more concerned about Indavara or the pursuing tribesmen.

'Watch his arm,' he told the Gaul as they helped Indavara the last few yards. Once they reached the *Fortuna*, the bodyguard's last surge of energy seemed to fade. His eyes rolled and his mouth dropped open; he looked about ready to pass out. Korinth and Desenna threw their lines aboard and leapt down on to the ship.

Cassius looked back. The closest warriors were a hundred feet away, bounding across the concrete with great leaps.

With Squint on the helm, Asdribar came to help as Cassius and Simo lowered Indavara on to the side-rail. Cassius held his right hand as long as he could, then let go. Simo kept hold of Indavara's tunic but lost his balance and fell on to the deck. As Indavara collapsed into Asdribar's arms, Korinth and Desenna were already pushing the ship away from the breakwater.

'Get on, lad,' yelled Squint.

'Sir, look out!' shouted Simo.

Cassius was about to jump but he turned and saw a javelin flashing through the air towards his face. He threw himself to the side, yelping as he landed on a sharp concrete edge.

He looked up to see a dozen Maseene coming at him. The

414

Fortuna was already three yards clear of the breakwater; too far to jump from a standing start.

'Master Cassius!' cried Simo.

Cassius got to his feet and set off for the end of the breakwater, doing his best to emulate the long, loping strides of the tribesmen. He heard a javelin whoosh past his right ear and saw it hit the water. The oars were out on the port side of the *Fortuna* but hadn't been lowered yet. He took a deep breath.

Cassius's last step took him straight off the end of the breakwater. He doubted it was the most graceful dive of his life but he got his arms out in front of him and arrowed deep into the cold, choppy water. Without even waiting for his eyes to clear, he turned towards where the ship would be and kicked out hard. Broad strokes took him deeper. He saw the *Fortuna*'s hull sliding past and oars striking the water above him.

He put in a spurt then let himself rise, hoping not to catch a javelin or an oar in the head. As he surfaced about ten feet from the rudder housing, something splashed into the water behind him. He snatched another breath and dived under again. One of his boots came loose and fell away as he made for the ship. He stayed as low as he could until he was in front of the rudder housing, then came up again. The top edge of the housing was two feet above him and the timbers slimy and wet, but he reached up and held on.

'. . . is he?' came the shout from above.

Cassius's first attempt to speak came out as a gurgle. He spat out salty water and tried again. 'I'm here. Go!'

'He's there!' cried Simo.

'Oars in,' ordered Asdribar. 'Pull away.'

'Hold on, sir!' added Simo.

'I intend to!'

Unable to see anything other than the hardwood an inch in front of his face, Cassius heard the oars hit the water behind him, then felt his legs being pulled towards the stern as the *Fortuna* picked up speed. All the strength seemed to have drained out of him once more and it was all he could do to retain his grip.

After what seemed an unnecessarily long time, the splashes of the oars ceased and the ship began to slow. Cassius managed to turn his head to the right. They were well away from the harbour. He could see the fisherman's hut, the two doors still open. A few Maseene on the Via Cyrenaica had stopped their horses to watch the ship.

The rudder housing shook as boots thumped down on to it and the scarred face of Korinth appeared above. 'Think you might enjoy the trip better on deck, sir.'

'Just pull me up, man,' Cassius replied, spitting out more water. Desenna appeared and the two of them took a hand each and hauled him up on to the housing. Korinth then gave him a leg-up and he clambered over the side-rail.

Simo was waiting there with a blanket, which he wrapped around Cassius. The Gaul beamed as he rubbed his master's shoulders, then anxiously inspected his nose. Had it not been for the others aboard, Cassius would have gladly embraced him. He settled for patting him on the chest.

'Nicely done, Officer,' said Asdribar. 'Welcome back.'

'Thank you, Captain.'

Asdribar plucked a Maseene javelin from the deck and examined the tip.

'I trust we're out of range now,' said Cassius.

'Indeed we are.'

Cassius looked back at the breakwater. The tribesmen were already returning to the shore, but hundreds more had gathered in the harbour. Cassius gripped the blanket and gestured for Simo to go and help Indavara, who was sitting by the hatch, cradling his left arm. The back of his tunic was wet through with blood.

Sitting on the steps just below the hatch were two women. Others peered out from behind them, all looking back at the town. Before Cassius could ask who they were, he saw Annia. She was lying on the floor just inside the deckhouse door. Clara had wrapped her in a cloak and was offering her some wine.

Opilio shouted from below. 'Oars in again, sir?'

Before Asdribar could reply, Noster spoke. The veteran was

416

by the port side-rail, looking back at the harbour. 'By Jupiter. He's still alive.'

'Who?' said Cassius, hurrying over to join him.

'Who else?' replied Noster.

Cassius couldn't believe what he was seeing. Carnifex – still with the half-crested helmet on his head – was up on his feet and staggering past the warehouses towards the dock. Indavara arrived next at the side-rail, ignoring Simo's protestations that he sit back down.

'It can't be—'

Then the Maseene saw Carnifex. With whoops and cries that carried across the water, the tribesmen surged towards the centurion.

'They'll tear him to pieces,' said Noster.

'That's about the only way to be sure you've killed him,' added Indavara.

The first javelin was thrown from some distance and struck Carnifex's cuirass. As he lurched sideways, a warrior drew his arm dagger and leapt on to his back. A second man stuck a knife deep into his throat, then was lost from view as the other Maseene closed in.

The last trace of Carnifex they saw was the crested helmet as it was tossed from warrior to warrior. Finally one of them threw it into the harbour. It floated for a moment, then sank.

'We leaving?' asked Asdribar.

'Yes,' said Cassius.

The Carthaginian gave the order. Within moments the oars were in the water and the *Fortuna* was under way.

'Sir,' said Simo. 'I'd like to get Indavara down below. I must stop this bleeding.'

'Of course,' said Cassius. 'Go ahead.'

He helped them as far as the hatch and was about to follow, but then glanced back at Noster. The veteran was still gazing at the shore.

'I'll be down in a moment.'

'Corbulo, did you come to the harbour last night?' Asdribar asked as he passed him.

417

'No. We were . . . delayed.'

'It was too dangerous. We had to wait at anchor.'

'I'm just glad you stayed,' replied Cassius.

'Your man Simo there can be very persuasive. Young Clara too. What happened? You were supposed to be here this time yesterday.'

A single day. To Cassius it seemed more like a week. The hut, the pit, the battle, the gorge, the flight through Darnis. He didn't know where to start.

Asdribar put a hand on his shoulder. 'Perhaps you'll tell me when you're ready.'

Cassius went and stood by Noster, who was looking beyond the leaping, cheering Maseene towards the beach by the warehouses; towards where Eborius lay.

'I'm sorry we had to leave him,' said Cassius.

'He was a fine officer,' said Noster.

'And a fine man,' replied Cassius. 'Finer than he knew.'

XXXV

The *Fortuna Redux* slipped gently into the cove under a sky streaked with orange and red. Asdribar himself was at the helm and – with just the foresail flying – he guided his ship to a tranquil spot sheltered by a promontory. Once Desenna and Korinth had the sail down, old Squint dropped the anchor from the bow. As the chain rattled through the block, Asdribar left Tarkel to tie off the tillers and made his way forward. Desenna and Korinth unshackled the foresail then bagged it up. Dismissed by the captain, they and the lad went below.

As the already slight wind died and the light faded, Asdribar and Squint stood in silence, watching the ship settle back on the anchor chain. With the *Fortuna*'s bow veering gently from side to side, Asdribar took a flask of wine from his tunic and the two sailors shared a drink. The only sign of life on the barren shore was a pair of white storks perched on a rock, watching the ship.

Eventually, the bow stopped moving. Asdribar tested the anchor chain with his boot; it was taut and still. Not wanting to alert anyone onshore to their presence, he'd already decided that the ship's lanterns would remain unlit. The captain took a final look around the cove, then glanced at Squint. The veteran nodded and the two of them made their away towards the hatch.

—●—

'Ow! Gods, Simo, you're just making it worse.'

Cassius pushed the Gaul away and wiped tears of pain from his eyes.

'I am sorry, sir. It really requires some specialist attention.'

'That bloody animal Carnifex. Knowing my luck I'll end up looking like some backstreet brawler. My nose was perfect. Perfect! People used to make comments. More wine, Simo.'

'The jug is empty, sir. I shall have to—'

'Ah, forget it. I shall take a walk instead.'

'I have the last of your clean tunics here, sir.'

Cassius let Simo dress him. Though he'd slept solidly through most of the afternoon, and knew he should have felt profound relief to have escaped Darnis alive, there was no sense of euphoria, only an unsettling disquiet.

As Simo buckled his belt, Cassius remembered what he'd pledged to do before the end of the day. 'Simo, Captain Asdribar told me about your efforts to ensure he waited for our return.'

'My prayers were answered, sir.'

Cassius didn't have the heart to take issue with him on that one.

'Perhaps. In any case, I thank you. There are some servants who might be glad to be rid of their master, especially one who berates them for simply doing their best. I am . . . fortunate to have you by my side.'

Simo straightened Cassius's tunic and gave a slight bow. 'Thank you, sir.'

'A promise – if we ever make it back to Antioch, you can take all that leave I owe you in one go. A week off – how does that sound?'

Simo seemed barely able to comprehend such a concept. 'Thank you, Master Cassius.'

'Not at all.'

Cassius walked along the passageway to Korinth's room. To everyone's surprise, the deck-chief had offered his bed to Indavara. Cassius knocked on the door.

'What?'

'You might want to try something more polite,' Cassius said as he entered. Indavara was sitting up on the bed. Looking at the state of him, Cassius immediately felt embarrassed by his earlier bleating and hoped Indavara hadn't heard.

The bodyguard's right leg was bandaged from ankle to knee and his toes were blotched with purple bruises. In order to cover both the gash on his brow and the more serious wound to the back of his skull, Simo had wrapped up almost his entire head, so only a few tufts of Indavara's thick black hair were visible. His left arm appeared largely unscathed – apart from a few scrapes and welts – but lay limply by his side, his hand at rest on the bed.

'I still can't believe you relocated that yourself,' said Cassius.

Despite Simo's protests, Indavara had decided to knock his shoulder back into place by smashing it against the *Fortuna*'s mast. It had taken three attempts.

'I believe Clara almost fainted,' added Cassius.

'It's not so bad. I've done it a couple of times before. Once during a fight actually.'

Shaking his head in disbelief, Cassius sat down on the end of the bed.

'This is worse,' said Indavara, pointing at his head. 'Can't lean back on it, can't lie down.'

He looked at Cassius's nose. 'You want me to re-break that for you? I've seen it done. Might set straighter.'

'Tempting though that sounds, I think I'll decline.'

'Do you know how Annia is?'

'No. I don't believe she's left the deckhouse since we came aboard.'

Cassius gazed idly down at the numerous grazes on his hands, largely a result of rolling around on the concrete breakwater. 'I wonder how all this will affect her – on top of losing her father. I suppose we should just be glad we got her out.'

'With a bit of help,' said Indavara.

'I'll start on my report tomorrow. I don't know what weight my opinion will hold, but I'll be recommending the highest post-humous honour for Eborius. What he did should be acknowledged. Remembered. What happened to him – on the beach?'

'I didn't see all of it. But he fought bravely. And if he hadn't kept Carnifex occupied, I'd never even have got back on my feet.'

421

'Only the gods know how you did. Simo said the skin at the back of your head was cut almost to the bone. Twenty stitches, wasn't it?'

Indavara nodded but then ground his teeth together. 'I have to remember to stop doing that.'

'Well if my socks are anything to go by, I'm sure Simo did an excellent job with the needle and thread.'

After attending to the wound, the Gaul had confided to Cassius that he'd seen an older, similarly sizeable scar hidden under the bodyguard's hair. Cassius had elected not to discuss Indavara's confession with Simo but he wondered, was this the injury that had caused his memory loss – left him with a gaping void instead of a past?

Cassius thought it unlikely there would be a better chance to discuss the matter. 'Indavara, listen—'

A quiet knock on the door.

'Who's there?' asked Indavara, with a valiant attempt at politeness.

'It's Clara, sir.'

Cassius got up and opened the door. He hadn't spoken to the girl yet and was pleased to see her blush as she returned his smile. It took her a few moments to remember why she was there.

'Sir, Miss Annia can't really move because of her feet, but she'd like to see you both – whenever it's convenient for you.'

'Now?' suggested Indavara keenly.

'Why not,' said Cassius, realising his chance had gone. 'Clara, tell your mistress we'll be there presently.'

With a little bow, the maid hurried away.

Indavara manoeuvred himself to the side of the bed using only his left leg and right arm.

'Sure you should be moving around?'

'I'm fine.'

Cassius put out his hand but Indavara got to his feet unaided. 'You go ahead.'

Cassius made his way along the passageway then turned, watching as Indavara struggled through the doorway. Though

Simo felt sure there was no break, Cassius had seen the condition of the right leg before the Gaul had applied ointment and bandaged it. The flesh on the shin seemed to have been almost flayed from the bone; such was the price Indavara had paid to bring the old centurion down.

Having barely noticed earlier, Cassius now realised the *Fortuna*'s hold had been transformed. The timber and twig bales had disappeared and every available space was occupied by the townspeople. Lanterns hanging from the roof cast an opaque glow over the morass of people and baggage. A few sat or lay alone but most were gathered in small groups. One woman was tearing up a loaf and placing equal-sized hunks of bread on three plates already covered with olives and dried sausage. Three children looked on expectantly.

Asdribar appeared from the gloom, shaking his head at the state of his beloved ship. Upon reaching the steps, he turned and spied something at the other end of the hold. 'I said no lamps! Just the lanterns. Whoever lit that better put it out now or I'll come back up there and throw you over the side!'

One of the children awaiting her dinner – a girl of no more than five – looked up at the captain and promptly burst into tears. Exasperated, Asdribar started towards the galley but then stopped and walked back to the little girl. He squatted down in front of her and smiled.

'Sorry about that, love. We sailors like things done a certain way.'

The girl squeezed up close to her mother.

'Tell you what,' said the Carthaginian. 'Why don't you sew my mouth up and then I won't be able to make a sound?'

Asdribar produced an imaginary needle and threaded it. 'Here you are. Careful now.'

With a reluctant smile, the little girl leant towards him and opened her palm.

Asdribar pretended to drop it. 'Oh. No, there it is.'

As the girl played along, Indavara caught up with Cassius and looked on.

423

Pouting, Asdribar pointed at his mouth. While the girl pretended to sew it up, he pulled all manner of faces, drawing laughs from all three children.

Cassius glanced at the other townspeople nearby. They were ignoring Asdribar's antics and seemed far more interested in Indavara. Word had spread perhaps: this was the man who had beaten Carnifex.

Asdribar took a piece of bread, pretended he couldn't get it in his mouth, then adopted a sad expression worthy of a pantomime performer.

With the little girl now chortling, he stood up and went on his way, looking rather sheepish when he realised Cassius and Indavara had been watching.

'I think you might have missed your vocation, Captain,' said Cassius. 'Perhaps it's time to give up the freight trade and convert the *Fortuna* into a passenger ship.'

'Not for all the silk in the East. Thank the gods this is to be a short trip.'

'Will we make Apollonia by nightfall tomorrow?'

Asdribar looked back at the crowded hold. 'Even if I have to take up an oar myself. By the way, I've organised another gathering in the deckhouse this evening – before we all go our separate ways.'

'You won't be taking Annia and Clara back to Rhodes?'

'I'm afraid you shall all have to make your own way home. You may not listen to the voices of the gods, Officer, but I do – and I know when I'm pushing my luck. Storms, rogue centurions, rampaging tribesmen . . .'

'Think of the money, Captain.'

'Oh I do,' said Asdribar with a smile. 'I do. And I'll need plenty of it to keep the crew quiet when I tell them we're wintering in Apollonia. See you later?'

'Of course.'

With that, the captain continued on his way.

Just as Cassius and Indavara reached the steps, Noster hobbled out of the hold. He was with a plain-looking woman made rather more attractive by her voluminous, curly brown hair.

424

'Sir, this is my wife. Octavia, this is Officer Corbulo, and that's Indavara.'

'A pleasure,' said Cassius. 'How's the knee, Noster?'

'It'll be all right, sir.'

Cassius turned to his wife. 'I'm glad you were able to get out of the town safely.'

'Octavia's been telling me we should leave for years,' said Noster. 'I suppose I should have listened. What do you think will happen to Darnis, sir?'

'I've no idea. I shall certainly be meeting the provincial governor in Cyrene. Hopefully something can be done.'

'I wonder if we shouldn't just leave it to the Maseene, sir. They were there before us, after all.'

'Right,' said Indavara quietly.

'Well, we can't really have that,' said Cassius, 'but I take your point. Misrule can be as bad as anarchy on occasion, but order must be restored. There might be a way forward, with a half-decent governor and a garrison of men like yourself. Would you like me to put your name forward?'

Noster's wife tightened her grip on his arm. The veteran looked at her and smiled. 'No, thank you, sir. My twenty-five years were up a few months ago. I was really only staying on for Centurion Eborius. Hopefully they'll give us a nice plot of land somewhere quiet.'

'Fair enough. You deserve nothing less. By the way, there's to be a get-together up in the deckhouse later. I'm sure the captain would be happy for you to join us.'

'Thank you, sir. We'll see you there.'

—■8■—

They found Annia lying in bed, covered by no less than three blankets. Cassius helped Clara bring over two chairs and though the maid betrayed nothing with her expression, she touched his arm when the other two weren't looking.

They sat down. Cassius was surprised – and felt strangely proud – when Indavara initiated the conversation.

425

'How are you, miss?'

'Better, thank you. Clara has been wonderful.'

The maid gave yet another of her neat little bows.

'And you two?'

Though the question was directed at both of them, Annia was gazing at Indavara. Aside from all the bandages, even the exposed areas of his dark skin were heavily marked; new damage upon old.

'Nothing a bit of rest and some hot food won't fix, miss.'

Cassius couldn't help feeling slightly jealous of the look Annia gave the bodyguard then.

She sat up higher in the bed. 'Officer Corbulo, having had some time to think, I can understand why you didn't disclose everything to me before. But I would ask that you do so now.'

'Gladly.'

Cassius described how the investigation had unfolded from the sighting of Dio onwards. Relating the events at the quarry, he spared Annia the worst of Carnifex's excesses, though he felt he had to tell her that the conspirators had been shown the head as proof of the assassin's work. Strangely, it wasn't this that produced the most marked reaction in the girl. That came when Cassius reached the end of his account, explaining how they'd captured Carnifex and taken him to the hut.

Annia looked away and covered her hand with her mouth. It took the attentions of Clara and a little wine before she could recover herself enough to speak. Cassius and Indavara exchanged glances and looked to the door but Annia motioned for them to stay. She took a handkerchief from Clara and wiped her eyes.

'How different things might have been had I stayed on the ship as you had instructed. Centurion Eborius and those other soldiers . . .'

Cassius knew a little about guilt; about how it could so easily flourish if it wasn't nipped in the bud.

'Miss, Eborius and his men made their choices a long time ago. When it would have been far easier to go along with Carnifex,

426

they chose to stand up to him. Whatever our involvement, such a confrontation was inevitable.'

Cassius wasn't certain of that, but he was certain Annia needed to hear it. It was right that she should regret her actions, but he couldn't allow the young woman to shoulder such a burden.

'Circumstances and the actions of others certainly played their part,' he continued, 'but, ultimately, one man is to blame for all the suffering we have witnessed. But thanks to Indavara here, Darnis, Rome and the rest of the world are rid of him.'

Annia dabbed at her eyes with the handkerchief. 'Hearing of some of the things my father dealt with, I certainly didn't consider myself an innocent. But I confess I had never expected to see such cruelty, such reckless hate. How could the gods allow it? Allow *him*?'

'I don't know, miss,' said Cassius.

'I wonder if I shall ever be able to forget that man. That monster.'

Cassius said nothing; he had already spent a considerable amount of time pondering the same question.

'Forget him, miss,' said Indavara flatly. 'Nothing but a bad man who got what was coming to him. Don't trouble yourself. He's not worth it.'

Annia seemed to take comfort from Indavara's words; they gave Cassius pause for thought too.

'Clara, bring it over now,' Annia said after a while.

The maid picked up a hardwood box and gave it to her mistress.

Annia opened it, took out two small silver discs and placed them on the bed.

'I didn't see my father until I was four years old. He was a centurion then, away fighting with the legions in the East. He gave these to me upon his return, a reward, he said, for me being so brave – with him absent and my mother ailing. As a girl I thought nothing of where they had come from but when I was older I realised they were medals. For valour. I once asked him why he hadn't given them to his men. A tribune had distributed two each to every centurion after a great battle, asking that they

427

select the men most deserving to receive them. Of my father's century, only twenty-five had survived. But he said every last one of them deserved it, so he kept them.'

Annia looked up. 'I should like to give them to you both. A symbol of my gratitude. First, for finding those responsible for my father's death; second, for getting me out of that awful place.'

'That is very kind, miss,' said Cassius, 'but we cannot accept. Those were given to your father.'

'You didn't know him. He would want you to have them. As do I.'

Annia took out one medal and offered it to Indavara. He glanced briefly at Cassius, then took it. 'Thank you, miss.'

Annia offered the second medal to Cassius.

He stood up. 'I appreciate the gesture, really, but I cannot accept it. Please excuse me.'

——8——

Later, with the singing sailors already in the galley for their own gathering, Indavara sat on the bed once more, running his fingers across the cold silver of the medal. He didn't care what the inscriptions said, nor did he care about the eagle – even though he knew what it represented. To him it was simply a gift from her, and a symbol of what he had done.

In the arena, he had been applauded and cheered by thousands, but those few words from Annia meant more to him than all of it, as did praise from Corbulo and men like Noster and Captain Asdribar and Master Abascantius.

A gladiator was little better than an animal; a well-trained beast kept only to fight and entertain. But a man – a man had a name, a reputation, a history.

A man needed a family too. Indavara thought of all those people from Darnis, of Noster and his wife; they'd been through so much together, their ties were so strong.

Sometimes at night, lying in the darkness, he would try and

summon a face – a brother, a sister, a father, a mother? His mind would play tricks, showing him those he'd known in the arena or since, never someone new or unknown. Someone from before.

Even a place would do. A familiar room or a courtyard perhaps, a river, a field, a forest? But there was nothing.

Indavara was still glad to have told Corbulo. In fact, he was surprised Corbulo hadn't asked him more about it yet – he talked so much about everything else after all. Indavara hadn't expected to ever tell anyone, certainly not him. But if they were going to stay together, work together, it was perhaps good that he knew. All the questions could stop – there was no reason to lie, to hide. Now Corbulo knew, perhaps he would understand.

Indavara looked down at the medal and used his tunic to wipe his fingermarks off the silver. This – this was something; something to keep and treasure. It would help him remember too; those few precious moments with Annia.

Once they reached Apollonia he would probably never see her again. The thought tore at him but Corbulo had been right; there was no future in it. Young ladies from rich families didn't pair off with rough, ignorant men like him. But he believed she liked him and respected him and admired him, and this was enough to bring a smile to his face.

The medal would go in the little pocket he had sewn into his pack, along with the two figurines of Fortuna.

A man had a history. He could make his own history now.

— 8 —

Having eventually dozed off, Indavara was later woken by Simo, who'd come to check his bandages before they joined the others in the deckhouse. Returning to Cassius's cabin to fetch him, they found him lying on the bed. Simo instantly busied himself by putting away a few odds and ends, but Indavara noticed Cassius wiping his eyes.

'This damned nose.'

When Simo had finished tidying, he offered Cassius his cloak. 'Shall we then, sir?'

'You go ahead, Simo,' said Indavara.

The Gaul looked to Cassius, who glanced at Indavara.

'Go on. I can help him up.'

Once Simo had gone, Indavara leant against the wall. 'Why didn't you take it?'

'The medal? Didn't seem right.'

'You deserve it as much as I do.'

Cassius just shook his head.

'This is about the bridge, isn't it? You've told Simo?'

'I don't think I can. By the gods, Indavara, the noise of it. And then that silence.'

'What if they had got across? You were right – the rest of us were too stupid or too scared to even realise it. They would have caught up with us and cut us down in moments. Would you prefer it if we and Eborius and the others had been killed? If they'd taken Annia?'

'Of course not. Logically . . . you're right. I know that. But it doesn't change the fact that I have to remember it. Live with it. What I did.'

'*You* didn't do anything. *We* did. Lose sleep over those bastards if you want. I won't. Any man that chose to side with Carnifex over Eborius deserved everything he got.'

Cassius gazed up at the black beyond the porthole.

'So, you coming?' asked Indavara. 'I can't get up those steps on my own.'

———◄8►———

Eleven people had crowded into the deckhouse. Annia was sitting up but was still covered with blankets. She had said little and seemed initially to resent the invasion of her quarters, but was now watching with amusement as Noster finally got the chance to have his drinking competition with Asdribar, Squint, Korinth and Opilio. The veteran's wife seemed almost as keen as the men on the cinnamon wine.

430

For his part, Cassius had decided to take it slow and amuse himself by exchanging the odd smile with Clara. Like her mistress, the maid had light blue ribbons in her hair.

Indavara pointed at the wall above the beds. Asdribar had already added two new mementos to his collection: a pair of crossed Maseene javelins. 'All that money spent on weapons and we ended up without a blade between us.'

'Yes, rather ironic,' replied Cassius.

'What about those lessons then?'

'Well, if you're willing, we can continue them—'

'—at the earliest opportunity?'

'Precisely.'

'I saw you with that chair by the way,' Indavara added. 'Good improvisation.'

'Like you said – him or me.'

Cassius noted that their glasses were empty. Simo beat him to the jug.

'No, Simo, allow me.'

'Very well, sir. None for me, thank you. I'm still recovering from the last time.'

'Nonsense,' said Cassius, filling each glass in turn. 'We have good cause to celebrate. Things might have turned out very, very differently.'

'*Fortuna Redux*,' said Indavara thoughtfully. 'The good luck that brings you home.'

'Well we eventually had the good luck,' said Cassius. 'Home?' He glanced at Indavara. 'Well, right now, this feels pretty close to me.'

The three of them clinked their glasses and took a long swig of wine. Noster's wife asked a question of Simo. He excused himself and turned towards her.

Cassius spied a space under the table and stretched out his legs. 'I remember back in Antioch – you complaining about how you were getting soft, not seeing enough action to keep you sharp. Had enough for the moment?'

'More than enough,' replied Indavara.

'By the gods, so have I. What a few months – that affair with the flag and then we get dragged into this.'

Cassius glanced across at Annia. 'You know neither of us is really good husband material, what with the Service despatching us on hazardous assignments to far-flung corners of the Empire. I fear we shall just have to accept casual assignations for the time being.'

'I think I can live with that,' said Indavara. He turned to Cassius with a conspiratorial grin. 'Tell me more about these hearth girls.'

Historical Note

As before, I thought some readers might be interested in the factual basis behind certain aspects of the story.

Client kingdoms like Karanda – the fictional territory featured in the prologue – were immensely important for the Empire. With the relatively small numbers of soldiers and administrators at their disposal, provincial governors couldn't hope to police every region and often relied on these local leaders. Agreements like the one Cassius delivers were of course generally weighted heavily in the Romans' favour.

I hope readers will forgive Indavara's shabby treatment of the Colossus of Rhodes. Long celebrated as one of the 'seven wonders', the fallen statue was indeed a favourite with the travellers who flocked to the popular island. We cannot be sure of its final fate but some accounts claim that in the seventh century it was sold to a merchant, who had it broken up and shipped to Syria. Historians have calculated that it was well over one hundred and twenty feet high (not including the platform). Weight estimates depend on the clouded question of bronze-thickness, but it is unlikely to have been less than ten tons.

Travel by sea was every bit as feared and genuinely perilous as I have suggested. The sailing season was widely considered to be between May and October. Long-distance trips outside this period were exceptionally rare and to be avoided at all costs. Apart from the danger of storms and the consequent wear on comparatively fragile craft, increased levels of fog and cloud made navigation using landmarks and stars far more difficult.

Captain Asdribar was of course given quite an incentive to depart immediately but skippers typically wouldn't leave port until the winds (and the omens) were favourable. The lists of ancient naval superstitions run to pages, another factor which suggests that securing passage by water would have been a haphazard, unpredictable affair. And, unless you were a Roman emperor, it would also have been extremely uncomfortable. Cassius was very lucky to find himself in a cabin; the majority of passengers slept on deck.

The character of Squint was born out of a passage from the letters of Synesius, a Greek intellectual from the fourth century. Having concluded a sea voyage to Cyrene, he wrote to his brother about the crew, commenting that 'the one thing they all shared in common was some bodily defect . . . they called each other by their misfortunes instead of real names – Cripple, Ruptured, One Arm, Squint; each and every one had his nickname.'

The corrupt naval officer, Commander Litus, is based on an individual of the same name from the fifth century, who was accused of taking bribes from pirates and slave traders.

Even given the unusual circumstances of her upbringing, Annia's character and behaviour must be seen as highly atypical. Although her father's status would have afforded her a level of influence denied to women from the poorer classes, the course of women's lives was in large part dictated by their fathers and husbands. As suggested by Cassius's attitude, the view of Roman men was that women should know their place and preferably stay there.

Cassius's pride in, and use of, his patron's letters accurately reflects the way in which the upper echelons of Roman society worked. Connections were everything, and letters of recommendation greased the cogs of army, administration and government. For example, Pliny tells us that military commissions were handed out first to dependents and friends, and that the person in charge of approving the appointments would need to know nothing more than the applicant's name! *Beneficia* was the word used to describe the interventions made by a powerful individual on behalf of someone else. In summary, who you knew was invariably more important than what you knew.

Darnis was indeed a Roman town on the coast of Cyrenaica.

Located in modern Libya, it is now known as Derna. Though I have invented the second earthquake, Cyrene was struck by such a disaster in AD 262. The emperor Claudius Gothicus made efforts to restore the city but it, and the province, never recovered their former status. Another earthquake struck in AD 365 and Synesius describes Cyrene as a ruin.

Africa had been comparatively peaceful for two hundred years but the third century did see a number of uprisings by various tribes. It is not easy to discern the reasons for these conflicts but corruption and water supply might easily have been contributing factors. The Romans were typically industrious in ensuring their lands were well-watered and we know that their activities disrupted the grazing patterns of nomadic local tribesmen.

The depths to which Carnifex and his cohorts sink are of course extreme, but Cyrenaica in particular was a hotbed of venality and there is considerable evidence of corruption across the African provinces. One example is that of Allius Maximus, a Roman administrator who tried to demand more than the normal six days of work from local peasants. When they refused, he sent a detachment of soldiers to seize and torture them. It is worth noting, however, that the peasants were able to despatch a letter of complaint to the then-emperor Commodus, who ruled in their favour.

Soldiers demonstrated a remarkable capacity for exploitation. Often put in charge of tax collection, they were masters of their assigned domain and duly milked every last drop. As well as operating 'protection rackets' they would – in lieu of payment – claim property, women or slaves for their own. Complaints of such behaviour came from across the Empire.

From Ammianus, we have the tale of one Romanus, a military commander stationed in Africa during the fourth century. Claims of negligence were made against him and a tribune named Palladius was sent to investigate. Palladius was also responsible for delivering the payroll and, upon arrival, received the usual 'kickbacks' that went along with such a duty. Working in conjunction with two local leaders, he made enquiries and eventually prepared a report in which the accusations against Romanus were upheld. Hearing of this, Romanus threatened to reveal that Palladius had accepted the 'kickbacks'. The tribune duly changed the report and claimed the charges against Romanus had been unfounded. The two local leaders? The emperor ordered that their tongues be torn out – for falsely impugning Romanus.

In examining the practices of the military in the later Empire, it almost seems that for many soldiers – officers in particular – financial gain wasn't just a benefit of military service, it was the raison d'etre. This type of behaviour seems to have reached a peak by the third century and some historians have suggested that such rank corruption was a major contributing factor to the decline of the Empire.

Though Carnifex is fairly disparaging about 'barefeet', there is in fact little evidence of what we would consider racism on the part of the Romans towards the people of Africa. Throughout the Empire, status was far more important than colour or creed and Africans played a leading role in Roman life; providing notable philosophers, orators, poets, generals and eventually emperors, the first of whom was Septimius Severus (who reigned from AD 193 to 211.)

The punishment of exile was limited in the main to the upper classes. There were two basic forms. If sentenced to *relegatio*, the exile maintained his citizenship and stood some chance of return. Barring a dramatic change of regime however, those suffering *deportatio* were unlikely to ever see Rome again. They lost both citizenship and property.

Remote spots such as islands like Sardinia were favoured, as were isolated locations in the African desert. Anyone who tried to violate their exile could expect far harsher and more violent punishment. In a society where reputation was paramount and the capital the absolute centre of all things, I would suggest that Cassius's description of exile as 'a kind of death' is fairly apt.

Once again I must express my gratitude to all the historians whose illuminating texts I used whilst researching the book; novelists like myself would be lost without them.

Acknowledgements

A tale of two cities this time, with *The Far Shore* being completed in Warsaw and Norwich between September, 2011 and June, 2012. Bizarrely, the the lowest temperatures were experienced in England (thanks to a very chilly house) which meant many early morning writing sessions clothed in several layers plus hat and scarf.

Over the past year, my agent David Grossman has again provided invaluable advice in matters both creative and practical. Editor Oliver Johnson expertly guided the third book from early draft to finished product. Thanks also to Anne Perry and all those others at Hodder & Stoughton who contributed; and artist Larry Rostant, who produced yet another striking and memorable cover. I must also mention the authors, reviewers and bloggers whose kind words have helped Cassius et al. reach a wider audience.

Lastly, sincere thanks to all the readers who have supported the *Agent of Rome* series so far; I do hope you also enjoy future tales from the third century.